# TWELFTH WINTER

## THE SEQUEL TO SUMMER OF TWO WORLDS

WRITTEN BY:
J. ARTHUR MOORE

ISBN: 978-1-952874-50-5 (softcover)
978-1-952874-51-2 (hardcover)
978-1-952874-52-9 (eBook)

Published by:

**OB OMNIBOOK**Co.

OMNIBOOK CO.
99 Wall Street, Suite 118
New York, NY 10005 USA
+1-866-216-99652
www.omnibookcompany.com

photo editing and design by Gian Carlo Tan

For e-book purchase: Kindle on Amazon, Barnes and Noble
Wholesale purchase: Ingram (615) 793-5000, Baker & Taylor (800) 775-1800
Book purchase: Amazon.com, Barnes & Noble, and www.jarthurmoore.com
and www.omnibookcompany.com

Omnibook titles may be purchased in bulk for educational, business, fund-raising, or sales promotional use. For more information please e-mail info@omnibookcompany.com

# AUTHOR'S NOTE

Contrary to common practice, names which this author uses in the series of stories which take place along or are related to the Virginia and Truckee Railroad in West Virginia, do have meaning.

The setting itself grew out of the author's hobby of model railroading and is in part duplicated in miniature recreations. There is, however, a real railroad of the same name and period located in the state of Nevada near Virginia City.

Most of the names of places and characters are from real people and places in the author's experience as a middle grades school teacher, or from places and friends who have been a part of the author's life experiences. All have been chosen from good memories and are a way of saying, "I haven't forgotten you, though we haven't seen each other in years and may never meet again."

Often main characters are created for specific people and stories are dedicated to those individuals. Yet in a sense all the stories which are created as a part of the Virginia and Truckee series are dedicated to life's memories and the people who have been a part of those memories.

# ARTWORK

All illustrative material – photographs, maps, drawings – are by the author. Front cover photograph and portrait of Michael were taken at Washington's Headquarters at Valley Forge National Park, Valley Forge, Pennsylvania. Back cover was taken at Hibernia County Park, Wagontown, Pennsylvania. The portraits of Adam and James were taken at the Lincoln Funeral Train Event at Stone Gables Estate in Elizabethtown, Pennsylvania. The photographs of Teddy and Miles were taken at the Devon Campus of the Episcopal Academy at Devon, Pennsylvania. Jason's photo was taken at his home in Nottingham, Pennsylvania. Additional setting photographs were taken of the author's model railroad layout, which represents in miniature the setting of the story, Snow Shoe, West Virginia, and the domain of the Virginia & Truckee Railroad of West Virginia.

Michael PC Freeman is represented by Michael Flanagan, Adam Tyler is represented by Paul Wunderlich, Teddy Latimer is represented by Teddy Leeds, Miles Hart is represented by Mike Henry, Jason Johnston is represented by Andy Wunderlich, and Brett Tompkins is represented by James Wunderlich. Paul, Andy, and James participate with the author in Civil War living history encampments. The remaining three were participants in camp programs run by the author.

# ACKNOWLEDGEMENTS

Since I have started working with Omnibook Company, three individuals have been key to the publication of my work. Andy Sullivan, Supervisor/Operations has been my personal company contact representative from the very beginning. As such he has coordinated every aspect of each project. This includes the assignment of designated design person, Gian Carlo Tan and my designated internet technical website developer/designer Shan Gabrielle. Gian's design work has been conscientiously and promptly carried out as he has produced outstanding books and marketing posters, among his many talents. The award-winning website is the ongoing work of Shan as it is constantly updated as new material comes available, including the development of book trailers and their addition to the website as he produces them. With the upcoming release of this, my tenth book, they deserve thanks and recognition for their continuing outstanding work.

Two others have helped with this book's development.

Medical Doctor William Loretan helped as medical advisor for the chapter Illness, to verify the content/historical accuracy of the details within that chapter.

Dennis Blank, a longtime live steam railroad operator and model railroader, has served as technical advisor for the locomotive and train action within the story.

For each of these and their contributions, I am truly grateful. Thanks.

J.A.M.

# DEDICATION

**T**welfth **Winter** is dedicated in His love and in friendship to Michael Flanagan, Paul Wunderlich, Teddy Leeds, Mike Henry, Andy Wunderlich, and James Wunderlich who have helped bring the characters of the story to life by representing them with their images, and to all who share in reading this story of changing worlds and new adventure.

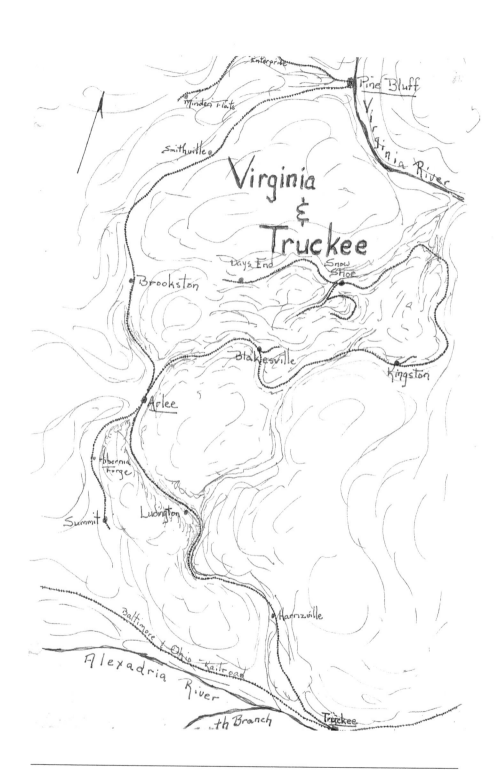

Virginia
&
Truckee

Enterprise
Pine Bluff
Minden Flats
Virginia River
Smithville
Days End
Snow Shoe
Brookston
Blakiesville
Kingston
Arlee
Hibernia Forge
Summit
Ludington
Harrizville
Baltimore & Ohio Railroad
Alexadria River
...th Branch
Truckee

# OTHER BOOKS BY
# J. ARTHUR MOORE

These books by J. Arthur Moore are also available on
www.jarthurmoore.com and from the publisher, Omnibook Company
at www.omnibookcompany.com/journeyintodarkness/ as well as
www.barnesandnoble.com, and www.amazon.com
Also available from Ingram Distribution w/returnability
[Ingram new accounts 1-800-937-0152]

Omnibook titles may be purchased in bulk for educational, business,
fund-raising, or sales promotional use. For more information
please e-mail info@omnibookcompany.com

# CONTENTS

# MICHAEL PC FREEMAN

# ADAM TYLER

# TEDDY LATIMER

# MILES HART

# JASON JOHNSTON

BRETT TOMPKINS

# JOURNEY'S END

The sun had not yet risen as the distant whistle pierced the morning air with its shrill cry. Approaching from the westward tracks, the light of the engine's headlamp glowed dimly in the mountain fog. The pounding of the steam in the pistons grew audible as the train neared the station platform, already alive with activity of waiting passengers and baggage wagons with loads to be transferred.

The sign at the end of the platform read "Truckee, West Virginia." This was the southern end of the Virginia and Truckee Railroad line which ran north through the West Virginia mountain country to its terminus at Pine Bluff on the Virginia River, a distance of about one hundred and twenty miles. Here at Truckee, railroad traffic transferred to the Baltimore and Ohio Railroad for travel eastbound or westbound.

The morning coach was arriving from the west. Steam blasted from the cylinders and air rushed into the brake lines as metal squealed against metal and the train slowed to a stop. The clunking sound of car couplings knocking together was followed by a brief quiet as the train came to a final stop.

During this brief pause in activity punctuated with the rumblings of steam in the engine's belly and the hissing of escaping pressure, trainmen climbed down to place stools on the station platform at the bottom of each of the cars' steps. Then controlled chaos broke loose as passengers clambered down then up depending on where they were headed, and baggage wagons were rolled into place to receive or send out various packages and shipments and personal goods.

A middle-aged traveler, very much annoyed by the harangues of his wife and the prattling of a half dozen offspring ranging from fourteen to four, descended the steps in tight-lipped silence. An older couple, comfortably married, followed, arm-in-arm, with weary smiles and enthusiasm in the sparkle of their eyes. They took time to see and appreciate the movement about them.

On the platform, children asked questions, or whined, or argued, or explored, or slept in their mothers' arms. Adults talked, or pushed their way through the crowd. Some were blind to the happenings around them. Some took in everything with the awe of youth or a first trip away from home. There were city folk and country folk, folk from the east and folk from the west, folk used to civilization and folk just off the frontier.

Amidst the commotion the small figure of the boy descended the steps. He was lost in a confusion of people and motion, which had never before been forced upon him in the short dozen or less years of his life. In appearance, he was a clash of civilizations. Long blond hair hung across his shoulders. Dressed in buckskin from his fringed shirt to his moccasins, and dark-skinned from continuous exposure to the sun, he appeared to be an Indian child, but his features were those of a white.

The boy looked again at the paper in his hand. He stood for a while in confusion as he gazed about to get his bearings. Then, folding it up, he tucked the paper back into his waistband. The boy carried a parfleche, a beaded bundle which contained his personal possessions. He also had a long package, wrapped neatly in buckskin and tied with rawhide strings.

Pausing for a moment, the boy watched toward the baggage car as a ramp was pulled out and a paint pony was led down. The pony was skittish and apprehensive, but made it safely to the platform. Then he glanced to the baggage wagon to make sure his travel trunk was there. Satisfied that all was well, he moved on.

Crossing the wooden platform, pushing his way through the crowd, he reached the train on the northbound track. He mounted the steps, entered the coach, and found an empty seat by a window. Placing his parfleche on the bench and leaning his long package against the side wall, he sat near the window and stared out at the crowd. Tears welled up in his eyes and slid unchecked down his cheeks as he watched the activity so unlike that which he had lived all his life. He cried quietly to himself. The boy was not aware of the figure that paused in the aisle by his seat.

"Michael?" The voice and the name were nothing to him and he ignored them.

"Prairie Cub?" His name startled him and he looked to see who spoke it.

The conductor in his dark blue uniform and gold name-plated hat, stood there. He seemed friendly. He even smiled.

"I'm Dan Seegers." He pushed the back of the next seat forward to reverse it, then sat down facing the boy. Folding his hands under his chin he explained, "Your friend Scot wrote that you were coming. Perhaps he told you of Jay Miller up at Snow Shoe." The boy nodded an acknowledgement. "Jay and I work together for the railroad. We and some of our friends have been taking turns watching for you." Dan stopped.

The boy gazed out the window again. They sat there in their own silence amidst the constant noise around them.

"Why?" the boy cried softly. Pleading eyes the color of a clear spring sky met those of the man. "Why am I here? My whole life is like it never happened. It is so far back and so long ago, I feel like it was a dream."

"Michael, I cannot help you with your hurt. I only know of you from what Scot wrote in his letter . . ."

"I am Prairie Cub, son of Thunder Eagle!" the boy cried.

The noise around them paused as people stopped to stare, then moved on. Again the noise.

"You are Prairie Cub and you are Michael. You have always known that. Now you are in Michael's world, though we will know you as both."

"I want to go back!"

"There's nothing to go back to." Dan could feel the heat of tears rising up in his own eyes and brushed them aside as inconspicuously as he could.

"I know that! Why did it have to happen?!" Tears flowed freely. He looked at the parfleche and ran trembling fingers across its beaded design. "This is my grandmother's gift before the last buffalo hunt." Tears puddled on his shirt and the body shook with the sobbing.

Dan, too, teared up. He tried to hide it. But his emotions were touched too deeply. He took out a kerchief to check his tears. The boy calmed some and wiped his eyes with his shirt sleeve. Dan placed a consoling hand on his wrist.

"Trust me. We will do all we can for you." He dabbed his eyes as he stood, very conscious of their redness and wanting to get away to himself. "Stay where you are. I'll be back later."

The boy watched him through the door to the open platform. The aisle emptied as the last of the passengers took their seats. Michael reached forward and reversed the seat in front of him. He did not wish for anyone else to sit there.

The engine's whistle cut the air with two sharp blasts. Pressure rushed through the brake lines under the floorboards. Brake shoes clattered loose and couplings rattled tight as the train began to ease into forward motion.

The boy leaned back against the seat. He closed his eyes. His mind drifted back to his life on the plains.

*       *       *

The engine's whistle sounded. The boy stirred from his sleep. Sitting up, he rubbed the sleep from his eyes and glanced at the passing countryside. It was a misty morning. The glow in the air meant the sun would most likely break through the mist and drive it away. Michael looked up as the conductor, Mr. Seegers, approached.

"How did you sleep?" the man inquired as he pulled the seat and sat down.

"Good," the boy replied. "Do you know how my pony is? I haven't seen him since two days back, except to watch him get off the last train."

"He's fine," the conductor assured. "I checked on him as soon as we left Truckee."

"How much further?"

"We should arrive in Arlee in five minutes. Look outside. You will see the engine yards as we pull into town."

The boy turned his attention to the window once more. The engine's whistle blew.

"There it is," Dan Seegers pointed.

The train slowed as it passed through the yards. Several locomotives stood on the tracks, some ready to go to work, others quietly unattended. The yards fell behind. Buildings passed by. The train slowed to a crawl.

Mr. Seegers stood to the aisle. "Hurry, Michael. Grab yer things and come outside." The conductor led the boy to the platform as the train rolled into the station area, alongside other trains already waiting on a pass track and siding. "Look there," Dan pointed. "See that engine, with the number 21?" Michael nodded. "Wave. That's Jay in the cab watchin' us in."

The boy waved. A stocky-built, bearded man waved back. He had a kindly smile hidden in his whiskers. As the train shuddered to a stop, the bearded engineer scrambled down the steps and passed across the end platform between two coaches to the station platform, hurrying to meet the boy as Dan guided him down the coach steps.

"I'll see ya later," Dan called. Toward Jay he added, "Don't forget the boy's trunk and his horse!"

"I won't," Jay returned. "You must be Michael," he approached the boy and offered his hand.

"Yes, Sir," the boy accepted. "And you are Scot's friend, Jay."

"The same."

"I'm glad to meet you. He's told me much about his time with you."

"Come on," the engineer said, "let's find yer horse and trunk. This train only sets here ten minutes."

With parfleche and bundle tucked securely in arm, the boy walked with the engineer toward the front of the train. The pony pranced, panicky, as it was led down the wooden ramp, but calmed as soon as its young master took the lead line and stroked the prickly muzzle.

"He looks good," Jay observed. "Now for yer trunk."

While the two wandered the platform and checked the baggage wagons, people finished boarding the train and baggage handlers finished loading personal baggage and freight. The train soon departed and continued its journey northbound. A second train soon departed leaving only Number twenty-one with its two cars, a coach and a mixed baggage.

"That's our ride home," Jay observed. 'We'll put yer horse on an you can ride in the baggage room with him."

They led the horse across the wooden platform and tracks until they neared the baggage side door. It was rolled open and a ramp slid out for the pony.

It was time to go on again. The journey's end was near. Yet now that Michael was already with Scot's friend, it really had reached its end. He watched as the baggage wagon was unloaded into the train and saw his trunk go on. Of-The-Wind whinnied for his master. The boy climbed into the baggage room with his pony and the door was rolled shut as the engineer returned to his locomotive. The few remaining passengers climbed aboard.

The engineer sounded the whistle and the fireman set the bell to ringing as the train eased out of the siding and crept onto the main line. Inside, Michael, still dressed in his buckskins, sat atop the trunk and stroked his pony's mane. The bundle of bow and arrows rested across the parflech which sat in the straw against the trunk.

The engine picked up speed. Arlee fell behind. Soon the train disappeared into the hills on its morning run to Snow Shoe.

# A New Beginning

A soot-darkened, gloved hand closed around the wooden handle of the cord overhead and pulled expertly on the line. The steam locomotive's whistle responded with a scream that echoed through the surrounding hillsides -- two long calls, a short blast, and a long wail that hung on the crisp autumn air. Twenty minutes passed. Through the open door to the locomotive's running board, the small country station of Blakesville closed rapidly as the train approached its scheduled stop. The engineer pushed the throttle lever forward to slow the locomotive. Across the cab, the fireman reached for a second line and set the bell to a rhythmic ringing. The movement of the pistons slowed as the large driver wheels slackened their speed. Concentrating on the approaching station area, Jay pulled gently on the brake lever as he guided his train into position to line up the cars on the wooden platform. Brakes squealed against the wheels. Surplus steam pressure hissed as it was released from the piston chambers. The train rolled to a gentle stop as the bell echoed its last and fell silent. The engineer pulled one last short toot to signal the brakes were set.

"Scott," the engineer spoke to his fireman, "Keep an eye on things for a while. I'm going back ta talk ta the boy. We'll take a few extra minutes here."

"I got it, Jay," the younger man responded. "I need ta draw some water inta the boiler and rake down the fire anyway."

The engineer crossed the cab to descend to the station platform while his fireman walked to the tender to open the water valve. Jay Miller was in his late thirties. A full beard, neatly trimmed, framed a friendly face. Eyes that sparkled with kindness, reflected, too, pride and confidence of a man at ease with his life's work. Ignoring the few passengers that were boarding or leaving the train, he strode directly to the first car, the mixed coach and baggage, climbed the front steps to the open platform, and entered the baggage compartment.

The brown and white paint pony snorted nervously at the intrusion and pawed at the straw. Stroking the pony's muzzle to reassure her, the boy looked to the door as Jay gently pushed it shut. A slight smile tugged at the corners of his mouth, but was not reflected in his eyes. Long blond hair hung to his shoulders, brushing the collar of his buckskin shirt. Crystalline blue eyes glistened with a sadness born of recent tragedy in his young life. Michael hung his arm across his pony's neck and leaned his body against the sturdy shoulder as the engineer stopped before him and gently stroked the bristly muzzle.

"Where are we?" the boy asked.

"We've stopped at Blakesville. We'll be goin on soon. But I thought we should talk some first."

Michael stroked the strong neck with his free hand as his pony swung his head and nudged him. The man walked to a nearby stack of crated produce and leaned against the boxes.

"Michael," the man began, "It's a very difficult thing you have ta do now, startin' over. We don't know each other except for what Scot's told you about me and written me about you. I know some of what's happened. When ya feel like it ya can tell me more of yerself."

"I'd like that," The boy smiled. This time his eyes smiled too.

"But again, so's folks don't come down hard on ya, we'll use the first an last names, Michael Freeman. When needed we'll put initials "P.C." fer Prairie Cub."

"That'll be okay."

The man smiled beneath his beard as he stood. "Guess it's time ta get this train on the move. Folks'll get impatient." He put his hands on the boy's shoulders. "You go ahead an change now an get yer trunk packed up. I'll check back at the next stop." He squeezed gently to reassure the boy that everything would be okay. "Ya take care, too," he added as he patted the pony on the neck.

"She is called Of-The-Wind," the boy volunteered.

Jay reached an apple from a produce crate. "Here, Of-The-Wind. It's been a long trip and ya deserve somethin' special."

The pony took the apple from the outstretched hand and crunched it gingerly as the engineer reached for the door knob and left the boy and his pony to themselves.

While Of-The-Wind finished the apple and pawed the straw impatiently, Michael removed his shirt and laid it across the top of the trunk to fold it neatly for storage. As he knelt in the straw and lifted the lid to lay it within, two sharp blasts of the engine's whistle cut the air. The floor vibrated as the car eased into motion. The shirt was laid reverently in the chest and a change of clothes was withdrawn. He fingered the cotton fabric of the shirt and thought again of Keith Summers, the storekeeper who had given it to him. Laying it across his knees, he picked up the bundle from where it lay beside the chest and the buckskin wrapped bow and quiver of arrows and thought of his people and especially of his parents, Thunder Eagle and Prairie Flower. His mind was flooded with memories of Grandfather and Granny-Woman, of life and death, of joy and tragedy and sorrow. Oh how his heart ached. A tear slipped down his cheek. Laying the precious bundle in the bottom of the chest and the wrapped bow on the floor in front, he stood and slipped his arms into the shirt sleeves. Brushing aside the tear, he walked to the platform door and watched the colorful foliage of the West Virginia mountain country flash its autumn beauty as the train rushed on. Again the whistle echoed through the hills. A dirt road flashed by. The boy turned back to finish changing and to pack and close the travel chest. He chose to keep his moccasins. They were more comfortable than the boots he left in the trunk. And they reminded him of the life he left behind.

The morning run of engine Number twenty-one continued to wind its way through the Appalachian mountain country. The consist of a coach and mixed baggage, painted yellow with green trim, bore the name Virginia and Truckee. Having departed earlier from the transfer point of Arlee, West Virginia, it was on its regularly scheduled return trip to the branch terminus at Snow Shoe. The rhythmic chugging of the locomotive echoed through the brilliantly colorful tree scape as the light cloud of wood smoke trailed behind, drifting off in a slight breeze.

Inside the engine cab, Jay Miller only partially concentrated on the track ahead. His mind was occupied with thoughts of the boy. He sifted again through the information his young friend, Scot Robinson, had written concerning Michael's previous life on the western plains as the son of a Sioux warrior. Tragic events had caused his father to send him back to the world of his white heritage. Now it was up to the engineer to help this boy to start over. He knew he could do it. He had liked the boy from the first letter in which Scot had spoken of him. From the moment he laid eyes on him earlier that morning as he transferred trains at Arlee, his heart went out to him and he promised himself that Michael would have the best he could provide. Automatically he reached up for the cord and the whistle cut in on his thoughts as he noticed ahead, the station and the nameplate for Kingston. For the moment concern for Michael was set aside as Jay concentrated on bringing the train into Kingston station.

Again, as the train waited for passengers to board or disembark, the engineer walked back to the baggage room. A baggage wagon was drawn up to the side and the large door was rolled open. As Jay ascended the platform steps and entered the car, he found the boy standing near the large door watching the activity. He had changed into a pair of suspendered trousers and a brown cotton shirt.

"Michael," the boy looked toward the voice. "Come here a minute." The boy crossed to the door which the engineer still held ajar. "How'd ya like ta ride up front with me?"

"You mean it?!"

"Certainly!"

"Okay!! Scot told me you taught him how ta run a locomotive."

"I taught him how ta run *this* locomotive." He led the way out onto the platform, then started down the steps. "And I'll teach you how ta, too."

"Yes, Sir!" he exclaimed in excited anticipation.

The boy dropped to the wooden station platform and followed behind the engineer. They headed for the steps to the engine's cab. As the two passed the locomotive's tender, the boy ran his hand along the metal of its sidewall and explored the feel of the large painted letters with his fingertips. Jay grabbed the handrail and pulled himself up to the engine cab. Michael followed close behind.

Introductions were made as the boy met Scott O'Donnell, the fireman. Collar length brown hair cascaded in natural curl from beneath a leather, visored cap. The fireman was of lighter build than the husky engineer and not quite as tall. His blue overalls were tinged with soot and dust. He greeted the boy with a firm handshake. Michael liked him right off. O'Donnell turned to check the gauges as Jay took his seat on the right side of the cab.

"Come sit here, Michael," the engineer invited.

He helped the boy climb up to sit on the front edge of the engineer's box. Gauges hissed. Steam rumbled in the boiler. Smoke drifted from the large diamond stack. Outside, the large baggage door was rolled shut and the conductor called, "All aboard!"

Jay replied with two sharp blasts of the whistle while Scott set the bell to a rhythmic ringing.

"See this lever?" Jay indicated the throttle. "Grab hold and I'll work it with ya."

Michael wrapped his left hand around the handle as the engineer enclosed the small hand in his own. He released the brake and shifted the Johnson lever into forward while he eased back on the throttle. Steam surged into the piston chambers and pushed on the drive rods. The large wheels began to turn. Wheels rumbled against the steel rails as the train eased into forward motion. It picked up speed as the noise of its movement picked up volume. The bell stopped. The throttle clicked into its position set. All relaxed and watched the track and the train's progress through the open doors to the locomotive's running boards. A cool breeze warmed by the heat from the boiler and mixed with cinders from the stack, flowed refreshing through the door openings and smudged faces with ash. On their way once more, the next stop was Snow Shoe.

As the train continued on its run and Scott threw on wood, raked the fire, and checked the gauges, Jay began to explain some of the workings of the engine. Michael tried to understand what he could, but it was all so unfamiliar. Rounding a curve along a hillside, the train slowed to a crawl. Suddenly a figure appeared alongside the track and climbed aboard as the engine picked up speed again.

The young man of about twenty-one who had boarded was introduced as Jamie Rhodes. He walked the tracks from Snow Shoe to this point each day to inspect their condition. Michael had been looking at some of the gauges with Scott. He moved out of the way and leaned against the engineer's box. Jamie leaned against the cab opening to the tender behind the fireman's box.

"How's it look this mornin?" Jay asked.

"It's definitely time for a day of maintenance. Rails are showin their wear and some rotten ties should be replaced."

"The bridge?"

"Chamber's Crossing looks good," Jamie reported.

Just then the train rumbled across a tall wooden trestle which spanned a cut about eighty yards across. The floor of the little valley lay some fifty feet down where a mountain creek cascaded down the mountainside.

Michael gripped the hand rail tightly as he peered over the edge of the footplate between the engine and its tender.

"Was that Chamber's Crossing?"

"That was it," Scott confirmed.

As the four talked among themselves it became obvious to Michael that each had already known of his coming. Except for the engineer, the others knew only that he was a friend of Scot Robinson's and had suffered some tragedy which included the loss of his family. He would be staying on for a while under the care of Jay Miller.

Again the engineer slowed the train as Jamie Rhodes moved to the steps.

"We're approaching the switch fer Snow Shoe station," Jay explained.

The track walker dropped to the ground as the train continued at a crawl, and ran ahead to throw the switch. The train eased off the main to the station track as Jay blew the whistle and Scott set the bell to ringing. Proceeding through two more switches, already set, it pulled in on the back side of the station building. Jay spotted the coach near the end of the platform and paused while he watched from the cab window for a trainman to set the brakes and uncouple the car. Passengers detrained and went around to the front benches to wait, if they had luggage in the baggage room. Otherwise they left the station area and went about their business. The signal was given for all clear and the engine with its remaining car moved on out of the station through another series of switches.

Jay explained, "We still have one more stop ta make at Day's End, about four miles down the track. It's the end of this line. Then we'll back up and pull in on the station side ta finish unloadin'."

\*     \*     \*

More than a quarter hour passed before the train was again easing in to the station at Snow Shoe. The engine with its single car stopped in front of the station building. It was very quiet compared to many of the stops Michael had made. The few passengers who had returned from Day's End disembarked from the coach end of the car and went their separate ways. Most of what remained was baggage or deliveries to be unloaded from the baggage area and placed in the station storeroom until arrangements were made for pickup. The boy sat on the fireman's box and watched from the window while Scott and Jay checked the gauges and prepared the engine to be uncoupled and put away. It was time for him to return to the baggage room of the mixed coach and retrieve his pony as his trunk and bow bundle were unloaded onto a baggage wagon.

"You wait here with Of-The-Wind while I take Twenty-one to the engine house, and I'll be back for you," Jay instructed. "Dan will stay with you and introduce you to the station master. I'll be about a half hour."

"Okay," Michael replied as he turned to the steps and descended from the engine's cab to the station platform.

*   *   *

Michael stood leaning against the corner of the station building holding Of-The-Wind's halter lead, talking quietly to his pony as he stroked her cheek. His long bundle lay on the bench nearby. Dan had introduced him to the stationmaster, Robert Coates. Jarrett, his seventeen-year-old son, had come in from the freight room and was with him on the platform, admiring the pony. The youth had yet to reach full height and stood just over five feet. He brushed his untamed brownish blond hair out of his eyes as he spoke.

"Wow, she sure is a beauty," the youth commented. "Can I touch her?"

"Sure."

Jarrett reached out to pet the pony's neck as she swung her head to look at him. He jumped back.

"It's okay," Michael assured. "She just wants to get to know you."

Jarrett reached again to run the palm of his hand down the smooth neck. "She feels so strong," he commented.

"She's my good friend. We've been through a lot together. I hope she'll be happy here and be able to run like she could before when we lived on the open land." Michael kissed her on her muzzle.

"What was it like where you lived?" Jarrett asked, stepping back from the pony.

"Someday after I've been here a while I can tell you about it," Michael replied. "Just now I'm waiting for Jay to find out where we go from here."

"Okay. I have to get back to my chores," Jarrett informed. "I'll see you again later."

"Thanks," Michael acknowledged.

As Jarrett walked off toward the freight room, Jay approached from the far end of the station platform.

"Meet a new friend?" he called.

"I guess," the boy replied as he picked up his bow bundle. "What about my trunk?"

"I've asked Ephram, the Wells Fargo agent, to drop it off on his morning deliveries." Jay caught up with the boy. "Just now let's get you and Of-The-Wind off to your new home and settled in. Follow me."

Leading his pony and carrying his bow in his other hand, Michael walked with Jay as they crossed from the station to head south on Main Street, into the heart of the south-side residential area of Snow Shoe. Three blocks later, Main Street ended at Cedar where they turned left toward Washington Street. Halfway down the block the two crossed to a small farm on the south side of the street, which occupied most of the block and reached back into the hills. Michael quickly surveyed the property from its lane back to the buildings, to its fenced meadows beyond with evidence of a stream in the distance, and felt a sense of comfort from within.

"Is this our home?" He asked as they neared the house.

"Yes," Jay replied. "This is your and Of-The-Wind's new home. Here, your pony will have the best of care and room to run, and you will be able to be with her whenever you want. This is Bill and Janet Tyler's farm. They have a sixteen-year-old son, Adam. He is looking forward to meeting you and your pony and will show you her new home in the barn. The Tylers have a spare room on the second floor that they've set up for you."

A two and a half story white wood-frame house stood back from the street at the end of the tree-lined lane. Situated on a small thirty-acre farm, it had a corner porch along the left side facing the front and the lane, and a two-story barn in the back. Out buildings included a chicken coop, smoke house, wood yard and shed near the back door, and a carriage shed across from the barn. A small apple orchard with plenty of fruit on the trees and on the ground, stood behind a large vegetable garden on the far side of the lane, across from the house. Four rows of sweet corn bordered the orchard side. A flower garden occupied the back end of the vegetable garden. Both gardens appeared somewhat mid harvest for the season, going barren for the winter months ahead.

The two stopped beside the porch so Michael could look the place over. He leaned the bow against the side of the porch and smiled to himself in the comfortable feeling that Of-The-Wind would have a good home here.

Mrs. Tyler was out the side door before the two were halfway to the steps. "Ephram has already been here and your trunk is in your room," she announced. "And this must be Michael." She rushed down the steps and pulled the boy into a motherly hug. He stiffened at the unexpected reception.

Janet quickly backed off. "I'm sorry," she said. "I didn't mean to make you uncomfortable."

"No one has ever touched me like that," Michael explained. "I didn't know what to do." He studied the woman before him. Her long reddish-brown hair hung unbound down her back. Of light build, she was an attractive thirty-something in a plain red dress with white highlights, covered from the waist down with a white apron.

"I'll be more careful." Janet eyed the boy with concern. "We'll get to know each other better, first.

"Jay, I see you have brought the boy's pony to her new home." She wiped her hands on her apron.

Michael responded, "This is my pony, Of-The-Wind."

She shook her head with a soft whinny as if to acknowledge the introduction, as Michael turned her lead to face the woman.

"Let's turn your pony loose in the meadow so she can run about and get used to her new home." The small group walked toward the barnyard gate to the meadow. "We can go back to the house and get a bite to eat. Then you can settle in. Adam and his pa will get home from the mountain later. Then you and Adam can show your pony her stall within the barn. We have arranged that she have a stall that can stay open to the meadow so she can go in and out as she pleases."

Jay opened the gate. Michael took the lead line off his pony's halter, led her through the gate, slipped off the halter, then released her to run the field. She paused and looked at the boy.

"It's okay," he soothed. "This is your home now." He patted her on the neck and she turned away at a slow walk. Looking back to see that her master was still there, she took a few quick steps then burst into an open run, finally free to go after being cramped up in baggage cars for so long.

The three turned back to the house. Halfway there, Michael turned back to watch his pony run. Satisfied that she was happy, he continued on his way to the house.

"Come on in and I'll show you around. I've fixed lunch for you both. Can you stay, Jay?"

"I have made time for this. The "Scott's" regular crew will take the afternoon run to South Camp and my crew will take the afternoon freight run, just a little late. But I'll have to get back for that by two this afternoon."

"Well come on in and let's have lunch. After you leave, I'll get Michael settled."

*     *     *

Shortly after lunch, Jay left for work and Janet took Michael up to his room. He placed his trunk in a back corner and stood the bow bundle against the corner walls behind. Removing the clothing Keith Summers had given him, he placed it in the chest of drawers. He put his moccasins in the trunk and removed the boots to be placed in the kitchen under the coat pegs by the door. He would just wear socks in the house. He noticed Mrs. Tyler left her shoes by the door and just wore socks and slippers. The trunk was closed and locked, the key placed under his clothes in the drawer.

Returning to the kitchen, Michael sat at the table to watch as Mrs. Tyler prepared an apple pie for the oven.

"Mrs. Tyler," he began, "Thanks for taking me in."

The woman unrolled the top crust across the pie, set the rolling pin aside, and slipped into a chair across from the boy.

"Michael," she looked straight at the boy, "you are more than welcome here. Adam is so looking forward to having a younger brother again. Some years back, Mr. Tompkins and his son, Brett, stayed with us for several months and he so enjoyed having Brett to hang out with. The Tompkins family has since relocated in the family home place at the west end of the street. They, too, are looking forward to meeting you."

"How many people know of my coming?" Michael asked.

"We're a fairly close-knit small town community here. At present, a handful of folks who work together with the logging company know of your coming. But, to my knowledge, Jay may be the only person to know however much of your story that Scot has told him. We figure it's up to you to share it when you're ready. Most just know that you are a friend of Scot Robinson's and that you have suffered a tragedy and lost your family. Jay has shared some of your story with us and with Mr. Tompkins, the owner of Stewart Creek Logging Company. For now we need to help you get settled in. We'll decide later where to go from here."

"What now?"

"Well, I have to finish dinner. You're welcome to spend time with your pony until Adam and his pa get home."

"Thanks." Michael stood from the table and headed out the door as Mrs. Tyler rose to finish her pie.

\*　　\*　　\*

The afternoon was spent in the field, riding Of-The-Wind, exploring the pastureland, sitting by the stream where it cut across the back corner of the meadow, and watching the fish and other wildlife, while the pony drank from the water and grazed nearby. As the sun slipped closer to the western horizon, Michael judged it was time to start back to the house. Slipping onto the pony's back, the two walked leisurely toward the barn. He glanced across the back fence line and noticed several holes in the ground that reminded him of the prairie dog holes on the plains. He would have to be careful that his pony didn't step in one.

The five o'clock whistles blew at the various industries on the outskirts of Snow Shoe and the boy and his pony were startled by the unexpected noise. Michael left his pony in the meadow, walked through the gate, and started toward the house.

Shortly after entering the kitchen, the front door opened and Adam and his father entered the front hall.

"We're home," Adam called. "Where's Michael?"

"He's in the kitchen with me," his mother shouted back.

The two rushed to the kitchen where Mr. Tyler greeted his wife with a kiss and Adam went straight to the chair across from Michael.

"Michael? I'm Adam." He reached across the table and Michael responded with a handshake.

"Hi," he replied looking the other in the eye. "Your mom says you're okay with my coming?"

"Okay! I couldn't wait!"

"We've been looking forward for your arrival," Mr. Tyler added, standing with his arm around his wife's waist. "Adam can show you the barn and what we've arranged for your horse, tend to his chores, then you can both clean up for dinner."

The boys left the house and headed toward the barn. Adam's height and stride easily outpaced Michael and the older boy had to hold back to allow the younger to keep pace. As they approached the barn, Adam noticed the halter and lead where Michael had left them on the gate post.

"Grab your horse's halter and lead and I'll show you where to hang them," he instructed.

Michael picked them up on the way into the barn.

"This is the tack room." Adam indicated a storeroom just inside the barn door to the left. He opened the door and led the way in. "Here's a peg where you can hang the halter and lead line." He indicated an empty peg near the back of the room.

Michael hung them up as indicated. Walking the center of the barn, he noted there were box stalls on either side, two to the left and three to the right. A side area near the back of the barn contained a grain bin and a pile of loose hay. Adam stopped at the second box stall on the left.

"This'll be your horse's stall," he explained. "It opens on the meadow and the door can stay open so she can go in and out as she pleases. The empty one beside hers is sometimes used for Cheyenne, our saddle horse, or our cow, Bessie."

Hearing her master's voice, Of-The-Wind entered through the open door and approached the boys.

"Adam," Michael introduced, "this is my pony, Of-The-Wind."

"She's a beauty," the older boy stated. "Let's get her some grain and hay. It's over here."

Adam showed Michael where the grain was as he filled a scoop from the grain bin and dumped it in the manger. Then he took up a fork and deposited a forkful of hay into the manger as well. A bucket of water was filled from the pump outside the back door and used to fill the tin-lined water basin in each manger. There was a soft rustling in one of the other stalls accompanied by the distinct mooing of a cow. The saddle horse occupied one of the remaining box stalls.

"I have to feed my horse and milk the cow, then throw down some hay for tomorrow, then we tend the chickens and the smoke house, and can go up to supper."

Working together, the two finished feeding the cow and horse then took up a bucket and small stool to milk the cow.

"Ever milk a cow before?" Adam asked.

"No," Michael replied.

"It's easy." Adam grabbed a teat and shot a stream of milk at Michael. "You want to try?" he asked as the younger boy jumped back.

"Maybe tomorrow."

Adam went on to finish drawing the milk into the bucket until all four teats had been drained. Michael watched in fascination. The bucket of milk was left just inside the barn door.

Afterwards, the two climbed a wooden ladder to the second floor of the barn, built into the wall in the back of the grain box area. There Adam showed Michael how to fork the hay for the next day down a hole in the floor above the pile below. Once finished in the barn, he filled a bucket with chicken feed and led the way outside to the chicken yard where he scattered the feed on the ground. The bucket was returned to the barn and the two returned to the chicken coop to gather the eggs in a basket that hung inside the door opening. Finally, Adam led Michael into the smoke house to be sure there was enough fuel on the fire to maintain a smoky burn to continue to cure the hanging meats. Once finished Michael was sent to retrieve the milk and the two headed for the house.

Setting the egg basket on the counter, Adam explained, "Ma, I want to take Michael to my room and show him my collection."

Looking up from the potatoes she was peeling, she replied, "Okay, but don't be long. Dinner will be ready soon."

"Come on Michael. Leave the bucket on the floor."

The two left the room, down the hall, and up the stairs to Adam's bedroom in the front of the house, overlooking the front lane.

"Wow," Michael wondered as they walked in. "Where'd you get all this stuff?"

He gazed about a room filled with railroad paraphernalia.

"I collect it. Have a seat on my bed. I'll show you."

Among other things, he had tie plates, spikes, a boiler plate from an engine the company had scrapped, a lantern, and old timetables and way bills. A railroad crossing sign hung on a side wall. He even had a white whistle post standing in a corner. Several old illustrated railroad calendars hung on the walls as well as paintings of trains running the countryside, and station buildings. A switch stand stood beside the wardrobe closet from a time when it was replaced by a newer one. Boxes contained ticket stubs and more schedules. Bookshelves contained railroad novels and history books.

"I guess you like trains," the boy observed. "How long have you been collecting things?"

"As long as I can remember." He picked a piece of charred rope from a storage shelf. "A lot of these things have a story." He held out the rope for Michael to hold. "Brett can tell you about this. It's what's left of the whistle cord from the "Scott" when it went through a forest fire some years back. We were both there."

The boy examined the piece of rope and offered it back. "Were you scared?"

He took the cord. "We were too busy to be scared. We were in the engine cab which had been mostly burned away, and Brett was the only one who hadn't been badly burned. He drove the train. You know how Jay is teaching you? Well, he taught Brett, too."

"Dinner!" His mother called from the foot of the stairs.

Adam put the rope back in its place. "Time to go. You can come look again some other time."

They left the room.

*　　*　　*

Following dinner, the family gathered in the living room where Mr. Tyler added some cord wood to the large Round Oak stove that kept the room warm on the cool fall evening. As the sun set and the house darkened, Mrs. Tyler lit the kerosene table lamps. She motioned for the boys to find places to sit while she and her husband settled on a cushioned sofa.

Mr. Tyler began, "Tomorrow's Adam's last day of the week on the mountain. He works at *The Herald* on Friday. I've arranged for him to take the day off so he can show you around, Michael. While Snow Shoe is a small town, it does have several small industries, a central business district, and another residential area on the north side of the tracks that is nearly twice the size of that here on the south side."

"Also," Mrs. Tyler joined in, "we're going to have to think about getting you enrolled in school. The town has an elementary school that has begun its fall session some weeks ago, and I suspect you are still school age. How old are you?"

"My parents found me near the end of summer many seasons ago and have guessed my age by the seasons. They would say this was my eleventh summer and I would be going into my twelfth winter."

"The school goes through the eighth grade so your age would put you in the seventh grade this year. But that would depend in part on how much you know in the various subject areas," the woman continued.

"What are subject areas?" the boy asked.

Adam stepped in at this point. "Schools teach different areas of information including reading, writing, figuring, and history. Did you ever go to a school before?"

"No. My father and Grandfather taught me what I needed to know. After the fight with the soldiers and my people's going away, I stayed with Trader Mattson at Keith Summer's trading post in the town of Savage, and he taught me to read and write and to do figures and count money. I do not know of this thing you call school."

"Michael," Mr. Tyler joined in, "we know some of your life from what Jay has shared with us from what Scot Robinson has written to him. But there is much we don't know. You just touched on events about which we know nothing. We won't ask questions. You can tell us what you want when you want. I can see that school is not something you are familiar with. Next week, Mrs. Tyler can take you to the school and see about getting you enrolled. The principal teacher will try to figure out which class will work best for you."

Adam cut in. "I'll help you with whatever is needed to get you in with your age group. Ma, you make sure they know that at school and put Michael in a class his own age."

"I'll do what I can, Adam. Let's not worry about that 'til next week. For now, just plan on enjoying tomorrow together."

"Thanks," Michael sighed.

"What about a game of dominoes," Adam suggested.

"Teach me?" Michael asked.

"Yes," Adam replied.

Mr. Tyler got the box of dominoes while the boys moved to the floor on either side of a low side table. The adults watched as the boys played and the older one taught the younger one the game. The evening slipped away and the hour came when all decided it was time to go to bed. The fire in the stove was banked to burn low for the night. The game was packed away. The parents closed up the house for the night as the boys headed upstairs to their rooms.

"Here," Adam offered. "Take this lamp from the table here so you can see where you're going." He handed the boy the lamp. "There's one for each room. You bring it back down in the morning."

"Thanks."

Before long everyone was settled in bed and Michael lay reflecting on the day that had just passed and all that had happened. It was hard to believe that he had only arrived that morning and so much had happened, that the morning seemed so long ago. He closed his eyes, thought again of his family, and softly cried himself to sleep.

# About Town

It was still dark when Adam stepped into the doorway to Michael's room, kerosene lamp in hand. "Time to start the day, Michael," he announced, setting the lamp on top of the chest of drawers.

"What time is it?"

"Six o'clock. Time to start chores. I'll be in the kitchen." He picked up the darkened lamp from the desk by the window and was gone.

Michael threw off the bedding and sat up, rubbing the sleep from his eyes. Reaching his clothes from the chair beside the bed, he dressed, made up the bed, and left the room to the kitchen, taking the lamp as he went. At the foot of the stairs, he blew out the lamp and left it on a side table in the hall.

"Mornin' sleepy head," Adam greeted as the younger boy entered the kitchen.

"Adam!" his mother chastised.

"Just kiddin'."

"Hi," Michael greeted. "I guess I have a lot of change to get used to. Only yesterday this time I was on a train." He took his hat and jacket from the rack and stepped to the door. "We have chores to do?"

"Yea." Adam reached for his hat and jacket and followed.

"See you boys at breakfast soon 's the chores are done," Mr. Tyler added.

The milk bucket and the egg basket were returned to their locations as the boys headed toward the barn. Of-The-Wind neighed with excitement as her master entered the barn. Michael went directly to her stall and entered to caress her mane and speak soft words of greeting in her ear.

"I'll feed the livestock," Adam stated. "Why don't you and your pony spend some time together."

"Thanks. We haven't had a chance in so long as we rode the train for days and really didn't have much time yesterday."

He led his pony out of the stall and into the meadow. The dark of early dawn just began to fade in the thin yellow glow across the eastern horizon. After standing a moment, he swung up onto her back and they raced across the meadow in a joyous run. He made it a point to avoid the back fence area where the holes were. As they crossed the meadow, the boy saw critters standing near some of the holes. They looked like prairie dogs, but were bigger and fatter. Adam entered the stall and walked to the open door to watch the two go, racing silhouettes in the predawn light. A smile of appreciation at the joy he watched, creased his face, and he stood there sensing the joy he was witnessing. Minutes passed and the tall lanky youth returned to his chores.

As Adam stood the hay fork in the haystack on the floor, he heard Michael and his pony return to the barn. The boy slipped to the ground, caressed his pony's neck, and whispered some words into her ear. He then reentered the stall from the meadow as his pony wandered off to graze.

"You two are one together," Adam complemented. "We're done here. Let's head up for breakfast." He picked up the bucket of milk and handed it to the younger boy, then grabbed the basket of eggs on the way out the door.

As the boys left the barn, Michael questioned, "I saw two boys along the creek in the distance. Why were they there?" He stopped and turned to Adam for an answer.

The teen paused and turned toward the hills. "Teddy Latimer has a trap line along the Lawrence Creek and into the hills beyond. It stretches nearly a half mile. He and his friend Miles Hart are checking to see if they caught anything before they head off to school."

The two turned once again toward the house, bucket and basket in hand.

"They're about your age. You'll probably meet them next week when you start school."

They ascended the back porch steps and entered the kitchen where breakfast was waiting on the table and the aroma of fresh-cooked bacon and potatoes, and coffee perfumed the air. The milk and eggs were left near the sink.

\* \* \*

It was a crisp autumn morning as Adam and Michael wandered out the lane toward Cedar Street. The Norway maples that lined the lane were vibrant in their yellow coloring as they continued to slowly shed their leaves with the occasional splash of color floating on the morning air in a slow glide to the ground. Each wore a light jacket against the chilly morning air as he walked the leaf littered gravel lane with dry leaves crunching under foot. Michael smiled as he noticed a grey squirrel meander across the path ahead, then scramble up a tree. It paused on a low branch, up against the tree trunk, and watched the boys go by.

"They'll be gathering for winter sleep soon," Michael commented.

"I've noticed they seem to be gathering quite a supply this year," Adam added. "The oak and walnut trees have very few nuts on the ground beneath. The squirrels get them as soon as they drop."

The boys reached the street and headed to the right toward Washington Street.

"Are the winters hard around here?" Michael asked.

"Generally we have snow before Thanksgiving and it lasts into March. Once the season starts we get very little rain or ice. It usually stays too cold and comes as snow. Sometimes it snows for days on end. Sometimes there are clear blue skies and bright sun, even though it stays bitter cold. Some years are worse than others."

They reached Washington Street and turned toward the center of town.

"This might be a hard year," Michael observed. "The animals usually know."

"I think you're right," Adam agreed.

The houses along the right side of the street were mostly alike in their design, two-story wood frame structures with a full width front porch and a one-story back section for the kitchen and woodshed. Most had a small barn and chicken coop in the back yard. Yards were narrow with shallow yards in front and more area in back. These were the original company houses for the lumber company beyond the creek which ran behind them. Larger properties with bigger homes stretched along the left-hand side of the street.

Adam pointed to the distant right. "See those buildings beyond the houses on the other side of the creek?" Michael nodded. "That's the Starkweather Lumber Company. Most of the logs that come off the mountain end up there. Most everyone who lives along Washington Street works at the company. More workers live on the north side of town on the other side of the railroad."

The boys continued toward the business district.

"Who lives in the bigger houses on this other side of the street?" Michael asked, pointing to the nearest property.

"Some of the foremen and other bosses from the big companies live there. It's close to their work. Company owners and businessmen from the stores in the business district live along Main Street, the next street over. There are a few company homes along Jeffers Street which backs up to the tracks for the Stewart Creek Logging Company. Most workers live on the north side of town."

They had arrived at Railroad Avenue where the firehouse stood across the street in front of them. The boys stopped so the younger could study the structure and its stable to the left of the main building. All doors were closed against the chill air. There was no sign of life.

Adam described, "The fire company has two engines, a pumper for pumping water and a ladder truck that carries extra hose and ladders. The second floor has a bunk room where the firemen stay when they are on duty. They have a full kitchen and living area on the first floor beside the engine bay area. There are matched teams of white horses in the stable building, four for each engine. They sure are beautiful when they're harnessed up and on a run. They're not bad in a parade either."

"Can we go in?" Michael asked.

"Another day when we have more time," Adam replied. "The street to the right," he continued, "goes to the Graham Barrel Company, then on to the lumber company. In between is an engine house for Number forty-six, the "Kidd," and its caboose, plus storage tracks of the fire train and the snow plow car. Number forty-six takes care of delivering freight cars to their various companies and businesses, and assembling freight cars into their daily freight train. The first business after the firehouse is Daniel Baldwin's Feed and Grain Company. We're going to go to the left here down Railroad Avenue."

The boys began to walk the business district. Adam pointed out each of the stores along the left side of the street. The right side of the street contained the millwork and hardware, each of which backed up on the railroad with spurs along the back of each for receiving deliveries by rail. Stores and shops lined the left side of the street with the Railroad Hotel taking up half a block on the crossroads corner with Main Street. To the right, Main Street passed between the millwork and hardware to cross the tracks to the station complex and on into the large residential area to the north.

Passing Main, the boys went on to the corner of Jeffers. The last business on the near side was the Wells Fargo Company with the livery stable on the right side of the street just past the hardware. Adam pointed out *The Herald* newspaper and press, just before Wells Fargo, where he worked on Fridays.

"This is where I'll be tomorrow. Evan Clanton owns the newspaper and puts it out each Friday. It's printed starting on Wednesday with last minute items finished in the morning and distributed in the afternoon. I help with the morning printing and use Mr. Clanton's horse and wagon to distribute during the afternoon."

The schoolhouse stood on the far side of Jeffers, a large red two-story wooden structure on about an acre of schoolyard.

"This is where I'll be next week?" Michael asked.

"Yea," Adam responded. "There are four large classrooms, two with an office upstairs for the older kids and two with an office downstairs for the younger kids. Each teacher as two grades."

They stood looking over the building and its schoolyard until Adam decided it was time to move on.

"Behind the school and the houses along Jeffers Street are the tracks for the Stewart Creek Logging Company. We can cut through behind the livery and I'll show you about. I work with my pa four days a week on the mountain at South Camp where they're cutting the final stand of trees off that section." Adam led the way past the livery corral to the company track leading out from the station area. "We're gathering material to lay a new line further up the mountain to cut a new area. It will become the new South Camp. Beginning next week, crews will clear the right of way and lay track while others will finish planting new seedling trees in the last areas that were cut."

Arriving at the track, Adam led the way left toward the building complex of the logging company. Stepping through a switch track, Michael looked ahead and saw several empty storage tracks to the right of the logging main, and to the right of that, a track that ran between the buildings to another behind. One of the storage tracks led into a car shop. A small office building stood across the through track to the right on the back side of the engine house.

"We'll stop in the office building first," Adam stated. He glanced toward the sun. "It must be nearing lunch time."

A shrill whistle shrieked from up toward the mountain and its call echoed back from the trees.

"That's the morning load coming down from South Camp," Adam announced pointing toward the mountain.

As the two watched, the plume of smoke marked the train's progress down the valley. There was a movement at the bend ahead. Michael could make out a carload of logs coming toward him. Soon he could see clearly the end of ten loaded log cars with the engine behind, backing slowly toward them. The whistle blew for the road crossing behind the boys toward the station, as they stepped further back to a safer distance from the tracks. The train rumbled slowly past, stopped at the switch, then continued on toward the saw mill.

"I'll show ya 'round another time. Ma must have lunch ready and she'll be lookin' for us."

They cut back across to Jeffers Street passing a noisy schoolyard where the children had been let out for noon break. Most were gathered in small knots, talking together and eating their lunches. Some had already gone off to the swings and playground or to the back yard area to start a game of baseball. An older boy noticed Adam and Michael and wandered to the front fence.

Leaning on the top rail he called out. "Adam! Whose yer blond girl friend?"

"Shut yer foul mouth, Jamison, or I'll shut it for ya!" Adam shouted in return.

Michael cringed at the sudden exchange.

"And you would just do that, too," the large stocky red head retorted. "Well come and get me." He turned and disappeared around the schoolhouse.

"He's not worth your time," Adam turned to Michael. "Let's go home."

"Why?" the younger boy asked. "What did I do to him?"

They headed home by way of Jeffers Street. Just past Pine Avenue on the same side of the street as the school, the boys passed a white church building with a tall graceful bell tower above the front entrance.

"Jamison's a bully," Adam informed. "He's always finding someone to pick on. But it's all talk. He can't stand up to anyone who would fight back. That's why he left. You are who you are and he'll just have to get used to it."

"Oh." He looked toward the church building. "Is that a church?"

"That's the Reverend Jesse Moore's Methodist church. We attend there on Sundays."

They arrived at the corner of Cedar and turned toward home.

*     *     *

At lunch, Mrs. Tyler asked the boys about their morning. Michael shared all he had seen and Adam shared the incident with Jamison Boyd.

"Do you want your hair cut?" Mrs. Tyler asked.

"No."

"Then it's settled. Jamison will just have to live with it. I'm sure you will make new friends and he will have to find someone else to pick on."

Following lunch, Adam asked if Michael would like to go fishing. They dug a few worms from the wood yard, took the fishing poles from the tool shed near the carriage barn, and headed out across the meadow to Lawrence Creek. Of-The-wind followed and stayed to graze nearby. It was a lazy afternoon with a few bites but no catches. The afternoon wore on until it was time for chores. The three wandered back to the barn, fishing poles were retired and chores took attention. Michael tried his hand at milking the cow. Mr. Tyler got home from work and it was time for dinner. The evening slipped by and the day came to an end.

Michael, having changed into his nightshirt, sat on the side of his bed and reflected. He had only arrived on the train yesterday, and already, so much had happened. It felt as though ages had passed. Life was so different. The life he had lived seemed but a dream. The Tylers were nice enough, but he missed his family and his people and his friends. He missed his life. Crossing the room to the window he knelt and rested his arms on the window sill and gazed out toward the barn and beyond. The landscape was bathed in moonlight from a broken moon. He looked beyond to the shadow of the mountain. Someday he would explore that too. New adventures awaited, but the past tugged at his heart. The boy rested his forehead on his arms and wept.

# SCHOOL AND NEW FRIENDS

The Tyler family stayed at home the weekend so the boys would have time together and Michael could have some time with Of-The-Wind. Adam put a saddle on Cheyenne and the two spent time each afternoon riding beyond the far side of the meadow into the lower hills of Fisher Mountain. He marveled that the younger boy road bareback, but said nothing. It was a quiet time, a comfortable time.

The household rose at six on Monday morning. The boys tended the chores. Breakfast of sausage and pancakes was served after which lunches were packed and Adam and his father left at seven for work at the logging company. Michael helped clear the table as Mrs. Tyler washed the dishes and placed them in the drainer to drip dry. Then she packed a lunch for Michael and they sat at the kitchen table to plan the trip to school.

"School starts at nine o'clock and lets out at three," she informed. "I figure we'll go over a half hour early and get you checked in."

"I'm not feeling too good about this," Michael offered. "I never had to stay inside on a fixed time before."

"Please give it a try." Sympathetic eyes gazed at the boy. "Look at it as a new adventure. Maybe make a friend who can help to pass the day." She lay a hand on his wrist. "I've packed some cheese for a morning snack when the school breaks for recess and a sandwich and apple for lunch. There's milk in the tin jug. Florence Miller teaches the oldest class. She's firm, but fair and very considerate of her students. Helen Wheatley is the principal teacher. She teaches the third level students and runs the school as well. Esther Forte is the secretary and runs the first floor office."

"Thanks for all the information, but I might not remember most of it." Michael stood from the table as the parlor clock struck the quarter hour past eight. "Is it time?"

"It's time," Mrs. Tyler agreed as she, too, rose from her chair.

Michael took his jacket and hat from the peg by the door. Mrs. Tyler reached for hers as the boy put his on. Picking up his lunch bucket and milk jug from the sink counter, he joined Mrs. Tyler as they headed down the hall toward the front door.

* * *

The boy and the woman entered the schoolyard gate and approached the front door. A number of children were already in the play area on the swings and seesaws, or the field playing baseball. Some stopped to watch the new boy enter the building, then returned to their play.

Just inside the large oak front double doors, a staircase went up from either side of the door to a second floor balcony hall. On each floor, a classroom opened off on the right and left side of the center hall and the office opened across from the front door. Mrs. Tyler led the way into the office.

Esther Forte looked up from her desk. A young woman in her late thirties, her light brown hair was put up in a round bun on the back of her head. She wore a dress with a floral pattern in shades of green. "Mornin' Janet. Is this Michael?"

The boy was surprised to hear his name from a stranger.

"Yes, Esther, meet Michael Freeman. Michael, this is Miss Forte," she introduced.

"Pleased to meet ya, Ma'am," the boy nodded.

"I'll need to get some information for his school records," Miss Forte stated as the office door behind her opened and Helen Wheatley stepped out. Her bearing was a bit formal, enhanced by her graying hair and wrinkle lines on a face used to smiling. As the principal teacher, she was the senior member of the staff and administrator for the school.

"Good morning, Janet," she greeted, just a little stiff in manner. "I'll take Michael upstairs and introduce him to Florence and see about where to get him started while you and Esther work on his records information."

"Thanks," Mrs. Tyler responded. "Adam said to be sure she knows he will help him at home and to put him in a class his own age."

"We can start him there and make changes if it doesn't work out."

"Thanks. I'll leave you with Miss Wheatley, Michael, and see you at home after school."

"Okay," the boy replied as a sudden sinking feeling hit the pit of his stomach. He followed the woman upstairs, casting one last look toward Mrs. Tyler.

"I understand you're twelve years old and have never been to school before," Miss Wheatley stated as they reached the top of the staircase.

"Yes, Ma'am," Michael answered, as she turned to the right and entered the classroom. He followed her in, finding them in a large room with high six-foot double-hung, multi-paned windows on three sides of the room. Three neat rows of wooden desks filled the center of the room to accommodate the two dozen students assigned to the class. An empty desk in the back of each row provided for any new students that might arrive during the year. Mrs. Miller rose from her desk in the front of the room as the two entered, and met them beside her desk. The front wall behind her desk had a chalk board full of notes, bulletin boards on either side and across the top, covered with student work, teacher display material, and along the top of the chalkboard, the letters of the alphabet in cursive.

"Florence," Miss Wheatley began, "this is Michael Freeman. He's living with Janet Tyler and her family. Michael, Mrs. Miller will be your teacher to start, until we are able to learn how much you know and the most appropriate grade level in which to place you."

"Pleased to meet you, Mrs. Miller," Michael nodded.

"I hope we will work well together," Mrs. Miller responded.

"I'll leave you two to settle in," Miss Wheatley said as she turned to leave. "It's almost time for Esther to ring the bell to call the students in." She was gone.

The teacher stood a comfortable height near five and a half feet tall. She was not a full-figure woman yet at ease with herself, standing relaxed with an obvious air of confidence. Wire-rim glasses and a firm square jaw line gave her a no-nonsense countenance. She spoke with a firm, but kindly tone.

"Michael," Mrs. Miller instructed, "we'll not have time to sort things out just now as the rest of the class will be in soon." She led him to a desk near her desk in the front of the room on her left. "This will be your seat for now so I can keep an eye on your needs, until you make a friend who can become your guide for the present. There's a cubby along the side wall where you can put your lunch, and coat and hat. I have gathered books for you to begin with until we decide what's best." She set the textbooks, a copybook, and pencil on the desk.

The bell on the rooftop began to ring and a sudden rush of footsteps and voices began to surge into the building and echo up the staircases and into the classrooms. Mrs. Miller returned to the door to greet the students as they arrived.

A voice called out as it passed through the room, "Hey everyone, Adam Tyler's girlfriend is here."

"Jamison Boyd!" Mrs. Miller's voice echoed across a suddenly silenced room, "You are totally out of order! You stand yourself in the back corner of the room until I tell you otherwise! Once more and your pa will be notified to take you home for the rest of the day and you well know he will not put up with your rudeness!"

Jamison left his things on his desk and walked to the back corner where he stood dutifully facing the corner wall. The class settled with full attention on their teacher, ready to begin the day's lessons.

"Students," she began, "I want you to welcome Michael Freeman to our class. He's come a long ways to stay with Adam Tyler's family and to become a member of our class. Stand and be seen, Michael."

He stood awkwardly, gazed across the sea of faces, then quickly turned and resumed his seat. He wished he could vanish and never come back again. Again, that sinking sick feeling flooded his stomach.

"It's time to start our day," Mrs. Miller stated. "We begin with the Pledge of Allegiance to the flag followed by the Lord's Prayer. Students," she turned to the flag above the chalk board. Placing her hand over her heart she began, "I pledge allegiance to the flag...with liberty and justice for all." Then facing the class, she bowed her head and began. "Our Father who art in heaven...Amen."

"Ma'am," a voice called as a boy on the far side of the room raised his hand.

"What is it, Teddy?"

"Is it all right if I move my seat and sit with Michael and help him to learn how we do our lessons?"

"That would be a great help, Teddy. Sarah," she spoke to the girl in front. "Would you please trade seats with Teddy?"

The move was made as the teacher introduced the younger boy.

"Michael, this is Teddy Latimer." Teddy offered his hand and Michael accepted. "He will take good care of any questions you have and guide you through the day's lessons."

Mrs. Miller went over the instructions on the chalkboard for each of the two classes, explaining the math assignments, page numbers, and practice work to be done in their copybooks. While the eighth grade students began their review practice, she worked with the seventh graders to explain and demonstrate the concepts involved in the situation problems they were to solve. For the next twenty minutes the teacher moved from student to student to check for accuracy and to re-explain concepts as needed. Teddy showed Michael the process needed to read each problem and select the ciphering process needed to solve it. It reminded Michael of his days working with Trader Mattson at the trading post and he was able to relate the problems to his work in the store. Teddy checked his work and confirmed its accuracy and the two worked quietly solving each problem and cross checking their answers and their work.

Mrs. Miller noted the boys' progress and smiled to herself that a good partnership was at hand and a friendship had begun. Michael, too, felt a new comfort as he worked with Teddy, and hoped they could be friends outside of school as well. This must be the Teddy Latimer that he had seen checking the trap line, and Michael sensed they might have interests in common. He felt himself relax and begin to feel more comfortable. The feeling in his stomach was gone, replaced by a growing confidence.

*   *   *

As the day played out, a subdued Jamison returned to his seat and ignored Michael during the rest of class. Mrs. Miller kept alert to any concerns Michael might have, but observed that Teddy was able to guide the older boy through the day's lessons. Reading and writing went well. Handwriting was challenging, but Michael figured he could take the workbook home and practice the cursive letter shapes. Grammar was a total loss. The whole concept was so foreign to his experience. Mrs. Miller offered to tutor him after school and try to teach him the basics so he could work at his own level on his classwork. Likewise, he had no experience with history. The teacher suggested that she get him the history books from the lower grades and he could read up on earlier history on his own and try to make sense of the assignments in class.

Teddy stayed with Michael during recess and lunch break. They took lunch seated under a black walnut tree. Another boy approached. Before they sat down, Teddy made the introduction.

"Michael," he began, "this is my friend, Miles Hart."

They exchanged handshakes, then settled under the tree to eat lunch. Both boys were close to five feet in height, give or take an inch, Miles the slightly taller of the two. Teddy's facial features appeared more refined and Miles' slightly more pudgy. Neither boy carried any extra weight as they both appeared used to an active lifestyle.

Michael observed that he was most likely the oldest of the three. Their conversation revealed that Miles had turned twelve the week school started and Teddy's birthday was coming up in December. While young for seventh grade, Teddy was a quick learner and had been advanced a grade two years previous. Both boys though similar in height, were shorter than Michael.

"Are you the two I saw working the trap line behind Adam's place Thursday morning?" Michael asked between mouthfuls of sandwich.

"Yea," Teddy replied.

"How'd ya know?" Miles questioned.

"I saw ya while doin' chores with Adam," the older boy answered. "Adam told me."

Teddy explained, "We were only there before school that day because we missed the afternoon before."

Miles added, "Good thing, too. Got two rabbits and a squirrel."

"Want ta work with us?" Teddy asked.

"Okay, I can help some," Michael accepted.

Following lunch the boys played baseball and Michael sat on the side and watched. It looked like fun. One day he would play, too.

As he sat and watched the game, Jamison walked by and paused to glare angrily at him, then moved on. Michael wasn't upset by it. He had friends and the confidence that the older boy was more mouth with little likely action toward someone equal in stature.

The school day ended with an invitation to join his friends later when they came by to check the trap line.

*     *     *

Michael sat at the kitchen table with an after school snack of milk and cookies. Mrs. Tyler sat across from him as he shared his first day of school.

"Mrs. Miller is a nice teacher. She offered to help me after school with grammar. It's something I never heard of before." He paused to finish a cookie and drink some milk. "She also got some books from other teachers so I can read about history. I was glad for my time with Trader Mattson at the trading post. It helped me to understand the ciphering problems."

"Tell me again about your new friends," the woman asked.

"Teddy Latimer asked if he could help me with my lessons, and at lunch I met his friend Miles Hart. They have a trap line out back along the creek." He continued with another cookie.

"I know them. They're good boys," Mrs. Tyler informed. She set her cup down. "Their fathers both work at the saw mill. They always stop here on the way to the trap line when they go right after school, to leave their books and lunch buckets. When they go home first, they're usually here within the hour."

There were footsteps on the porch.

"That should be them. Ask them in for a snack."

Michael went to the door even as there was a light rapping on the wood, and let his friends into the kitchen.

"Have you eaten?" the woman asked.

"No, we wanted to come right over," Miles replied.

"We hope Michael can come with us to check the trap line," Teddy explained.

"He'll go with you," Mrs. Tyler confirmed. "First, here are some fresh baked cookies and milk." She poured the milk and set the glasses in front of each boy as Michael slid the plate of cookies in their direction.

"Thanks," they chorused.

A short time later, they were finished and ready to leave. Michael put on his coat and hat and the three left, pulling the door shut and banging the screen door behind. Teddy picked up a grain sack he had left on the porch, and slung it over his arm.

"How long have you had your trap line?" Michael asked as the three walked toward the creek behind the carriage shed.

"We started last summer," Teddy replied. "It's sort of a shared thing to earn some extra money to help our parents be able to buy things they might not get otherwise."

They approached the creek and the first trap.

"Whatever we get," Miles added, "we skin and salt and take to the general store. Harvey Jenkins buys them and collects them in his store room. When he gets enough to bale, he sells them to a tannery in Brookston and ships them out by train."

"There are some boys on the north side of town who have trap lines, too." Teddy paused to check the first trap. It was empty. "Even with their skins, it takes a while for Mr. Jenkins to collect enough for a bale."

They moved on to the next trap. It held a dead rabbit. Miles removed the rabbit and put it in the sack while Teddy reset the trap. Michael watched. While the trap line followed the creek, most traps were several yards away from the water. The third trap was sprung, but empty. Teddy reset it and they moved on. A raccoon was taken from the forth and the next was empty. Nearly an hour passed as the boys advanced along the half mile. In the end, they had collected a coon, two rabbits, and a squirrel. It was time to head back.

*   *   *

"How was your first day of school?" Adam stood behind the cow with his elbow resting on its hind quarter while Michael tried his hand at milking.

"It was okay, especially after Teddy Latimer volunteered to sit with me and help me with my classwork. At lunch hour I met his friend, Miles Hart. They're the ones you told me about last week. They came over after school and we walked their trap line." Concentrating on getting the milk into the bucket, Michael didn't look up.

Finally, he got the last drop of milk, stood up, and handed Adam the stool.

"When the class first came in to the room," Michael continued, "I was standing with Mrs. Miller near her desk, and that Jamison went by and made another remark about my being your girlfriend. Mrs. Miller stood him in the back corner of the room. He didn't bother me the rest of the day."

They left the cow stall, put the milk by the door and the stool outside the box stall, and went on to do the rest of the chores.

"You know he's all mouth, don't you?" Adam stated.

"I noticed. If it looked like someone was going to fight back, he ran off and disappeared in the play area. Since Teddy and Miles became my friends, I don't worry about his words."

The livestock was fed, fresh bedding was thrown into the box stalls, and the next day's hay thrown down. The boys headed for the house and stopped to feed the chickens and collect the eggs along the way. The last chore they did was to check the fire in the smoke house to keep it low in flame and as smoky as possible. The pile of cut wood was mostly trimmings from apple trees to give an apple flavor to the meat.

At dinner, Michael again shared his day with the Tylers. Afterwards, all retired to the living room, Mr. Tyler tended the stove, the boys again played dominoes, and the parents read. The day slipped toward night and the lamps were lit. As the nine o'clock hour approached, game and reading materials were set aside and all retired to their rooms. Before Michael changed into his night shirt, he opened his trunk and pulled out his warm red capote and hung it in the wardrobe. Cooler weather would soon arrive.

The boy reflected on the day and thought of the days ahead. He had never had a routine before. Now each day would have its sameness – up at six for chores, breakfast, then Adam and his pa were off to work at seven. There would be time with Mrs. Tyler until leaving for school at 8:30, tutoring with Mrs. Miller after school let out at three, home for homework and some free time with Of-The-Wind, chores, dinner, time with family, bedtime, then start again the next morning and do it all over again. Once more, Michael knelt by the window and looked out at the faintly lit moonscape. He thought again of his past life and its people – gone. Forever? Resting his arms on the window sill and his chin on his arms, Michael gazed toward the mountain and wondered what adventure might lay ahead.

Moments later, he stood, crossed to his bed, crawled in, and lay on his back with his hands beneath his head. He closed his eyes and exhaustion pulled him into sleep.

*     *     *

The week drifted on and settled into its routine, including ongoing insults from Jamison whenever he found the opportunity, away from the presence of any of the teachers, but always with an audience of other children. Michael tried to ignore the teasing. But the more he did so, the more intense it became.

"Aren't you going to do something?" Teddy asked during the Thursday lunch hour.

"I have an idea," Michael replied. "But it depends on stopping Jamison from getting away every time he says something."

"What if I can get my friends to form a circle around you both so he can't get away the next time he says something," Teddy offered.

"That should work." Michael packed his lunch bucket as he finished his lunch, then stood to go watch the baseball game.

Teddy wandered the school yard talking to a number of his friends.

They gathered near the ball game and settled to watch. Some took part in the game and between innings spoke quietly to teammates. Mrs. Miller had playground duty and watched the game from the playground as she supervised the children on the play equipment. Between the noise of activity on the swings and other equipment and the cheers from the game, the sound level was quite loud. Jamison slipped up behind Michael and spoke so all nearby could hear.

"Our girlfriend here has to watch the game. She's too timid to play."

The reaction was electric. The game stopped abruptly and Teddy's friends from the sidelines and the field quickly surrounded Jamison and Michael so that the older boy could not move away. He tried to run off and was quickly blocked by the surrounding students. Mrs. Miller noticed the commotion and started to walk to the gathering to prevent any trouble. She stopped when she heard Michael speak and decided to watch instead.

"Jamison," he began, "where I come from my people have two ways of dealing with people like you. Sometimes, they just kill their enemies. But in your case, they would challenge you to a feat of strength or skill. I challenge you."

There was silence as Jamison cringed and tried to get away. At the word challenge, he took notice.

"What challenge?"

"We stand with our right foot touching and lock arms. Then, whoever forces the other to move his foot is the winner. If you win, you can go on saying whatever you like. If I win, you never say an unkind word again and we try to become friends."

There was a collective gasp of breath as all listened to the details of the challenge and Jamison stepped closer, relieved that his younger opponent did not intend to beat him up.

"I'll show you." Michael took Jamison's arm and helped him to lock forearms together, then guided him into placing their feet side by side.

"You ready?"

The taller boy nodded.

"When Miles says 'go' we start."

"Okay."

A dead silence came over the crowd, which had grown as others became aware that something was happening. Mrs. Miller watched in awe. Never had she seen an argument settled without a fight. Others from within the building came out as they heard the silence, saw something was happening, but no battle stirring up the dust, and became deeply curious. "Go!"

It was over in an instant as Michael pushed then quickly pulled his opponent off balance and Jamison stepped wildly to try and keep from falling. Too late. As he tumbled backward to the ground, Michael caught him with his free hand and prevented him from hitting the dirt.

Wild applause erupted. "I never..!" Mrs. Miller whispered to herself. A startled Jamison, standing with Michael's hands still on him to prevent his falling, starred in disbelief. Michael let go and offered his hand in friendship. At first, Jamison just starred at it, then slowly reached out to accept. This time he looked at the younger boy with respect and cracked a smile.

"You won. I learned something today. Thanks." He shook the offered hand with a strong grip. "If you mean it, I would like to be your friend. But I wonder."

"What?" Michael asked as they released their grip.

"Why is your hair so long?"

"Where I come from, my people all let their hair grow. It is a sign of strength."

"Oh."

The bell on the schoolhouse rang to call the students back for the afternoon session. Lunch buckets and game equipment were gathered and the mass moved toward the schoolhouse doors, in noisy chatter about what they had just witnessed. Mrs. Miller followed the students into the building, amazed at what had happened and at a loss for words to comment. As she passed her colleagues, they quietly shook their heads as they followed their students into the classrooms for afternoon lessons.

*     *     *

As the week ended, Jamison learned that Michael didn't play baseball because he wasn't familiar with the game. Thus, at recess and lunch hour, the stocky red head offered to teach his new young friend how to play the game. It wasn't long before they both joined a team and took part.

As the days slipped by, Michael and Jamison enjoyed their new friendship on the ball field. Each had his own circle of friends and was comfortable not going beyond baseball. For Jamison, his changed respect for Michael had consequences. More boys his own age felt a new respect toward him and in turn, took him into their circle of friends.

# The Revelation
# and the Hunt

Mrs. Tyler finished adding the vegetables to the roasting pan, arranged them around the roast, put on the lid, and placed the covered pan into the oven. She closed the oven door as the kitchen door to the side porch opened and Michael arrived home from school. She turned to the counter to move the plate of cookies to the table, then retrieved the pitcher of milk from the ice box and a glass from the dish drainer. Michael dropped his school books and jacket on the side chair beside the back door. They met at the table.

"How was your day at school?" she asked, pouring herself a cup of coffee and taking a seat across from the boy.

"Jamison and I joined the ball game today," he pulled out a chair and sat down, "and I actually hit the ball during the game."

"I'm so glad you two have a friendship." She poured a glass of milk and placed it on the table. "How are your lessons coming."

The boy took a sip from the glass. "Mrs. Miller let me read from the lower grade books during history class and gave me a set of review questions based on my reading while the rest of the class worked from their books. Teddy helped me with words I did not understand. I'm still confused with what she calls grammar, but she keeps trying to help me after school." He reached for a cookie and took a bite. Once swallowed, he continued. "But it's only the end of the second week, and so much has happened."

The front door opened and Adam was home. Entering the kitchen, he kicked off his shoes along the wall under the line of coat pegs.

"Another Friday," the teen called, "and another issue of *The Herald* is out." He reached out and hung his jacket and hat on the peg beside the porch door, then pulled up a chair at the table. "They smell good, Ma." With that, a cookie disappeared.

After he finished a second cookie and a glass of milk, Adam stood from the table and turned to Michael. "Let's do chores a little early and go riding in the back meadow," he suggested.

Finishing his own snack, Michael agreed, "Fine by me."

Grabbing their hats and jackets, the boys headed out the door.

\* \* \*

Adam slipped the bridle over his horse's head, then led Cheyenne out of her box stall and tied the reins to a ring on the outside wall. He then brought the saddle from the tack room, threw the blanket onto her back then lifted the saddle in place. Reaching under her belly, he grabbed the cinch strap, pulled it forward, and tied it securely. Adam led Cheyenne out to the meadow by way of Of-The-Wind's box stall where Michael waited patiently on his pony's bare back.

"You don't use a saddle or blanket or bridle?" the surprised youth finally decided to asked.

"Never have," Michael replied. "We've always traveled together like this. I grab a handful of her mane and my knees tell her what I ask." With that, he turned his pony away from the barn door and started to walk into the meadow.

Adam mounted his horse and followed.

"Let's head for the gate at the far corner of the meadow and take the trail into the hills of Fisher Mountain." He moved ahead to lead the way. "I never go fast in the meadows because of the groundhog holes."

"Is that what they're called?"

The boys rode leisurely across the grassland, pausing whenever their horses chose to graze. Far ahead, groundhogs stood on the dirt mounds beside their holes and watched the boys' approach. Near the fence line, a rabbit stopped to watch. As the riders came nearer, each disappeared into hole or underbrush. Arriving at the gate, Adam pulled alongside to reach down, slide the drawbar back, and swing the gate open.

"The first few acres of this timber belong to our farm. We'll pass a stone corner marker and then we're on logging company property." Adam explained. "They've never logged these hills. Their railroad tracks are up the mountainside about a mile from here."

The two rode on along the trail, deeper into the forested landscape.

Michael pointed at the sound of movement to their left. "Deer."

Adam turned and drew Cheyenne to a stop. Michael did likewise. They paused for a moment as they watched a yearling fawn and its mother wander through the underbrush. In the distance, a small buck studied the boys, then moved on with the other two.

Adam pointed out the marker as they crossed onto logging company property. "Except for the marker, you wouldn't know there's any difference out here. The forest is the same."

The trail began to rise up into the hills. The silence was intense and wrapped the two in a sense of peace. A slight breeze stirred and was gone. A distant whistle echoed off the mountainside.

"That's the afternoon train coming in from the logging camp. Pa should be home within the hour." Adam turned his horse. "It's time we started back."

Michael turned Of-The-Wind to lead the way back down the trail. They had been out nearly an hour, so the boy picked up the pace. Less than a half hour later he reentered the meadow and paused while Adam closed and secured the gate. Minutes later, he dismounted from his pony and turned her loose to wander to the water trough near the corner of the barn by the gate.

"I'll get the eggs and meet you at the house," the boy announced. He left the meadow by way of the gate.

"Okay," Adam acknowledged. "I'll be along shortly with the milk."

*   *   *

As the dinner table was cleared of dirty dishes and leftovers, Michael left the kitchen. Moments later he returned with two buckskin bundles, a long one held together with leather laces and a smaller fat one with beaded design also tied with leather lacing, and placed them on the empty table. He stood beside the table and waited while the family finished putting leftover food in the ice box and began to wash the dinner dishes. Adam and his mother were at the sink and his father had just closed the icebox door.

"What's this?" Mr. Tyler asked.

The others turned from the sink to see what he had asked about.

Michael stood by the table and responded. "What has Jay told you about me?"

Mrs. Tyler dried her hands as she crossed the room toward the table. "Michael, Jay told us you were coming from the frontier, had suffered a personal disaster, had lost your family, and needed a place to live and start a new life. That's all we know about you." She rested her hands on the back of her chair.

"He didn't tell you who I was?" The boy stood watching each face and its reaction to his words.

"Only that your name was Michael PC Freeman," she replied. "And that's how I registered you at school."

Adam and his father approached the table. The family sat down.

"We have learned," Mr. Tyler added, "from what you said last week that there was some sort of fight. But you don't have to explain if you don't feel comfortable."

Michael pulled out his chair and sat down. "The PC in my name is who I really am. My name 'Michael' is from a memory of long ago. 'Freeman' was given me by Jay so I would have a white man's name and start to live in the white man's world."

"What do you mean by this 'white man's world'?" Adam asked, a look of puzzlement on his face. His parents, too, had a look of bewilderment as they waited for Michael's answer.

"These bundles are from my real life," he began, but made no move to open them. "I have been told that my real parents died many years ago when my parents figured I was about three summers old." The family was confused and listened silently as Michael continued. "The only family I have any memory of are my father, Thunder Eagle, my mother, Prairie Flower, Granny Woman, and Grandfather. Grandfather died over the summer. They are Sioux. The name they gave me is Prairie Cub, the PC in my new name."

"Holy cow!" Adam exclaimed in a quiet whisper.

"We had no idea!" Mr. Tyler stated softly.

"Are you okay talking about this?" Mrs. Tyler asked. "Because this is so fascinating and we really care about you and want to hear your story."

"You won't tell anyone? I don't want others to know. They might think I'm too different and not want me around."

Adam spoke for his family. "Whatever you tell us won't go any farther than this table. You are part of our family now and your story will stay with us only."

His parents nodded in agreement.

"Does anyone else know?" Mr. Tyler asked.

"I have not told anyone. My friend, Scot Robinson, who stayed here once, wrote to his friend, Jay, and told him about me and asked if he could help me find a new life when my real life was taken from me. His closest friends only know that they have helped me to find that new life. Because I was born white my parents sent me back to the white man's world after the soldiers' fight forced them to flee. I am Sioux, it's the only life I've known. But now I must live in the world of my birth, and it's so hard." His voice cracked and tears welled up in his eyes. For a moment he couldn't talk.

Mrs. Tyler reached out a consoling hand and placed it on Michael's hand. "It's okay. Take your time and stop whenever you need."

There was a brief silence as each controlled his own emotions and reaction to the poignant personal history being shared with them.

Michael continued, "These are who I am." He ran his fingers across the beadwork. "Granny Woman made this for me before the last buffalo hunt. She explained that this is the eagle spreading his wings over my tepee to protect me from the dark clouds and the thunder bolt." All gazed at the beaded design as they understood its significance.

The boy turned the bundle over, untied the leather laces, and opened the buckskin folds to reveal the contents. He went on to explain. "These are the last clothes my mother made for me. After my people were driven into the mountains to a temporary village, my father hunted the deer to make the buckskins for her to make my clothes." He picked up a pair of eagle feathers that rested atop his clothing. "The tribal counsel awarded these to me because I killed the cruel captain who led the attack against our people. My father gave them to me the last time I saw them in the mountains where they were camped as they prepared to leave for the cold of winter in Canada." Laying the feathers aside, he now took up his hunting knife. "After I gave my original knife to my new friend, Lawrence Kaymond, my father traded for this new knife and my mother made its sheath." He went on to reveal beadwork, flint arrow points, his medicine bag, and other possessions kept within the bundle.

Michael left the bundle open so the family could view his possessions as he turned to his bow bundle and opened it to show his bow and arrows in their quivers. "My father helped me to make this bow when I was younger and my mother and Granny Woman made the quivers. Grandfather helped me with the arrows. We gathered the flint from the flint hills and he showed me how to chip and flake the stone to make the points."

There was silence as the boy stopped and the Tyler family gazed in astonishment at all that lay before them.

"Why are there feathers on your bow? Are you any good with it?" Adam broke the silence.

"They are eagle feathers. They give it the strength and accuracy of an eagle in flight. And I am good. I can take down a rabbit on the run," he replied.

All chuckled as the question broke the tension of discovery and all began to relax.

"Are those stone points on your arrows?" Adam continued.

"Yes. They're made from flint stone gathered among the rocks in the hills. My grandfather taught me how to chip the stone to form the arrow point and to flake the edges to make them sharp."

"Can we touch?" Mrs. Tyler asked.

Michael nodded and his new family carefully fingered his possessions as they discovered the story behind the newest member of the family and a family bonding began to strengthen.

"You know, Michael," Mr. Tyler confirmed, looking the boy in the eye, "you are a very special part of this family. And we realize at the same time, we are only your temporary family as your real family lives in a different world, the world you grew up in. That will always be the core of who you are."

Michael smiled, "Thanks. That means a lot. I'm glad I told you this tonight."

"Can we go hunting tomorrow?" Adam asked. "Want to see you shoot your bow."

"Sure," Mr. Tyler agreed. "There's nothing special that needs doing other that your chores."

"Will you wear these clothes?" Adam suggested.

"Of course not," Michael replied. "And you're not to say anything about them either," he reminded the teen.

"Okay. But I'd sure like to see you in them some day. Before you get too big for them to fit." He smiled.

"Maybe."

"I have dishes to finish," Mrs. Tyler commented. "Anyone planning to help?"

While the family helped with the dishes, Michael hung the bow and arrows on the beg beneath his coat and hat, then folded the buckskins and added them to the parflech. He then repacked the bundle to be returned to the trunk in the bedroom.

*   *   *

Saturday dawned with a low-lying fog carpeting the creek and lowlands. By the time chores and breakfast were finished, it had burned off and the sky was a clear blue with some distant wispy clouds floating along the western horizon.

Michael took his hat and jacket from their peg, stuffed his feet in his boots, and prepared to go with Adam. The older boy took his father's new Winchester rifle as the younger slung his quivers of bow and arrows over his shoulder and hung his hunting knife around his neck.

"Bye, Ma."

"Bye, Mrs. Tyler."

"You boys take care and good luck. With two such hunters, those critters don't stand a chance." She smiled as she watched the boys depart and the door close behind them.

"Let's wander the meadow into the hills beyond and watch to see what game is about," Adam suggested as the two walked toward the gate.

Of-The-Wind saw them approaching and met them at the gate. Michael took time to talk to his pony and caress her neck. At first, the pony followed behind as the boys walked across the grass. But soon she stopped to graze and let them go on.

The boys froze motionless as a groundhog stood by his hole and surveyed his surroundings. Slowly Adam raised his rifle and took careful aim. But before he could pull the trigger, the critter dropped into his hole and disappeared.

"Not what I would want," Adam whispered. "But one less critter digging holes in the meadow would have been okay."

They continued on at a slow walk, carefully watching for any sign of wildlife. As the boys advanced across the meadow, Michael paused to string his bow and drew an arrow from the quiver. He knocked the arrow to the bowstring and lay a finger across the shaft to keep it in place for when the need might arise. They continued on. Arriving at the back fence line, Adam led the way through the fence rails on to a deer trail leading into the wooded hills at the base of the mountain. Squirrels scurried about the leaf-carpeted woodland floor, busy gathering nuts for their winter stores. The boys ignored them looking for bigger game. A rabbit dashed from the underbrush and Michael drew back his arrow and took aim, following its motion through the trees. But there were too many trees in the way. He relaxed the bow and kept the arrow ready for another opportunity.

An hour passed with nothing in sight. "Should we check the creek? Would anything be looking for water?" Michael whispered.

"It's worth a try," Adam agreed.

Turning eastward, the boys stalked quietly through the woodland toward the water. Michael signaled a halt and pointed ahead to a point near the water's edge. A doe was drinking while a majestic buck stood watch, sniffing the air and gazing into the woodland far to the right of where the boys stood. Adam nodded and Michael drew back his arrow as he slowly raised his bow. A yearling fawn appeared beside the doe and approached the water to drink. The younger boy looked to the other who slowly shook his head 'no'. He relaxed the tension on the arrow and held his shot. The two watched the family of deer as they drank, then turned back into the underbrush.

"I really didn't want to shoot," Michael whispered.

"I didn't want you to," Adam agreed. He glanced toward the sun. "It's getting on toward noon and ma will have dinner on the table in another hour. We can take our time going back and maybe we'll see something."

As the two neared the edge of the trees in sight of the rail fence, something stirred in the bushes. As they watched, a large rabbit wandered to the grass near the fence and started to nibble. Adam nodded and Michael drew back his arrow and took aim. The arrow struck the rabbit behind his left foreleg and drove deep into the body. The rabbit dropped quickly. There was no struggle.

"We can gut him here," Adam suggested, "then take him to the wood yard to skin him."

Approaching the dead rabbit, Michael lay his bow on the ground and drew his hunting knife to open the body cavity and clean out inside. First, he cut out his arrow, wiped it clean in the grass, then returned it to its quiver. Once finished, the knife was wiped clean in the grass and returned to its sheath. Standing, the boy unstrung his bow and returned it to its quiver as Adam picked up the rabbit and they headed across the meadow toward the gate and the wood yard.

Of-The-Wind ran across the grassland and walked beside her master as they crossed to the gate. The boys passed through the gate and Adam secured it shut. The pony nuzzled Michael in the back looking for some attention and was rewarded with soft words and a stroking of her muzzle, then turned to the field and stopped to graze.

*　　*　　*

After skinning the rabbit, Adam took it in to his mother to be washed and stored in the ice box for a future stew and Michael took the skin to the barn to be stretched on a plank of wood and salted down. He would give it to Teddy the next time the boys checked the trap line.

Sunday morning ushered in a new month. The sun was just peeking above the trees on the eastern horizon as the boys climbed the porch steps and entered the kitchen. Adam set the eggs on the counter as Michael left the milk bucket on the floor by the ice box.

"Love the smell and sizzle of bacon," Adam commented as he moved behind his mother and watched her turn the sizzling strips in the fry pan.

"Why don't you show Michael how to skim the milk and bottle it," his mother suggested.

The teen moved to the counter and reached for a clean pitcher against the back wall. "You've seen this before, right?"

"Yea."

He picked up the bucket. "Notice the top of the milk is thicker. That's the cream." The bucket was tipped slightly as the cream poured of into the pitcher. "We pour it off separately. Pa uses it in his coffee and ma uses it for baking and making butter."

As the milk thinned, Adam set the bucket back down and poured the cream into one of the smaller milk jars from the counter. Using the empty pitcher, he poured the skimmed milk into the pitcher until it was full. Then he emptied it into one of the larger quart jars. "We bottle the rest of the milk separately." The pour was repeated until the bucket was empty. "Usually there's about a pint of cream and a couple of quarts of milk." He put all in the ice box, then rinsed out the bucket in the sink, pumping clean water from the hand pump beside the sink basin. The eggs were placed in a ceramic bowl and added to the ice box.

Michael put the empty containers by the porch door.

"Thanks, Boys," Mrs. Tyler commented. "Let's finish setting the table and enjoy breakfast." She moved the food to the table as the boys finished setting out the flatware and plates.

Mr. Tyler returned from the living room where he had tended the stove and reset the dampers.

"Today will be another first for you, Michael," he stated as he pulled his chair up to the table.

All sat down and started to pass the food platters around the table.

"I don't suppose you have churches where you lived," he continued.

"I never heard of churches until I lived in Savage." The boy reached for the platter of scrambled eggs. "They built one there near the edge of town. Adam showed me yours when we walked the town two weeks ago."

"We attend church on Sundays," Mrs. Tyler added. "Do you know what they're for?"

"That's where you talk to your God?" Having spooned eggs onto his plate, he passed the platter to Adam.

"A good way to put it," the woman acknowledged as she poured her orange juice and passed the pitcher on.

"We dress up for church in a suit," Mr. Tyler informed between mouthfuls of scrambled egg. "I think we can find the suit Adam outgrew last year if you're willing to wear it."

Adam put his fork down and swallowed a mouthful of fried potato. "Why don't you sit with me and do as I do to get an idea of a church service. Ma can find my old suit for you."

"I don't know," the boy replied. "I don't want to do anything wrong." He drank from his orange juice.

"Please give it a try," the teen asked. "If you find it upsetting, you can slip out of the service with me. We'll sit in the back, just in case." He looked to his father. "Is that okay, Pa?"

"I think that's a good idea, Son."

The family continued with a leisurely meal and conversation about church, and Michael's recollections of special religious ceremonies with which his people celebrated. The conversation ran longer than expected as the family was fascinated by the vivid remembrances the boy shared.

They finished breakfast and Mrs. Tyler went to the hall closet and found Adam's old dark blue suit. "Adam can help you with the tie."

Michael took the suit and left for his bedroom to change.

The family cleaned up from breakfast, then each in turn dressed for church. Adam stopped in Michael's room to tie the black bow tie. All gathered in the living room.

"You really look good in my old suit," Adam complimented.

Michael stood there in the three-piece dark blue wool garment, obviously very uncomfortable.

"I guess this looks good to you, but I feel like a trussed up turkey." He ran his finger around his neck behind the shirt collar. "Sure am glad you don't dress like this all the time." He sat down on a side chair.

"You did a good job on the tie, Son," his father praised. "Why don't you do our morning reading." All found a seat, Adam in a chair near Michael, and his folks on the sofa.

"Anything special?"

"How about Psalms 121."

"Okay." He took the Bible from his mother and thumbed through it until he located the passage. "I will lift up mine eyes unto the hills…"

Michael listened, closed his eyes, and thought back to the foothills of the Rockies and his last ride with Grandfather. A tear slipped down his cheek and he self-consciously wiped it away with a coat sleeve. Mrs. Tyler noticed, and her heart went out to the boy. Her husband's attention was focused on his son's reading.

The parlor clock struck the quarter-hour past ten.

"The service is at eleven so we better leave by ten-thirty," Mr. Tyler stated.

Mrs. Tyler returned the Bible to its shelf under the end table by the sofa. Mr. Tyler checked the living room fire while his son tended the one in the kitchen.

# ON THE TRAIN WITH JAY

Weeks passed. October drifted towards November. Cooler temperatures arrived and the leaves fell and the landscape took on the barren look of the oncoming winter season. Scattered showers were occasionally mixed with sleet. Some mornings began with a light coating of frost or misty fog, which generally burned off after a couple of hours. Michael's routine wore on as his schooling advanced with the help of his friends and his teacher, the three walked the trap line on a regular basis, he hunted with Adam on their Saturdays and became accustomed to the Sunday routine. His days started and ended with the chores he shared with Adam. On some afternoons or mornings before school he helped Mrs. Tyler in the gardens, harvested vegetables for winter storage in the cold cellar, picked apples, or made a quick trip to the garden to pick some corn or other vegetables, or dig a few root vegetables for dinner. He enjoyed time with Of-The-Wind, and Jay checked in on occasion – sometimes stopping at the house and sometimes talking with Adam or his father at the logging company. On one occasion, after the third week, the engineer had come to dinner at Mr. Tyler's invitation and spent time with the family and walked to the barn with Michael to visit his pony and learn how the boy was doing in his new life.

The last Friday of October dawned raw and overcast. It was a teachers' day and there was no school for the students. Adam asked if Michael would want to work with him at *The Herald* that day. As the parlor clock struck the half hour at 6:30, there was a knock at the front door. Mr. Tyler put his coffee down and walked down the hallway to answer it. He opened the door.

"Mornin', Jay. What a surprise. Come on in to the kitchen."

"Thanks, Bill."

The two walked to the kitchen where Mrs. Tyler promptly poured a cup of coffee and placed it on the table.

The boys looked up from their breakfast.

"Hi, Jay," Michael greeted. "It's great to see you again." All paused to find out what brought this visitor at this hour of the day. "What's happening?"

Jay sipped the coffee. "Thanks, Janet." He glanced toward the woman and nodded. "Sorry to come over at the last minute, but I just learned that the students have today off for teachers' meetings."

"That's right," Mrs. Tyler confirmed.

"It's been a long time since I've had any time with Michael and wondered if he could spend the day at work with me."

"Wow! Could I?" he looked to Adam first and then to Adam's parents.

"That sounds like a great offer," Adam quickly confirmed.

His parents looked to each other and nodded. "I think that would be fine," Mr. Tyler agreed.

"Wear old clothes, you'll get dirty." Jay continued to enjoy the coffee.

"I really don't have any other clothes," Michael stated.

"I'll get a set of Adam's old clothes from the attic," Mrs. Tyler offered.

"If it's okay with you folks, we can stop at the general store on the way to the station and I'll get him a pair of coveralls." Jay looked to Mr. Tyler for an answer.

"Put it on our account," the man agreed.

"I'll take care of it," Jay said. "Thanks. If you all are ready to leave, we can all walk together. The train is scheduled to leave at seven. The boy won't need a lunch. We'll take care of him for the day."

Michael beamed with excitement as all prepared to leave. It was cold out, so he wore his red capote.

"You all have a great day," Mrs. Tyler waved as the group left out the front door.

"We will," the boys chorused

"You, too," Mr. Tyler replied.

The four turned toward Main Street and walked together to Railroad Avenue. There, Adam and his father turned toward the logging company and Jay and Michael headed the opposite way toward the store.

"We'll make this quick," Jay stated as they entered the store. "The train is in the station, ready to go."

In the store, the two went directly to the coverall display where Jay held up a pair for size. Not quite. He grabbed another which appeared as though it should fit.

"Put this on my account, Harvey. We're running late."

"Okay, Jay. You have a good day."

Returning to Main Street, the two crossed to the station and headed straight to the train, which sat steaming and hissing, ready to leave at a moment's notice. The few remaining passengers hastened to climb aboard.

"Michael," Jay instructed. "Take these to the baggage room and change. Leave your coat on a peg on the wall. It will get dirty in the engine." He reached the grab iron and started up to the engine cab as Michael climbed the steps to the platform outside the baggage room. "Come up to the engine when we stop at Day's End," Jay called.

"Okay."

The boy entered the car while the engineer pulled himself into the engine cab. Dan watched from where he stood by the coach steps.

"All aboard," he called, then climbed the steps to the open platform on the coach.

Jay replied with two sharp blasts of the whistle and Scott set the bell to its rhythmic ringing. Number twenty-one eased into motion as steam blasted through the pistons and the large drive wheels began to turn. The morning train to Arlee moved slowly as it backed out of the station on its way to its first stop at Day's End. Jamie waited at the switch to the main, which he closed as the train eased through. Continuing at a slow speed, it allowed for the twenty-one-year-old to run to the engine and climb aboard. It then picked up speed and disappeared as it curved into the hills west of town.

\*　　\*　　\*

Michael stood on the end platform of the baggage room and watched as the train approached its first stop. As soon as it came to a complete stop, signaled by a single sharp blast from the whistle, the boy climbed down and hurried to the engine, and Jamie dropped down to uncouple the engine and run ahead to throw the switch for the pass track. As soon as Michael entered the cab, Jay shifted the Johnson bar into reverse, blew three short calls on the whistle and eased the engine back past the switch. Jamie threw the switch and the engine slowly passed forward to the rear of the train, which would be pulled backwards on the run to Arlee. Closing the switch, the young man ran to the switch at the other end of the track and threw it for the engine to pass through. Once clear, the switch was closed and the engine backed to the coach and was coupled to the train. Meanwhile, the few passengers getting on or off did so as the baggage handler took care of baggage, freight, and the mail. Dan signaled departure.

Jay put the train back into motion as he eased back on the throttle and let out two blasts on the whistle.

"Sit here with me, Michael," he instructed. "Today you are running the train."

Beaming with excitement, the boy did as instructed.

"First, we'll run open throttle as we fly past the station at Snow Shoe with bell and whistle. We stop on the far side of Chamber's Crossing to drop Jamie off. After that we return to this speed until we approach Kingston, then I'll help you to bring us into the station there." He set the throttle into its notch then let go. "This is the brake." The man wrapped his hand around the handle on the brake stand. "I'll work it with you." Michael nodded. "Remember the crossroad whistle?"

"Yea."

"We're coming to the crossing at Main Street. There will be a white post beside the track with a W on it. Start the whistle when you see it."

Michael reached up and grabbed the whistle handle as he watched out the open door to the running board. The post appeared in the distance. As the train approached it, the boy pulled on the whistle – two long blasts, a short one, then a single long wailing call. He released the handle as the station and Main Street flew by and Jarrett waved from the platform. Michael waved back.

"Great job!" Jay complimented.

"A little more practice and you'll sound like an engineer," Scott added.

The boy smiled. He shivered within with excitement. He felt a sense of warmth and joy he hadn't felt since he left his home. This presence in the company of this friend of Scot's was like traveling with Grandfather and learning the lessons he had shared with his grandson as Grandfather taught him new skills. Never in his wildest dreams did he ever imagine that he would be learning how to drive the locomotive that Scot had driven when he had been stranded in Snow Shoe and taken under the care of Jay Miller.

Jay stopped the train to let Jamie off.

"Enjoy your day," Jamie waved as he left.

"Thanks, I will," Michael waved back.

Once again, the train picked up speed and raced on through the mountain country. For the next ten minutes, no words were spoken as the engineer and the fireman focused on their work and the boy gazed out at the passing country, standing on the footplate with his hand firmly grasping the door frame to the engine cab.

"We'll be arriving at Kingston soon," Jay interrupted his reflections. "Come on back and have your seat." Michael returned to the engineer's box and resumed his place. "Put one hand on the throttle and the other on the brake."

Michael did as instructed. The engineer wrapped his hands around the boy's.

"We ease in on the throttle and wait on the brake until we get closer to the station." The man pushed in a couple notches on the throttle.

The train began to loose momentum.

"One long blast on the whistle to tell folks we're comin' in."

Michael let go of the throttle to reach up and pull the whistle cord.

"Okay. Now push in on the throttle and ease on the brake."

The man guided the boy's hands in coordinated motion as the pistons slowed and the brakes squealed, metal on metal, and the train began to slow.

"Easy for a smooth stop." Jay guided the boy's hands as the two pulled the train into the station and it slowed to a full stop. "Take her out of power." He put the Johnson bar lever into a central position and set the brakes. "One short blast to say we've stopped."

The boy reached up and jerked the whistle cord for a short screech. Stepping down from the engineer's seat, Michael wandered to the top of the steps to watch the activity on the station platform.

"Nice work," Jay complimented.

Michael looked at the man and smiled. "Thanks. You sure have about the greatest job ever."

"Want ta give me a hand?" Scott asked. "You can pass me some firewood. We need to feed this old girl so we can keep on goin'."

Michael moved to the tender and started to pass wood to the fireman.

"That's good." He shut the door and checked the gauges.

"All aboard," Dan called from where he stood with one hand on the railing for the coach steps. He climbed up while Jay acknowledged with two blasts on the whistle.

"Ready, Michael? We do this all again in reverse order."

Michael returned to his seat as Jay set the Johnson bar into forward position and the two placed their hands on the brake and the throttle. Scott started the bell to ringing as Jay eased the throttle back, steam pushed through the cylinders, and the train began to move.

"The crossing."

Michael blew the crossing. The train picked up speed. Kingston was lost from view.

\*     \*     \*

The morning run continued on toward Blakesville. Michael watched the approaching countryside through the open door to the locomotive's running board. A cool breeze blew in the opening and was heated by the heat radiating from the firebox and boiler as it caressed his face and stirred his hair. A tingling sense of excitement warmed from within as the boy felt a rising thrill and joy in the shared running of the locomotive. Jay removed his hands and allowed Michael to hold the controls by himself. Together they had set the throttle and had let go of the brake handle. A whistle marker post approached, the engineer nodded, and the boy sounded the whistle for the crossing.

"We'll be approaching Blakesville soon, Michael," Jay announced. "Why don't you bring her in by yourself. Remember what we did at Kingston."

"Are you sure?" Michael asked.

"I'm here if you need," Jay replied.

The throbbing noise of the train reverberated through the floorboards, and echoed off the hillsides as it rushed forward through the countryside.

"Blakesville is a ways around this bend, Michael. Begin your slowdown."

Michael began to ease in on the throttle and the engine responded. The drivers began to loose speed. He engaged the brake ever so slowly. Rounding the bend brought the station into view about a mile ahead. The boy eased off on the throttle a click at a time as the train responded and continued to slow.

"Doing good," Jay praised. "Now begin with the brake. Remember, we have the weight of the train pushing as we slow and will need growing help from the brakes."

At a quarter mile out, the boy continued to reduce the throttle and increase the brake. The train continued to slow.

"Now close the throttle and let the train coast." The slowing train approached the station platform. "Ease the brake to a full stop."

Metal squealed against metal as the train entered the station. Slowing to a stop, there was a sudden light jerk as its final stop was short and sudden. Michael sounded a short whistle blast.

"Not bad, Michael. Folks got a little bit of a shock at the end, but they've had that before and are used to it. We hold here about five minutes, then we'll move on toward Arlee."

Michael glanced at Jay and felt a sense of pride when his look was greeted with a smile of 'job well done.' He beamed back.

Jay continued. "You can take her out from here, then I'll take over as we get nearer to Arlee. Take a break. Coffee? Water?"

The engineer handed Michael a tin cup and he drew some water from the water keg on the front of the tender. He leaned against the front metal and watched as Scott added wood to the fire. On the station platform a few workers boarded the coach after a family and two men got off. The baggage car was serviced.

"All aboard," Dan called.

Michael reached for the whistle cord and responded with two sharp blasts. Jay acknowledged with a smile and sat back as the boy ascended the engineer's seat, released the brake, shoved the Johnson bar into gear, and eased the train into forward motion. Steam pressure exploded from the cylinders as the drive rods pushed against the big drive wheels and they began to turn. The train picked up speed gradually as Scott sounded the bell and the station soon fell behind. The bell stopped. The boy brought the train up to speed and set the throttle in its notched position.

Michael stepped down and turned to Jay. "It's all yours."

"Thanks, Michael. You did a really good job." The two smiled at one-an-other and the boy again felt that rising tingling of excitement and sense of accomplishment.

This day had become one of adventure and wonder at doing something he never dreamed of in his wildest imagination. Reflecting back on the day he stood in the cab of another locomotive, in another world with his friend Scot Robinson, and Scot's telling him of how he had learned to operate a steam engine, this steam engine. Now he knew the sense of pride and accomplishment that Scot must have felt when he told Michael of his experience. Michael knew he had letters to write once he returned to the house later in the evening.

*   *   *

Nearing the end of the Snow Shoe branch, the train passed through Ramsey Hills followed by Guyer's Cut as it traveled toward the switch onto the main line. Soon the switch came into view. Jay brought the train to a stop about fifty feet from the switch, blew a short blast on the whistle to signal the brakes were set, and checked his watch.

"The northbound freight should pass through here in the next five minutes," he announced.

After four minutes of silence a distant whistle signaled the oncoming freight. Within seconds, it roared into view. Michael subconsciously counted the cars, fourteen. The train flashed by in a blur of speed, sound fading into the distance as its smoke, too, trailed off into the air.

The brakeman, Charles McKenzie, stepped down from the baggage end of the combine, and walked over to throw the switch. Jay eased the train slowly onto the main line, moving at a crawl until McKenzie closed the switch back to the main and climbed aboard. Picking up speed, the train soon pulled in to Arlee station, right on time, ten minutes before eight. After a five-minute pause to allow passengers to get off and baggage to be unloaded, it pulled onto the pass track where Charles uncoupled the train to allow the engine to go to the engine yard to be turned and serviced for the return trip back to Snow Shoe. A service locomotive pulled the train past the yard switch before Twenty-one returned to couple on to the front end of the cars.

In the engine yard, Michael climbed onto the back of the tender and helped fill the water tank by opening and closing the fill lid. There was plenty of wood for the round trip. He watched from the engine cab as Jay pulled onto the turntable and the ground crew pushed into the push poles at either end and rotated the engine a full turn to leave the table back the way it had come. Returning to the station, the train was positioned for its return trip.

In the mean time, the southbound train to the Summit branch had pulled out onto the main to allow the train, heading north to Snow Show, to pull ahead on the pass track.

Michael watched and wondered at the timing and coordination of it all. The Summit train backed back to its position on the pass track, then all waited as the remaining trains pulled in. All was done by the clock to be ready for the north-bound to Pine Bluff access to the station track by 8:15. At 8:15 two trains arrived, one on either side of the station, each in the opposite direction. They waited for ten minutes for the exchange of passengers and baggage, then continued on their separate ways. New passengers boarded the train and baggage wagons loaded their baggage and outgoing mail bags to the baggage room. After another ten minutes, both trains departed to their respective branch lines.

Michael leaned against the back of the fireman's seat as he watched the men at work for the departure.

"Wow," he observed, "that was a lot of work in not a lot of time!"

Scott replied, "With four trains coordinating schedules to be at the same station at the same time, everyone has to be precise."

Jay set the throttle and turned to the boy. "You saw this the morning you arrived. It happens two times each weekday, once around eight in the morning and again around five in the evening. At mid day it's only the two main line trains. There's also an eleven o'clock passing of mail trains north and south." He turned back to give his attention to the approaching switch.

"I'll get it," Michael offered as he started down the steps.

"Go with Charles and watch this time," Jay instructed. "You can help with switching when we get back to Snow Shoe station."

"Okay."

Once clear of the switch and underway again, the engineer continued his explanation of train movements.

"When we return to Snow Shoe, Bob Leary and his crew will have brought the morning load from the logging camp to the saw mill and returned the empties to the Stewart Creek main for the midday run. They will then break for lunch. After we run to Day's End and return to Snow Shoe station, we'll leave the passenger train at the station and service the engine with wood and water, turn it on the wye track and leave it in front of the company office."

The rocky landscape closed in on either side of the train and the noise of its passing echoed loudly off the rocks as they passed through Guyer's Cut. Coming out at the far end, the train's progress echoed off distant hills as it passed through the Ramsey Hills and on through more valleys and hills rising through the mountain country.

"Crossing," Jay announced nodding toward the boy.

Michael stepped forward from the fireman's box, reached up to grab the whistle cord and sounded the crossing. He even managed to get a short wailing echo at the end. Smiling to himself, he stepped to the back of the engineer's box and took up a position watching the countryside approach through the open door to the front.

Keeping his attention on the track in front, Jay continued. "We'll take an early lunch in the office then trade trains. We will take the "Scott" and its log cars up the mountain and pick up the loaded cars from the camp and leave the empties. Bob Leary and his crew will take the "King" and finish assembling the afternoon freight run. Another locomotive, "Kidd" Number forty-six, serves the local industries as needed and has its own caboose for its crew. It will double head with number twenty-one for the freight run. During the morning Ryker Kimball and his crew have assembled the train from the outgoing cars from the local business as they swapped in the incoming deliveries and empties. While we service the "King" they will pull the freight onto the main line and wait."

"Why do you trade engines?"

"It's more for variety and to prevent boredom."

"Oh."

Kingston came into view and all attention was given over to the station stop. Jay supervised as Michael brought the train in, waited for the few passengers and baggage exchange, then continued east. Again, the stop was a bit rough and the start began with a slight jerk. But he thrilled at the job and felt a continuing inner joy at this new adventure.

\*    \*    \*

The 11 o'clock early lunch break passed quickly. All too soon, they pulled out with the logging train and watched as Bob Leary and crew headed toward the station with the "King." Jay took charge of the trip up the mountain explaining that it was a whole different kind of trip and a different type of trackage.

"Michael," Jay instructed without taking his attention off the track ahead. "You can work with Scott on this trip and learn about the job of fireman. The first part of the trip will be onto the lead of the switchback, just shy of two miles ahead."

"What's a switchback?" the boy asked.

"It's a switch we will pass then back through to continue the journey up the mountain. There isn't room to put a curve on the mountain to change our direction around the mountainside. From there we'll back up the mountain the rest of the way to the new logging camp."

"Pass the wood," Scott requested.

Michael crossed to the tender and began handing pieces of firewood to the fireman, who tossed them into the open firebox door. Closing the door, he motioned the boy to the gauges.

"See this clear glass with water inside?"

"Uh huh."

"This indicates the level of the water in the boiler tubes." Pointing to another gauge, Scott continued. "This dial indicates boiler pressure. If the water level gets too low, the pressure will rise dangerously high and could cause a boiler explosion. To prevent this I have to open the water valve on the tender and add more water whenever the water level gets down to this line." He indicated a mark on the glass. "It's getting close now. Do you see the valve wheel on the front of the tender?"

Michael walked over to the tender to check it out. "Here?"

"That's right. Can you open it slowly and I'll tell you when to close it."

"Okay." The boy opened the valve as instructed and waited.

"Close it now," Scott instructed as he watched the level in the water gauge.

Michael turned the valve shut and returned to the fireman's box and, resting his elbow on the seat, leaned against its side.

The train rumbled across the switch and Jay eased into a screeching stop. Smoke hissed from the stack and steam rumbled in the engine's belly as a crewman dropped from the last empty flat and threw the switch. The train backed slowly through the switch as the crewman climbed back aboard. The switch was left open for the return trip back down from the logging camp. Picking up speed, the train continued another two plus miles to the location of the logging camp. Jay sounded the whistle to announce their arrival. For the camp crews, it was also the signal for the midday lunch break.

Jay backed the train into the empty siding, uncoupled the engine, then moved over and coupled onto the loaded flatcars which had end stops and loads of pulp wood.

As the engine coupled and came to a stop, and Jay sounded the whistle to announce the brakes were set, he explained, "At the end of the week, the midday load is made up of all the cuttings from the week's work. This load will be stored on an extra track at the saw mill and ship out next week, Monday, for the paper mill at Ludington. All the logging companies along the V&T send their pulpwood there. The empties will be returned on Tuesday to be stored at the saw mill until used again next Friday." He crossed the cab to the steps down. "Come on." He started down. "We stay over here a half hour break. Horace, our cook, has coffee and baked goods."

Michael followed his friend down the steps as Scott raked down the fire then joined them.

*　　*　　*

The afternoon passed quickly. The pulp load was delivered to its storage track and the "Scott" was serviced, coupled to the logging empties with the addition of the company combine and caboose, and parked on the logging main, ready for its last run of the day. Bob Leary's crew was back from the freight run and had taken a coffee break while waiting for Jay to return. Jay, Scott, Dan, Charles, and Michael left the train and crossed the yard to the office. It was crowded as all took their coffee tins from the table, poured a cup, then gathered to exchange information. Scott found an extra for Michael.

"The freight consist has been broken down and all cars delivered," Bob informed. "The "King" is serviced and waiting with its coaches at the station for tonight's run to Arlee." He sipped from his cup.

"Michael, this is the end of your day." Jay turned to the boy, cup in hand as he sipped his coffee. "Bob leaves directly for the camp for the last load and any from the crews who wish to leave the mountain for the weekend." He paused as he drank. "Some have families here in town, some have a room at the hotel, and some will go to Arlee for the weekend." The man emptied his cup, wiped it out with his kerchief, then placed in back on the table. He wiped out Michael's cup when he finished and put it away. "Get your coat from where you hung it when we come over from the train and I'll walk with you back to the Tyler's."

Michael took his coat from where he had left it on the coat rack in the corner of the room and joined Jay as they walked out the door, leaving the noise of conversations behind. Once outside, he was suddenly aware of how quiet it was for the first time since arriving at the station in the early morning. He was also quite cold in the afternoon chill without the warmth of an engine's cab or the inside of the office.

They started across the company yard toward Railroad Avenue.

"Did you have a good day?" Jay asked as they left the company property.

"I sure did," Michael beamed. "It seems so long ago that we stopped at the mercantile and got my coveralls. Thanks," he looked at the man beside him, this friend of Scot Robinson's who had taken on the challenge of helping a boy from another world to find his way in this, the world of his birth. He smiled and the man put a protective hand on his shoulder, and smiled back.

As the two approached Main Street, they heard the screech of the "Scott's" whistle as the train started once again to climb the mountain for the last load of the week.

*    *    *

Upon arriving at the Tyler's, Jay stayed a while as Michael shared his day with Mrs. Tyler and the man filled in any missing pieces of information upon request. It would be a while before Adam and his father returned from their respective jobs. Jay explained that the Friday evening train always left late, after the train came down from the mountain and the town's industries let out for the weekend. He usually stayed over with friends who owned the Railroad Hotel in Arlee, for the train's return on a later schedule on Saturday morning. There was only one more weekend run, on Sunday evening when the workers from the various industries in Snow Shoe returned.

Jay left to return to the hotel for dinner, then the station to be ready for the evening run. Michael hung his coveralls on a peg beside his bow and arrows and coat. His hat joined the coveralls. His boots were left on the floor beneath. After washing off the dirt and soot of the day, the boy helped Mrs. Tyler by setting the table for dinner.

Mr. Tyler and his son arrived home from their two different work locations, shortly past five. The boys tended their chores. All gathered for dinner and, once again, Michael shared the day's adventure. Afterwards, as the family retired to the living room, he asked for paper and envelops so he could write to his friends back home, then excused himself to his room so he could write his letters. All would be sent c/o Keith Summer's Trading Post in Savage, Montana Territory.

Michael set his writing materials on the desk near the window and lit the lamp. The first and longest was written to Scot Robinson. It told of all that had happened since leaving by train back in September, with great detail about this day on the train with Jay. His letter to trader Walter Mattson contained a brief summary of life in the white man's world and questions about his family. Keith Summer's letter was more general, but asked to be sure his letters to Scot and Trader Mattson could get to them.

Carefully Michael reread each letter to be sure he hadn't forgotten anything, addressed each envelop, then slipped each into its envelop and set all aside. They would not be sealed until morning in case he chose to add something.

The boy changed into his nightshirt, throwing his clothes on top of his trunk. There was a knock at the door. Adam peaked in to say 'good night' for himself and his parents, then moved on after Michael acknowledged.

As he had done on many previous nights, Michael knelt on the floor to gaze out the window at the moonlit landscape. This time as he looked toward the mountain, he knew what was there. It had been part of this day's adventure. He thought of his friends whose letters lay on the desk and of the life they once had shared in the past. His heart ached for his other life, yet felt, too, a growing joy for his new life as well. He now had two families, and loved them both so very deeply. How he wished his family were with him here, and his friends as well.

"Great Spirit," he prayed. "Watch over them all and keep them safe." Suddenly overcome with grief he wept, "I miss them all so much." And the tears flowed freely.

Michael returned to his desk, picked up another sheet of paper, and wrote another letter. 'Dear Father and Mother, …' all were signed 'Prairie Cub.'

# SNOW

October slid into November. Most days were overcast. A few saw light snow flurries with a thin coating of snow remaining on grass and shrubs from day to day. Michael's afternoons with Mrs. Miller began to pay off. Grammar started to make some sense. Cyphering became a problem with the introduction of the study of fractions. Between Teddy and Adam with their added help meeting new words in reading, his reading improved as well. Teddy's patient guidance during class enabled spotty success, but only because Michael was able to see some short-term patterns and to make some lucky guesses in his classwork. Adam's extra help and patience at home eventually enabled Teddy's help at school to make some sort of sense. Jamison became a welcome friend among his peers as his friendship with Michael strengthened in their shared interest in baseball, though the colder weather limited game opportunities. Following Michael's Friday with Jay, Friday afternoons became a regular visitation as the engineer stopped during the hours between the afternoon run for the logging company and the evening train to Arlee, to see his young friend when he returned home from school and to catch up on the week's events. Other afternoons were shared with Teddy and Miles as they checked the trap line. On some days, the three gathered at Teddy's to skin the animals caught and salt them down for the storekeeper. Many Saturdays found time with Of-The-Wind, either quiet time in her stall or walking or riding in the meadow, and time sharing interests with Adam, even an additional look at his collection with the stories behind the items.

A light snowfall began during the lunch hour on the first Monday of November. Many of the older boys were focused on their baseball game. Younger children played on the swings and other playground equipment. Several children kept busy individually or in group play such as dodge ball.

Miles was up to bat. As he wiped a snowflake from his nose, the pitcher released the pitch. Instinctively he swung, but missed.

"Strike two!" the catcher called.

"Not fair," Miles called back as he stood with the bat hanging at his side.

"Give him another chance!" Jamison hollered from his position as first baseman.

"Okay," the catcher agreed.

The game continued. Miles took his stance, bat ready, eyes on the pitcher. He did his windup and released the ball. Miles swung and caught the edge of the ball. It bounced wildly on the ground as Miles dropped the bat and ran for first base. The pitcher reached for the ball as it took a sideways bounce toward the infield. Miles arrived at the base as the third baseman captured the ball on a roll and tossed it back to the pitcher. The bell rang and recess ended.

As the boys gathered the game gear and headed to the schoolhouse with the rest of the children, Jamison commented to Miles. "That was one wild hit." He smiled. "It sure bounced out of reach."

"Thanks," Miles replied. "Just a lucky shot." He grinned at the older boy.

Michael caught up with the two. "Do you think this snow will amount to anything?" he asked.

Jamison observed, "I've seen major storms begin like this and last for days."

"Where I once lived," Michael continued, "there was once a storm that started like this one day then suddenly blew into a blizzard the next. Our people were lucky. They had enough food and firewood to last a few days. It was so deep …" He stopped suddenly before he said something that would reveal the nature of his village.

"So deep what?" Jamison asked as they approached the schoolhouse door.

"It came to your waist and you could hardly move," Michael thought quickly.

They entered the building and went to their classroom for the afternoon session.

*     *     *

"Mrs. Miller said you could skip this afternoon's lesson?" Teddy asked.

"The teachers are having an after school meeting to prepare for the possibility that there will be no school tomorrow," Michael replied.

The three boys continued along Railroad Avenue on their way home. Snow continued to fall lightly, but it had started to accumulate on the grass, shrubs, and the roofs of buildings.

"Let's go by way of Washington and Maple Streets so we can drop off our schoolbooks and pick up the sack to check the trap line," Miles suggested.

"Good idea," Teddy agreed as they crossed Main Street.

"When we get to the Tyler's," Michael added, "Mrs. Tyler will have hot chocolate and cookies. We can get a quick cup of hot chocolate, check the trap line, then stop for a snack afterwards."

Turning up Washington Street, the boys observed two firemen taking firewood into the firehouse. Another was feeding and watering the horses. The boys waved and the men waved back.

"You ready if this becomes a big one?" one called.

"I'm ready if we get off from school!" Miles called back.

"Even if you're all busy having to shovel the snow?" another added.

"That's fine by me!" Miles returned.

They moved on. Pausing at their homes toward the middle of the first block, Michael waited on the walkway as each of his friends dropped off their books and lunch pails and Teddy grabbed the grain sack. They continued on toward Cedar Street and the Tyler farm. By the time the three entered the lane to the house, a good half inch of snow had accumulated on the lane's surface as well as fence rails, tree limbs and all structures. Dropping the bag on the porch, they entered the warmth of the kitchen and the welcome aroma of hot chocolate, and dropped their coats, hats, scarves, and gloves in a pile by the door.

"Hi, Boys," Mrs. Tyler greeted. "I've already poured your chocolate and the cookies are on the table."

"Thanks," the boys chorused.

"But we'll just stop long enough for the chocolate and eat after we check the trap line," Michael explained.

"I hope you won't be long." She lay a clean towel across the plate of cookies. "With this snowfall, it will get dark quickly."

"We'll hurry," Teddy assured as he drained his cup. "Let's go now."

Bundling up once more, the three were out the door and on their way to the trap line. Of-The-Wind saw them coming and rushed to the corner of the fence line for some attention.

"I'll meet you at the third trap," Michael announced as he turned away to greet his pony. As he ran his hands along his pony's neck and caressed her muzzle, he spoke softly to her. Then the two walked together along the fence line as they followed along the direction of the trap line. Nearing the location of the third trap, the boy patted his pony on the neck and whispered, "See ya later, Girl. Meet you in the barn for chores."

He slipped through the fence rails and turned to hurry and catch up with his friends. It was a quick trip to check all traps. They were all empty and undisturbed.

"Guess all the critters have gone in out of the storm," Teddy commented.

"I sure would," Miles agreed.

"Let's hurry back to the house," Teddy suggested. "It's cold out here and the warmth in the kitchen sure felt good."

They hurried back to the house, dropped the sack on the porch, and rushed inside.

"That was quick," Mrs. Tyler observed. She took the pot from the stove and refilled the cups, then removed the towel from the cookies.

"The traps were all empty," Michael explained as he reached for a cookie.

"The critters have more sense than you boys," Mrs. Tyler smiled. "They know when to stay warm." She filled her own cup, placed the pot back on the stove, and sat down at the table. "How is the snow doing?" she asked.

"I'm not sure," Miles responded. "It sure has been steady and is now starting to accumulate."

"I've seen a storm start like this and stay the same for days," Teddy stated. "Even though it's light, if it doesn't stop, it can get a couple feet deep. And if the winds start up, it can drift mighty high."

All drank their hot chocolate and munched on their cookies in silence as they thought about what had been said.

"We've got to get home," Miles broke the silence as he rose from the table to put on his coat.

"Thanks, Mrs. Tyler," Teddy added as he, too, left the table to bundle up for the trip home.

Miles reached for the doorknob. "Bye," the two chorused.

"Bye," Michael and Mrs. Tyler responded.

"See you tomorrow," Michael added.

The door closed behind the boys and they were gone. Michael hung his clothing on their pegs and returned to the table. The two sat down and drained their cups.

"Do you have any homework?" Mrs. Tyler asked. She stood and started to clear the table.

"Mrs. Miller said we wouldn't have any in case the storm got bad and we had extra work to do because of the snow." He gathered his friends' cups and took them to the drain board.

"Why don't you bring in extra firewood and tend the living room stove while I start dinner," the woman suggested. "Then take some time with your horse until Adam and his father get home and it's time for chores."

"Thanks." The boy bundled up and headed out to the wood pile.

*       *       *

The storm kept on through the night without any change in its intensity. By morning, well over a foot had fallen and still it continued. The boys had finished their chores and the family was at breakfast when there came a knock at the front door.

"I'll get it," Adam volunteered. He went to the door and brought Mr. Tompkins back to the kitchen.

"Have a seat, Teddy," Mrs. Tyler invited. "I'll get you some coffee." She went for the coffee and a cup while Mr. Tompkins hung his coat on the back of the chair, stuffing scarf and gloves into a pocket. He set his hat on the chair by the door.

Adam returned to his seat and continued his breakfast. All waited to hear what their guest had to say.

"Bill," Teddy began, "I think we're going to go to the snow schedule today. The storm can only get worse and the longer we wait, the less we can get around." He sipped from the cup.

"Thanks, Janet," he acknowledged, then continued. "We'll take extra food and clothing supplies to the camp first thing with the short supply train consist of box car, combine, and caboose. Any who live in town will come back to be with their families, and they'll have to report to the company for snow removal duty. Those remaining will take care of the camp and keep the tracks clear in the camp and along the top half mile of the line. Those down here will keep the equipment clean and the company yards clear as well as the bottom half mile of the line. When not in use, the engines and caboose will be stored in the engine house. We'll borrow crews from the other industries to work with some of ours to keep the station, passenger equipment, and local tracks clear. I know the town council has arrangements with the local merchants to take care of the business district and homeowners to take care of their properties and the sidewalks and streets that adjoin them." He finished his coffee and Mrs. Tyler offered to refill it.

"Thanks, Janet," he declined, "but we need to get started before the snow gets much deeper. I'm really grateful that it's not any heavier."

Mr. Tyler reached for his coat as he instructed, "Adam, you and Michael stay here to help your mother and begin snow removal around the property." Finishing with scarf, gloves, and hat, he turned to Mr. Tompkins who had already bundled up. "Let's go and get things underway."

The two men headed down the hall and out the front door.

"You know the routine, Adam," his mother stated. "You can explain to Michael as you go along."

"Yea, Ma," he replied. To Michael he explained, "We start at the barn to clear the lane and walks, then clear the front walk and our side of the street."

The two bundled up in coats, scarves, gloves, and hats, then headed to the side door.

"Shovels are in the barn," Adam instructed.

The boys stepped out into the cold to begin their work, letting the screen door slam shut behind them.

\*     \*     \*

The community mobilized and anyone who had lived in Snow Shoe during the previous winter and before, knew what had to be done. The morning was spent in snow removal. After a long midday break, all was repeated throughout the second half of the afternoon. Around seven-thirty in the morning, Jay and his crew took the "King" a half mile out in either direction to check the track and determine if it was safe to make a morning run. Considering the condition of the track and the rate of snowfall, they decided a quick run was feasible.

The engine was coupled to the train, ready to go in reverse to Day's End. Two long wailing screams from the whistle announced to the community that the train would be leaving in ten minutes. Few showed up, but Jarrett put the mail in the baggage room. Five minutes later, two sharp blasts announced that the train was leaving. It backed slowly from the station and headed out onto the main, then quickly picked up speed and disappeared westbound. Fifteen minutes later it returned, slowed to see if any more passengers had arrived, then, seeing none, picked up speed and headed out eastbound. Nearly three hours later, the train returned and dropped its cars at the station. A few passengers had come in on the train and the day's mail was delivered. The crew took the engine, turned it on the wye, serviced it for wood and water, and started toward the engine house. The engine started to back into the engine house but paused over the ash pit. Scott dumped the hot ashes from the bottom of the firebox. With the remaining steam pressure, Jay backed the "King" into the empty track in the engine house, then released the remaining steam pressure in a cloud of steam, and shut her down. The "Scott" and the caboose had already been parked on the second track inside the structure. Here they would remain until the weather cleared and the lines could be reopened to the mountain and to Arlee.

*   *   *

The storm lasted for three days. Thursday dawned with a misty overcast, but no new snow. The morning was spent in one final snow removal operation. Snow Shoe and its industries and businesses reopened as best they could. The sawmill and the barrel company started up and operated as long as they had materials. Each ran out within a day and shut down until new supplies could come available.

The logging company loaded crews and tools onto its log cars and began the trip to the camp, to clear the track on the way.

Jay's crew steamed up Number twenty-one then went over to the saw mill storage siding to pick up the plow car. Meanwhile, Ryker and his crew fired up Number forty-six, picked up their caboose, and moved to the main in front of the station. Jay took the plow car to the main and positioned the "King" in front of the "Kidd," and the two double-headed to push the plow and open the line to Arlee. Adam, Michael, and Jamie joined the crews and rode in the caboose, to be available if extra help might be needed.

"Have you done this before?" Michael asked the two older youth.

"This usually happens several times each winter," Adam explained.

Jamie added, "It could take all day depending on how hard the ice has built up on the rails." He stepped to the front window to watch progress as the plow train got underway. "We'll know in a minute how hard the trip might be."

Jay sounded two blasts on the whistle. Ryker acknowledged with two of his own. Steam shoved the pistons in both engines as the drivers began to turn and the train got underway. The loud chuffing was slow and steady as the pair of locomotives began to push the plow car forward. The train maintained a slow and steady speed with each engine's chuffing sounds slightly out of synch with the other. At a half mile out, the plow hit the wall of snow that covered the tracks and began to slice through it sending snow flying off both sides of if its wedge.

The boys watched in awe as the snow flew out and disintegrated into a cloud of white mist.

"This is a light dry snow," Adam stated. "If it stays this way, it will be a good trip with little resistance." He watched forward over Jamie's shoulders as he knelt on a chair behind him.

Michael took up a position at the front window across from the older two. He watched the snow fly from his side as the train made slow and steady progress. "What happens when we get to Chamber's Crossing and go over the bridge?" he asked.

Jamie explained, "It should be pretty easy going since the snow will just drop off either side of the bridge."

"What about the barrels I've seen on the little platforms along either side of the bridge?" Michael observed.

"They're water barrels for fire emergencies," Adam replied. "The water has probably already frozen and split them open. They'll just fall into the valley and be replaced next spring."

"Oh."

"Chamber's Crossing coming up," Jamie announced.

The boys watched in wonder as the train pushed across the bridge and broken barrel staves flew to either side, mixed in the white mist of flying snow. Progress continued without pause for several more miles. Then, suddenly, the train burst into clear track.

"We're nearing Kingston," Jamie announced. "This is where we take our first break." He moved from the window and settled onto a bench beside the table. "We'll stop here and the crews will come back for a coffee break."

At that moment Michael became aware of the aroma of coffee. Until then, he had been too focused on the plowing operation to realize the air had that familiar smell about it. The train slowed and the boys moved to the table. At that point, they tended to the pot-bellied stove in the middle of the car with a huge coffee pot on top.

"Let's find the cups," Adam offered.

Searching the cabinets built into the base of the cupola, Adam found a stash of about a dozen tin cups. He passed them to the other boys who set them out on the table. Jamie turned his attention to the stove and checked the fire. The wood pieces smoldered hot and didn't seem to need more fuel.

The train eased to a full stop and each engine signaled the brakes were set. Soon a commotion arose as the two engine crews mounted the platform steps and crowded into the caboose.

"Sure smells good," Ryker stated as he took up his cup and Adam poured.

Soon all were settled wherever he could sit or lean or stand, as each enjoyed the warmth of the coffee.

"I hope it goes this well all the way in," Scott stated.

"It sure would make this day good," Charles added.

"Jamie," Ryker stated. "You know where the water tank is and the extra coffee in the storage cabinet."

"I remember," the youth confirmed.

"As we get underway, will you make up a fresh pot for when we stop at Blakesville?"

"Sure thing, Mr. Kimball."

"Time to move on," Jay announced.

The crews left and headed back to their locomotives. Quiet returned to the room.

Jamie took the coffee pot to the rear platform and quickly dumped the grounds and dregs and returned to the table before the train began to move. He refilled the pot with water from the water tank mounted on the wall in the back of the caboose, took the bag of fresh coffee from the cabinet and refilled the basket, then returned the prepared pot to the stove. Checking the fire, he added a couple sticks of wood and stirred it up to a hot flame so the freshly prepared pot could come to a boil and allow the coffee to perk.

Meanwhile, the younger boys returned to their places by the windows to watch as the train got underway once again. All settled to the rhythm of the moving train.

The snow continued to fly off either side of the plow wedge and dissipate into a fine mist. About a mile short of Blakesville there was an earsplitting explosive crash and the train came to a dead stop, throwing the boys crashing through the front windows of the caboose.

Michael's heavy wool coat and hat protected him from the broken glass, but the impact against the window ledge knocked the breath out of him and left him with sharp pain in his ribs. The weight of Jamie's body slammed Adam through the glass. His hat protected his head, but his arms and hands were torn by the shards of broken glass and bled freely. The chair took part of the shock to his body as it splintered on impact. Jamie flew off Adam's back and landed in the doorway with scrapes to his hands and a cut on the side of his head where it struck the doorframe.

"Help me," Adam called weakly as he was unable to move from the window opening.

Jamie pushed himself into a seated position, too dazed to get himself up.

Michael carefully pushed back from the window and stood testily as pain cut through his side and he worked his way toward Adam. Gently the younger boy worked to free his older friend from the window wreckage and move him to a bench by the table.

"Keep your arms on the table and don't try to move them," he instructed. "I need to stop the bleeding and make sure there's no glass in your cuts."

Looking up at Adam's bleeding arms and Michael's attempts to help him, a dazed Jamie barely whispered, "There's bandages in the cabinet across from the coffee."

"Thanks," Michael replied as he opened the cabinet in search of any medical supplies. He found bandages, salve, tincture of iodine, and towels.

"Lift your arms about a foot." He lay a towel on the table and eased Adam's arms back down. Carefully picking out some small shards of glass, he worked to clean the arm with the worst damage, then covered it with a clean towel, patting it gently to absorb the blood. He did the same with the other arm.

"Do you smell smoke?" Jamie asked. He had recovered his senses and stood up to check it out. "It's the stove." He checked out its odd position with smoke wisping from the chimney pipe. "The impact knocked the stove but the stovepipe kept it from falling. It's leaking smoke near the top. The coffee pot flew onto the bench on the other side. Amazing! It's standing up! Only some of the coffee splashed out. The cups are scattered about the floor."

"Can you get me some water?" Michael asked.

Jamie found a bucket in the back room and drew water from the tank. "Here," he offered as he placed it on the floor by Michael's feet.

The boy took another towel, soaked it in the bucket, wrung it out, then sponged the blood from the first arm.

"Ow!" Adam cried.

"What?"

"It feels like you just stabbed me with a knife."

Carefully Michael opened the wound and fished out a small splinter of glass. "Better?"

"Yea."

Next he took the salve and gently applied a small amount to the wounds, then folded bandaging to place across them. "Jamie, can you hold this for me?"

The older boy gently held the bandage in place while Michael took a roll of material and firmly wrapped in around Adam's arm and hand. Once finished, he did the same for the other arm and hand. "Now you stay put and don't move from your seat."

All watched apprehensively as the bandages began to soak red with continuing bleeding. The tightness of the bandaging took effect and the bleeding slowed, then stopped.

"Sure am glad to see that slow down," Jamie sighed in relief.

"You and me both," Michael added. "Keep the towel under those wet bandages. You might get ta feelin' faint from loss of blood. Just put yer head down if need."

"Okay. Thanks. Where did you learn what you did?"

"Last summer I had an accident and got cut by glass from a lamp chimney. Not as bad as you. My friend's pa fixed me up and I watched how he did it. He had to sew my cut together. You might need some sewing, too. But you're going to have to wait for a doctor."

"Are you okay?" Michael turned his attention to Jamie.

"Scraped some and banged my head, but I feel okay now."

Michael stood up from his kneeling position beside Adam.

"Ugh" he grunted as he grabbed his side and nearly doubled over in pain.

"You better sit down, find a position where it doesn't hurt, and stay put yourself."

Jamie helped Michael to find a bench and ease himself into a sitting position where the pain wasn't so intense.

"No one's come back from the engine crews," Jamie observed. "I wonder if they're okay."

"Can you check?" Michael asked.

"If you two promise to stay put, I'll go see."

"Yea," they both agreed.

The young man left to check on the engine crews and the damage up front. Moments later Jay rushed into the caboose, greatly concerned by what he had learned from Jamie.

"What happened!?" he asked.

"You tell me," Michael replied. "There was a crashing explosion and everything suddenly stopped! What happened up front?"

"We hit ice," Jay explained. "Fortunately we were going slow and the only damage is a crushed snow plow car and broken front coupler. We all got banged up some but nothing major."

"We went through the front windows," Michael explained. "Adam's cut up pretty bad and needs a doctor as soon as possible."

Jay gazed at Adam's wrapped arms. "It looks like you found one."

"It's just temporary. What are you gonna do?"

"We're thinking on leaving the plow car here and returning to Snow Shoe. We'll telegraph the company office and tell them what happened. They can send the "Dalton" with its snow blade and helper engines to open the rest of the line. When they finish, they can crane the plow car onto a flat and take it to the shops in Arlee for repairs. We can pick it up on a later freight run and tow it back to Snow Shoe. I hear you're not feelin' too well either."

"I hurt my ribs."

"Let me check it." He lifted the boy's shirt to look and gently touch.

"Ow! Hurts like crazy."

"Lot's of color. And you might have cracked something."

As he stood to go, Jay noticed the stove.

"Where's the coffee?"

"Sitting on the bench behind you."

"Glad the stove's still standing. We might have had a fire here, too." The engineer started toward the door. "Adam, you mind the doctor, here. We'll get you both to Doc Blevins as soon as we return to Snow Shoe."

"Thank you, Sir. Can't wait," Adam responded.

"I'll send Jamie back and we'll get underway shortly." He left the car and quickly descended the steps.

Jamie returned to the car followed by Dan Seegers.

"Not much need for a conductor up front, besides it was getting crowded and I decided to ride back with you boys and keep you from getting into any more trouble." Dan took a quick glance about the car.

He spotted the coffee pot where it sat on the bench, then reached for a bloody towel on the table beside Adam. "I'll borrow this." The conductor picked up the coffee pot, wiped it off, and placed it on the table. Then he wiped off the bench and sat down, leaving the dirty and bloody towel on the end of the bench.

"I know what happened up front. Will someone tell me what happened back here? I see broken windows and chair, blood, a crooked stove, and cups across the floor. And I see three boys, all wounded in some way. I think you got the worst of this accident."

"Well, it's like this," Jamie began.

Three short whistle blasts cut through the air and the car shook and moaned as loud chuffs pushed driver wheels into motion and the train began its slow journey back to Snow Shoe.

# HOLIDAY PAIN

Upon returning to Snow Shoe, Dan Seegers took all three boys to Dr. Blevins office on Railroad Avenue, next door to *The Herald*. Jamie's scrapes didn't require any treatment. The doctor gave him an ointment to use to help the healing process. Michael did not appear to have any broken or cracked bones, just a really severe bruising that went deep to the bone. Time and rest with restricted activity were prescribed. Adam needed a few stitches in the worst of his cuts. They were to be cleaned at least twice a day and dressed with antiseptic ointments to help prevent infection and aid healing. The stitches could be removed in seven to ten days depending on how fast the wounds healed. Afterwards, Doc Blevins drove the boys home in his carriage. Adam was too weak from the loss of blood to walk the distance. Jamie was dropped off at Maple Avenue to walk the rest of the way to his home. Adam and Michael were dropped off at the side porch near the kitchen door. Doc waited to make sure that Michael got Adam into the house before turning around and heading for home.

Each engine crew took its locomotive to the Stewart Creek facility where each was serviced. Ryker's crew took Number forty-six back to the saw mill yard after leaving the caboose in the company car shop for repairs. There the "Kidd" was stored in its single stall engine house on its designated siding between the saw mill and the barrel company. Jay's crew put Number twenty-one back in the company engine house where the "Scott" and its caboose had already been put away for the night. After all was settled, Jay went to the station and sent a telegram to the V&T headquarters office in Arlee to report the accident and the location of the plow car in the ice east of Blakesville.

\*     \*     \*

By late Friday afternoon, Stationmaster Coates had received a telegram stating that the line had been reopened to Arlee and the plow car had been delivered to the shops to be repaired. Schedules were to return to normal the following Monday. The Friday issue of *The Herald* reported that life would return to normal on Monday with all industry and businesses opening on schedule and school back in session.

Monday dawned with a brilliant sun glinting off a white wintry landscape. Even bundled up, the trip to the barn for morning chores was bitter cold. There was little Adam could do with his forearms completely bandaged. He watched as Michael fed the livestock, milked the cow, tended the smokehouse fire, and collected the eggs. They rushed their return to the kitchen to get to its warmth as soon as possible.

"Boy this sure feels good – sooo warm," Adam stated as he unbundled and hung up his coat and all.

"And it smells so good, too," Michael added, as he turned from hanging up his things, and took his seat at the table.

Breakfast was consumed with little conversation.

"Adam," Mr. Tyler instructed as he bundled up to face the cold, "you will stay home this week and help around the house while your cuts heal." He picked up his lunch bucket and started toward the door. "If you heal enough during the week, you might be able to work at *The Herald* by Friday."

"What am I going to do all day," the teen asked.

"You can keep me company," his mother offered. "And when Michael gets home from school, you might be able to help him understand his fractions," she suggested.

"I'd sure be grateful," Michael added.

"You all have a good day." The father continued down the hall and was gone as a blast of cold air signaled the opening and closing of the front door.

\*       \*       \*

As the week passed, both boys continued to heal. Adam was a good teacher. Michael began to understand the mysteries of fractional numbers. The weeks of after school lessons in grammar paid off to the extent that he could now participate in regular class time lessons without the extra tutoring. He had also consumed the content of the lower grade history books and could now join his classmates in their history lessons. The boy felt a sense of accomplishment as the wintery weather advanced into the holiday season. His bruising healed as did Adam's deep cuts. Stitches came out and bandaging was reduced to the worst of the injuries.

The plow car returned as part of the Friday freight run, a week after the accident.

The weeks since the first snow had seen a mix of sunshine and overcast with a few scattered snow showers, but little additional accumulation. It remained cold so the snow showed little sign of melting. School let out midday on the Wednesday before Thanksgiving. There was a noisy exodus as the children poured from the building and headed off in their various directions toward home.

It was Jamison's turn to take firewood in for the classroom stove.

"Want some help?" Michael offered as he followed the older boy out of the building.

"If you want, that would be great," the older boy responded. "We might get in a little extra for the start of next week."

"We'll help," Teddy offered as he and Miles followed their friend from the building.

"Thanks," Jamison accepted. "Leave your school things in the hall. They'll stay dry there."

The four boys gathered firewood from the front of the playground where each week's delivery was dumped. Boys from each of the four classrooms gathered wood for the next day's supply. With each of the four taking in an armload of wood, only one trip was needed to complete the task.

"I owe you next time it's your turn," Jamison stated as each emerged from the building with books in hand. "Have a great Thanksgiving weekend. See you next week."

"You, too," the other three chorused.

The boys headed off toward home, Jamison toward Main Street and the north side of town, and Michael and his friends up Jeffers Street toward Maple and a first stop at Teddy's house.

"Can we do a quick check of the trap line before we all head for home?" Teddy asked as they turned down Maple.

"I'll tell my ma," Miles stated. "Then we can go directly toward the Tyler farm."

The two left their books at their homes and Teddy picked up the feed sack. They headed on to Washington Street then south to the farm.

\* \* \*

Michael dumped his armload of wood into the wood box next to the kitchen stove.

"I'll make another trip for the living room stove," he stated.

"Thanks," Mrs. Tyler said as she turned the pork chops in the cast iron frying pan and put the cover back on. "What about some extra so we don't have to get any tomorrow." The woman turned to the boy.

A blast of cold air rushed in from the hall as Adam and his father came in through the front door. Adam had spent the day at *The Herald* getting out the holiday edition. His father had met him there and the two walked home together.

"Can Adam help?" Michael asked.

"Help what?" the older boy asked.

"Get in extra firewood," his mother replied.

"Sure." He put his lunch bucket on the table and followed Michael out the door, while his father paused to hang up his coat and hat.

"It's good to be home and have a few days off," Mr. Tyler addressed his wife as he crossed the room to greet her with a kiss and a hug.

Mrs. Tyler slid the pan to a cooler area on the stovetop. Then she took the pot of boiled potatoes to the sink to pour off the water and prepared to mash them in readiness for dinner.

Mr. Tyler tended the stoves while the boys finished bringing in a supply of firewood. In short order, warm coats and outer wear were placed on their respective pegs near the door, all washed up for dinner, and dinner was moved to the table.

\* \* \*

Thanksgiving Day dawned with low clouds and steady snow flurries. Following chores and a breakfast of sausage, eggs, home fried potatoes, and home made donuts, the family gathered in the kitchen. Mrs. Tyler worked on preparations for an early afternoon dinner. She had been up since six o'clock in order to prepare the turkey and get it in the oven for the hours of slow cooking that made it so tender. Mr. Tyler read the newspaper, which had come out Wednesday because *The Herald*'s offices were closed for the holiday weekend. The boys focused on a game of checkers. From time to time the boys and the man paused to attend to whatever need the woman requested.

"You boys need to check on the dining room stove," Mr. Tyler suggested as mid morning wore on. "We want the room warm enough for a comfortable dinner."

"Sure, Pa," Adam stated as he jumped two of Michael's pieces and removed them from the board.

"Darn!" the younger boy exclaimed in surprise. He stood from the table to do as asked. Adam followed.

"Bill," his wife turned from the stove having just slipped a string bean casserole into the oven. "You might start setting the table for dinner."

"Okay." He lay the newspaper down.

Mr. Tyler joined the boys in the dining room and started to take the place settings from the china closet while the boys raked down the fire and added two pieces of wood to the stove.

The smell of wood smoke and the warmth of the fire drifted throughout the room, blending with the food aromas wafting in from the kitchen. Adam closed the door on the stove and turned to the silverware box on the buffet cabinet to take out the flatware for the table. Michael turned from the stove and stood staring at the scene in front of him. In his mind he reflected on his mother's preparation of food for their family in the winter of the year with help from Granny Woman. Thunder Arrow, Grandfather, and he would never be helping prepare the meal in any way. They would have hunted the game and brought it home for the women, and the women would have done all the preparations. As a boy, he might have responsibility for the fire, but not cither of the men. Here, the whole family worked together to prepare and set out the food. He had begun to take his new life for granted. He hadn't thought of his family in days, and it worried him. His letters would take a long time to make their journeys back home and a long time to receive replies. The boy had become so caught up in his life in Michael's world, he had forgotten his real world, the world of Prairie Cub. It came as a sudden awakening and emotional shock.

"I have to check on Of-The-Wind." Michael made a sudden dash to the kitchen, quickly pulled on his boots, bundled up in coat, hat, scarf, and gloves, then suddenly dashed out the door, closing it securely behind him.

Adam and his father hurried to the kitchen as Mrs. Tyler watched the boy through the window as he ran to the barn.

"What happened?" she asked turning to her husband and son.

"I don't know," Mr. Tyler replied as he and Adam joined her to watch out the window.

"We were setting the table," Adam began, "and he turned from the stove and just stared at us with a blank look on his face." He started toward the door. "Should I go after him?"

"No, Son," his father replied. "I think he is in need of some time to himself. It may be that his past suddenly caught up to him. A lot has happened in recent weeks." He walked to the table. "There was a look of shock and bewilderment on his face as he stood there in the dining room." He sat down. "I think he is suddenly filled with unexpected emotional pain."

\*　　\*　　\*

Michael closed the barn door and walked to his pony's stall. While the door was always open to the meadow, Of-The-Wind was busy feeding on her grain when the boy entered. She immediately walked to the inner gate and reached her head over for his attention. The boy opened the gate and entered. He wrapped his arms around her neck, buried his face in her mane, and cried his heart out. The two stood there in locked grief. The pony rested her muzzle on his shoulder and stood patiently waiting for his next move.

For the moment, he was Prairie Cub, lost from the world that was his heritage, frightened at the sudden realization that he had become so wrapped up in this new world that he had started to forget who he really was.

"I'm afraid," he whispered to his pony. "I'm afraid I'm loosing who I am and will be too comfortable in this new life. I don't want to loose myself. I can't do this."

They stood there a moment longer. Suddenly, the boy slipped onto his pony's back and directed her to the open door. They wandered out into the midday cold, the boy bent forward with his face in the pony's mane as she meandered aimlessly across the meadow, pushing herself through the knee-deep snow. His tears froze on his face and he rubbed his eyes to dislodge the flakes of ice. The two continued out into the meadow, brushed silently by the falling white dust, struggling slowly through the weather as it quietly coated him and his pony in white. Wracked with an emotional pain he could not control, Michael gave his pony her head and let her go wherever she wanted. They wandered the meadow to the back gate. There they paused.

"Why!" he whispered to no one in particular. "I want to go home. I want my family." Fresh tears flowed and froze. He sat up and looked across the landscape, a constant world of white. In the distance the farm buildings stood in dark silhouette against the world of white.

Of-The-Wind started to force her way back toward the barn. As they neared the building, Michael saw that someone stood in the door to his pony's stall. In his blurred vision through his tears, it looked like Prairie Flower wrapped in a robe. But it couldn't be. It was Mrs. Tyler. She stood patiently and silently, bundled in coat and gloves with a scarf covering her head and wrapped around her neck, making no attempt to say a word. Noticing the moisture of tears on her cheeks, Michael slid to the ground, rushed into outstretched arms, and buried his face in her embrace. He shook with his sobbing as she guided him into the barn and held him tightly. The pony wandered to the water trough, broke the ice with her hoof and drank, then wandered into the barn.

The woman stood unmoving and said nothing as she continued to hold the sobbing boy in her firm embrace.

"I want to go home," Michael cried softly.

"I know you do," she replied quietly, never shifting her stance or her embrace.

"I can't stand this. I can't forget."

"Come," Mrs. Tyler whispered as she shifted her embrace and turned the boy to walk to the barn's interior.

She found the milk stool and sat down cradling Michael in her lap. There they remained for several silent minutes while the boy cried his heartache and slowly quieted.

"Michael." He looked up into a tear-dampened face and suddenly was aware of how deeply she cared for him. "Michael, we have all become so wrapped up in our daily lives that we have all taken your life with us for granted. And in that, we have forgotten your great loss and the deep grief that is a part of that." She brushed his hair out of his eyes as she leaned his head against her shoulder. "I and my family will never let that happen again. I think you forgot, too, and suddenly realized that today, and it frightened you."

He nodded without looking up.

"We need to do something that will keep you always in touch with who you are."

For a moment they sat there in silence. The boy stirred.

"Shoes," he whispered.

"What?"

"I hate shoes. They feel like a prison to my feet."

"What do you suggest?"

"Can I wear my moccasins?" He sat up and looked upon her face. "And can you learn how to make another pair for when mine wear out? I can get a deer and clean and tan the hide to make the buckskin for making them."

"I can do that. You can wear the ones that are in your trunk. Maybe I can get a piece of rawhide to cut an extra sole to make them last longer since you walk on harder surfaces than just the ground outside."

She smiled at the idea and the boy smiled back.

"You do know that this whole idea of Thanksgiving was created by the colonists and the Indians from up in New England." Mrs. Tyler stated.

"I had forgotten. But it was in one of the history book stories I read."

"Are you ready to go back to the house and have dinner?"

"Okay. Do we have to say anything more when we get there?"

"No. Bill and Adam understand what happened. Bill even said as much. While I finish fixing dinner, you go upstairs and get your moccasins. Will they be all right out in this weather?"

"They always were."

"Then you won't ever need to wear shoes again. If anyone asks, you just tell them you always wore them in the past. They're more comfortable."

Michael stood up and offered his hand for Mrs. Tyler.

"Thanks," she accepted as she took it and gently pulled herself up from the stool.

Of-The-Wind offered a soft whinny as the two started toward the door.

"Take care, Girl. I'll be back for chores this afternoon."

She tossed her head in reply, then stood and watched as the two left the barn.

# SHARED SECRET

The light snow of Thanksgiving Day continued through the night and strengthened to a full blown blizzard during Friday. Over the weekend it began to die out to overcast late Saturday and a hazy sun throughout Sunday. By Monday the community found itself once again on a snow schedule. The town lay under a thick blanket of snow with deeper drifts throughout, sparkling under the morning sun. A brilliant glare brought hat brims down over squinted eyes, already hurting from the brightness. Pathways had been dug to the roads where morning traffic had trampled the snow and packed it hard in the middle. The Monday routine began slowly as businesses dug out and mill workers helped open the central work district and the railroad before starting up the saw mill. Crews from the logging company and the railroad dug out the yard areas. The railroad had not yet opened the line into Arlee, so the morning train had been canceled. Over the weekend, as the storm raged, trains had been canceled and those who had left for the holidays were unable to return. Manpower was affected at the mills. Those present had that much more to do and cleanup took extra hours. Nevertheless, preparations for a late train were underway as all local trackage was cleared by hand with the help of the plow car pushed by Numbers twenty-one and forty-six. A trip was made to Day's End to clear the line that far. The Stewart Creek locomotive "Scott" took on the plow car and a crew train late in the morning and left with a double track crew to open the line to South Camp. School had cancelled for the day and the students worked to help their families with the cleanup.

Michael and his friends had brought their lunches so they could walk over to Snow Shoe Station to get the latest news from Mr. Coates. The three boys walked leisurely down Jeffers Street to Railroad, turned toward Main Street and followed it across the tracks to the station. The snow crunched under foot as they crossed the wooden platform and entered the warmth of the waiting room.

Once inside the door, the boys left their lunches on a side bench. Miles pulled off his gloves, tucked them under his elbow, rubbed his hands briskly and blew into them trying to take off the chill. "Boy, is it cold!" he blew.

Teddy stamped snow from his boots and crossed the room toward the potbellied stove. "The heat sure feels good!" He removed his gloves, stuffed them inside his coat, and stretched his hands over the stove. "Come over here, Miles. This'll warm ya."

As the two warmed themselves at the stove, Michael stomped the snow from his moccasins and headed toward the ticket window to see if the stationmaster was in. "Mr. Coates!" he called.

"Over here, Michael." The reply came from the freight room across the hall. "I'll be there in just a minute."

Michael paced to the front door and looked at the track through the window. About a quarter mile out toward Arlee, the tracks disappeared under the drifted snow. The line was open toward Day's End.

The stationmaster returned from the freight room. "Mornin', Boys." He crossed to the office area behind the ticket window. "Any news from Jay on plans for this morning?"

"Haven't seen him yet," Michael replied as he checked the fire in the stove. "Want me to add some wood?"

"Yes, thanks."

Miles passed two pieces of firewood to his friend who placed them onto the hot coals in the potbellied stove, then closed the door. The telegraph key clattered briefly and Mr. Coates acknowledged.

"Hold on. News coming in."

He sat down with paper and pencil and the boys crossed the room to the ticket window to listen and watch. The key began to clatter its message as the stationmaster focused on getting the message on paper. The boys waited patiently. Several minutes passed before the sender signed off and Mr. Coates replied.

"Looks like we're getting some help from the other end." He turned to face the boys. "The company was able to clear the main line over the weekend. They're sending the "Dalton" with its helpers and crew to open the Snow Shoe branch. They left a half hour ago."

"We'll go tell Jay at the Stewart Creek office," Teddy volunteered. "Thanks."

The boys turned from the ticket window, drew on their gloves, picked up their lunch buckets, and headed toward the center hall and out the back door.

\*     \*     \*

Jay and his crew had just sat down to lunch as Michael and friends arrived.

"I see you brought lunch," he observed. "Join us."

"Okay," Miles replied as the three sat down at the table and pulled their sandwiches from their lunch buckets.

"Mr. Coates just got a telegram from the company offices," Michael announced.

"They're sending the plow train to open the branch line," Teddy quickly added.

"Any time information?" Scott inquired.

"Left a half hour ago," Miles cut in.

The boys settled to eating their lunches.

Dan Seegers thought aloud, "It will probably be close to five this evening before they arrive."

"Number twenty-one needs to be serviced before we go anywhere," Scott stated between mouthfuls.

Jay finished his coffee and set the cup down. "We have lots of time. Let's clean off the passenger cars and get the train set in the station ready to go to Day's End. We'll wire Kingston and ask them to let us know when the "Dalton" gets there. That will give us an hour to let folks know we're leaving for Day's End, make the trip, then hold here until the line is cleared. We'll telegraph Arlee and let them know we'll be coming in ahead of the return of the plow train so they can let our folks there know to be at the station for the return trip."

"Sounds like a plan," Scott and Dan agreed.

"Jamie's on the mountain with my trainman and brakeman," Jay said. "If you boys want to ride along and help as needed, you'd be welcome. We'll get Jarrett to take charge of the baggage room. Miles, you and Teddy go over to the mercantile and pick up the outgoing mail. Michael, go to the Wells Fargo office and let Ephram know we leave in an hour for Day's End."

The boys packed up their lunch buckets, left them on the table, and prepared to depart on their assignments.

"I'll have Jarrett meet us at the station and ask his sister to let your folks know you're with us," Dan stated.

"We'll lay over in Arlee for a half hour and take dinner at the Railroad Hotel," Jay added.

"Okay," Michael acknowledged as the boys left.

The engine crew packed and left for the "King" and Scott took the coffee pot from the stove for the engine cab.

\*    \*    \*

Jay positioned Number twenty-one's water fill hole under the spout of the water tank and Scott flipped open the cover, reached for the chain, and drew it down. Following a sudden explosive splash, water poured into the hole. Scott waited for it to fill and overflow before he released the spout to be pulled back up by the counterweights. He closed the lid with a clang. The locomotive then eased forward to the woodpile as the boys ran across the company yard from the train station, having returned from their errands. They joined Jay and helped throw firewood to Scott on the tender while the fireman placed it in the deep well of the wood load. Once finished, all gathered in the cab and Jay shifted the Johnson bar into forward, released the brake, and pulled back on the throttle forcing the pistons and drive gear into motion. Heavy smoke billowed from the stack as the steam hissed from the piston chambers and the wheels slowly turned. The engine moved toward the station where Dan Seegers was already supervising as Jarrett worked with Ephram to unload the Wells Fargo wagon and passengers began to arrive. Soon the train was assembled and Jay sounded the whistle to announce its departure in another ten minutes. Evan Clanton approached and informed Dan that he wanted to gather a news story about the storm for the week's edition of *The Herald*. The two stood and visited for several minutes while waiting for passengers and baggage to load, as the newsman began to gather informational notes for his story. Several families that had come to visit family for the holiday boarded to return to their homes and places of business. Evan boarded the coach. In the absence of the brakeman, Michael ran ahead and threw the switches.

"All aboard!" Dan waved toward the engine and climbed aboard. With three short blasts of the whistle, the train backed out and left for Day's End. As the engine moved through the switches, the boy climbed back aboard, leaving the switches set for the return trip.

Quiet settled on an empty station platform. Mr. Coates wandered out from the station to return the baggage wagon to the baggage room door.

*     *     *

The train returned in twenty minutes and sat waiting for the plow train to arrive. The switches were reset in the closed position. The boys gathered in the engine to enjoy its warmth and quiet conversation. Steam rumbled in the boiler and hissed from the piston chambers while smoke drifted light from the stack.

A distant whistle announced the pending arrival of the plow train. As the boys watched, three columns of smoke announced the approach of a triple header, pushing its way through the snow.

"Awesome!" Teddy remarked as the train came into view.

"Michael," Jay asked, "would you go to the switch, wait for the plow train to pass, then throw it for us to pull out?"

"Okay."

"You two can go to the baggage room with Jarrett and Michael can work with Scott."

The three left for their duties. Michael had no sooner gotten to the switch than the "Dalton" and its plow train approached and passed through the switch. Within five minutes the passenger train eased out of the station and slowed, once through the switch, for the boy to climb back on board. It quickly picked up to a slower than usual running speed, and was soon out of sight.

*     *     *

By week's end, routines had once again returned to normal. Accumulated snow depth averaged about a foot, give or take a couple inches. Industry and business ran on schedule and the students were once again in school. A light snow began Wednesday mid morning. By early afternoon, a light wind blew up.

Whirlwinds of falling snow danced across the schoolyard. A steady north-westerly wind had already drifted over all traces of earlier activity in the yard. Yet a warm glow from the windows and a white smoke whipping from the chimneys at either end of the building and the office area in the middle, confirmed activity within the wooden structure.

Suddenly, the central doors burst open and the afternoon air erupted with the boisterous excitement and laughter of about eight dozen children headed homeward. Some turned off down the street immediately while others paused to await friends. Small knots gathered to talk briefly and go their separate ways.

Michael stood by the street and waited for his friends. The brim of his hat was tied down over his ears with a long knitted scarf Mrs. Tyler had made for him. His red capote was tied snugly. Fur-lined gloves warmed his hands. School books were wrapped in brown paper and tucked under the coat.

Teddy Latimer was the first to join him, kicking at the snow as he crossed the schoolyard, and called a question when he judged himself within ear shot. "Hey, Michael! What'er ya gonna write on fer yer Christmas writin?"

Michael turned to his friend. "What? Can't hear you."

"What'll ya write on?"

"I don't know yet. My people never knew of Christmas. I'll have to find out what it is, first."

Teddy looked back to the school, embarrassed. "I fergot," he apologized.

There was an awkward silence while the two waited for Miles. It was his turn to fill the schoolroom's wood box and Jamison was helping.

"What do you want ta do?" Michael changed the subject.

Teddy scanned the slope of Fisher Mountain. He, too, was bundled warmly against the storm. "I guess there's too much storm ta walk the trap line. It'll be dark soon."

"Hi! Guys!" Miles called as he bounded down the schoolhouse steps, writing book in hand. "Thanks, Jamison," he acknowledged as the older boy followed and turned toward home. Jamison waved back in reply. "What's up?" Miles asked as he drew closer.

"We could just check the near part of the line, up behind the farm toward Lawrence Creek," Michael offered.

"Sure," Miles agreed.

"Okay," Teddy added. "Let's go straight away and leave our books on the back porch. We'll get best light if we go now. Can we grab an empty feed bag at your place, Michael?"

"Sure."

The three bent into the wind as they turned up Jeffers Street to Cedar Avenue and headed toward the Tyler farm. Two inches of new snow had accumulated on top of the twelve inches of snow that lay on the ground from the previous storm, with combined drifts up to two feet snuggled against the sides of houses and trees. The streets were temporarily empty. But even as the boys turned into the side yard at Tyler's, neighborhood children reemerged from their homes with sleds, or gathered in yards to construct snow forts and snowmen. Mrs. Tyler waved from the back door as Michael and his friends left their books in a protected corner on the back porch.

"Where ya all goin?" she asked.

"Ta check the lower trap line," Michael called back.

"How are ya gonna get to the traps under all the snow?"

"We pulled them and set them on top of the snow when we walked the line on Monday."

"Be careful. See ya back fer supper."

"Okay." He turned again to catch up with his friends.

"We'll just check the lower pasture hedgerow and the creek," Teddy offered.

"Okay," his friends chorused.

The first trap was staked about four hundred yards beyond the barn. Of-The-Wind forced her way through the snow to the fence line as they passed and followed for a short distance before turning back toward the barn.

Miles ran ahead for a quick check. "Nothin here," he called.

They moved on. The third trap had been sprung, but was empty. After resetting it, the trio continued. A young muskrat was in the fourth. It had died and the carcass was stiff and cold. Removing the prize, Teddy reset the trap, placed his catch in the sack, and they trudged onward. The seventh trap held a frightened coon, tired from struggling and slowed by the cold. It stared at the boys through dark pleading eyes.

"You don't need this coon," Michael stated. His sympathetic eyes met the animal's.

"Why not?" Teddy questioned, looking about for a suitable club.

"Coon hides don't bring much now," Michael suggested. "And your pa has a good job with the saw mill." He kept eye contact with the terrified animal.

Teddy paused and looked at the injured creature caught in the steel jaws. Miles, too, watched the animal.

"I think Michael's right," Miles offered.

"Yea," Teddy accepted with half a smile. "Do ya think he'd make it if we turned him loose?"

"Our Mother the earth cares for her own," Michael stated. "Be quiet. I'll tell ya when, then open the trap."

The boys nodded acknowledgement. Michael gestured and they slowly lowered themselves to kneel motionless in the snow. A windy silence wrapped about them to be broken by the soft voice with words his friends could not understand from a world he had left behind. In the language of the Sioux, Michael spoke to the coon. The chain on the trap drew taught as the animal backed away. The dark eyes of the wild met the gentle blue eyes of the boy caught in a reassuring stare as the boy moved slowly closer. The other two watched in awed silence. The coon tensed, bared its teeth, and hissed a feeble warning. A gloved hand moved slowly toward the creature. And all the while, the soft reassuring voice offered comfort.

The eyes remained locked on one-an-other as the gloved hand gently stroked the fur. Quickly sharp teeth sank harmlessly through the tip of the thumb as the two friends stifled a surprised warning. The voice continued to soothe and the glove continued to softly stroke behind an ear. The animal released its grip and jumped aside at the sudden movement from the other two boys. Michael signaled his friends with his free hand that it was all right, as he moved even closer to the animal. Then, stroking the back of the coon's head, he closed in a firm grip on the nape of the neck where its mother would have held it as a baby, to carry it to a safe location. Gently lifting the creature, he clamped the other hand to its belly, locking the injured paw with two fingers.

The coon screamed and struggled to tear at the hands, but was held firmly from behind. Michael moved it to slacken the chain, and nodded for the others to open the trap. As soon as it was free of the jaws, he released it. Bounding off on three legs, it disappeared into the storm without so much as a glance backward. The boys watched it go. It was a few moments before either spoke and before they felt their own tenseness ease from their muscles.

The youngest of the three spoke. "Where did you learn ta do that?"

"Do what, Teddy?"

"Ta talk ta creatures an git close ta them like that."

"Grandfather taught me since I was small."

A gust of wind whipped at the snow and for a brief moment, the whole world disappeared into white. Suddenly the three were aware of approaching darkness.

"We best go back, now," Miles observed. "The day's nearly gone and the snow will bring on an early dark."

Teddy reset the trap. The three stood and glanced at the track left by the departing coon. It had already blown away leaving no trace of the animal's flight.

"Come on," Miles urged. "I can't see where we've been, but we can still follow the edge of the pasture to the barn."

Twice they stopped to check their bearings before they finally reached the barn. Neither of the boys spoke until they had retrieved their books from the porch and started toward the street. Mrs. Tyler poked her head out as they left the porch to check on their safe return, then waved them on. She ducked back inside to await Michael. Rounding the corner of the house, the small group was hit by a strong wind from the north and a furious swirling of snow so thick it hid them from each other. They stopped and waited for the wind to pass and the snow to settle.

"Our folks'll be worried we're so late," Miles observed. He brushed snow from his coat collar and pulled it closer around his neck. "We best hurry."

"See you in school tomorrow," Michael paused as the other two turned toward the street.

Miles and Teddy bid their friend a good evening as they separated to travel Washington Street toward home. Michael paused to watch them go. Teddy turned back a moment as Miles went ahead and Michael raised a question.

"If your pa says okay, come on back after supper," Michael suggested to his friend. "May be if you could tell me about Christmas, I could think of a story for Mrs. Miller."

"Sure," Teddy accepted. "See you around seven."

Michael watched his friend disappear into the swirling snow, then turned back to the walkway, mounted the porch steps, and entered the warmth of the house.

"Is that you, Michael?" Janet called from the kitchen as the boy pushed the door shut, cutting off the sudden swish of snow and wind that had followed him into the house.

"Yes, Ma'am," he replied.

"Come on to the kitchen and get warm."

Michael entered the warmth of the kitchen where Mrs. Tyler was busy at the range.

"Could you fix the fires for me?" she asked.

"Okay, soon's I set my books on the steps and hang up my things."

\*    \*    \*

The living room stove was finished and the boy had just returned to the kitchen when the door opened to the wind and snow, and Adam and his father entered the house.

Mr. Tyler hung his coat on its peg as he spoke. "Michael, Jay gave me these letters for you this afternoon."

Michael set the plates he had taken from the dish drainer, on the table. There was a shiver of excitement from within as he reached for the letters. It had been such a long time since he had sent his letters to friends and family in Montana Territory. Adam and his parents knew this and they paused to watch and share the boy's excitement.

Michael stared at the two envelopes to see who had sent which. He ripped open the first and spread the paper on the table. The message was brief.

> *Comin ta see ya. Bringin gifts n news. Thars two letters in Mr. Summers envelop and some bout yer folks.*
>
>                          *W. Mattson*

Quickly, the boy laid the first letter aside and tore into the second. There were two sheets of writing. Both were in Keith Summers' hand. He studied them both carefully. Adam's family sat and watched intensely, wanting to ask questions, yet remaining respectfully silent.

*27 October 1882*
*Keith Summers*
*Summers Freight Company*
*Savage, Montana Territory*

*Prairie Cub,*

> *Your letters arrived yesterday. Today I sent Trader Mattson with a small pack train of blankets, food goods, shells for their guns, bolts of cloth, knives, and cooking pots to your people's village in Canada, along with your letter to your folks. We've been in touch once in the months since you left. Your people have found a quiet valley to settle in and have been welcomed by the Canadian officials. Game has been plentiful. There are scattered settlements who have done some trading*

*with them for food crops. They do not know how long they will be able to survive there and do believe that sooner or later, they will have to return to the United States and eventually settle on a reservation. They will avoid this as long as they can.*

*Savage continues to grow as the railroad continues to bring new people to the territory. Construction has moved far to the west and the Robinsons have gone with it. Your friend Scot wrote to ask if I had heard anything from you. I wrote back that I had not, but would let him know as soon as I did. I'm sending him a letter today to share your news and give him your new address.*

*I'll hold this until Mattson returns.*

*K. S.*

Michael read the letter to the family, then lay it down and took up the second page.

*24 November 1882*
*Keith Summers*
*Summers Freight Company*
*Savage, Montana Territory*

*Prairie Cub,*

*Mattson returned yesterday. He has spoken to Thunder Eagle and Prairie Flower as well as Granny Woman. They were all so grateful to learn of your new life and sorry to learn of your pain. They love you deeply and miss you so much, but know you need to thrive in your new world and hope that you will. Thunder Eagle has taken four deer for you and Prairie Flower has tanned the skins. They sent them back with Trader Mattson along with a pack mule loaded with a variety of trade hides, and he will bring them to you in the weeks ahead. In the meantime, he made a stop at Fort Pierre to ask about your and his friend, Trapper Murray and his boy Lawrence. Mattson will look them up in St. Louis on his way to Snow Shoe. He hopes to arrive in Snow Shoe sometime near the end of December.*

*We all miss you and hope you are well.*

*It is my wish to invite you and the Tyler family to visit here in Savage during the spring of the new year. We can all retreat to the old trading fort to enjoy time together. If I can, I will arrange for your family to come from Canada and will get word to the Robinsons and to Trapper Murray. I have already sent an invitation with Mattson for him and his boy to winter at the fort and trap along the river. They can stay in the old barracks. I'll let you know if they decide to come.*

*Mattson has given me a note for you and I will send these out on tomorrow's train.*

*Know you are loved and missed by many.*

*K. S.*

Tears of joy and of homesickness welled up in the boy's eyes. He laid the pages together and stared at them momentarily. He looked up at the family.

"He's coming!" he cried. "He's coming here!"

"Who's coming, Son?" Janet asked. Moved by the burst of emotion, she slipped a finger alongside her nose to interrupt a tear. Her husband and son tried to hide their feelings of emotion as well.

"Trader Mattson's coming! He's coming all the way from Montana Territory to see me! He'll have news of my people!" Michael's excitement was boundless as he picked up the letters and the papers trembled in his fingers.

"Who's Trader Mattson?" Adam asked, wrinkling his nose in his puzzlement and an attempt to hide a tear.

"He's a friend of Michael's," the boy's pa explained.

"He's a mountain man from the great Rockies," the younger boy added in a voice of controlled importance.

"Oh," Adam whispered.

"That's good news," Bill stated. "I'm sure we'll learn more in a day or two. But jest now, I'm feelin' hungry. Let's eat."

"We forgot chores," Adam announced.

"You can do them after dinner," his father stated.

Michael folded the letters and tucked them into his shirt. Then he picked up the plates and continued to set the table. Mr. Tyler pitched in to help while his son washed up.

\*      \*      \*

The boys had previously returned from the barn. Mrs. Tyler had just finished up the dishes, her husband had poured himself a cup of coffee, Adam had just fed the stove and replaced the stove lid, and Michael sat at the table studying the letters. There was a knock at the door and the woman went to open it.

"Teddy, come in." She closed the door. "What are ya doin' out on a night like this?"

"I come ta talk ta Michael 'bout a school assignment." He brushed the snow from his coat as he peeled out of his extra warmth.

"He's in the kitchen, Teddy. Hang yer wet things behind the range ta dry."

They walked to the kitchen where the boys exchanged greetings, then excused themselves to Michael's room.

"You boys don't be up there too long. Ya have ta get up fer school tomorrow," Mrs. Tyler admonished.

"We won't, Mrs. Tyler," Teddy assured. "What ya got?" he asked Michael as they started up the stairs.

"Letters from friends. Here, take a look." He handed the papers to Teddy.

As the two entered the bedroom, Teddy flopped across the bed and spread the papers to be studied. Michael perched in the corner on the lid of his trunk. They remained this way for several minutes, Teddy studying the letters and Michael studying his friend. Teddy looked up.

"These say you have parents?" he questioned, puzzled. "I thought they were gone. And why do they call you 'Prairie Cub?'"

"They are. They're in Canada when we were separated. I'll tell you about Prairie Cub later."

"Who's this Mattson?" he asked.

"He's a friend who helped me when I was alone," Michael replied. "He's a trader from the mountains. Some would call him a mountain man."

"Gee," Teddy sighed, "and he's comin' here?"

"Yea," Michael confirmed, taking back the letters as Teddy held them out. "Hey, what about Christmas? You said you'd tell me."

"Okay," the younger boy rolled over onto his back and locked his hands behind his head. "It's a holiday that remembers the birth of a baby named Jesus. He was God's son who came to earth to save people from evil and forgive sins. When he was born there was a bright star in the sky and kings came to bring him gifts." Teddy rambled on telling of shepherds and angels and Herod and all he could remember of the story of Christmas. Michael listened intently with his arms locked around his pulled in legs and his chin resting on his knees.

When Teddy finished, there was a moment of silence. The quiet voices of Mr. and Mrs. Tyler and their son Adam could be heard through the floor register from the kitchen below, though words were incoherent murmurings.

"That helps," said Michael. "I'm glad you told me. I still don't know what I'll write, but I'll know when I do if it is right."

"Do ya think...?" Teddy hesitated.

"What?" his friend encouraged.

"Do ya think ya kin ever tell of yer people and what it was like 'for ya come here?"

"I don't know," Michael stared toward the ceiling. "Jay said if people know how different I am, they might not like me and might make fun of me."

"I don't think yer much different," Teddy encouraged. "Brett Tompkins grew up in Baltimore, an he's not much differ'nt. How differ'nt kin it be ta grow up in Montana Territory. And why did they call you Prairie Cub in the letters?"

"That's who I am."

"What?!"

"Do you know anything about my people?" the older boy asked.

"Not really," Teddy admitted, "only that they were differ'nt and lived in the wilderness."

Michael slipped to the floor and knelt beside the large trunk. He opened the latch and reverently lifted the lid.

"This is who I am." Carefully he removed several bundles, wrapped in buckskin and tied with rawhide laces, and spread them on the floor.

Teddy rolled over to hang from the side of the bed for a better view. There was surprise in his dark eyes and intense curiosity. "What is it?" he asked.

"You know my red coat?"

Teddy nodded.

"It's really called a capote'. Mountain men make them from wool trade blankets."

"That's why it looks so different!"

"Yea." He untied a large rectangular bundle and spread its contents. "These are my clothes which my mother made from deer skins." There were a shirt, leggings, breechclout, ankle ties, and moccasins.

"Those are like what you wear!" he pointed to the moccasins.

Teddy was bewildered at the strangeness of what he was seeing. He slid from the bed for a closer look. Hesitantly, he reached for the shirt.

"It's okay. You can pick it up," Michael assured him.

Teddy fingered the soft texture of the deerskin. Then he noticed the bundle with a beadwork design. He ran his fingers over their textured surface.

"My grandmother made it," Michael explained. "It's called a parflech. Inside are the last clothes my mother made and some other things I cherish." He turned it over, untied the rawhide laces, opened up the folded deerskin, and paused as Teddy explored the materials with his eyes. "My bow and arrows are hanging on a peg in the kitchen. I've used them to go hunting with Adam."

Puzzlement on Teddy's face gave way to discovery. "Yer people are Injuns?" he ventured.

"My people are Sioux. You know my initials 'P.C.'?"

"Uh huh."

"They're for my Sioux name. I am Prairie Cub, son of Thunder Eagle."

"But ya don't look like no Injun."

"It's a long story, Teddy. I was born white, but I was adopted and raised by my parents who found me on the prairie when I was very little. Are we still friends?"

"Yea. You bet. No wonder ya know about wild critters like ya do. Does anyone else know?"

"Jay Miller and some of his friends and the Tylers. That's all."

"Aren't ya gonna tell the rest of us?"

"Not yet. I trust you won't tell either."

"No Way! That's a promise!"

Teddy continued to study Michael's prized possessions. Questions were asked. Storied were told. Finally things were rewrapped and put away. The trunk was closed and latched. It was time for Teddy to start for home.

# THE VISITOR

The second Friday morning of December dawned overcast with a ting of orange-yellow brilliance on the eastern horizon at the edge of the clouds. As the day brightened, the overcast began to break up and the rising sun played peek-a-boo with the scattering of clouds. That afternoon during the time between school dismissal and chores, Michael sat at the kitchen table with paper and pencil, working on ideas for his Christmas story. Jay stopped as had become his habit.

Michael answered the knock at the side door to the porch. "Hi, Jay."

The man entered, removing cap, coat, and gloves, and placing them on the chair beside the door. "Hi, Michael, Janet."

Mrs. Tyler brought a cup of coffee to the table as the engineer pulled out a chair and sat down.

"Thanks, Janet."

"Welcome, as always. Help yourself to the cookies." She returned to the sink where she continued to peel potatoes for dinner.

"What ya workin on?" Jay asked.

"I have to write a Christmas story for the week after next. We are to read our stories to the class as part of our last day before the holidays."

"Any ideas?"

"Teddy told me about the baby Jesus and what happened when he was born." He took a sip from his glass of milk, then continued. "My people never had any of that. I'm trying to figure on something that I can use for a story. But nothing yet."

"Knowing you, you will think of something," the man soothed. "I had a telegram from Hank Johnston today. I think you'll want to ride with me on tonight's train." Turning to Mrs. Tyler, he continued, "If it's all right with you folks, I want to take Michael with me tonight. We spend the night at the Railroad Hotel with the Johnstons and return with the morning train."

Turning from her work at the sink, the woman replied, "I suppose you have a reason for this, Jay?"

"Hank sent word there's a need for Michael at the hotel and asks if he might be able to come for the night."

"It must be important for him to ask. I'll let Bill know when he gets home. You need to pack an overnight bag, Michael."

The front door opened and a blast of cold air rushed down the hall before it closed again.

"That you, Adam?" his mother called.

"Yea." He entered the kitchen and hung up his coat and hat stuffing gloves and scarf in a pocket.

Michael passed him on his way to his room to pack.

"What's the rush?" the older boy asked.

"Goin' to Arlee with Jay tonight."

"What's up?" Adam looked to his ma.

"Jay got a message from Hank Johnston that Michael's needed there for some reason."

The boy looked to the man. "I can't rightly say just now," Jay answered.

Adam sat down as his mother poured a glass of milk and he reached for a cookie.

Michael bounced down the steps and into the kitchen, dropped his carpet bag on the floor by the back door, and grabbed his red coat and dressed to leave.

"You can't wait to get out of this house," Mrs. Tyler teased.

"I just got in and you're leaving without helping with chores," Adam added.

"We've a train to take out," Jay stated, He winked as he rose from the table and reached for his coat.

"See ya tomorrow," Michael said as he headed out the door with Jay close behind.

*   *   *

Michael stood by the engineer's seat, watching out the front door to the running board, as the train approached Arlee station. His bag rested on the floor near the back of the seat.

"Pull the whistle," Jay instructed.

Reaching up for the wooden handle, the boy pulled a long wail to announce the train's arrival. Surveying the crowd standing around on the station platform, Michael saw a businessman who looked familiar. He seemed to be searching the car windows of the approaching train looking for someone. The dark brown dress coat with bow tie, light colored shirt, contrasting vest, and boots were natural enough. But his pants looked to be buckskin and he wore a greenish felt hat with a broad brim.

As the engine eased past the man, Michael saw his bearded face and the old involuntary twitch of the left eye, and the surge of recognition brought a burst of tears as he grabbed the door frame, swung out of the cab onto the footplate, and shouted, "Mr. Mattson!"

The man gazed at the boy who shouted from the engine cab. Recognition brought a look of astonishment and a broad smile.

"Prairie Cub!" he shouted back as he rushed to catch up to the moving locomotive as it slowed to a stop.

"Catch!" Michael tossed his carpet bag as he scrambled down the steps from the still moving engine.

Walt Mattson dropped the bag beside his feet as he reached for the boy and pulled him into an emotional bear hug.

"See you all later," Jay called from the cab as he released a short blast from the whistle. There was no response. The two clinging to each other were no longer aware of anything other than their reunion.

*　　*　　*

Mrs. Johnston reentered the kitchen from the dining room full of hotel guests. She set the empty tray on the sideboard as she turned her attention to those gathered at her kitchen table.

"Mr. Mattson arrived on the morning train, Michael." She pulled out a chair and sat down. "Jay had told us to watch for him and explained who he was. We immediately set aside Jay's room for you two. He had planned ahead to spend the night with the rest of his crew in the train crew bunk room above the station building's freight room."

"Thanks," the boy replied. "But can't he stay with us?"

"I appreciate the offer, Michael," Jay stated. "But you two have some catching up to do."

"I finally get to meet you, Michael," Mrs. Johnston's son, Jason added. "You left the same morning you arrived. I've heard a lot about you and your life in Snow Shoe from when Jay spends the night. When Pa told me you were coming because Mr. Mattson was here, I couldn't wait."

Mr. Johnston added, "I knew from what Jay had said that Walt here was a very important part of your life, so as soon as Nancy notified me that he was here, I wired Jay and asked if he could bring you with him this evening."

"This is so great!" Michael beamed.

"Mr. Mattson," the fourteen-year-old asked. "How do you and Michael know each other?"

Throughout the conversation, the old trader just sat and watched and listened, amused by the fuss his arrival had create. He sat up to respond.

"I used to be a trader for the mountain folks. We met at my last rendezvous last spring. Later, I became a freight hauler, then manager for the Summers Freight Company and we met again. By the end of the summer, Michael was working for Summers, too, and we became very close friends. I'm also Mr. Summers' contact with Michael's family." He put his arm on Michael's shoulder and gave a sideways hug.

"I thought his family was gone," the teen picked up. "That's why he's living with the Tylers in Snow Shoe."

"It's a long story, Jason," Jay spoke up. "We'll let Michael tell you some day when there's more time."

Michael felt an inner relief that the questioning had ended.

"Michael," Mr. Mattson turned to the boy. "The things I wrote you about are in our room. When we've finished dinner, we can go up and I'll bring you up to date with everything."

"Please excuse me while I see to the hotel's guests." Mrs. Johnston left the table and headed for the dining room.

\*     \*     \*

"I put a spare cot in your room, Michael, so Mr. Mattson could stay here with the family," Mrs. Tyler explained to the boy and his friend who stood at the bottom of the hall staircase. "Leave your bags in the room and I have lunch ready in the kitchen. Adam and his pa are out hunting and should be here shortly."

"Thanks," Michael replied as he picked up the carpet bag and Mr. Mattson picked up his large duffle bag.

"She seems like a real nice lady," Mr. Mattson said as they started up the steps. "Is she a good second ma to ya?"

"I never thought of her that way, but she really is."

Michael led the way to his bedroom. "This is home for now," he stated as they left their bags inside the door and headed back to the kitchen.

Adam and his father had returned by the time the two entered the warmth of the room. A plate of sandwiches and a pot of steaming tomato soup were on the table, which had already been set for five. Mr. Mattson inhaled the aroma of warm tomato and wood fire.

"Smells good, Ma'am."

"Sit down everyone. I'm bringing the coffee pot to the table. Adam can grab the cream from the ice box."

The father, son, and guest introduced themselves to each other, then pulled out their chairs and settled to lunch.

"Mr. Mattson, can you tell us about yerself?" Adam asked.

Mr. Mattson glanced at Michael.

"It's okay. They know."

Over lunch, Walt Mattson shared life with Prairie Cub and his people over the past summer. He added some new details that the boy had not yet spoken of, including the day of the battle and his travels to Canada. In the course of the conversation, he brought Michael up to date as well.

"When we received Michael's letters at the freight company, Mr. Summers quickly put together a small pack train of supplies for his people so I could take his letter for his folks. The trip took a couple weeks from Savage to Canada and back, including a couple days while I stayed on. I even got a chance to go hunting with Thunder Eagle. Even though I had given him a fine rifle, he preferred to use his bow."

Adam smiled. "Michael's the same way when we go hunting."

"I'd guess he'd be like his pa," Mattson responded. Continuing, "Thunder Eagle had taken four fine deer, three large buck and a large grown doe. Prairie Flower had carefully tanned the hides and sent them with me for Michael. They're in my duffle in the bedroom."

"I know he has his clothes his mother made. If you want, Michael, I'll make you a coat from them for colder days that don't require the extra warmth of your red coat," Mrs. Tyler offered. "Perhaps I should make it a little larger so there's room for you to grow. If there's enough leftover material, I can try to make that extra pair of moccasins we once talked about."

"That would be great!" the boy replied.

"On the way here, I headed to St. Louis to try and find our friends Trapper Murray and his son Lawrence," Mr. Mattson picked up his story. "I was worried that they had already left for the trapping season and that I would miss them. They had, but I was lucky and caught up to them as they were leaving Fort Pierre. We camped the night together and I told them of what had happened to you and your people. Then I told them of Mr. Summers' invitation to trap the Yellowstone and stay the winter at the trading fort. Lawrence begged his pa to say yes so they could be there when I return and learn of my visit here. Trapper Murray agreed. I'll see them after I return." He paused to enjoy some soup and his sandwich. There was quiet as all digested the news with their lunch, and waited for more.

"The railroad has moved on toward Idaho Territory and I haven't seen the Robinsons since you left. But Mr. Summers has been able to keep in touch with letters sent with various shipment handlers who direct supply shipments sent by train. Scot put a note in one of his pa's letters to tell you 'hi' and he one day hopes to ride a train back to visit you and his friends in Snow Shoe from that summer he spend here back in '80. Do you know that Mr. Summers is trying to get everyone together at the old trading fort come next spring?"

"It was in the letters he sent," Michael shared.

"I have every intention that we will all go," Mr. Tyler shared.

"How did you get to see the Kaymonds?" Michael asked as it occurred to him there was no train from Savage to Fort Pierre.

"I traveled by horse and pack horse to the fort, planning to continue that way to St. Louis and get a train there. But after meeting the Kaymonds on the road, I sold the horses and took the stage from Fort Pierre to St. Louis. It was much faster."

All continued quietly with lunch. Finishing his sandwich, Mr. Mattson washed it down with the last of his coffee. "Michael," he asked, "did you bring your pony with you? I haven't seen her since you left."

"She's in the barn. I'll show you."

"We'll see you later," Mr. Tyler acknowledged. "We'll let you two have some time to yerselves."

Michael and his friend bundled up and left for the barn.

\*　　\*　　\*

Michael sat on his bed and watched as Trader Mattson removed the contents of his duffle bag. He noted with great pleasure when the man withdrew his mountain buckskins. They immediately brought a flood of memories of the boy's past life and a hope that he would return one day soon. There were the blankets that made up his bedroll from his journey. Carefully stored in the bottom of the bag were the four skins that Prairie Flower had tanned for the boy. Folded in with them were other items he didn't know about. Thunder Eagle had made a dozen new arrows with fine flint points and Mr. Summers had sent along a fine new hunting knife with sheath. He took them all with reverent care as the man passed them to him, and placed them on top of his trunk in the corner of the room.

"Thanks," the boy said quietly. "They are really special treasures."

"I truly understand," Mattson acknowledged. "I look forward to when I will see you wearing your new coat." He smiled. "You now have extra arrows for your hunting and a knife to clean your deer."

"I should have my coat for when we meet again in the spring. How long can you stay?"

"Mr. Summers said I can stay as long as I need, as long as you need."

"I would have you stay forever, but I know I can't." He leaned forward with his elbows on his knees.

The man settled back on the cot and it squeaked under his weight. "I will stay until I feel I need to go for both our sakes. We'll take it a day at a time. What have you been up to?"

"Do you remember Scot?"

"Yes."

"Did you know he was here once and Jay looked after him, back when he was trying to find out where his pa had gone?"

"I had heard something about his being lost from his pa, but never heard the full story." Mr. Mattson adjusted the pillow and lay back on the cot.

Michael kicked off his moccasins and shifted back on his bed. "When Scot was here, Jay taught him how to run the locomotive he runs."

"I noticed you were in the engine when you arrived last night. Is he teaching you, too?"

"Yea. I'm gettin' some good. When we're out on the branch line he lets me run it. It's the greatest job in the world! I love it!"

"Better than a buffalo hunt?"

"No way. I'd go home this instant if I could. But I know that Thunder Eagle is right. I have to stay for him and some day be able to help my people." He yawned.

"Tired?"

"Yea."

"Me, too. We'll take time together tomorrow."

Mr. Mattson stripped to his johns and Michael changed into his night shirt. The boy blew out the lamp and the two settled in for the night.

# SETTLING IN

"Michael?" Adam stood in the doorway, a shadow in the early morning darkness. "Ya gonna help with chores?"

The younger boy stirred and pushed the covers off. He shivered as he sat up to the side of the bed. "Yea." He grabbed his clothes. "I'll get dressed downstairs where it's warm."

"Ya want any help?" Mr. Mattson asked as he pushed back the blankets and sat up.

"Sure," Adam responded.

"Meet you boys in the kitchen. Go get warm."

Moments later, the trader arrived in the kitchen as Michael finished dressing and slipped into his moccasins.

"Mornin', Janet," the man greeted.

"Mornin', Walt. You going with the boys?"

"I'll supervise." He smiled.

"Breakfast 'll be ready when you get back." She turned to the pancake batter she was mixing as the three bundled up and left for the barn.

"What are you two doing today?" Adam asked as they walked across the barnyard.

"Don't rightly know just yet," Mr. Mattson replied. "We'll figure it out as we go."

Once in the shelter of the barn, Adam instructed their guest on feeding the animals while he climbed up to throw down hay for the day and Michael milked the cow. Chores went quickly. Michael and Mr. Mattson collected the eggs while Adam fed the chickens and tended the smokehouse fire. They all hurried back to the warmth of the kitchen.

The aromas of breakfast added to the warmth of the kitchen as bacon, pancakes, and biscuits were set to the table. Mrs. Tyler took the milk to the side board and quickly poured off the cream from the top into its separate bottle and the rest of the milk in its bottles, then set the milk in the ice box and the cream on the table.

All commenced to enjoy their breakfast over the next several minutes with little conversation.

"You're welcome to come ta church with us, Walt," Mr. Tyler offered as he scraped the last of the syrup from his plate with a last forkful of pancake.

The trader drained his coffee and placed the cup on its saucer as he asked, "Would it be all right if I spent some time with Michael while you're away, then we could all share time together when you return?"

Mr. Tyler glanced at his wife. She nodded. "We can do that." He stood to place his plate on the drain board beside the sink. "Will you boys check the fires before we leave?"

"Okay," Adam answered. "Come on, Michael."

"Thanks," Mr. Mattson said, following the example and taking his plate to the sink.

The stove door clanked in the large Round Oak stove in the living room as the embers were raked out and new wood added to the fire. Mr. Tyler tended to the kitchen range as his wife washed the dishes and placed them in the drainer to drip dry.

The parlor clock chimed the hour at ten as the family finished bundling up and left for the walk across to the church on Jeffers Street. Mr. Mattson poured a cup of coffee and the two settled at the kitchen table.

He added some cream from the small jar. "This is a treat," he commented. "I rarely get real cream."

At first they shared what each had done since the last time they were together near the end of summer. To the boy, it seemed like ages ago. So much had happened. If was hard to believe that less than four months had passed since he left his home. For a moment, neither spoke.

Then Mr. Mattson asked, "How is yer schooling goin'?"

"It's been hard some. Both Teddy and Adam have really helped with my reading and arithmetic, and my teacher with that thing they call grammar. So I'm doin' okay." He went on to tell briefly of early problems with Jamison and some of his school work and the efforts to resolve each. He told of his friends and their trap line. Finally he spoke of his most recent challenge.

"We have an assignment to write a story about Christmas to be read to the class on the last day before vacation. Their Christmas is so different and I can't think of a story to write."

"I know of the Christmas story," Mr. Mattson commented. "One thing about it caught my attention. It's the whole thing about gifts. God's gift to man was the baby, Jesus. Then the kings came and they brought gifts for the baby. The shepherds came to worship the baby, but they had no gifts. Is there something in that you can work with?"

"I hadn't thought of that," Michael reacted. He got up from the table and went to the sink for a cup. Returning to the table, he poured himself a cup of coffee, added some cream, and sat back down. "Thanks." He sipped thoughtfully. "I'll try to think if I can do something with that idea."

"When did you start drinking coffee?"

"Sometimes when I'm with Jay and they have their coffee, I'll get some, too. You remember, I had it with you at the freight company."

"The folks know?"

"Not yet."

The clock struck three-quarter past noon.

"What time do you usually get back from church?" He refilled his coffee cup.

"Service lasts an hour. There's a social hour for visitin' after. We usually get home near one-thirty ta two." He finished his coffee and placed the cup back on its saucer. "Sure wish we were back home and could wear our real clothes again."

"You haven't worn yer's?"

"No. I haven't told folks about who I really am. Only the Tyler family and one friend have seen my clothes and possessions. Hey! Ya wanna check the trap line? Or we could go hunting?"

"Let's walk the trap line. The folks should be back by then."

The two bundled up and left the warmth of the kitchen.

\*    \*    \*

Adam placed three chunks of firewood into the large living room stove, adjusted the damper to hold back more heat, then returned to the table he and Michael shared and their game of dominoes.

"Walt, what would you like to do tomorrow?" Mr. Tyler asked. "Adam and I will be at work in the logging camp, Michael will be in school, and Janet will be here, baking Christmas cookies, I think." He sat in his gentleman's chair with the Friday paper in his lap.

Walt rested on the couch leaning back into its soft cushions. "One day this week, I'd like to go to school with Michael. But tomorrow, if it's all right, I'd like to go to work with you and Adam."

Mrs. Tyler rocked lightly in her wooden Boston rocker. She paused in the knitting on which she had been focused. "Not up to getting your hands in cookie dough?"

"I really haven't cooked except on a camp fire in a long time. I'll pass, respectfully." He smiled.

The boys only half listened to the conversation as they worked out positioning for their domino pieces. Michael picked up on the mention of school.

"I think Mrs. Miller would find it really interesting if you visited the class and told stories of life in the mountains. Just don't mention my people."

"I do hope you will share your story before too long. Your classmates will be fascinated."

"I'll think on it. No promises."

The men discussed schedule for the next day and agreed Mr. Mattson would need to find more rugged clothes for the day. He had his work clothes from the freight company. Another hour drifted by during which Mrs. Tyler concentrated on her knitting project. Then it was time to bank the fires for the night and head up to bed. Michael picked up his night shirt from where he had left it in the kitchen after dressing in the morning, and headed up to bed, wishing folks good night along the way. The Tylers headed for their bedroom off the kitchen. Adam took his lamp and passed Michael, leading the way up the stairs, and Mr. Mattson followed. Adam stopped in Michael's room first to provide light so Michael could light his lamp, then headed across the hall to his own room.

"You can see the mountain from the window," Michael pointed out as they entered the room. "I was up there once on the day I spent on the railroad with Jay." He turned back to his bed. "Haven't been back there since." He changed into his night shirt as Mr. Mattson gazed out the window at the moonlit landscape.

"A new adventure," the man commented as he turned to his cot and slipped off his clothes to his johns. "You climb in and get warm. I'll get the lamp."

The room darkened and the boy could hear the squeak of the cot as his friend settled his weight on it and slipped under the blankets.

"Night, Mr. Mattson."

"Night, Michael."

\*     \*     \*

Michael sat at the kitchen table with paper and pencil while Mrs. Tyler shoveled the freshly baked ginger bread cookies onto the cooling towel. No words were spoken as each focused on the task at hand.

The boy turned over ideas in his head reflecting on the comments Mr. Mattson had made about gifts. He started to write.

*Gifts, a Christmas Story*
*Michael P.C. Freeman*

*I just recently learned about the Christmas Story with the baby Jesus, the angels, the shepherds, and the kings. It had never been a part of my family's life. But something about it had. Christmas is a time of giving. God gave his baby son, Jesus, to the people of the world. The angels gave song. The shepherds gave reverence. The kings brought precious things as gifts.*

*Gifts have been a part of the life of my people, too. When someone would ask a favor, he always gave a gift in return. A gift might be given as a sign of respect and a sign of friendship. It might be given from one family member to another as a sign of love and affection. Most gifts are created by the giver. Sometimes it's a deed done to show thanks or to help a friend. . . .*

Michael had his Christmas story. It still needed to be expanded, fully developed, and finished. But it was started and he knew how it would grow and become a finished work in time for the last day before Christmas holiday.

At dinner that evening, Mr. Mattson shared his adventure on the mountain with added details from Adam and his father. Michael shared his afternoon triumph with the beginning of his Christmas story assignment. Mrs. Tyler served a sampling of her day's baking in a plate of Christmas cookies. Mr. Mattson decided to return to the mountain, explaining that it would give Michael time to work on his story while it was fresh. But he wanted to go to school with the boy on Wednesday.

Michael would ask Mrs. Miller the next day and tell her some about his visitor from the frontier.

The visit was a great success. Classwork was done during the morning session and the afternoon session was reserved for a living history lesson from one who had lived it. The students were so fascinated, they begged the trader to return for another day of stories from the frontier. He agreed to return early the following week, Christmas week, if their teacher sent a note with Michael that they had finished each day's work to her satisfaction.

On Thursday, Mattson was back on the mountain. He had enjoyed working with one of the cutting crews and decided, if it was okay with Mr. Tompkins, he would work with that crew on a daily basis as long as he stayed on with the Tylers. On Friday, he worked with Adam at *The Herald* and learned how to hang the wet papers as they came off the press. He also tried his hand at the press and, after a couple trial runs, managed the right pressure for a clean print. Evan Clanton took advantage of the frontier trader's presence and interviewed him for a feature story in the following week's edition of the paper.

\*     \*     \*

"We usually go hunting on Saturdays," Adam informed at breakfast. "Want to go today?"

"I didn't bring my rifle on this trip." Mr. Mattson cleaned the piece of sausage from his fork. "But if you have one I can borrow, I'd love to go hunting. I want to see Michael's skill with his bow. Now he has new arrows from Thunder Eagle."

After helping to clear the table, Mr. Mattson and the boys bundled up, took up their weapons, and set out for the hunt. Mr. Tyler had an older rifle which he lent to Mattson. They crossed the barnyard to the gate to the meadow where Of-The-Wind met them, eager for some time with Michael. The four trudged through the snow together across the meadow to the back gate into the forest. There, the pony watched as the three ducked through the fence rails and started up the deer trail. The day was cold and overcast without any breeze. The woodland was silent except for the crunching of the snow underfoot as the hunters moved forth.

The three moved in single file with Michael in the lead. The boy had an arrow knocked on his bow and locked between his fingers. Each of the others had his rifle at the ready in case anything significant stirred in the forest. Slowly they advanced along the trail keeping alert for any sign of movement. A rabbit darted within the underbrush, its white fur blended into the snow, nearly invisible. No one made any attempt to take it.

Suddenly, a wild turkey burst from the bushes to the right. Just as quickly, Mr. Mattson brought up his rifle and fired. The bird fell. But the sound of the rifle shot startled a buck grazing in a small clearing and he darted through the trees. In the instant, Michael raised his bow as he pulled taught the string and let fly his arrow. The buck dropped as the arrow struck behind the foreleg and the animal stumbled to the ground. Adam stared in amazement as these two, experienced from the frontier, reacted so swiftly to bring down their game.

"Wow!" he exclaimed. "You two are fast!"

"I think we're done here," the man stated. "We've Christmas dinner. Adam, you take the turkey and I'll help Michael with the buck."

The teen walked over and picked up the bird by its feet. "It sure is a big one," he commented. "And heavy, too."

Michael unstrung his bow and slipped it into its quiver. Using the new knife he'd brought with him, he carefully cut out his arrow using the smallest possible cut to preserve the skin. He wiped the arrow on the snow and returned it to its quiver, then did the same with his knife. Pulling a pair of rawhide laces from his pocket, he tied the front and back legs in pairs. In the meantime, Mr. Mattson searched for a stout pole with which to carry the deer back to the house. He found a useful tree branch and trimmed it to fit the need. With Michael's help he slipped the pole between the tied legs and prepared to carry it back.

"You two ready?" the man asked.

"Yea," the boys replied.

The three picked up their kills and started back the forest trail toward the house.

\*    \*    \*

Mrs. Tyler saw the returning hunters from the kitchen window and informed her husband. The two stepped out into the side yard to gaze in amazement at the triumphant trio and their prize game.

"It looks like we have Christmas dinner," Mr. Tyler remarked.

"I guess so," his wife agreed. "I can take care of the turkey. It's no more than an oversized chicken. Hang in on the porch for now. Can you take care of the deer?" She looked to Michael and his friend.

"We've done this before," Mr. Mattson replied. "Michael and I will clean it and hang it in the barn until this afternoon. Then we'll skin it and butcher it, and hang the meat in the smokehouse."

"If you have an empty barrel," Michael added, "I can tan the hide."

"Look out behind the carriage barn. I think there's one there," Mr. Tyler informed.

"Thanks."

"Adam," his father instructed, "get a piece of feedbag line and hang the turkey on a flowerpot hook."

"Okay."

As the Tylers returned to the house, the hunters carried out their assignments. Adam took care of the turkey while Michael and Mr. Mattson took the deer behind the barn and gutted it. Taking it into the barn, they hung it by the tied back feet from a rafter to await further work. Michael sought out an empty feed bag to recover the heart and liver to take to the kitchen for Mrs. Tyler to cook during the afternoon as a delicacy.

Soon, all had cleaned up and settled to the table for lunch.

\*     \*     \*

Following lunch, the boys and Mr. Mattson left to the barn to take care of the deer. Adam mostly ran errands while the other two did the work. Adam fetched the barrel as well as a saw to cut the antlers from the head. The other two skinned the buck and tossed the hide into the barrel. Adam fetched large metal tubs for the meat as the two butchered the animal. The head was removed and cut open, and the brains dumped into the barrel. Adam was sent for several buckets of water for the barrel as well as a bucket of ashes from the stoves. All was added to the barrel and stirred until thoroughly blended into a murky soup that completely covered the deer skin. Michael explained that it would soak that way with occasional stirring for about a week before the process would continue. At that point all the hair will have fallen from the hide and the plain skin would be worked until it was soft.

When finished, the carcass was placed in a wheel barrel along with the innards from behind the barn and taken to the creek side of the meadow and dumped. Scavenger critters would feed on it and it would be gone by spring. The tubs of meat were taken to the smokehouse and the meat was hung to slow cook and smoke to preserve it for later use in the winter months. Adam added fuel to the smoke fires and closed the door to keep the smoke in. By the time they returned to the house, his mother had prepared the turkey for the oven, wrapped it in butcher paper, and placed it in a tin cooler box in a shaded corner on the porch to set in the cold for the week until it was time for baking.

# A History Lesson

All attended church on Sunday and enjoyed quiet time -- reading, handwork, table games, conversation -- during the afternoon. As the week before Christmas began, Walt returned to the mountain on Monday. That afternoon, Mrs. Miller sent a note home with Michael that the students had earned their second visit from Mr. Mattson. He and Michael excused themselves to Michael's room to plan for the following day.

"What do you think," Mr. Mattson asked. "Should I dress in my wilderness clothes and give them a real look at the frontier?"

"I'd like to see that," Michael responded. "It will bring back memories of life as I once lived it."

"How about it? Why don't we both show them who we really are?"

"I'm afraid," the boy answered. "I don't want to loose my friendships. You will leave and go back to Savage. I can't."

"Michael," the man looked him in the eyes. "I truly think you underestimate your friends. I think they will respect you all the more for who you are and for the life you once lived and lost. They might even envy you that you did it and they can't."

"I want to tell the Tylers. I want them to be there, too." He stood up from his bed, prepared to go down and talk to the family.

"Let's do this together." Mr. Mattson rose up from his cot.

"Okay."

The two left the room and went down to the living room with the family.

"We're thinking of doing something very different tomorrow," Michael stood facing the family. "And I really want you with me."

Mr. and Mrs. Tyler looked at each other then to Adam. "If you need, we will tell Mr. Tompkins we need to stay home tomorrow," Mr. Tyler stated.

"We're thinking on going to school as we really are, in our clothes from home, to tell the class our true stories," the boy ventured.

"I *do* want to be there," Adam stated.

"We *will* be there," Mrs. Tyler confirmed. A sudden catch of emotion cut short her last word.

"Adam," Mr. Tyler instructed, "run over to the Tompkins' and tell Mr. Tompkins we need to be in school with Michael tomorrow. Then go to the hotel and tell Jay what's going to happen. I think he'll want to get Ryker's crew to take Number forty-six for tomorrow morning's work so he and his crew can join us at school."

"Sure, Pa." He headed for the kitchen to bundle up, then left to carry out his instructions.

"I didn't expect all that," Michael said. He looked to Mr. Mattson. "But I surely would like Jay to be there, too."

His friend smiled. "Your teacher has no idea what she's in for. What about it, you think Of-The-Wind would like to be part of this? Maybe I could borrow Bill's horse and we could both ride over."

"We get there before the bell and no tellin how folks will react," Michael commented. "I think I like this."

"You think Adam will want to tell Evan Clanton?" Mrs. Tyler asked. "I know he will be really upset if he hears about it afterwards."

"I'll ask him when he gets back," Mr. Tyler answered.

"Come on Michael, Prairie Cub," Mr. Mattson said. "We've work ta do."

The boy smiled at the mention of his name.

The two left the room to return to the bedroom and lay out their clothes for the big day.

*   *   *

Tuesday dawned with sun and clouds and milder temperatures in the upper thirties. The air was dry and quiet, no breeze. The ground remained covered with several inches of snow and curbside piles over a foot deep.

As they finished morning chores, Adam gave Michael her halter for Of-The-Wind so she could be tied while at school. He showed Mr. Mattson the tack room so he could saddle Cheyenne. Both were left in their stalls until after breakfast and the outside door was closed on the pony's stall.

Mrs. Tyler fixed a generous warm breakfast so all would be well fed for the day ahead. Michael and Mr. Mattson retired to the bedroom to dress. The boy wore his newest clothes his mother had made last. He repacked the parflech in a long bundle so he could lay it across his pony's neck and carry it across his shoulder.

"Can you attach these to my headband," he asked handing the man the two eagle feathers Roaring Wing had awarded him as coup. Mr. Mattson worked them into the leather ties that held the headband together. As he tied his leggings to his rawhide belt and pulled on his shirt, the boy became acutely aware that he had grown since arriving in Snow Shoe. The leather ties on his leggings used to hold up the extra slack for growth, became mere decoration. His leggings at full length no longer had any slack. The boy wore the new knife that Mr. Summers had given him. Mr. Mattson gave Michael a bright red trade blanket to wear on the way to school to help against the cold.

The two went down to the kitchen.

"Oh, wow!" Adam exclaimed as the frontier pair entered the room. "You look unbelievable!"

"This is such a treat," Mrs. Tyler added. "I would never believe this if I hadn't seen it myself."

"It's surely one thing to sit at the table while you show us your things," Mr. Tyler stated. "But to see you wearing it is a whole other wonder."

Michael took down his bow and arrows from their peg and added them on his back.

"Adam, you leave now and tell Evan Clanton," Mr. Tyler instructed. "We'll meet you at school. We'll leave first and I think we'll see Jay and his crew there early. You two follow on your horses about five minutes before the bell. That should reduce the time you are out in the cold."

\*　　\*　　\*

The older boys fought a snowball battle on the ball field, attacking a snow fort that had been built weeks ago. Younger children played on the playground equipment or at small group games on the playground. Two of the teachers stood near the corner of the building supervising. Jay Miller approached with Scott and Dan, neither dressed in his work clothes. Following them, Adam and Mr. Clanton came, the reporter lugging a large camera and the boy carrying a satchel of glass plates. The Tylers entered the schoolyard gate.

Mrs. Miller hurried over, a look of concern on her face.

"What's happened, Janet?" she asked. "Why are the engine crew and Mr. Clanton here? Where are Michael and Mr. Mattson?" There was a slight panic in her voice.

"Everything's okay, Florence," Mrs. Tyler assured. "But you're about to have a history lesson unlike anything you can imagine. We need to be present for this and Mr. Clanton will be telling about it in Friday's paper."

There was a sudden silence in the schoolyard as a few children looked up the street and saw the approaching riders, and nudged their friends to look. Mrs. Miller and the other teacher looked past the Tylers at the horseback riders, and gaped in unbelieving astonishment.

"Florence, you asked Mr. Mattson to speak to your class again." The teacher nodded, speechless. "Well he has decided that your students will see him as he truly is and Michael has decided to do the same."

A voice called out from the group of students. "Hey, Prairie Cub! You're gonna do it!"

"Teddy, what do you mean?" Miles asked in complete confusion.

"We're all gonna find out who Michael really is," Teddy answered as he worked his way to the front gate.

"You know about this!?" Mrs. Miller turned to her student in surprise.

"Yes, Ma'am. And now everyone will know just how special this kid is." His smile beamed the pride he felt in knowing Michael's story and knowing now that he was going to share it.

The school bell rang and students reluctantly filed into the building. Mrs. Miller stood transfixed as she watched the two draw near. Her colleague entered the building with the students leaving her to follow. Seeing their teacher wasn't going in just yet, the students lined up at the door and waited.

Teddy returned to the class.

"Is he for real?" Jamison whispered.

"He sure is," Teddy replied proudly.

Mr. Clanton had set up his camera during the commotion and made an image of the gathering at the gate. He wasn't able to ask anyone to hold still and hoped that his timing and the light of day would allow for a good image.

"Adam, this is one fantastic story," the newspaper man whispered. "Have you known about this before?"

The two traded plates for the camera. "Yes, for some weeks now. But we gave Michael our word that we would let him tell his story when he felt comfortable."

The riders stopped in front of the teacher.

"I am Prairie Cub, son of Thunder Eagle. And this is my good friend and trader among mountain men, Walt Mattson. We are here to share who we really are with your students."

A collective gasp escaped from the gathered students as they reacted to the introduction.

Mrs. Miller regained her composure as she invited everyone into the warmth of her classroom.

"Please let the grown folks into the room first," she instructed her students. Mrs. Tyler led the way in to the classroom as the others followed. Michael and Mr. Mattson dismounted and tied their horses to the fence. Mr. Tyler covered each with a blanket he had brought from the barn for keeping each warm.

The three followed the class into the building.

\*     \*     \*

The day's opening exercises were quickly forgotten as extra wooden folding chairs were brought into the room for the guests. Student desks were doubled in order to create the extra space needed along the sides of the classroom. Mrs. Miller moved away from her desk to allow Mr. Mattson and Michael to lean or stand in front of it.

"Do you have a map?" Mr. Mattson asked.

The teacher pulled down a wall map of the United States from the roll that hung above the chalkboard.

"Let me begin," he stepped to the map. "Here is the Montana Territory," he pointed. "Here is the Yellowstone River and here the Powder." Then moving his finger, "Here is the trading fort and just north of it, the town of Savage." Facing the students, he continued. "This is where we live, Prairie Cub and me. There is a special breed of men known as mountain men, who live in these mountains and hunt and trap for a living during the winter months of the year. At the end of the season, we gather near the Powder River for a Rendezvous, a camp where we share skills in competition and song and dance and gambling, too. I am a trader and go to these gatherings to sell trade goods. I first met Prairie Cub and his family there this past spring when they came with mountain friends, Trapper Murray and his son, Lawrence."

The students sat in wrapped silence as they learned the story of their classmate and who he really was and how he came to live in their community with the Tyler family. Jay and his crew were equally attentive as they, too, learned the story behind the boy they had been asked by an earlier friend, Scot Robinson, to help. Mr. Clanton frantically took notes as the story unfolded. It would be a unique feature in this week's paper, requiring a tremendous run of extra copies for distribution locally and in towns all along the railway.

Mattson continued. "His father, Thunder Eagle turned out to be a remarkable marksman with a rifle. We met again at the trading fort owned by Keith Summers when I started hauling freight for his company. North of the fort, the Northern Pacific Railroad is being built. The railroad had a work camp there for months. When it moved west, the town of Savage was built there and the Summers Freight Company built its business there. I am the company manager. Just now, I am here on unlimited leave to see Prairie Cub and to bring him gifts from his family. As you can see, while he has been raised by his Sioux family and that is the only family he has ever known, he happens to have been born white. And that's why he's here. I'll let him tell the story."

Mr. Mattson sat back on the top of the desk and Prairie Cub picked up his story. "My people set their summer village outside the fort each year. We would trade with other nations and sell our buffalo hides to Keith Summers for trade goods. This year the railroad was there so we set up a few miles to the south. I had a vision while we were at the Rendezvous, and in it Grandfather was dead and the village was destroyed. When we got to the fort, Grandfather explained its meaning. Our people would be driven from our way of life violently, but he would die before that happened. And he was glad that he would die in the old ways before that happened. And he did."

Some in the class became emotional and a few tears glistened on some faces. The boy continued to tell his story – the promise his father asked of him, his friendship with Scot Robinson, the coming of the soldiers, the night before the battle when his father wanted him to go and he begged to stay, the compromise, the battle, the death of his friend Little Slow Walker, the hasty departure from the fort, life in Savage, the last journey to visit his family, Scot Robinson's offer to help him go east to live with friends who had helped him when he was lost.

The morning slipped by quickly and the lunch hour was upon them. But no one was hungry. All were caught up in the boy's story and fascinated by the reality behind these two people who were not who they appeared to be. By early afternoon, it was decided to take lunch in the classroom, to continue as soon as the boy and the man had eaten. Jay and his crew had to leave.

"I surely had no idea as to all you have lived and lost," Jay said as he excused himself. "I wish we could stay to hear all, but we do have to get back to work. I am so glad that Scot asked us to help. Michael Prairie Cub Freeman, you are special, and we love you so very deeply."

He quickly turned and left before his emotions could be detected.

"We'll see you later," Scott said in parting.

"Take care," Dan added.

Then they were gone.

During the afternoon the conversation shifted to lifestyle, questions, sharing and explaining clothing, weapons, the possessions in the parflech and the story behind its making, and the last gifts that Mattson had brought. When asked about the feathers in his headband, Prairie Cub answered with pride.

"My father gave them to me the last time I saw him. Our chief, Roaring Wing, had awarded me coup, which is an honor these feathers stand for, because it was my arrow that killed the captain who led the soldiers against our people."

There were whispered comments of awed respect.

School dismissed. Many lingered with more questions and wanting to spend more time in the presence of such unique individuals. Mr. Clanton asked to take some images of the two and of the boy with the Tyler family. He would catch up with Jay and his crew at the station, on his way back to the newspaper office. Students in the younger grades stopped to look at the horse and the pony tied to the schoolyard fence and wondered about the visitors in Mrs. Miller's classroom. A few stopped in to her room to gawk at the visitors and say 'hi.'

Finally, it was time to go.

"I'm so sorry what happened to you and your family," Jamison said as he started toward the door. "But I'm really glad I get to know you as a friend. I'm sorry for how I treated you at first. It was so unfair."

"We're friends now," Michael soothed. "And that's what counts. See you in class tomorrow."

"Thanks," Jamison said as he left the room.

"You look exhausted," Mrs. Tyler observed. "It's time to go home."

"Thank you so much, both of you," Mrs. Miller acknowledged. "This certainly was a very different lesson. None of these students is likely to forget this day for many years." She rolled up the map. "See you tomorrow, Michael." There was a brief tenderness in her voice. "And I'll always know that behind the boy I have in class there is another named Prairie Cub."

"Thanks."

"We are glad this day went so well," Mr. Mattson added. "There was some hesitation before we decided to do this."

"We are all so glad you did," the teacher replied. "Thanks."

Adam left with Mr. Clanton. His parents remained to leave with Michael and Mr. Mattson. The four left the building together.

The teacher followed to the classroom door where she stayed to watch them descend the stairs and leave the building.

"We'll ride slowly so we can walk together," Michael advised.

"Fine by me," Mr. Mattson added.

Mr. Tyler removed the blankets before the two mounted their horses. "I'll take care of these and put them away when we get home," he volunteered.

Untying the leads from the fence the two frontier friends mounted, and guided their horses to the street and a slow walk homeward.

*   *   *

As the three worked at the evening chores, Michael took a scrap of board and stirred the mix with the deer skin in the barrel just outside the tack room door. Mr. Mattson took a look at the contents.

"The hair is starting to fall out," he observed.

"Maybe by the weekend," Michael predicted.

Adam looked in and asked, "How did you do this in your village?"

The younger boy replied, "We'd do several skins at a time and do them in a pit. Barrels weren't usually available." He set the wood stick aside for next time. "Once the hair's off, it has to be softened. I'll show you later."

The horse and pony were given extra grain for their day in the chill air, and a brushing. Gathering up the milk and eggs, the three headed back to the warmth of the kitchen. Along the way, they checked in the smokehouse to tend the fire and see how the deer meat was progressing.

Entering the warm kitchen, each hung his outer clothing on their pegs and went to the sink to wash up for dinner.

As he dried his hands, Michael shared, "I sure was glad to have you all in class, today." He hung the towel on its dry bar and approached the table. "I was nervous at first. But as we went on, it was easier." He sat down. "I wasn't expecting the rest of the class to be so quiet."

"Everyone was fascinated by your and Mr. Mattson's stories." Mrs. Tyler placed the biscuits on the table and sat down. "No one had any idea about what they were gonna hear. They were particularly shocked when they saw you both on horseback dressed in your regular clothing. It sure wasn't what they were expecting, especially when they were only expecting a return visit by Mr. Mattson."

"Anyone for ham?" Adam offered the platter.

"Thanks." Michael accepted it, put a slice on his plate, and passed it to Mr. Mattson.

The family continued with their meal in quiet.

*   *   *

The family settled in the living room for the evening.

"Checkers or dominoes?" Adam asked as the two settled at their gaming table.

"Checkers," Michael stated. "I need to get good enough to beat you at least once."

The two laughed.

"When is the last day of school before the winter break?" Mr. Tyler asked.

"Thursday," Michael answered.

"Mr. Clanton wants me at the newspaper tomorrow through Friday," Adam announced. "We have to put the paper to bed by tomorrow noon and start printing tomorrow afternoon. It will take an extra day to print all the extra copies needed for this edition." He divided the checker pieces according to color and gave Michael the red pieces to set up. "He's printing hundreds of extra copies for this week's circulation."

"I guess they'll get to know me wherever we go from now on," Michael stated without looking up from placing his game pieces on the board.

"Don't worry," Mr. Tyler offered. "The story will be old in a week and no one will remember it."

"Pa's right, ya know," Adam confirmed. "Most folks are interested as they read the story. By the next day, they're thinking of other things." He checked the board for completed layout. "You go first."

The boys became focused on the game while Adam's father picked up the book he was reading, his mother picked up her knitting project and both continued in silence to follow their interests. Mr. Mattson worked on the leather project he had started. When asked about it earlier, he simply responded that he hadn't decided yet.

Several minutes passed with checker jumps and 'king me's' until the game neared its end.

"Guess this isn't my time to win yet," Michael moaned.

"You're getting close," Adam encouraged. "When you beat me, I want it to be real. So I'm not gonna help ya, just give lots of practice so ya can continue to get better."

He started to reset the board.

"Ma?" Michael hesitated.

Mrs. Tyler nearly dropped her knitting as she froze mid stitch. All stopped what they were doing. They stared at the boy as he continued.

"Mr. Mattson asked me a while back if you were a good second ma to me. I've thought about it since. You have really been like a ma and I never really gave it much thought. I guess I'm sorta lucky. I do have two sets a folks. You and Mr. Tyler have been like I'm your son and Adam's brother. Today you were at school for me, all of you, just like family. So I'm thinkin' that now, you are family. I have two families, my real folks who are in Canada, and you, where I live for now. I have two homes."

Mr. Tyler's voice was hoarse, "Michael, I am proud to call you son and so honored that you think of me as a second pa."

"And I'm sure glad ta be your brother," Adam added.

"Well I'll be," Mr. Mattson spoke up. "I had no idea that any comment of mine could start such an idea ta happen." His project lay untouched in his lap. "It's time I think about headin' back home, and leave this new family to grow on itself."

"But you're part of my family," Michael protested, "and I don't want to see you go. I know that you will someday. But not just yet."

"Walt," Mrs. Tyler added, "You have become like family, too. You are such a part of Michael's life and have become a part of our lives as well. We all know you have to go, but please, wait until after the holidays."

"I can do that," Mattson agreed. "Come the new year, I'll begin my journey homeward."

"Speaking of the holidays," Mr. Tyler spoke up. "The local industries shut down Thursday at noontime for the holiday week. While Adam has to work, what say you and Michael and me go pick us a tree for Christmas on Friday?"

"What are you gonna do with a tree?" Michael asked.

"That's right," Mr. Mattson realized. "You were never around anywhere during the winter where people celebrated Christmas. Well you will have another new experience this year." He smiled at the boy.

Mrs. Tyler continued an explanation. "We bring an evergreen tree into the house and decorate it as part of our holiday tradition. We'll show you as we prepare this Friday and you can learn in the process." The parlor clock struck the hour. "Time to turn in. It's been a long and tiring day."

# CHRISTMAS

The days passed in regular routine. Wednesday was a little awkward at school with classmates looking at Michael with a new respect and unsure just how to treat him. But with Teddy showing no new deference toward his friend, others began to relax and by afternoon, Michael was just their classmate again. Thursday dawned gray and overcast with temperatures in the low thirties. School was a half-day. Christmas stories were shared, followed by a sing-a-long of carols and a party at which each student received a small box of Christmas hard candies from the teacher. Michael went home at noon by way of the newspaper office in order to see what Mr. Clanton was doing with the story. The image taken at the gate had turned out well and was the lead from the front page with a headline, "Local Boy Has A Remarkable Back Story." The 4-column image had a caption referring to a full page insert with story and more pictures. The insert page had the story on one side and a full page of ads on the back. It had already been printed that morning. The final edition of the paper had started printing at noon the previous day and would continue throughout the afternoon and finish printing on Friday. Mr. Clanton gave the boy a proof print of the story side to keep. Michael took it with him.

Next he went to the mercantile where he had asked Mr. Mattson to meet him by coming off the mountain with the midday log load. He had a wad of his money from the pay Mr. Summers had given him for his work at the freight company. The money had been stored in his trunk since he had no need to spend it. Now he wanted his trader friend with him as he did some Christmas shopping. The two consulted each other on gifts as each made selections for the family members. They also took advantage of Tracy, Harvey Jenkins' extra holiday helper who did gift wrapping. They asked Jenkins for an empty grain sack to carry their gifts in so Walt could slip them into the bedroom as they entered the house. Michael explained Mr. Mattson's early arrival as a request to spend some extra time together.

That night, Mr. Mattson told Adam to bring home a half dozen copies of the paper for him to take back for friends at Savage. Teddy and Miles stopped Friday morning to check the trap line. Michael and Mr. Mattson went with them. It was a good day with two coons, a muskrat, and a rabbit. All traps were left sprung until the day after Christmas, when they would be reset once again. The four took the catch to the wood yard and worked together to skin them. Mr. Mattson bought the larger coon skin to use to make a hat. The carcasses were dumped with the deer remains and the boys bagged the remaining skins and left for home. The trader chopped a wood slab from a large tree round in the wood yard and went to the carriage barn to find the tools to stretch the coon skin on the wood and salt it down. It was left to cure outside the barn door.

Later in the morning, Michael and the two men headed for the woodlands to find a pine tree for the parlor, while Mrs. Tompkins went to the attic to bring down the tree stand and Christmas ornaments.

That evening, Adam reported *The Herald* had gone out on time and every local issue had been sold as soon as the local issues had been delivered to the train station newspaper stand. Clanton had agreed to another printing for Saturday. He gave Mr. Mattson his copies and returned to the newspaper office after dinner to help with the second run.

*     *     *

The night sky was still filled with a myriad stars, but absent of any moonlight, as the boys and Mr. Mattson strolled to the barn for Saturday morning chores. The man checked his coon skin and was satisfied. Michael and Mattson checked the deer skin as they entered the barn.

"I think it's ready," the boy observed.

"Now to find a nice round piece of timber to break it on," Mr. Mattson added.

"There's an extra wagon tongue standing beside the carriage barn," Adam offered. "Will that work?"

"Let's go look," the elder agreed.

They walked across the barnyard to the south end of the barn and examined the timber.

"It's round enough," Mattson determined. "And it's used enough that there aren't any splinters in the wood. We need to take it into the barn and lay it across the center walk from stall to stall."

The three hefted the wagon tongue and carried it into the barn.

"Stand it here until after chores," Mr. Mattson instructed.

They stood the timber against the cow stall and began the morning chores. Michael fed his pony and milked the cow. Mr. Mattson fed the rest of the livestock and climbed up to throw down hay while Adam fed the chickens and gathered the eggs

"If you boys want to bring in firewood, I'll take the milk and eggs," Mr. Mattson offered.

"Okay," Adam agreed. "We'll need to check the fire in the smokehouse after breakfast when we come back to work on the deerskin."

"Before we go," Michael added, "I need to hang the deerskin on the barrel's edge to start to drip dry." With that, he took the scrap board, fished out the skin, and hung it over the side of the barrel.

The three left for the house.

The eastern horizon was tinged with a brilliant yellow-red glow, wiping out the stars, leaving but a ghostly star mass on the western horizon, about to vanish with the growing daylight. On the way to the house, the boys each grabbed an armload of cordwood while Mattson went on to the back porch with the milk and eggs. There, he held the door while the boys entered the kitchen. Then he followed, allowing his back to ease the screen door closed. Once inside, he used his foot to guide the inside door closed.

*   *   *

Following breakfast, Adam and friends headed back to the barn while his parents started to work on the tree decorations. The process started with making a batch of popcorn for stringing. The sun was up in a brilliant blue sky as the three approached the barn. A distant cloud bank appeared on the western horizon.

Entering the barn, Michael was greeted by Of-The-Wind and paused at her box stall to give her some attention, and an apple he had brought from the bowl of fruit gathered with the tree decorations Accepting the treat, she stepped back to munch on the apple and watch preparations.

"First, we need to set up the wooden beam," Mr. Mattson instructed.

The boys worked the back end with the cross tree while the man worked the front. They lifted it into place, resting each end on the top edge of a box stall. The cross tree on the back end was lined up on the wall to secure the whole from rocking.

"We hang the hide across the beam and begin to work it back and forth to soften it," Michael instructed.

Mr. Mattson lifted the skin from the barrel. It had already begun to stiffen with drying. He hung it across the beam. The pony turned away and wandered out the door into the meadow.

"Adam, you watch while we begin to work it, then you can give it a try," he advised.

While the teen watched, the other two began to drag the hide back and forth across the wooden beam to break down the fibers and soften the skin. They worked it for several minutes, then turned it over.

"Your turn, Adam." Mr. Mattson stepped aside and passed his end to the older boy.

The two boys continued the operation. Within the hour, the skin continued drying and began to become pliable and soft. By the time the three had taken several turns and the hide itself had been flipped over several times, the buck skin had become as soft as the four new skins Michael's mother and Granny Woman had prepared and sent for him.

"That was sure a lot of work," Adam observed. "And it sure is soft. Just like your clothes."

"Let's clean up," Mr. Mattson said.

The wagon beam was returned to its place beside the carriage barn and the barrel taken behind the barn, emptied, and left upside down where it had been in the first place.

Back in the barn, Michael took the hide from its resting place on the milk stool and handed it to Mr. Mattson.

"Would you please give this to my mother when you see her again," he asked. "I want her to have something that I made."

"I'll take it back with me. But we both might be seeing her at the same time if everyone is able to get together come spring."

"If that's what happens, I'll be so glad to be able to give it to her."

"If so, it'll be in my room at the freight company."

"Let's tend the smokehouse so we can get back to the house," Adam offered. "I think we'll be able to have venison roast for next week."

The three left the barn.

*   *   *

It was lunchtime by the time the tanners returned to the kitchen. Adam's parents admired the product of their work.

"It's hard to believe that this here buckskin was walking in the back woods a week ago," Mr. Tyler observed.

"This is how your people lived," Adam added. "You hunt the game for food, but you use his skin to make your clothes."

"That's a simple way to put it," Mr. Mattson stated. "In Prairie Cub's world you are one with the natural world."

"Wow. I keep learning new things about you," Adam concluded.

"Smells good, Ma," Michael observed. "Hot soup and sandwiches? And popcorn, too."

"Somethin' quick so you can help string popcorn and cranberries for the tree and we can decorate it after we eat," Mrs. Tyler explained.

Following lunch, the family gathered in the parlor and worked the afternoon preparing strings of popcorn, paper cutouts, and some store-bought ornaments to decorate the tree. The tree had been stood in a small, galvanized bucket placed on top of a wooden tree stand with guidelines on four sides to keep it upright. A red, flannel, tree skirt covered the stand and bucket, leaving the top of the bucket open so water could be added. The bucket had been filled halfway.

A warm fire burned in the fireplace, noisy in its crackling coals and dancing flames. Unlike the living room where the fireplace had been closed up and the Round Oak stove added into the chimney above the mantle for its extra warmth, the parlor fireplace had been left open for its comforting ambiance.

Adam showed Michael how to fold pieces of paper to apply scissors and cut out varying shapes of snowflakes and snowmen and Santas. The tree was wrapped in popcorn chains with cranberry highlights mixed in and decorated with the paper cutouts. To this was added an assortment of store-bought colorful glass balls collected over the years and an occasional piece of fruit. The fruit, apples from the cold cellar and oranges from the mercantile, was for eating on Christmas day. Once finished, all stood back and admired the tree.

"Time to gather the greens," Mr. Tyler announced.

While Mrs. Tyler fixed a pot of hot chocolate, her husband took the menfolk to the tool room in the carriage barn to get hand clippers and cut greens from the shrubs around the front porch. He demonstrated how to selectively cut branches from the holy bushes and small evergreens so as not to leave noticeable holes in the foliage. Taking an empty water bucket along, the four collected fresh clippings to use to decorate the parlor.

Back inside, all took a break with hot chocolate and cookies before returning to the parlor to finish decorations. A small, wood-carved manger scene was taken, carefully wrapped piece by carefully wrapped piece, from its small wooden chest and placed in the center of the fireplace mantel. The set consisted of the baby Jesus in his manger and Mother Mary and Joseph on either side. The mantel was finished off with small pieces of holly and pine. A couple of large pine cones were added from the collection of ornaments. Greens were added to window sills and the tree skirt beneath the tree. The decorative boxes that had contained the ornament collection were closed and stacked in a corner of the room behind the tree.

All stood back to survey the finished room.

"This is so beautiful," Michael admired. "I never saw anything like it before in my life."

"Truly amazing, Bill and Janet," the frontiersman added. "This is something Michael and me have never had the chance to witness. I am so grateful that we are able to now."

"Walt, we are so honored to be able to share this with you."

"Thanks, Janet." He pulled the boy close to his side and squeezed a token bear hug. Michael reached around the man's waist and added his own hug in return.

\*　　\*　　\*

Following dinner, the family gathered in the parlor to enjoy the beauty they had created.

"Shall we finish off the tree with the Christmas packages?" Mr. Tyler suggested.

"Good idea," his wife agreed.

Each in turn left the room to return with his gifts and carefully arranged them under the tree. Mrs. Tyler made a few shifts to add balance to the layout.

Mr. Tyler added wood to the fire and stirred it up to throw off a greater warmth into the room. All gathered on the floor in front of the fire. Adam retrieved the checkers game from the living room and the boys settled on the floor close to the fire and quickly lost themselves in the game. The adults settled back against whatever piece of furniture was close and leaned back against it. They were content to watch the boys at their game. After a short while, Mrs. Tyler left for the kitchen. She could be heard working at the range with a pot and utensils. After a while, she returned to the room with a tray of cups filled with hot chocolate and a bowl of popcorn. She set it on a side table and each helped himself. The mixed aromas of chocolate, popcorn, and wood smoke filled the air, and all were satisfied. The adults discussed plans for the days ahead. Finally, the parlor clock struck the hour and it was decided to turn in for the night. Mr. Tyler banked the fire for the night and set the screen in front to keep any hot coals from popping out into the room. The boys each took a lamp to his room. The Tylers headed down the hall to bank the fires in the kitchen range and the living room stove, put out the lamps in each room except one from the kitchen which they took to their room.

Soon the house settled to quiet as each climbed into bed to reflect on the day's memories, and drift into sleep.

*    *    *

The western clouds of the previous morning moved in over night and left an inch of new snow for Sunday morning. The family arose to a day of light snowfall and the brightness of a blotted out sun. The morning began with chores, then a bundled up walk to church for morning services and the noontime social hour. A light ham dinner followed into an afternoon of food preparations for Christmas Day. Mr. Tyler brought the turkey in from its cool box, unwrapped it, and placed it in the sink. Mrs. Tyler retrieved previously mixed cookie batter from the ice box and set out baking sheets for the boys to bake cookies. Mr. Mattson offered to make the biscuits, something he had become quite good at in his kitchen at the freight company with added practice in Horace's kitchen on the mountain. Mr. Tyler pitched in fixing potatoes to be boiled and, when finished, took care of tending the various fires throughout the house. Each passed the afternoon intensely focused on his part in the preparations for the Christmas feast. After the cookies had been baked, mince, apple, and pecan pies were prepared and set in to bake. The turkey was the last to be readied and placed in the oven. All the prepared vegetable dishes were placed in the ice box to be cooked the following morning. As the cookies came out of the oven, they were placed on cooling towels. Finished pies were set out on cooling racks. Finally, the fire for the oven was banked down for a cooler, long term baking temperature for the turkey. Once placed in its roasting pan and into the oven, cleanup began. While the adults worked to clean up the kitchen, the boys were sent to the dining room to prepare the table for Christmas dinner. Extra place settings were readied on the buffet cabinet for any who dropped by to visit. The fire in the stove was fed just enough to keep it warm throughout the day. The bedrooms above would benefit from the extra heat drifting up through the floor registers. The boys would have a warm wakening the next day.

Evening chores were done. A deep chill set in as temperatures dropped. Adam saw to it the horses had their blankets for the night. Bedtime brought a sense of excited anticipation for the day ahead. The household settled for the night and dreams of a wondrous day to come.

*    *    *

Christmas Day dawned gray and overcast with a chill clean air and no new snow. The house was warmed by the many extra fires and the mixed aroma of turkey cooking and wood smoke. As the family gathered in the morning darkness in the brightness of the warmly lit kitchen, the boys bundled up to get the chores done as quickly as possible. While they were out, Mrs. Tyler prepared a light breakfast of warm oatmeal and toast while the menfolk tended the fires to active flames and increased heat. The boys returned and all gathered around the kitchen table.

"The house feels really warm," Adam noticed as he hung up his outer garments and washed up for breakfast.

"It smells good, too," Michael added.

"We've a big meal preparing for dinner," Mrs. Tyler informed, "So I thought you might like a quick breakfast so we can go to the parlor and check out the presents."

"Merry Christmas," Mr. Tyler greeted.

"It is such a blessing that we can be together this day," Mr. Mattson remarked. "I am so blessed to be here with your family and to know that Michael truly has a home here. And I am so looking forward to our gathering at the old trading fort this coming spring."

The family consumed breakfast with little further conversation, gathered the dirty dishes on the drain board, then retired to the parlor.

The flames leaped brightly in the fireplace, radiating a comfortable warmth as all gathered on the floor in front of the tree.

"Let's see what we have here," Mr. Tyler began as he reached for a colorfully wrapped package from under the tree. "Adam," he announced. He passed the gift to his son.

Michael beamed within as he recognized the gift he had gotten. Adam looked at the tag. "From Michael!" Then proceeded to shred the paper. "A hunting knife! Wow!"

The next gift went to Mrs. Tyler. "A locket!"

"Look inside."

"Oh, my gosh! How did you?"

"I stopped at *The Herald* and asked Evan to show me his images. I picked out the one of the family and asked if he could print one small enough for the locket. He did."

She proudly turned the locket so all could see. Inside was the picture from the class session of the whole family, all four of them."

"I need to get one to take back with me," Mr. Mattson exclaimed.

Mr. Tyler carefully selected the next gift. It was for the frontiersman. He looked at it suspiciously it being shaped somewhat like a book. Tearing open the paper in anticipation, he found a custom crafted wood frame with two images. Suddenly, the man could not speak. He just turned it for all to see. One image was the gathering at the gate, The second was of all five of them gathered in the classroom, with the wall map in the background.

"You got your picture," Michael smiled.

Walt Mattson brushed a tear aside as he barely whispered, "Thank you so much."

The gifts continued. Among the remaining gifts, Mr. Tyler received a new scarf from his wife and a pocket knife from Michael. Adam received a pair of gloves from his mother and a flint and steal fire starter kit from Mr. Mattson.

"You learn how to use that and you will never be without a fire," the trader shared. "If I don't get a chance to teach you, Michael can." He smiled.

Michael received writing paper and envelops from Adam. "I know how important it is for you to write to your family and friends," the older boy reacted to his younger brother's grin. From Mr. Mattson he received a handcrafted leather billfold. "Now you don't have to keep your money all wadded up in your pocket," he explained, and was rewarded with a hug.

Mrs. Tyler gave Mr. Mattson a pair of warm woolen socks she had knitted during their evenings in the living room.

"Walt, here's an odd looking box." Mr. Tyler passed a long slender box.

"It's from Michael," he observed. Carefully unwrapping the paper, he lifted the lid on the box and withdrew a hunting knife in a sheath with beautifully crafted quillwork. He knew it immediately. "This is the knife your mother crafted the sheath for. Why?" Once again, the man was caught in unexpected emotion.

The family watched on in wonder and curiosity.

The boy could hardly speak as he, too, became emotional, and answered with great difficulty. "That has my mother's love for me. It holds, too, my love for you. My mother will be greatly honored when she next sees you wearing it and knows you are held with honor by my family." He reached for his friend and buried his face in his arms and wept. "And with it I will always be with you and also with my family and my people." His voice was muffled and barely audible. The two wept together, clasped in a brief eternity, and in that moment, within his mind, Michael was home again.

The family wept quietly in the emotional weight of the giving.

Moments passed. Mr. Tyler broke the silence. "There are still three small packages here. I set them aside as I was passing out the other gifts. You want to say anything, Michael?"

"They have names?" the boy asked.

"They do."

"I hope they will stop later today. I asked Jay if they could come by later this afternoon."

"Then I expect they will." The packages were left together in the middle of the tree skirt.

"Dinner should be ready by noon," Mrs. Tyler announced. "For now, I have hot chocolate on the range."

Michael stood up and moved toward the door. "I'm ready for something warm to drink."

"I'm with you, Brother," Adam joined in.

The family retired to the kitchen for refreshment.

"We'll clean up here later," Mr. Tyler instructed.

Mr. Mattson very carefully folded the wrapping paper from Michael's gift and slipped it and its gift tag into his shirt pocket. He placed the knife back in its box and returned the cover on the box, then placed it on the box with the photo images alongside the rest of his gifts. He followed the family to the kitchen.

*    *    *

Dinner was moved to the dining room table at noon.

"Ma, it smells so good," Michael complimented.

Mr. Tyler carved the turkey while all watched in anticipation. The table was spread with dishes of mashed potatoes, turkey stuffing, string bean and mushroom casserole, sweet potatoes, gravy bowl, biscuits, and cranberry sauce.

"Everyone start whatever dish is near you and pass it to your right," Mrs. Tyler instructed.

Food started around the table. The platter of turkey soon followed as Mr. Tyler placed the carving set on the plate with the bird, set it aside, and sat back on his chair.

"Janet, you've outdone yourself," Mattson complimented.

"Don't forget, this has been a family project as everyone has helped get it started yesterday." She broke open a biscuit, buttered it, and bit into it. After a minute she continued, "and that includes these wonderful biscuits you made."

Several minutes passed in quiet as everyone focused on the food.

"Ma, this is so good," Adam added after a while. "I know we all worked on it, but you saw to it all was done right."

"Honey," her husband spoke up. "I've got to hand it to you, we all did a great job."

She smiled.

A leisurely hour slipped away as the family enjoyed the Christmas dinner. The pies and cookies awaited on the sideboard buffet top. When all had finished with dinner, the dessert dishes were passed around the table and each selected what he desired and passed the dishes on. Once around the table, they were returned to their places.

Another half hour passed when it came time to clear the table. All was taken to the kitchen except for the desserts. The adults worked together to clean up and put leftovers away, while the boys tended the fires throughout the rooms.

There came a knock at the front door. Michael rushed to answer it.

"I knew you would come. You guys come on in out of the cold." He closed the door. "Ma, Jay's here with Scott and Dan."

"Show them where they can throw their coats in the living room and take them to the dining room. We'll be right there."

"Thanks, Janet," Jay called as he and his crew threw their coats and hats on the living room couch and followed the boys into the dining room.

Mr. and Mrs. Tyler followed with a fresh pot of coffee, a pitcher of cold milk, and another of cream. Mr. Mattson went to the side board and started passing out cups and glasses. Adam joined him and passed out small plates and forks. Then the two started the dessert dishes around the table.

"We sure weren't expecting all this," Dan spoke up.

"Well," Mr. Mattson commented, "we can put it all away and retire to the parlor."

"Not complaining," Scott put in. "I wouldn't want to miss these fine desserts."

"Have you had dinner?" Mr. Tyler asked.

"Yes, thank you," Jay responded. "They served a splendid holiday feast at the hotel's dining room."

The boys enjoyed second servings of pie, which they finished off with another selection of cookies. They were stuffed and left the last cookie only half eaten.

"Eyes bigger than your stomachs?" Mattson asked.

"Yea," Michael barely managed.

"When everyone is finished, we can retire to the parlor and enjoy the tree." Mr. Tyler pushed back his chair and paused.

"You boys want to start cleaning up?" Mrs. Tyler asked.

"Sure, Ma," Adam answered.

The two cleared their own places to the kitchen, then returned for whoever else had finished. The Tylers led the way to the parlor as the boys took the last of the dirty dishes to the kitchen. All gathered in the parlor as Mr. Tyler added wood to the fire. He then picked up the three remaining packages from under the tree.

"Do you wanna hand these out, Michael?"

"Thanks."

The boy took the packages and handed one to each guest.

"While we check these out," Scott said, "You can look into these." He handed the boy three packages that he had in a paper sack that sat by his chair.

Quiet anticipation awaited the opening of the gifts.

Michael received a pair of engineer's gloves from Jay, a cap from Scott, and two large red bandanas from Dan along with a gold plate for his cap that read "engineer."

"Thanks, guys."

The engine crewmen opened their small jewelry boxes that Michael had gotten from the mercantile to find a finely shaped piece of flint in each.

"What's this?" Jay asked.

By way of an answer, Michael left the room and brought back one of his arrows from the quiver in the kitchen.

"Do you see this point?" He held out the arrow.

The three studied the piece of stone on the arrow, then compared it to the one each held in his hand.

"They're arrow points," Scott announced.

"I had them in a bag in my parflech," Michael explained. "I made them last summer with Grandfather when I was making my arrows. These are extras. They are the last things we made together before he died."

The importance of the little pieces of stone were suddenly realized.

"Thanks, Michael," Dan acknowledged. "I know now what a treasure they are. I think back to the first day we met on the train. These are your past life."

The boy smiled at the connection.

Each man returned his stone point to its felt-lined box and slipped it into a pocket.

"Thanks," Jay and Scott responded.

The visitors remained an hour as all spent their time together in quiet conversation about recent events from news along the rail line to the school visit of the previous week to the latest from the logging camp.

# CHRISTMAS JOURNEY

Christmas Day slipped into the past as vacation week advanced to Tuesday. The day dawned a crystal clear black with a sky studded with a million specks of light. The air was brittle cold and deathly still. The three walked back toward the house, Mattson carrying the eggs and milk and the boys grabbing firewood from the woodpile. Back in the kitchen, the fuel was delivered to the kitchen range and the parlor fireplace. The eggs were carefully placed in their ceramic bowl and placed in the ice box. The milk was separated and followed. The warm aroma of sausage and fresh deep-fried donuts mixed with the warmth of the hot fire.

The family gathered at the table as the parents brought the food and handed it to the three to pass around, then took their seats with the others.

"Since industry is closed until after New Years, we have these next days to ourselves," Mr. Tyler stated. "Any ideas?"

"Pa," Michael suggested, "could we take the train to Arlee and visit the Johnstons?"

"Yea," Adam agreed. "That would be a great idea." He broke off a piece of his donut and wiped up some egg yoke with it.

"I'll send a wire and see what day would be good for them." He cut off and ate a slice from his sausage. After swallowing, he added, "Why don't you boys go over to Jenkins' and see if there's any mail?"

"Okay if we take the horses?" Adam asked.

"Sure. The exercise will be good for them."

Finishing breakfast, the boys excused themselves, bundled up, and left for the barn.

Michael entered Of-The-Wind's stall and slipped the halter over her muzzle. The pony immediately pranced excitedly, knowing they were going somewhere. Adam saddled Cheyenne and the two were led to the barnyard. Michael slipped onto his pony's back as his brother mounted his horse. They headed out the lane at a walk.

"Let's go past Teddy's and see what time they plan to walk the trap line," Michael suggested.

They turned to the right at the street and headed down Washington to Maple, then across to the Latimer house. They found Teddy engaged in a snowball fight as he and one group attacked a neighbor's snow fort, defended by another group of friends. The two boys stopped to watch. Snowballs flew thick back and forth between the two groups. The assault failed and the attackers retreated. All took a break.

"Hi," Teddy greeted. "What's up?"

Michael responded, "Just checking to see if you're walking the trap line today to reset the traps." His pony snorted and shook her head, impatient to be moving on.

"Not today. Having too much fun." He scooped up a handful of snow and worked it into a snowball. "How 'bout we stop after breakfast tomorrow?"

"Okay. We might not be home. We're takin' the train to visit friends in Arlee this week, just not sure which day. If we're gone, go without us."

"All right. See ya later." He rushed forth with his friends for another assault on the fort.

Michael and Adam moved on. Leaving the snow battle behind, they advanced to the corner of Main Street and turned toward the business district. Dismounting in front of the general store, the boys tied their horses to the hitching rack and entered the store.

"Mornin', Mr. Jenkins," the two greeted.

"Hi boys," he acknowledged, looking up from an order sheet he was working on. "Be right with ya." He reached two cans of beans from the shelf behind him and set them with the other items beside the order. The man walked to the center of the counter.

"Is there any mail?" Adam asked.

"Funny thing about that," Jenkins retrieved two envelops from the postal boxes in the caged area at the end of the counter and returned to the boys. "These came in on Saturday's train addressed to 'Prairie Cub.' It just so happened that I was staring at the image on the front page of the newspaper when the mail arrived, or I'd have no idea what that meant. I guess these are yours, Michael, Prairie Cub?" He reached out with the letters. "And now I understand earlier mail addressed to 'Prairie Cub' that yer folks have picked up at other times."

"Yea, that's me." The boy accepted the letters with a smile. "I guess a lot of folks are kinda' wonderin'." He studied the envelops for an indication of who had sent them. One had a railroad post office postmark from the Northern Pacific Railroad. The other, from Savage, Montana Territory. "They're from Scot and Mr. Summers!" he exclaimed as he tucked them in his shirt pocket inside his coat. "Let's go home so I can read them." Michael quickly turned toward the door, shouting back as an afterthought, "Thanks, Mr. Jenkins."

"Bye, Boys," the man waved.

Dashing to the street, Michael grabbed his pony's lead line, flung himself on her back, and took off toward Main Street. Adam was close behind. Of-The-Wind readily broke into a run as they rushed home, and all too soon, found herself back in her stall as the boy headed toward the house, not waiting for Adam to unsaddle his horse.

The boy burst into the kitchen dropping his coat on the floor, as he rushed to his chair pulling the letters from his pocket.

"What's happened, Son," a concerned Mrs. Tyler asked, turning from the pot she was attending on the range.

"Letters from home!" Michael explained.

Adam burst through the door. "You just left me in the dust, Brother!" he exclaimed. "I put yer pony's halter away." Hanging his coat on its peg, he picked up Michael's coat as well. "But I understand." He grinned and headed to his seat at the table. Without further comment, he sat and watched his brother devour his mail.

Opening the letter with the RPO postmark, he spread it on the table to read.

*December 6, 1882*
*Idaho Territory*

*Dear Prairie Cub,*

*We received your letter a couple weeks ago, but been very busy building snow sheds through the mountains. At one point, two weeks back, our train was stranded in a snow shed for five days in a fierce blizzard that shut down everything and completely blocked the tracks with ten foot drifts. The railroad has borrowed a steam driven rotary snow plow that blows the snow off the tracks. It took them days to* get to us so we could return to the construction camp. Everything is stopped for now as the snow has us confined to camp. We're not sure when operations will begin again. That gives lots of time for letters.

Pa an' me was so glad to get your letter. I'm glad Jay and his friends have been able to help you. The Tylers sound like really great people. When I was there, I stayed with Jay in his hotel room while we worked to find my uncle and news on where my pa had gone. I know you are Michael now and living in Michael's world. But for Pa and me, you'll always be Prairie Cub. We've not been back to Savage since the railroad left after I last saw you when we took you to the town and planned your trip east. When Mr. Summers forwarded your letter, he sent a note that plans would follow to try to get folks together one day. He also said that Walt Mattson would be going to visit you. I hope he got there all right.

It was great to read that you've been in the cab with Jay and Scott and learnin' to run the "King." Ain't it the best darn job in the world! I loved my time in Snow Shoe. It looks like you're lovin' it, too. Tell Jay and Scott and the rest hi for me. I think of them often and do miss them. I miss you, too, and sure do hope Mr. Summers can make somethin' happen so we can be together again. I miss your people, too, and still wear the necklace Prairie Flower gave me.

Does anyone other than Jay know about our life here on the frontier? I know from your letter that you miss it terribly. I hope it's not forever.

Write when you can. As soon as I learn more of how you're doin' I'll get another letter off to you.

I love you Prairie Cub,
Scot

"It's from Scot Robinson, my friend with the railroad who once stayed here with Jay some years back."

"I remember there was a boy staying with him back about 1880. He's about a year younger than me."

"Will you read his letter?" Mr. Tyler asked.

"Sure, Pa." and he began to share his letter with the family.

After all had heard and reacted to Scot's letter, Mr. Mattson offered, "If you have letters to go back, Michael, I'll take them when I leave next week."

"You're leaving?"

"I said I'd stay until the new year. And that is next Monday."

"Oh." He opened the second envelop. It held two letters.

*December 5, 1882*
*Savage, Montana Territory*

*Prairie Cub,*

*I am told there is a letter coming from the railroad camp in the next day or two and was given a letter from Lawrence and his pa. I am putting my note in with Lawrence's letter and will send all when I have them. You are sorely missed here, yet we all know that it has to be this way. By the time you get these letters, Walt Mattson should have arrived in Snow Shoe. I hope you have enjoyed a warm and happy visit. I have told him to stay as long as he likes or you both need.*

*There's not a lot of news. The Kaymonds are having a good season. As you know, I own ten miles of territory along the river. There are branches off the Yellowstone on my lands with beaver dams and communities and they are doing well with beaver pelts. And since they are the only trappers permitted on my lands, they won't hurt the beaver population.*

*I expect that Walt has shared with you that I hope to get your family and the Robinsons to gather at the old fort come springtime, and hope you and the Tylers will come, too. The Kaymonds will stay on and wait to return to St. Louis closer to summer. We might even convince Mrs. Kaymond to join us at the fort as well.*

*Savage continues to grow as more settlers come west and buy up land for farming. It's too many and too fast as far as I'm concerned, even though it is good for my business.*

*Looking forward to seeing you again and to meeting your new family.*

*KS*

The family waited in anticipation for Michael to share Keith's letter. He did so, then picked up the letter from Lawrence.

*Summers' Fort*
*Montana Territory*
*December 4, 1882*

*Prairie Cub,*

> *Pa and me was so excited to get your letter. We are happy to know that you are well.*
> *I liked reading about your day on the train. It must have been very exciting. We've had a good year trapping. Here on Keith Summers' lands are many beaver and beaver pelts are bringing good money. The fort is a good place to live. We have our own room and full use of the kitchen. There is also a large gathering room where we can skin our catch and stretch the hides. There's plenty of scrap wood from Mr. Summers' building projects for stretching the skins and this whole big room to set them aside in without worry about weather or wild critters. The old trading post still has some sale items that usually include anything we might need. We keep a ledger on the counter of anything we take and Summers will use it when he buys our pelts. Since we live here, he buys pelts at the end of each month and squares with the ledger. It's so much easier than waiting til the end of the season and trying to find a buyer for the whole season's catch.*
> *Mr. Summers tells us he's trying to bring us all together come spring. I really hope it works. We're planning to stay and see if that happens.*
> *Write again when you can. I'll try to write, too.*

> *Your friend,*
> *Lawrence*

Again, Michael shared his letter.

"Hearing from your friends makes me homesick, too," Mr. Mattson admitted. "I'll be sure they get your letters."

Michael gathered together the letters and returned them to their envelops, then put them back into his pocket. "got anything ta drink, Ma?"

"Just a minute and I'll have this hot chocolate finished." She returned to the range and moved the pot from its cool spot near the edge to a spot over the heat, and began to stir the mix again.

"I'll take a cup of coffee now and head off to Wells Fargo to send the wire. It should be answered quickly since Hank is the agent there."

Mrs. Tyler brought the coffee pot to the table along with several cups.

"If it's okay with you, I'll go along, too," Mr. Mattson offered. "I could use the exercise."

Each poured himself a cup of coffee while the boys waited for the hot chocolate. They finished, placed their cups on the table, and stood to take down their coats.

"See you all later," Mr. Tyler announced. The men headed down the hall. A blast of cold air followed by the bang of the closing door announced their departure.

*   *   *

Word came back that Friday would be the best day to visit. Teddy and Miles stopped the next morning to reset the trap line. The boys went along and they worked in pairs to reset each trap. With all four working the line, they finished quickly and returned to the house for refreshment. All gathered in the parlor. Teddy and Miles got to see and admire the tree. They also enjoyed time with Mr. Mattson as he shared stories of life on the frontier and times with Prairie Cub before the battle and afterwards, too, when he became Michael's teacher to help him enter the white man's world.

Thursday became a day with preparation for Friday's trip. Mrs. Johnston followed up with an invitation to spend the night so Jason would have more time with the boys. Adam made arrangements with Brett Tompkins to tend to chores while the family was away. Mrs. Tyler added instructions for Brett to take home the milk and any eggs he gathered and give them to his ma.

Friday started extra early. The boys got up and tended chores at 5:00am. Michael shared his carpet bag with Mr. Mattson as the two packed for overnight. Breakfast at 5:45 with cleanup to follow enabled the family to be on the road to the train by 6:30. They walked the dark snow-packed streets with canyon-like walls along either side where the snow from recent storms had been thrown. At the station, Jay called the boys and Mr. Mattson to the engine.

"Would you three care to ride up here til we get to Blakesville? This is so Walt and Adam can experience what you and me get to do from time to time."

"Okay with you two?" Michael asked.

"I'd sure like to," Adam replied.

"There's a first time for everything," Mattson agreed. "You boys go on up and I'll tell the folks. I'll leave our bag with your folks in the coach."

The boys climbed into the engine cab while Mattson walked back to let the Tylers know.

Dan put the stool on board and signaled the departure. Jay acknowledged with three short whistle blasts as the train eased backwards toward Day's End.

"Welcome aboard, Walt and Adam," Scott greeted. "Is this your first time in an engine cab?" He checked the water level as he spoke.

"Yea," the two chorused. As they watched the track beyond the tender, they saw Jamie standing at the switch.

The train rumbled through the switch and kept slow so Jamie could close the switch and board the steps to the coach. Picking up speed, the train hurried on to its first stop.

"Michael," Jay invited. "Would you like to take her into the station and do the run-a-round?"

"Sure would," the boy replied. He climbed up on the front of the engineer's seat, then eased the throttle back to running speed and locked it in.

"You run this thing?" Mattson asked in surprise.

"Sure do," the boy replied.

"He's getting' pretty good at it, too," Jay spoke with pride. "Whistle post coming up," the engineer announced.

"Got it," Michael replied as he reached for the wooden handle on the whistle cord.

Pausing long enough for the post to pass the engine's tender, he pulled two long wails, a short chirp, and a final drawn out cry that echoed off the landscape.

"You're good!" Adam observed.

"If I weren't standing here as my witness, I'd never believe you can do this," the trader spoke admiringly.

Michael grinned with the pride he felt at sharing his new talent with his friends.

Shortly after, the Day's End station came into view and the boy eased in on the throttle as the train began to slow. Applying the brakes lightly, he slowed the train even more. The station grew nearer in its wonderland snow scape. The boy closed the throttle all the way and began playing with the brake as it squealed steel on steel and the engine gradually slowed past the platform and he lined up the coach with a final lockdown of the brakes and release of steam pressure from the piston chambers. He reached up and sounded one sharp blast on the whistle. The train stood still with its rumbling in the boiler and soft swoosh of dark smoke from the stack.

Jamie dropped from the steps of the car in front of the engine, uncoupled the locomotive, and walked through the six-inch snow, over to throw the switch. The youth waved all clear and Michael acknowledged with three short whistle blasts as he again shifted the Johnson bar into reverse. Easing back on the throttle, the boy backed the engine slowly through the switch, paused while Jamie closed it and climbed up on the front of the engine while Michael shifted into forward and eased past the train to the switch in back. Jamie threw the switch for the engine to pass through, then closed it for the engine to back up to couple to the back of the train for the run to Arlee. Jamie climbed back onto the coach, Dan gave the signal, and Michael put the train into forward motion.

"Adam," Scott spoke up, "can you pass me some firewood to feed this old gal?" He lifted the latch on the firebox door with the toe of his shoe and pushed it open.

Adam passed firewood, one chunk at a time until the fireman said he had enough. Mattson observed the boys' activity with a sense of respect as he stood out of the way by the cab doorframe behind the fireman's box.

Michael sounded the crossing as it passed and brought the engine up to speed and locked the throttle in place. He watched the approaching track and passing landscape through the open door to the running board.

"Doin' real good," Jay complimented as he sat back on his seat against the cab wall.

"Jay," Mr. Mattson spoke up, "this sure has been a new experience for me. Did you teach Michael all this?" he stepped back to the door frame across from Adam and held on with his right hand for balance.

"I did," the engineer replied without taking his eyes off the track ahead. "And I taught Teddy Tompkins' son, Brett, his first summer here and Scot Robinson when he was here back in '80."

"Why?"

"It gives them a sense of accomplishment and personal confidence. And sometimes it even saves live."

"How so?"

"When Brett first came here back in the summer of '79, he was in the cab of the logging company's engine, the "Scott". When the train ended up running through a forest fire."

"I was there, too," Adam volunteered.

"Yes you were," Jay concurred. "I believe you saved Brett from serious injury by pushing him to the floor under your own body and paid the price with some serious burns." The teen nodded. "The engine crew suffered severe burns and smoke and both men passed out. It was Brett who ended up taking the train through the fire and bringing it to a stop on the other side."

"That is some experience," Mattson remarked with a sense of awe.

The train flew past Snow Shoe station, snow flying on either side in the passing train's windstream, as Michael whistled the Main Street crossing. Further on, the boy slowed the train as it rumbled across Chamber's Crossing bridge, then eased it to a near stop as he watched back for Jamie to drop from the coach steps. The youth waved and the boy acknowledged with a short crisp toot and brought the train back up to speed.

"What was that all about?" Adam asked.

Michael answered, "Jamie walks the bridge and the tracks to Snow Show to inspect their condition. He reports any problems to Mr. Coates, the stationmaster, and he orders out track crews as needed. On the return trip, he reports to Jay."

"Our next stop is Blakesville," Jay informed. "Scott and I will take it from there and you three can go back to ride with the family. I hope this has been a good experience for you and Adam."

"You bet it has," Adam replied.

"Most impressive," the frontiersman acknowledged. "I wouldn't have missed this for the world. I'll share this with Keith and the folks back home. I know when I see Scot again, he will be real happy to know that Michael is following in his footsteps."

The familiar landmarks told Michael that his next stop was close at hand. He began the train's slowdown before rounding the curve into the view of the oncoming station. Minutes passed as the boy brought the train to a smooth stop, blew the single whistle blast, then stepped down from the front of the engineer's box platform.

"It's all yours, Jay. And thanks so much."

"You're welcome, Michael. It's such a pleasure to watch you and the joy you share in the greatest job in the world." He stepped down from his seat to step out onto the footplate and watch his guests descend to the platform to walk back to join the Tylers in the coach.

\*     \*     \*

After miles of flying through the wintry landscape with snow blowing alongside the coach windows, the train slowed to a stop, then switched onto the main, to finish its run to Arlee. Within minutes the large, two-story, freight and office building slipped by as the train came to rest at Arlee station. The family party stood and reached their bags down from the overhead rack, then followed the crowd to the door to the open platform then down the steps to the wooden station platform. Within the minute, Jason was at Michael's side to guide the family through the noisy crowd and across the street to the hotel. Newly arrived visitors continued to pour into the noisy hotel lobby as Jason led the family down the center hall and into the quiet of the kitchen.

"Whew," Mrs. Tyler exhaled, "What a challenge. Quiet at last." She set her bag on the floor, removed her hat, and slipped out of her coat.

"Ma's gonna be busy for a while checking in guests," Jason announced. "Hang your things on your chairs and have a seat at the table." He turned to the kitchen range. "She made hot chocolate and coffee with Christmas cookies so you can rest here a while before she comes in."

The family sat down. Cups and plates were on the table along with a platter of cookies. Jason brought the coffee pot to the table, poured hot chocolate into a pitcher, and placed the pitcher on the table.

"Hi," he introduced as he pulled up a side chair. "I'm Jason. I met Michael and Mr. Mattson a few weeks ago when he came down with Jay to pick up his frontier friend." He poured himself a cup of chocolate. "Ma said to relax and enjoy the cookies while she checked in the guests.

Because of the holiday, she has a local girl, Sharon, helping her. But it will probably take a while." He reached for a cookie.

"Thanks, Jason," Mr. Mattson spoke up. "Best enjoy the refreshments." He poured himself a cup of coffee and took some cookies on a plate.

The rest of the family followed his example and momentarily ate in quiet.

Jason continued, "Jay planned ahead to stay over to the station's second floor bunk room tonight and the Tylers have his room. We put extra cots in my room for Mr. Mattson and the boys. It'll be crowded. You can bring your things up the back staircase and get settled, then come back down in about a half hour for breakfast. Pa should be back from the station by then and ma should have the new guests checked in. Any without previous reservations have to go elsewhere, we're full up. Put your coats on the wall pegs."

Everyone hung up their outer garments and picked up their bags to follow the teen up the back stairs.

*   *   *

The Tyler family gathered for breakfast in the kitchen. The dining room was packed with guests. Sharon and Mrs. Johnston shuttled the serving dishes of food back and forth to the dining room while Mr. Johnston tended the kitchen.

"You sure have a busy place this morning," Mr. Tyler observed. "Are you sure it was a good idea for us to stay over?"

"It's been like this all week. With Christmas and New Year being on Monday, most folks have an extended weekend and want to make the best of their time together. Tuesday was changeover as the first group left and the second started to arrive. It looked worse than it was when you came in. Most folks were just dropping off their room keys and gathering for breakfast." He paused to dig into his fried potatoes and wash them down with coffee. He continued, "Most will leave right after breakfast to spend the day with family and return late in the evening. We don't serve lunch and dinner is by reservation." He paused to continue eating.

Michael spoke up, "Mr. Johnston, these are my folks, Bill and Janet Tyler, and my brother, Adam. You already met me and Walt Mattson."

"I'm sorry, I should have introduced myself. I'm Hank and my busy wife, Nancy, and our son, Jason. It seems with all Jay has said that we've already known each other. Sure is nice to finally meet you folks. I've taken the day off. I just had to be at the station this morning to help my associate get everything transferred between the company wagon and the baggage car. He has taken it from there."

"We have this day," Mrs. Tyler stepped in. "How does everyone want to share it?"

Mrs. Johnston entered the kitchen with empty serving dishes. "I, for one, would like to get to know you folks," she offered.

"I want to show Michael and his brother the train yards," Adam added.

"I'd like to go with you, too," Mattson requested.

"I'm with Nancy," Mrs. Tyler put in. "You menfolk can do your own thing."

Mr. Tyler observed, "It looks like it's you and me, Hank. The women will enjoy their visit. And Jason will take the other three on a great adventure."

"Is breakfast about finished, Nancy?" her husband asked.

"We're just starting to clean up. Most folks have gone and the rest are leaving shortly." She left to pick up more empty dishes as Sharon brought a stack of dirty plates to the drain board.

"We're goin' now," Jason announced.

"Bye," Mr. Mattson waved as the four bundled up for their morning adventure.

The foursome closed the door behind them with a loud slam of the screen door, as they headed across the street to the station, now quiet as the morning traffic had finished passing through.

"All the morning trains have gone," Jason shared as they stood on the empty platform. "Jay went back to Snow Shoe. The Summit train returned to Summit. The southbound went on to Truckee and the northbound on to Pine Bluff. Freight traffic will be running morning and afternoon and a northbound and southbound at mid day. Follow me, I'll show you the roundhouse and the shops."

Jason led the group up the track leading to the engine yards. It entered the service yard on the backside of the roundhouse. The group followed it around to the far side where it came around to the yard office. The office building had a storeroom at one end and the office area at the other. Jason led his friends into the office from the back door.

The morning was spent wandering the buildings and exploring the yards. After meeting the office manager and one of the shop foremen, they left by the front door into the turntable yard. The turntable serviced twelve tracks that fed into the twelve stalls of the engine house, two that entered the repair and service shop, a lead track to the main yard track, and several outside storage tracks that held parked equipment cars. One, near the office, held the "Dalton" Number fifteen with its huge wedge snow plow.

"That's the snow plow that opened the line to Snow Shoe the last big storm when the plow car was in the shop being repaired," Michael announced.

"It gets a lot of work during the winter months," Adam added.

"That's its designated storage track when it's not in use," Jason informed.

Many of the roundhouse stalls were empty as their locomotives were in use. At one, Number three the "Miller" had been pulled out and sat idle with smoke from a newly lit fire drifting from its stack. After a quick walk-through of the roundhouse interior, Jason led the way around the turntable pit to the shop building. On the way, the group checked out the forge car and the steam shovel on their outside storage tracks.

Staying out of the way of the mechanics, the four checked out the machine shop with its belt-driven lathes, drill press, and other equipment. The air reverberated with the noise of the running equipment and machinery and the voices of men at work. In the main shop, an engine sat over an inspection pit wherein workers were checking out the underside of the boiler. It's cab had been removed and the backhead gauges and piping were being repaired or replaced. New piping lay on the locomotive's running board waiting for installation. On the track furthest from the machine shop, a new box car was being built.

"This is where they repaired the plow car when it was wrecked in the first snow storm," Adam announced.

A tender rested on the track closest to the machine shop, waiting for a new coat of paint to dry. It still needed to be re-lettered with road name and engine number.

Leaving through a front door of the shop, Jason led the way to the large wrecking crane with its service tender then beyond to the engine servicing tracks with coal bunker, firewood stacks, oil tank, water tank, and sand house. There were sidings where various passenger equipment and cabooses were stored.

Jason point out two special cars, the "Walton", a parlor car for special excursion trains, and the "Lage", the railroad president's car for the company president, Philemon J. Marlow's personal use when traveling the line.

"This is such a fascinating place to live, Jason!" Mr. Mattson exclaimed. "There's so much happening all the time."

"There's still another yard area," Jason informed. "The freight yard is across the main out behind the hotel. That's where they bring in the cars from various parts of the railroad and rearrange them into trains going to other areas where they are to be delivered. They're all the time working on moving cars there."

"Can we walk by on the way back to the hotel?" the man asked.

"I'd like to see that, too," Adam spoke up.

Having crossed to the opposite side of the service yard, the four walked back past the opposite end of the roundhouse and crossed over to the freight yard. Number twenty-eight was at work selecting specific cars and relocating them to an outside track on which a train was being assembled.

"Tom Jennings and his crew will have those cars sorted and the train will go out this afternoon so the cars can be delivered to their destinations between Arlee and Pine Bluff. A separate train will serve just the businesses in Pine Bluff to go shortly after the first," Jason explained.

"What time do we need to be back for lunch?" Mr. Mattson asked.

"That should be our next stop," Jason replied.

The hotel stood about a block from the end of the freight yard. Arriving on the back porch, each stamped the snow from his boots before entering.

"It's so warm!" Michael exclaimed as he stomped the snow from his moccasins and they entered the warmth of the room. "I didn't know I was cold until I came in."

The others smiled.

"I know what you mean," Adam added. "It is cold outside. I was just so busy with everything, I didn't notice."

Each hung up coat and hat, stuffing scarfs and gloves in coat pockets. They then followed the sound of voices and found their parents gathered in the parlor across from the front entrance to the dining room. A fire in the fireplace radiated warmth into the room. Mr. Mattson found a chair while the boys gathered on the floor in front of the fire.

"This feels sooo good." Adam reached the palms of his hands toward the heat.

"You bet," Michael agreed.

"Walt, did you all have a good tour?" Mr. Johnston asked.

"I have a much greater appreciation of that that is the railroad," he stated. "I imagine that when the Northern Pacific chooses its headquarters that it will be Scot's father's job to plan all this out for them."

"Is everyone ready for lunch?" Mrs. Johnston asked.

Murmurs of agreement circulated the room.

"Shall we, Janet," she acknowledge.

"Let's."

"We'll call you when we're ready."

The women left the room.

\*    \*    \*

The afternoon was spent at home. The boys found two sets of dominoes and laid out their game on the floor in front of the fire. The adults visited in the comfort of the parlor furniture gathered at the end of the room nearest the Christmas tree. There they brought each other up to date on their lives' events over recent weeks, then years in general. The evening meal, a pork roast with roasted vegetables followed by apple pie, was taken in the hotel dining room with the few guests from two families who chose to return for the evening. Following dinner, the guests returned to their rooms and the family retired to the parlor.

"Nancy, I'm so glad we could do this," Mrs. Tyler remarked. "Michael, thank you for the idea. This has been a great trip. I hope you folks will be able to close for a personal vacation and come visit us in Snow Shoe."

"That's a wonderful idea," Mr. Johnston agreed. "Honey, by mid January visitors die off and we could take a weekend then."

"Janet, we'll work on it. It will also depend on the weather. You could get snowed in again at any time."

"That's quite right, Nancy," Mr. Tyler concurred. "Hank, why don't we mark our calendars for the second weekend of January if all goes well. That way we have a plan. We can change it if needed."

"Agreed. Okay, Honey?"

"Yes, okay."

"Yes!" Jason exclaimed.

"Folks, I've really enjoyed this," Mattson announced. "But as the Tylers know, I'll be leaving at year's end. I have a job to get back to from which I have been given very generous unlimited leave. I also have letters to deliver and a spring event to help put together. I'll be passing through on the morning train come Tuesday and will probably only have time to say 'hi' as I get off Jay's train and onto the southbound. This truly has been a memorable trip."

"We are so glad to have shared in this," Mr. Johnston added. "You will be missed and we wish you a safe return to your home."

"How are you boys doin' with yer game?" the trader asked. "Ready fer bed, yet?"

The clock struck the three-quarter hour.

"When the clock strikes nine?" Jason asked.

"Okay," his mother agreed.

Fifteen minutes later, the clock struck the hour and the boys picked up the dominoes and returned them to their boxes. There were 'good nights' around and the boys retired for the night along with Mr. Mattson. Their parents closed down the house, banking the fires for the night, then took their lamps and left for their rooms as well. Darkness settled in as the lamplight drifted down the hallway.

\*     \*     \*

The women arose early to prepare a warm and generous breakfast of hotcakes, sausage, eggs, peeled oranges, juice, hot chocolate, and coffee. The families gathered in the warmth of the kitchen for their own six o'clock breakfast. A second breakfast would be served for the hotel guests at seven, in time for the eight o'clock trains. It being Saturday, there was no inbound train from Snow Shoe. The Friday night train had laid over and would return on Saturday soon after the northbound and southbound trains departed.

"I know you boys will want to go over to the station early so you can watch the train activity," Mrs. Johnston shared. "So as soon as you have eaten, you may go. Jason, your chores will be here when you get back."

"Yea, Ma. Thanks." He smiled. His mother smiled back.

"Michael," Mrs. Tyler instructed. "Be sure you have your bag and keep track of it. Adam, you do the same."

"Sure, Ma," the boys chorused.

The boys ate and left.

Mattson remained behind. "I think Michael is adjusting well, Folks. I hope I'm right."

"He is, Walt. And he isn't," Mrs. Tyler spoke out. "As long as he's so involved in what's going on and distracted from his loss, he handles it well. But he has a deep-set fear that he will forget who he is because he is becoming so used to life as it has become. And it pains him deeply. Sometimes he breaks down and has to go off by himself and mourn."

"I have seen this happen," Mr. Tyler agreed. "Thanksgiving was particularly hard. He has acknowledged that Thunder Eagle was right and he needs to live in the world of his white heritage. But he still wants so terribly to go home. He has accepted us as his second family and Jay has been so supportive of him. This all helps. But at the end of the day, he is still Prairie Cub."

"There is so much we don't know about his story," Mr. Johnston spoke up. "Much of what you are saying is completely new to us. And we are so glad to be a part of his new life in any way we can."

"Hank, I probably shouldn't have said anything. With the time rapidly approaching when I must leave, I so hope that he is doing well. But I have seen in the evenings when it is quiet and we are settling in to bed for the night, there is a certain quietness that comes over the boy. It didn't occur to me that you are not aware of all that Michael has been through. It's not for me to say. Perhaps one day, if he and Jason come to know each other more, he will share his story with your son. You did get a copy of last week's Herald?"

"We have it somewhere," Mrs. Johnston responded. "But no one has bothered to look at it. Hank, you usually don't bother with it but stick it in the wood box for when you need it to start a fire."

Mr. Johnston went to the living room to check and returned with the paper, still folded from when he brought it home with the mail. "Haven't needed it yet since the fire hasn't been allowed to go out since winter weather set in."

"The front page, Hank," Mattson directed.

The man opened the paper and gasped in astonishment. "'Local Boy Has a Remarkable Backstory'," he read. "And there's a picture with him and Mattson in buckskin clothing!" He turned the paper for his wife to see.

"That's who Michael really is," Mattson explained. "That's who we both are. You'll understand a lot more when you read the story. After we leave this morning, show it to Jason."

"Oh, my gosh!" Mrs. Johnston whispered. "I had no idea!"

The parlor clock struck the three-quarter hour.

"The train's due in fifteen minutes," Mr. Johnston announced. "We need to get going. Just leave everything, Nancy. We'll clean up when we get back."

"We completely lost track of time," Mrs. Tyler responded. "Didn't even finish breakfast."

"Here," Mrs. Johnston offered. She grabbed a picnic basket with hinged tops at either end and laid several cloth napkins inside with one opened across the basket's bottom. Then she stacked hotcakes in one end and sausages in the other. "You can roll these together and eat them on the train."

"The basket!?" Mrs. Tyler asked.

"Now we have to come visit so I can get it back." She smiled.

"Okay."

The men helped their wives into their coats as all bundled up and quickly left the room for the station.

*   *   *

Jay had pulled his train onto the pass track, facing north, ready to pull out toward Snow Shoe. The Summit train had been positioned behind it.

"He can't leave until after the main line trains have gone through and passengers have been able to change trains." Mr. Johnston checked his pocket watch. "They'll be another five minutes before they arrive."

"You don't have to get on the train until they leave," Jason informed. "There's a ten minute wait between trains."

"Thanks for having us," Michael shared with the Johnstons. "I sure was glad we could make this trip."

"We're glad, too," Mr. Johnston returned. "You all have a safe trip home. We hope to see you again early next year."

Whistles from the distant north and the distant south screamed in the morning air.

"Trains comin'," Jason announced.

The group stood in the midst of the noisy commotion that suddenly erupted all around them as the trains pulled into the station and crowds emerged from the station building and baggage wagons were rolled out from the freight room. The trains screeched to a stop and passengers surged from within and from without as people got off and others pushed to get on. The noisy chaos lasted about ten minutes until whistles blew and bells began to ring, steam hissed from piston champers, drivers began to push, and trains began their noisy departure to the north and to the south. Gradually picking up speed, they soon disappeared into the distance and a quiet, once again enveloped the station area. Engine twenty-one and its two-car consist waited quietly, with rumblings in its boiler and the whoosh of smoke from its smoke stack.

"Bye, Guys," Jason said as he hugged each In turn.'

"Bye, Jason," they replied.

The men exchanged handshakes and the women hugged. Then the Tyler party moved toward the train as the Johnston family waved good-bye. Minutes of quiet were soon interrupted by Dan's call, "Board!" two sharp whistle acknowledgements, the rhythmic ringing of the bell, and the loud chuffs as the wheels began to turn. A switchman stood at the end of the pass track and waved to the engineer as the train pulled out onto the main, then slapped the points of the switch back into the closed position and locked the switch handle in place. The Johnstons stood and watched as the trailing smoke diminished into the distance and finally drifted into nothingness.

They turned, pulling each other close together with their son held between, and walked back toward the hotel.

# Reluctant Good-Bye

It was midmorning when the family turned in to the farm lane. The brilliant white snow scape reflected the warm rays of sunshine in a crisp chilly air.

"Boy am I cold," Adam shivered as he rubbed his arms with his gloved hands.

"I agree," his mother said as she, too, rubbed her arms.

The men carried the carpet bags.

"Let's hurry inside and get the fires going," Michael suggested.

"Unless I'm mistaken," Mr. Mattson observed, "there's smoke coming from the chimneys."

Everyone looked up.

"Heat!" Adam exclaimed and dashed for the front door.

"Do you think Brett did that?" Mrs. Tyler asked, glancing at her husband.

"It would be just like him," Mr. Tyler replied. "Let's hurry in and get warm ourselves."

The three picked up the pace and quickly got inside.

Once in the front hall with the door closed and wrapped in a sense of warmth, Mr. Mattson sniffed the air.

"Coffee," he stated.

"That would be just like him," Mr. Tyler said. "He's worked with Horace since the very first day he came on the mountain. He makes a perfect pot of coffee, too."

All rushed to the kitchen where the boys had already discovered the coffee, put out the cups and cream, thrown off their coats, and set to the table with their hands wrapped around a steaming cup of coffee.

"Ummm," they sniffed with closed eyes.

"There's a note," Mrs. Tyler discovered as she hung up her outer garments, set Mrs. Johnston's picnic basket on the counter, and picked up the paper. "It's from Brett," she read, " *'I kept the fires going each time I stopped for chores so the house wouldn't cool down. There's a pot of coffee on the warming plate I made fresh this morning. Thanks for letting me take care of things for you. Brett.'"*

"I met him while I was on the mountain," Mattson informed. "He's a Hell-of-a-nice young man. His pa's one of the nicest boss men I ever met. Haven't met his ma, but she can't be any differn't." He hung his things up, poured a cup of coffee, and sat to the table.

The Tylers quickly joined them.

"I knew Adam drank coffee in the camp," Mr. Tyler observed. "When did you start?"

"On the engine with Jay, but before that, at the trading company with Mattson and Mr. Summers."

"Oh," Mrs. Tyler remarked. "Well you're welcome to drink it here any time."

"Prefer your hot chocolate. Just isn't any right now."

"I'll take care of that." She stood to start a pot of hot chocolate and placed a cookie tin on the table.

Everyone helped themselves and munched on cookies in silence. As soon as the chocolate was ready, the boys drained their cups and offered them for chocolate refills.

\*　　\*　　\*

At lunch, Mr. Mattson asked for time with Michael during the afternoon. The two bundled up in their coats and gloves with their side brims snuggly tied down over their ears with their scarfs, then left to the barn.

"Let's take a walk," the frontiersman suggested. "I've not seen much of the hills out back and only walked the trap line once."

They wandered to the barn. Of-The-Wind was excited to see them and danced to the stall door to reach out for Michael. She was rewarded by the boy's gentle touch and soft voice.

"She's such a good pony," the man remarked. "You've been through a lot together."

"Can she walk with us?"

"Of course."

The two entered the pony's stall, walked through, and left by the outside door. The boy slipped onto her back and the three walked in that fashion out into the meadow and its foot-deep snow, resulting in slow progress and high deliberate pacing each step of the way.

"Grandfather and me would ride into the hills and up to the high ground where we could look across the land." He paused to gaze about the meadow and the hills beyond. "Can't do that here. Not enough land."

"I understand," the man acknowledged.

"I miss those times. I miss Grandfather. Do you think he came with me and can watch over me here?" He looked to his friend.

"You told me once that Grandfather is with you." He looked up at the boy. "And he is with you here as well."

They smiled at each other, then the boy looked to the mountain.

"Can we see how high we can go?"

"We have all the time you want."

The boy rode in silence as the man walked alongside. They meandered across the meadow to the back gate, the only sound, the crunching snow. Stamping the snow down behind the gate, Mattson dragged the gate open, forcing it through the snow, and they passed beyond the meadow. Michael dismounted to walk beside his friend. With one hand on his pony's shoulder, he slipped the other around the man's waist. They walked the deer path in silence in this manner.

"Your thoughts?" Mattson inquired.

"I'm getting to like it here, but I'll always miss my family and my people and my home." He paused and walked in quiet thought. "I love my new family very much. I feel a part of them. I feel safe."

No more words were spoken as they continued to trudge on, leaving the record of their passing in the snow behind. The trail sloped upward and the two continued to advance.

"I'm glad to hear that, Michael. Your family will be glad, too, and very much relieved." He glance toward the boy momentarily. "They have worried greatly. Thunder Eagle has said he believes he did the right thing. But it hurts and he sometimes has second thoughts."

There was a quiet moment while the boy thought about what was said.

"I know my father was right. And it does hurt – all the time. I miss them so much." He squeezed the man beside him and felt comfort in his presence. "I'm so glad you're here and wish you didn't have to go. But I know you do."

A rustling in the bushes caught their attention as it shook snow from the branches. The pony looked as well.

"A rabbit," the man observed. "It's just standing there watching us. It does sort of blend its white coat to the snow."

"He knows he's safe. I don't carry my bow and arrows." He grinned.

They walked on and the rabbit moved on as well, leaving its tracks in the snow as it followed the human tracks for a short distance then cut away.

"Tell Mr. Summers 'thanks' for me. I really look forward to seeing everyone again come spring." He gazed ahead up the mountainside. "As much as I can't wait for it to happen, I know there will be great pain and I won't want to leave and return to this home. It's good that this family is going, too." For a moment, he walked in quiet thought. He leaned his head against the man's arm. "I belong to two families. They are so different. I am so glad they will meet." He glanced toward Mattson. Their eyes met. "I will be able to return here because I will be with family."

They had been climbing the slope for nearly an hour when they decided to pause and look back.

"I had no idea we had come so far." The boy exclaimed. "See our tracks? We have left the record of our passing and grandfather can see we are here." He gazed beyond the tracks at the scene below. "With the leaves gone, you can see how big the town is. From here you can see both parts. And look, you can see the pointed bell towers of the churches and the water tower in the engine yard. I've never come up this high before."

"Can't you see it from the train?" Mattson asked.

"I've only been up there once. Leaves were still on the trees and I didn't look."

The two found a large tree trunk lying on the ground and moved to wipe off the snow and sit on it. Of-The-Wind wandered close by and pawed the ground, breaking through the white crust for something to eat. A raccoon stirred in the distance. It looked toward the boy and began to advance. Mr. Mattson watched its approach with apprehension.

Michael noticed it limped on three feet. "It's okay. I know this coon and it knows me. I freed it from one of Teddy's traps a while back – with Teddy's help."

The coon advanced to within a few feet. There it sat down and studied the two who sat in front of it. After a moment, it turned and walked away.

"I'm glad to see it survived. I'll let Teddy and Miles know I've seen it and it's okay." He stood. "Wanna go further?"

"Sure." He stood and faced up hill.

The two continued to climb, the undisturbed snow dragging at their feet. The pony followed close behind. Mattson took the lead and Michael followed with his pony. The walk had gone more than a mile beyond the farm and high up the side of the mountain. They approached a deep cut in its shoulder.

"I don't think you can see the town from the logging train," Mr. Mattson called out. "The tracks are down here in this cut, which seems to run at least a mile along the mountainside." He stood on the edge and waited for the boy.

Arriving at the edge of the steep drop, the boy stopped and starred down a manmade canyon about twenty feet deep, that ran along the side of Fisher Mountain for more than a mile.

"Never been up here before," the boy informed. "Some of those rocks along the side look pretty close."

The two sat down on snow-covered rocks on the rocky ledge and gazed upon the steep passage with the railroad tracks along the bottom. No more was said for several minutes as they took in the spectacle. Of-The-Wind took one look and turned back down the slope, pausing several feet down to explore the ground for something to eat. Eventually, the boy stood up, paused for one last look, then turned to follow.

"I'm ready to go home, now."

The man stood and followed.

The walk back was slow and unhurried. They followed the trail they had left in the snow on the way up. Once again they came upon the distant gurgling of the creek.

"Let's check the trap line," Michael suggested.

As they turned toward the sound of water, the pony hurried ahead. Pausing at the water's edge, she lowered her head, broke the thin ice with her hoof, and slowly drank, while the boy searched out the closest trap. It was sprung.

"I'll leave it for now. Teddy might not get up here again until Tuesday after the holiday. We can just follow the creek and walk the line."

The afternoon was getting late.

Arriving at the gate, the boy starred at the tracks leading from the barn. "Only two sets, a pony and a man. Wonder why."

They passed through the gate and Mr. Mattson forced it closed again. Again, Michael mounted his pony to ride back to the barn.

"I sure did enjoy this walk," the boy stated. "It was almost like being home again." Once again, he shared a grin of joy with his friend.

"It was a good way to spend the afternoon. I feel content that we shared this together." He paused to gaze about the meadow, as though to commit the moment to memory, then moved on.

Darkness had begun to dim the light of day. There was movement in the barn as the three returned. Michael slid down from his pony's back as they entered her stall.

"Hi," Adam greeted. "Thought I'd start chores before it got too late. Would you two feed the chickens and gather the eggs?" He stepped from the cow's stall. "I've milked Bessie and fed the livestock, including your pony." Dropping the milk stool outside the stall, he continued, "I'll follow you and we can check the smokehouse then head up to the kitchen."

"Very thoughtful of you, Adam," the man complimented. "But first, I need to get my coonskin off the board so I can take it with me. It's cured enough I can wrap it in butcher paper and pack it tonight."

Mattson removed the coonskin from the board and they left the barn and turned toward the house.

*   *   *

Mr. Mattson stated that Sunday would be a day with the family, doing whatever the Tylers chose to do. The day dawned with a silent snowfall, falling straight without any breeze, adding a new clean coating to the landscape. By daylight, about an inch of new powder covered the yard, adding a challenge to the walk to the barn. As the boys headed out to do their chores, the men brought in several loads a wood from the stacks in the wood yard, to be sure to have plenty for several days. Extra was stacked on the porch, outside the kitchen door, for easy access in the course of the next few days. The snowfall gave every appearance of another several days event. But the rate of accumulation slowed as the morning advanced and it was decided to attend church and stay for the social gathering, pending a change in the weather. The weather held and the streets ran heavy with foot traffic as the residents gathered for services at the various churches scattered through the community. Besides the Methodist church on Jeffers, there were a Catholic church, a Presbyterian church, and a Baptist church in the residential community on the north side of town. The afternoon was spent in the comfort of the parlor. The boys had their dominoes game and talked Mattson into getting down on the floor with them and joining in the game. The parents managed a running conversation with those on the floor between periods of quiet when they read their books at hand or broke to their own conversations and thoughts about what they might do for the new year. They talked about the Tompkins family's forthcoming visit, only two weeks away. It was still early afternoon when Mrs. Tyler thought about what to prepare for dinner.

"Adam, didn't you say the venison had cured so that we can cut a roast from it?"

He looked up from the game. "It looks ready to me."

"Why don't you boys and Walt see if you can cut out a roast for today? There's a clever as well as a butchering knife on the butcher block counter out there. You can take a wash pan out, cut out a roast portion, and bring it back for me to roast for tonight. If I put it on now, it'll have a good three hours to cook."

The boys set aside their game and went with Mr. Mattson to bring back a piece of venison for the evening meal.

\*   \*   \*

Following a dinner of venison, cooked limas, baked potato, and biscuits, the family spent the evening in the parlor until the clock struck the hour of nine and all began to make ready to retire for the night.

Outside, the snow continued to fall in an imperceptible dusting, adding little accumulation by the end of the day and going into the night. That night, 1882 slipped quietly into 1883.

\*   \*   \*

As the new year dawned, the snowfall continued. Overnight, about three inches of new snow had accumulated. The lack of any significant winds resulted in little or no drifting. The boys trudged back to the house from their morning chores, stamped the snow from their feet on the porch, and entered the kitchen. Hanging their coats and hats on the wall pegs, they kicked off their boots, and slipped into their slippers and moccasins. Michael had decided to accept the use of an old pair of Adam's boots in order to save his moccasins from the constant dampness of the snow.

"It's really cold out," Adam observed as he took his seat at the table.

"The snow keeps coming down," Michael added, "but it's not getting real deep real fast." He took his seat and reached for the hot chocolate. "Maybe we'll be lucky and it won't close the railroad or the town."

Mrs. Tyler brought fresh deep fat fried donuts to the table.

"These are the best, Janet," Mr. Mattson complimented. "Horace makes fantastic donuts at the company camp, just not quite like yours."

"My mother passed this recipe down and I've been very careful not to make any changes." She went back to the range to plate the scrambled eggs, fried potatoes, and bacon.

Breakfast was placed on the table and all gathered around to enjoy it.

"I think we're gonna be stuck in the house," Mr. Tyler announced. "It's a good day to spend with Walt. Maybe he'll share a story or two about life in the west."

There was a knock at the door.

"I'll get it," Adam jumped up from his seat and rushed to the door. A blast of cold air swooshed down the hall and was gone as he opened and closed the door. "Jarrett, come in." The teen entered and the door was quickly closed. "What brings you here?"

"Come on to the kitchen, Jarrett," Mrs. Tyler called. "Get warm and sit down with us for something to eat, or at least some hot chocolate. Michael, get him a cup."

Michael reached a cup down from the cabinet, passed it to his mother, and she placed it on the table near the teen. Jarrett pulled up a side chair, hung his coat and hat on the back, and sat down.

"Thanks." He took the cup in his hands and held it for a moment for his hands to enjoy the warmth, then took a sip. "This morning my pa received this telegram for you folks." He handed the paper to Mr. Tyler.

As the man read the wire a look of astonishment crept across his face.

"I find this so incredibly hard to believe! Jarrett," he turned to the teen, "was there one for Jay as well?"

"Yes, he'll meet you all at the station."

"What's this all about?" Mrs. Tyler asked.

"There's a holiday special train coming out from Arlee. It's the private train of Mr. Philemon J. Marlow, the President of the railroad. He wants to meet us all. Hank sent the telegram. He says that Mr. Marlow saw the story in the paper and when he found out that Mattson is leaving tomorrow, he ordered up his train to come out today."

"When does it arrive?" Michael asked.

"Expect to be here around ten this morning."

"Well I'll be!" Mr. Mattson exclaimed. "I never expected anybody of any importance to want to meet me!"

"It's still early," Mr. Tyler observed. "So take your time and enjoy breakfast. You, too, Jarrett."

Mrs. Tyler brought an extra place setting to the table and the youth helped himself to breakfast as Adam passed him the platters.

The hour slipped away. Jarrett ate his fill and excused himself to return to the station and help clean up for the train's arrival. The family finished breakfast, cleared the table, washed up and changed into their Sunday best and prepared for an early start to the station.

"I wonder why he's coming," Adam thought out loud as he bundled up for the cold.

"I hope he's a nicer man than the last railroad boss I met at Savage. He tried to kill me."

"What!" Adam exclaimed.

"I'll tell you another time."

The five headed down the hall toward the front door and left the house for the walk to the station.

*   *   *

Jay, Scott, and Dave were gathered on the station platform, waiting with the Tyler family for the train to arrive.

"Michael, ya wanna check to be sure the switches are set for the train to pull directly into the station?"

"Sure, Jay."

The boy took off at a slow run to check the switches to direct the train from the main onto the station track. He set them both then hurried back. A whistle screamed in the distance to announce the train. Soon its smoke became visible above the trees. Two columns of smoke signaled a double header train.

"I wonder why two engines," Scott thought aloud.

Momentarily the lead engine came into view and Scott knew the answer. "Dalton", Number fifteen lead the way with its gigantic wedge snow plow, clearing the track all the way from Arlee. Snow caked the plow blade and covered the boiler and part of the engine's cab. The loud syncopation of the two chuffing engines filled the air with its noise, accompanied by the screech of brakes and the hissing of releasing steam as the engines slowed and brought the train to a stop. The consist included a box car, combine coach, the president's car, and a caboose. The conductor and trainmen quickly set the stools at the bottom of the steps and waited for the occupants to step out. The first off the train were track crew from the coach car. They headed for the station where Mr. Coates would have coffee for them. All watched in anticipation for Mr. Marlow to exit his car. Movement was observed through the windows. Finally the president came out with his private secretary.

Dressed in a brown, three-piece suit with white shirt and bow tie, black boots under his pant legs, and a brown Stetson hat, the man appeared impressively important, even if he was a bit heavy around the middle. His height, just under six feet, made him look less heavy. His secretary wore a derby hat and green plaid two-piece suite. They were both quite impressive looking, adding a dark bushy mustache for the president and a clean-shaven assistant with round wire-rimmed glasses.

As he stepped down from his car, the president addressed the engineer. "Jay Miller, I understand from the news article that you have something to do with this boy's story." He advanced to shake the engineer's hand. "And I see, too, that there is a Mr. Mattson here from the frontier." He greeted Mattson as well. "I found your story in the paper most fascinating and really want to learn more about Michael and you all. Would you all come aboard and gather in my sitting room." He extended a hand in the direction of the back platform steps.

"It would be an honor," Jay responded.

"This way, Folks," the secretary indicated.

All followed Mr. Marlow to the back platform of the car, up the steps, and into a warm and plush sitting area at the back end of the car. A fire crackled warmly in a fireplace located in the center of the wall opposite the door to the platform. The room was furnished with an assortment of pillowed sofas and arm chairs. There were plenty of seats for everyone. As the family and the engine crew filed in, each found a seat and stood by it.

Mr. Marlow stood by a velvet gentleman's chair near the fireplace. "If you are warm, feel free to take your coats off and put them wherever it's convenient. I want you to be comfortable, no formalities." He sat down. "I read Michael's story in the paper last week and wanted to meet you all to see if there is anything I can do to help." He paused as his guests peeled out of their coats, dropping them across the backs of their chairs, and took a seat. "One of my agents at the station mentioned that you had visited the Johnston family this weekend, so I stopped to see Hank on Saturday afternoon. He informed me that Mr. Mattson is returning to Montana Territory tomorrow, so I knew I had no choice but to come out today."

As the president was speaking, there was movement outside and the train shook as an engine coupled to the back.

"Are we moving?" Adam asked.

"No, Adam. My crews are pulling the "Dalton" and its support cars and caboose and getting them together to return to Arlee. We needed them to get here. Now they'll go back and do some finishing cleaning along the way. They have more work to open the main line this afternoon." The man sat forward and leaned his arms across his knees.

There was a moment of interruption as the caboose was separated from the back of the president's car and taken to the main line to be connected to Number fifteen and its train. The train was turned on the wye behind the station and the engine serviced in the yard. Fifteen minutes later the "Dalton" sounded its whistle as it left to return to Arlee. In the meantime, Mr. Marlow continued.

Turning to the boy, "Michael, are you getting along okay out here?"

"Yes, Sir." Michael sat up straighter in his chair. He was self-conscious of the suit and the discomfort of the closed collar and its tightness around his neck. "My second family has been really good to me and I've learned a lot." He looked toward his mother. "Ma got me in school shortly after I got here and I'm doin okay." He looked again toward the president. "A friend of mine, Scot Robinson was here about two years ago. Jay helped him back then. When I needed a new home, he contacted Jay to see if he could help me, too."

"Are you happy here?"

"I'm okay. But I miss my home, always."

"I understand, Michael. I sense folks here accept that and are doing all they can for you."

"Yes, Sir. They surely are."

"Mr. Mattson," he turned to the frontiersman. "I understand that you are a major part of Michael's life on the frontier. Can you tell me more?"

"Yes, Sir." He glanced toward the boy as he spoke. "I work for Keith Summers, the owner of the Summers Freight Company. I came here to bring gifts and information from Michael's Sioux parents and to see for them that he is doing okay." Looking back toward their host, he continued. "His parents have had serious doubts that they made the right decision to send him back into the world of his birth, even though they firmly believe that it was the right thing to do." Looking back at Michael he concluded. "I can tell them that he is going to be okay." He cracked a smile. Michael smiled back.

Marlow paused as he thought a moment on what had just been shared. He sat back in his chair and subconsciously brushed his mustache to either side, then turned to his engineer.

"Jay," Mr. Marlow continued. "You have been the solution for these two boys' needs. I commend you."

"Thanks." He turned his attention from gazing about the luxury of the car to its owner. "I saw a boy, lonely and lost, when Scot came here two years ago. Our stationmaster, Robert Coates, told me he had come to meet his uncle, but there was no uncle." He stopped to scratch his beard. "I live at the hotel and worked it out with the owner, Clara Stauffer, for Scot to stay with me while we tried to locate his uncle. He did odd jobs for her to earn his keep. I was finally able to track down his uncle who then took him west to find his father." He looked toward Michael. "Now Scot has asked me if I could help Michael." Glancing toward the Tyler family, he continued, "Because the Tylers had taken in Teddy Tompkins and his son, Brett, while the father was getting started with the logging company, I asked if they might want to help Michael. I told them as much of the boy's story as I had learned from Scot and they immediately said yes." He returned his attention to Mr. Marlow. "He now has a second family, but we all know he has another name and another life that will always be dear to him."

The president turned toward the boy. "You are quite the story, Michael. And it's obvious there are many here who care about you very deeply."

"I know, Sir. And I'm very grateful."

Looking toward Mr. Mattson, the man continued. "I understand from Hank that there's to be some sort of reunion in the spring?" Marlow asked.

"Yes, Sir," Mattson explained. "Mr. Summers is going to try to get everyone together at his old trading fort as spring sets in. He already has one family that Michael knows, Trapper Murray Kaymond and his son Lawrence, living at the fort." He shifted his weight to sit back into the cushion of the chair. "He invited them to spend the trapping season there and set their trap lines on his property. Michael's Sioux family is planning to come down from Canada where they currently live in safety away from the U.S. government." Mattson looked to Mr. Tyler. "And the Tyler family has agreed that they will all go this spring when final arrangements have been made."

"What of Jay's crew?"

"They're not a part of Michael's other life and we haven't given it any thought." Mr. Mattson looked toward the engine crew. "Would you want to go if it could be worked out?"

"We sure would," Dan spoke out and the others nodded as they looked from Mattson to Marlow.

"Charles," he turned to his secretary. "Be ready to take some notes as we explore some ideas." The man turned his attention to Michael. "You have a very remarkable story. I am particularly impressed with your connection to my railroad. I know Jay." He glanced a quick smile toward the engineer as he sat up and settled back into his chair. "He's not just anybody. He's very devoted to the people in his life." He shook is head lightly up and down, watching Jay as he spoke. "I happen to know that some years back when Brett Tompkins first came to spend the summer with his father, that Jay taught him how to run a locomotive. It's no secret." Marlow looked back toward Michael. "The story is in an old edition of *The Herald* how that boy, having been taught by Jay, was key to saving lives and a whole train during a forest fire that summer. I dare say he taught Scot when he was here and has taught you as well. Since you will probably grow up and stay here, for a while anyway, I expect you'll be looking for a job with the railroad. Maybe even an engineer's job."

"Wow! That's the best job in the world!" the boy exclaimed.

Marlow smiled at the boy's enthusiasm.

"You've done well, Jay." He looked around at the gathering. "We've been here a while, you folks thirsty?"

"We don't want you to go to any bother," Mr. Tyler remarked.

"No trouble at all. Charles," he looked toward his secretary," go out to the icebox in the galley and bring everyone a sarsaparilla."

The man stood up, with his finger he pushed his glasses back up on his nose, and left to do as asked.

"Here's the crazy part of what I've come up with." He looked from face to face, watching for reactions as he spoke. "I have a friend in Pullman, Illinois, who makes train cars. They're not just any car. His name is George Pullman and he makes Pullman Palace Cars. Ever hear of them?"

"I saw one on one of the trains I was on out of Chicago," Mr. Mattson volunteered. "They're special cars with built in beds so you can sleep on the train over night."

"Yes." He watched the engine crew. "Well we've ordered a pair for the Virginia and Truckee. They're due in next month."

Charles arrived with the beverages and passed them around. He had already removed the lids. Each enjoyed his drink as he began with an exploratory sip.

"This is really different," Adam remarked. "I never had anything like this before. It's really good." He held the bottle in one hand as he continued to follow the conversation.

"Thought you would enjoy them," Marlow commented. Sitting forward in his chair once more, he continued. "It seems we might be able to do something special for your endeavor. If you agree, I can assign a temporary crew to take over for your crew, Jay, and make special arrangements so you can go, too."

"Thank you Mr. Marlow." He set his bottle on the floor beside his foot and leaned both elbows on his knees.

"Here's the catch. You're going to have to work your way."

"How?" He sat back with renewed interest as he once again, picked up his bottle.

"Do you trust the "King" to go west and back?"

"What!?" He took a sip from the bottle.

"How about we put together a special train and you take these folks to Savage." The man gestured toward the gathering. "After all, there are railroad connections all the way." His voice picked up on the excitement he began to feel for his own idea. "We can set up for sidings to lay over along the way and I'm sure Mr. Summers has a siding for his trading company."

"Can I take my pony?" the boy asked.

"Of course, Michael. Your train can have a baggage car for supplies and horse stalls, a Pullman Palace Car for sleeping while you lay over, our parlor car for seating and dining during the day, and a caboose for the crew. The palace car even has a lavatory room at each end."

""That's a very different sort of train," Jay observed. "That's a lot of train for just the family and my crew, though I realize there is more crew than just the three of us."

"The parlor car will have my steward who will handle the kitchen duties and the maintaining of the Palace Car. You will have to coordinate with him on supplies, and see to his needs."

There was a period of extended quiet as some picked up their drinks and nursed their contents.

"Why would you do this," Jay asked looking at his superior.

Mr. Marlow leaned his head back and stared momentarily at the ceiling of his car. Then he sat up and looked his engineer in the eye. "Call me crazy. Because I can? And because I find myself caring about this boy's story and the turn of events life has thrown at him. And, because I see this group of friends rallying around him to create a cocoon of support."

For a moment, no one spoke. Some continued to nurse their drinks. The boys finished theirs and offered the empties to Charles with 'thanks'. He nodded in return and placed their bottles on the tray at his feet. His glasses slid forward as he bent down and he slid them back.

"Charles," Marlow stood up. "Can you arrange some notes for putting this into motion while I take my guests on a tour of my car."

"Certainly." The secretary moved to a desk in the back corner of the room to compose his notes based on the previous conversation, while everyone stood and stretched.

"You folks come with me down this side hall and I'll show you the layout of my car."

All began to follow, the boys in the lead. As they passed the tray en route behind the boys, they left their empty bottles with the two already there.

*   *   *

Walt Mattson entered the kitchen with the boys close behind. The chores had been done early and breakfast had just been placed on the table, so all hung up their coats and hats and settled to the table. The parlor clock struck the three-quarter hour before six.

"I can't believe it's already time for you to go," Michael lamented. "I know you haf ta, but wish you didn't."

"I know, Michael. It has been a great month and I am so glad I was able ta make this trip." He paused to take a drink from his coffee and wash down the fried potatoes.

"You are most welcome to come back any time," Mr. Tyler invited. "Bring any who might be able to come with you."

"Thanks, Bill."

"Ya have my letters?" the boy asked.

"Sure do." He patted the front of his shirt. "And I'm wearing your knife as well. I'll be sure to share your gift with Prairie Flower when I next get there to deliver your letter." He looked from the boy to his plate and continued with his breakfast.

Finishing off a forkful of egg the boy followed up, "Once she knows you have it, she might make me another sheath. You can tell here about the knife Mr. Summers sent and she can get the sheath from him."

"I will."

"I'll miss you," Adam admitted. "I'm sure glad we'll get to see you again in the spring."

"I find it so hard to believe that Mr. Marlow is providing a train for the journey!" Mrs. Tyler exclaimed.

"Like he said," Adam added, "he can."

"But I really don't know why he would," Mattson wondered. "Michael's story must have had some affect on him."

There followed a period of quiet while all concentrated on their breakfasts.

The world outside the windows was a soft moonscape as the quarter moon drifted toward the western horizon and a thin streak of light brightened in the east. Snowfall had stopped the previous day. The morning promised to be bright and crispy cold. Walt Mattson's duffle bag stood waiting by the front door. Departure time drew near. The parlor clock struck the half hour past six.

"It's almost time to go," Mrs. Tyler observed. "Are you sure you have everything, Walt? Michael, go check the room."

Michael pushed out his chair and hurried toward the hall and the stairway to the bedroom. His footsteps sounded on the ceiling above the dining room as he rushed to the bedroom, paused to look around, dashed in and out of the room, then headed back down the stairs. He reentered the kitchen carrying a red blanket.

"You forgot yer blanket."

"Isn't that the one you wore to school?" Mattson studied it from where he sat.

"Yes, Sir."

"It's yours to keep. That's my gift to you to remember me and our times together by."

"Oh."

"What a treasure," Mrs. Tyler shared.

Mr. Tyler stood and directed, "It's nearly time to leave for the station. There's just enough left to clean up from breakfast."

All pitched in to move dishes and leftovers to the countertop near the sink. Mrs. Tyler took some butcher's paper and wrapped up the leftover sausages from breakfast. She took out an empty flour sack and stuffed it within. Next she wrapped up supplies of biscuits and cookies to add to the sack, then found a small lunch jug to fill with coffee.

"Walt, take this with you to eat on the train as you travel."

"What about the coffee jug?"

"I'll get another at the mercantile."

It was time. All bundled up warmly for the walk to the train station. As the family turned toward the front door, Michael rushed to the frontiersman and wrapped his arms around his waist. Mattson automatically smothered the boy in a tight and emotional rendezvous bear hug. The two stood there for a brief eternity, tears flowing freely from each one as the finality of separation grew near.

"I love you," the boy cried. "I hate this having to leave you!" He sobbed uncontrollably. "I want so much to go home. But I can't!"

"I know," the man soothed. "It won't be too long and we'll be together again, all of us."

Adam wiped his eyes with his coat sleeve and started to the door. His parents followed. A cold blast of air shot down the hall as the three left the house. The man and the boy stood alone a moment longer. Michael pushed apart and wiped his eyes. The man put his arm across the boy's shoulder, picked up his duffle bag, and the two started down the hall.

*   *   *

The train stood noisily at the station, the front of the engine coupled to the front of the train, set to run in reverse to Day's End. Escaping steam hissed from the cylinder heads as boiling steam rumbled in the engine's belly and smoke drifted from the stack. Jay stood on the station platform, talking to Dan Seegers, at the bottom of the steps to the coach platform. He turned as the Tyler family approached the station and watched as Michael and Walt entered the building to get Walt's train ticket to Truckee. The engineer approached the family.

"Mornin', Bill, Janet, Adam. It's a hard day."

"We know," Janet replied. I wish it weren't so, but know that's not to be."

"We have a very hurting boy, Jay," Mr. Tyler added, "and there's nothing that will take away the pain."

"I'd arrange for you all to go with us to Arlee and even on to Truckee, but I know fer sure that it would only make it that much harder, even unbearable."

"Thanks," the couple acknowledged. "We appreciate the thought," Mr. Tyler added. "And we know you are so right," his wife concluded.

Janet glanced toward the station building then turned back to Jay. "We're gonna wait here until you've gone by from Day's End, walk together to work with Adam and his pa, then I'll drop Michael off at school on this first day of school for the new year, so he can play with his classmates and take his mind off his pain. The boys are supposed to check the trap line after school. Hopefully that will keep him busy until Adam gets home from work and it's time for chores." She paused to glance toward the station again. But the line of people coming out with their tickets suggested it might be a few more minutes. "I think he'll be okay for the evening. I worry about tonight when he goes to bed and his room will seem so empty."

The two emerged from the station and walked toward the family.

"Walt," Jay extended his hand, "it has been an honor to meet you and get to know you." They shook hands, "We all know you will be missed. I am so grateful we have the springtime journey to look forward to. Time for me to go back to work." He turned and walked back to the locomotive. At the top of the steps to the cab, he paused to wave. All returned his farewell.

Mattson bid farewell to the family with a handshake. He hugged Michael tightly, then stepped back and picked up his duffle bag from where he had left it on the platform beside Adam.

Placing his hand on the boy's shoulder, he asked, "Please stay with the family. This is awfully hard on me, too. I'll sit by a window and wave as we fly by from Day's End."

The boy nodded his acknowledgement. It hurt too much to talk. His mother put an arm around his shoulder and pulled him to her side with an affectionate hug. He leaned his head against her body as he watched his last connection to home walk away toward the train. Walt mounted the steps, waved and the family waved back, and disappeared into the car.

# SICKNESS

The Johnstons visited the second weekend of the new year. They arrived on the Saturday morning train and returned home on the Sunday evening train. Hank and Nancy had the spare room and Jason stayed in Michael's room. All enjoyed a leisurely weekend on the farm. The boys played outside in the snow making a snowman and throwing snowballs at each other. After lunch, Teddy and Miles joined them. They took a walk in the meadow, knee-deep in the snow. The boys showed Jason where their trap line had been as they struggled through the deep snow, explaining that they had just pulled the traps the previous Saturday. The Johnstons met Teddy and Miles when all came into the house for warmth and snack. It was a short meeting as the boys returned to the outdoors so all five could enjoy a snowball fight which ranged around the buildings and the barnyard. The adults spent the day in the house, visiting, the women in the kitchen mostly and the men in the living room. Dinner included a venison stew and the story of the hunt from Michael and Adam.

Jason had read the newspaper article. The three retreated to the bedrooms following Teddy and Miles' departure for home. After a stop in Adam's room to receive a private presentation of his collection, the boys retired to Michael's room where Jason asked questions stemming from what he had read and Michael shared answers and his personal possessions. Adam enjoyed listening to the answers to a story he never tired of hearing.

Sunday included church and a chance to catch up with Teddy and Miles during the social hour.

Winter advanced toward February. A week after their visitor had departed on the train, Jarrett delivered a telegram announcing that trader Mattson had arrived safely back in Savage. He would write later after all Michael's letters had been delivered. Meanwhile, the heavier snows of the season brought storms that lasted for days with strong winds, greater accumulations, and deep drifts. Life slowed down. Shoveled pathways became steep white canyons. Logging crews became track-cleaning crews. Industries shut down for extended days on end for lack of materials. Train service was cut off for days at a time. When a train could get through, it was usually a double-header mixed freight with the coach cars and a caboose attached to the back, with priority shipments of food and household goods to keep the towns along the branch alive until the heavy snow season passed. School was open many days when industry was closed, because the kids could walk and it kept them busy with their lessons, though excused when family needs arose.

On the first Saturday of the new year, Teddy decided that the winter snow was getting too deep to keep up the trap line. Snow depth along the creek bed had risen to a foot, more or less with deeper drifts. The boys trudged the line with empty sacks to search out the twenty traps and collect them for the season. They carried sticks to set each off as it was found. Once tripped, the chain that secured it was unhooked from the stake, which was frozen in the ground, and the trap collected in the bag. Adam went along to help. Yet even with the four of them, it took most of the morning and early afternoon. By the time they trudged through the foot-deep snow and dug around the area to find a trap, then released it and stowed it in the sack, nearly a quarter hour was gone. It was early afternoon before all twenty had been found and collected.

Teddy and Miles stayed for a hot soup and sandwich lunch followed by challenge games of checkers with breaks for hot chocolate and cookies. Michael's friends left as their dinner times drew near. The day had been cloudy and dismal, and afternoon light dimmed early. Teddy and Miles picked up the bags of traps from the back porch and headed off towards home.

During the following week, the logging crews managed to load one full train of ten cars for shipping to the saw mill. But, because temperatures lingered in the single digits for several days, the points on the track switches froze and in took much of Thursday morning for the "Scott" to get up the mountain. The crew had to build a small fire at each switch in order to thaw it out to be operable. Likewise, switches everywhere which had to be used, had to be thawed out first. For the next two weeks, small fires were maintained to keep switches operable.

For Michael, life kept him busy in a quiet sort of routine. Each morning, he and Adam were up in the dark before dawn to travel the narrow white canyon to the barn to do chores. They had to keep the snow shoveled out in front of the barn doors in order to open and close them and access the barn. A canyon path was maintained to the chicken coop and the smoke house. On the Monday following the pulling of the trap line, the boys moved three chords of firewood to the side porch, outside the kitchen and stacked it along the railing. This made it readily available for the house and created a temporary windbreak against the weather. It also meant one less access path to maintain. During most days, Michael attended school. After three months with extra help and effort on his part, the boy had caught up to a point where he took his daily lessons with his classmates. On occasion, Mrs. Miller would have to help with a new grammar concept and Adam would help with unfamiliar concepts in figuring. Afternoons were varied. His first letter was a brief note from Mr. Summers to say 'thanks' for Michael's letter, how much everyone enjoyed the newspaper article, and to let him know that Mattson had left with a delivery to Canada and the boy's people. In winter weather, it would take weeks. Michael wrote a letter back. He also became interested in reading, especially Mark Twain. He borrowed books from his teacher to read each afternoon before Adam got home. After evening chores and dinner, he played checkers or dominoes with Adam while his pa read and his ma worked on knitting or needlepoint projects, and an occasional book. His checker game had become much more challenging as he began to beat Adam on occasion. During the day, while he was at school, Mrs. Tyler worked on creating the deerskin coat. She sent Michael to the mercantile one afternoon for two yards of satin cloth to use for a liner. Each Friday, the boys took an order for groceries and other sundries to pick up at the mercantile on their way home from *The Herald*. School was operating on half days on Fridays and the boy spent his afternoons at work with Adam. Jay continued his Friday afternoon visits by picking Michael up from the newspaper office and walking home with him to the farm. Due to a lack of regular train service to Arlee, he sometimes stayed for dinner and spent the evening.

The third Wednesday of January dawned gray and overcast, yet dry, no snow, and still, no wind. Following chores and breakfast, Adam and his pa left for work. They expected to spend most of the day doing maintenance on buildings and equipment. The flat cars were being rotated through the shop for inspection of brakes and wheel sets and lubrication of journal boxes. The "Scott" was out of service for boiler inspection and annual maintenance of its operating systems. Logging operations were halted and the crews sent home; only a small maintenance crew of those without families maintained the camp and cared for the horses. Michael spent some time in the kitchen reviewing the latest concept in figuring before bundling up and leaving for school. Many of the children in the school were suffering colds and it was just a matter of time for sickness to spread among their classmates. By the end of the day, Michael had picked up a slight cough and began to feel tired.

He announced his return home with a round of heavy coughing as he entered the front door.

"Is that you, Michael?" Mrs. Tyler called from the kitchen.

"Yea, Ma," he responded between coughs.

The boy entered the kitchen and struggled to hang up his outer clothing.

"Ma, I don't feel good." He collapsed onto the nearest chair and grabbed the table edge for support. "I'm so cold."

The woman rushed to his side and instinctively put a hand to his forehead.

"Yer burnin up with fever." She looked at his drawn face. "Yer white as a ghost, too. Put yer head down and rest while I brew some tea."

"But I'm freezing!"

Shivering with cold, the boy lay his arms across the table and rested his head on top, as he continued to heave with coughing and his body trembled with cold. His mother rushed to the stove, put a pot of water over the hottest surface, and added firewood to increase the flames within. While the water began to boil, she went to the cupboard where she kept her tin of tea, took it down to fill the tea strainer, then hung it in the pot. As the pot came to a heavy boil, she moved it to the cooler corner and took down the cannister of sugar. Shortly thereafter, she poured a cup of tea over a spoonful of sugar and placed it on the table in front of the boy.

"It's hot. Sip very slowly." She stood by to help as needed.

Wrapping his hands around the cup for its heavenly warmth, the boy slowly sipped the tea in very small amounts as it burned his tongue. It took a long time to finish the liquid.

"Okay. We're goin' upstairs to yer room and yer goin' ta bed."

There was no resistance. Michael found himself too weak to stand on his own and allowed his mother to support his weight as they moved slowly down the hall and up the staircase to his room. She pulled back the covers on the bed, helped the boy strip to his johns and lie down on his back. After pulling up the bed covers, she went to a blanket chest in the hall and brought in two more blankets.

"Now you stay put under these blankets, even if you get hot and start to sweat." The woman spread the blankets across the boy and pulled them up to his chin. "Sweatin's good when you have a fever. I'm goin' fer Doc Blevins. You stay put."

She left the room and hurried down the stairs. A short time later, the front door banged shut as she left the house. The boy drifted into a half sleep. He could hear the crackle of the fires downstairs but felt only half conscious to the world around him. Time passed. He became aware of voices and shapes hovering over him.

"Michael, can you hear me?" a man asked.

He could only nod his head.

"Did this start suddenly?"

Again, he nodded his head.

"Did you ever have a cold like this before?"

He nodded and shook his head 'no.'

Doc Blevins put his hand to the boy's forehead. "He's burnin up with fever." He stood and turned to the woman. "You give him anything?"

"Hot tea."

"That's a good start, but we have to get this fever down." He turned to the boy. "You sleep. I'll be down stairs."

Michael nodded and the two left his room to settle at the kitchen table.

"Coffee?"

"Please."

Janet brought coffee for them both as the doctor explained. "We have a situation here that never occurred to me, but it's something I'm aware of." He sipped his coffee. "Michael may be a white boy living in a white community, but his body has the health of an Indian boy."

"What do you mean?"

"He has only had diseases common to his native people. He never had a cold like we're used to. His body's having a hard time handling it. We're lucky it's a cold."

"How so?"

"The measles and chicken pocks haven't shown up yet this school year. He's probably had a cold of sorts in the past, but not been exposed to these diseases yet. They will kill him." He looked from the coffee in his hand to the woman. "When we win this battle, and I'm sure we will, he cannot return to school until spring and warm weather are fully here."

"Ma!" There was a loud thump on the ceiling.

The two rushed to the bedroom. "We're coming, Son!"

They burst through the doorway to find the boy sprawled on the floor. "I was so hot!"

His mother pulled back the covers as the doctor carefully lifted him from the floor and lay him back on the bed. His body was soaking wet with sweat as she lay the covers back over him.

"The sweating is good, Michael," Doc Blevins assured. "It will help to break your fever. But we can't wait long. We have to get your fever down."

"Sassafras," the boy whispered. "My mother used to make sassafras tea."

"Do you have any sassafras trees on the property?" Blevins asked.

"I don't know. Certainly not near the house." She looked longingly at her son. "I have to ask Adam and his pa soon's they get home."

"We'll sit here with you for a while," the doctor said. "You try to go to sleep."

The boy starred at the ceiling with unfocused eyes.

"Is he…"

"No. He'll blink shortly, then probably fall asleep."

Momentarily, Michael closed his eyes, heaved a heavy sigh, coughed once, then settled to heavy breathing.

The two sat, Blevins on the side chair and Tyler on the side of the bed. They watched the labored breathing of the boy as they sat in silence.

The front door opened to a blast of cold air and the stomping of feet.

"Ma?"

"In Michael's room!"

"What's wrong?" Mr. Tyler called as the two rushed up the stairs. They froze with a look of horror as they stared at the helpless form lying unresponsive on the bed.

Michael burst into a fit of coughing, shaking his whole body, but not awakening him.

"What happened?" Adam asked, fear in his voice.

"He's collapsed with a cold," Doc Blevins answered. "But for him, it's a crisis. He has a white man's disease in an Indian boy's body."

"Oh, my God!" Adam responded.

"What can we do?" Mr. Tyler asked.

"Do we have any sassafras trees on the property?" his wife asked.

"Along the meadow creekside," Adam answered.

"Quickly get some roots," the doctor instructed. "We need to brew some tea."

"I'll be back as soon as I can." Adam left the room and hurried down the steps. The back door slammed shut behind him.

"Why sassafras?" Mr. Tyler asked.

"He said his mother made it when he was sick," the woman explained. "I'm going down to heat some water."

Doc Blevins spoke up. "We have to get his fever down." He looked from the boy to the father. "We're lucky. He's probably had colds before, but not this type. His body has some experience to fight back. But I told your wife, he can't return to school until warm weather returns. There are other sicknesses these kids get in the winter months that will kill him." He stood. "We'll try the sassafras tea and see if there's any improvement. If not, we get drastic."

"How?"

"Pack him in buckets of snow. That we have plenty of."

The two turned to the door.

"Is it okay to leave him?"

"For now, he's sleeping."

Gathering in the kitchen, the adults sat with their coffee while they waited for Adam to return and the water to heat. Steam boiled from the pot and Mrs. Tyler got up to move it to the side. The door opened and the teen entered with a bucket of sweet-smelling sassafras roots.

"You have no idea what it took to get through the snow and dig these." After hanging up his outer garments, he dumped the contents into the sink and pumped some water to wash off the roots.

"Take a knife and cut them into little pieces," his mother instructed. "Then dump them into the pot."

After the water returned to a boil, the sweet smell of tea began to drift on the air. The woman dumped a quarter cup of sugar in the pot and stirred. She then strained the contents into a cooking pan, dumped the root pieces in the sink, and returned the tea to the pot.

Grabbing a cup she ordered, "Let's go."

The other three followed as she led the way up the stairs to the bedroom.

"Prop him up in bed," the woman instructed. "Let's see if we can do this."

The men eased Michael into a sitting position as Mrs. Tyler poured a cup of tea and handed the pot to her son. The boy opened his eyes to see what was going on and accepted the cup with the help of his ma and tentatively tried to drink. At first it ran down his chin until he became more conscious and could control his drinking. He gingerly sipped the hot liquid.

As the men continued to support him and he continued to drink a second cup, it was obvious he was still dripping wet with sweat and the bed was soaked. The doctor put a hand to his forehead.

"There's no change. I'll stay with Michael. Can you two get some buckets of snow?"

The boy and his pa hurried down stairs. They each took a bucket from the kitchen closet and went out the side door to the yard beside the porch. They took turns with the shovel on the back porch and quickly filled both buckets. Dropping the shovel beside the door, they hurried back in to the bedroom.

"What next?" Adam asked.

"Pull off the covers and pack him in snow." The doctor stepped back with the pot of tea and took the cup from Mrs. Tyler as she ripped the bedcovers from the bed.

"What are ya doin'?" the dazed boy asked.

"We have ta cool ya down," his pa explained.

The father and son took opposite sides of the bed and poured the snow alongside the boy's body.

"Get another," the doctor ordered.

The two rushed down the stairs to comply.

"It's cold!" Michael shouted.

"Good," Blevins replied. "As soon as yer fever breaks, we'll drag you out of the snow and get you warmed up."

A second dose of snow was dumped across the half naked body as the boy went into spasms of coughing. The doctor put his hand on the boy's forehead.

"No change yet."

All sat quietly and waited. The boy continued to shiver and shake under the packed snow. Several times over the next hour, the doctor checked for temperature. Several times he solemnly shook his head. Finally, there was a smile on the doctor's face.

"It's working!" he announced. "Get a dry blanket for him." The woman retrieved a dry quilt from the blanket chest. "When I tell you, take him off the bed, strip off his wet johns, and wrap him snuggly in the quilt. Then carry him downstairs to the kitchen by the range. And, Janet, bring the tea."

"Please, I'm so cold." Again he shook with coughing.

Blevins put his hand on the boy's head. "Not just yet, Son. I know yer cold. Please wait with us."

Minutes passed as the doctor monitored the temperature and waited for it to drop. He felt the boy's chest. "He's still warm."

Finally the doctor felt the heat release itself from the boy's body and nodded his head to proceed. Mr. Tyler lifted his son from the dripping wet bed and placed him on the quilt in his mother's arms. As Adam reached for the saturated johns, she folded the quilt around the boy, supporting him on his feet. Her husband took him up in his arms and carried him to the kitchen. The others followed.

"Once Michael's settled in the kitchen, will you and yer pa please tend to his room?" the woman asked.

"Sure, Ma."

"Throw everything on the side porch, including his mattress, and mop up the room," she instructed. "Take the mattress from the spare room and make up his bed fresh with clean bedding from the blanket chest in the hall."

"We have this," her husband replied.

The two left. A short time later, they struggled down the stairs with the mattress, piled with all the wet bedding and clothes, and remnants of snow. Doc Blevins opened the door for them. Returning to the bedroom with the mop, they grabbed some clean towels from the linen closet and proceeded to mop up the room.

The woman had brought her wooden rocker into the kitchen for Michael to sit in near the heat of the kitchen range. The doctor sat beside him and monitored his temperature to make sure it didn't spike again. The boy continued to have fits of coughing, but far less violent than earlier in the afternoon.

The two returned from upstairs with the snow buckets, wet towels and mop. "Done," Adam announced as they deposited all on the side porch and closed the door for the night. All gathered for hot coffee and chocolate. For the boy, it was sassafras tea.

"The tin of cookies is on the side board," Mrs. Tyler announced. The parlor clock struck the hour. It was nine in the evening. "I'll fix dinner if you want," she offered. "But I'm okay waiting until breakfast and to getting everyone to bed."

"I think the patient is out of the woods," Doc announced. "If it's okay with you folks, I'll head fer home." He stood to reach for his coat and hat. "Don't hesitate to send Adam if anything changes. I'll be back in the morning."

"Breakfast?" the woman asked.

"Breakfast," he confirmed. "'Night." He wrapped his scarf around his neck, pulled on his gloves, and was gone as a sudden draft of cold air announced his departure.

Bill Tyler turned to the boy. "If yer ready, I'll carry you to your room and you can find a clean pair of johns and crawl into bed. I'll spread this quilt on yer bed fer extra warmth. In case ya still feel cold." He put a hand to the boy's head to be sure he hadn't any more fever.

"Sure, Pa. I'm ready."

The boy stood and his pa scooped him into his arms and left the room. As the two left the room, Adam turned to his mother.

"What now?"

"We'll leave this all for morning," his mother stated. "Good night, Son."

"Night, Ma."

They each took a lamp and left the room.

*    *    *

Doc Blevins returned to the house early the following day, in time for breakfast. Before he even took off his coat, he asked to check on Michael.

"He's in his room and wide awake," his mother reported.

"I'll be right back." The doctor hurried up the steps to the bedroom. "Mornin, Michael."

"Hi, Doc," the boy grinned. "Thanks, for takin' care of me yesterday. When can I get out of bed? And when can I go back to school?"

The doctor pulled up a chair beside the boy's bed.

"Michael," he looked the boy in the eyes, "you can get up whenever you feel like it."

"Now? fer breakfast? I'm starved."

"Yes. We can go down to breakfast together. But, no, you can't go back to school."

"Why?" He threw off his covers, sat up, and reached for his clothes.

"We have a medical problem. You have never grown up around kids with common childhood sicknesses. Your body has no immunities."

"So?" He stood to pull on his shirt and pull up his pants.

"So. Their sicknesses, which they will get over, will kill you."

The boy dropped suddenly onto the side of his bed. "What!?"

"When you grow up in a community, your body gets used to the illnesses that are common to that community, especially during your childhood. Yet even at that, there are many children who die from the same diseases others recover from. But if you don't grow up in that community, your body never gets those experiences that make it able to survive. And those same diseases will kill that body. Your body had never been exposed to the diseases these kids will get. It can't survive. Until the weather warms up in spring, you need to protect yourself and stay home. We'll talk more downstairs. Your parents already know this and we'll have to work out some changes."

The boy stood up, put his feet in his moccasins, and started toward the door. Blevins met him there and they left for the kitchen.

The doctor hung his outer garments on the sidewall pegs and settled to the empty seat at the table. "Smells good, Janet."

"Thanks. It's good to see our boy up and feeling better."

"He knows we have some changes to work out," Blevins shared. "We can do that after breakfast."

Breakfast was eaten in quiet as the platters were passed around the table. After all had their fill, the table was cleared and a pot each of coffee and hot chocolate were brought to the table along with a platter of freshly made, and still warm, heavy donuts.

All helped themselves and the doctor began. "Michael's lack of immunity is very serious and we will have to take serious actions to protect him. I will see his teacher this morning and explain the situation to the class. You'll need to put a table on the front porch for whichever classmate brings his assignments each day and picks up his work from the day before. Janet, you and Adam will most likely become his teachers to help him with his work each day. Any of his friends who want to visit will have to be darn sure he's not sick and no one in the class has been sick for that friend to catch anything. If we're really lucky, these precautions will make it possible to make it to the warm days of spring when the danger will pass." He paused to enjoy his coffee and donut.

"What happens if we get sick?" Mr. Tyler asked.

""If it's no more than a cold, I think we're safe. This incident has probably given Michael stronger protection against colds."

"I sure didn't see this comin'," Mrs. Tyler commented as she stood to put the leftovers away from breakfast. "Wait 'til we see Jay this Friday."

"If I see him before you," Blevins offered, "I'll be sure to tell him he needs to talk to you, that Michael was sick this week." He stood to get his coat and hat. "Time to head for my office, then go over to the school."

Pulling on his coat and hat, he started to the door. "Thanks, for breakfast folks," he waved. "And you take care, Michael."

The door closed behind him.

"Time for us to go, too," Mr. Tyler announced.

"Your lunch buckets are on the side board," his wife pointed out.

"See you later, Ma." Adam picked up his lunch. "Checkers this afternoon, Brother." He grinned at Michael.

"Bye, Pa. You, too, Brother," Michael waved. "Yes, checkers."

The two left the kitchen down the hall to the front door. They were gone.

*　　*　　*

Michael and Mrs. Tyler were busy in the kitchen, working on a batch of chocolate chip cookies. There was a knock at the front door.

"I'll get it, Ma."

"No you won't. Remember what Doc Blevins said and stay here in the kitchen. I'll get it." She lay the spatula on the cooling towel and went down the hall.

Michael moved to where he could see the front door.

"Teddy, Miles, good to see you. Won't you come in out of the cold?"

"We brought Michael's assignments," Teddy informed.

"But we don't think we should come in," Miles added. "I have a runny nose and don't want to get Michael sick again."

"Step in enough to close the door. Put his schoolwork on the side table. I appreciate your caution. Just the same, let me get you each some of the cookies we made this afternoon. Wait here."

"Hi, Guys" Michael waved from the kitchen.

"Hi, Michael," they chorused. "We're gonna pick up yer work in the mornin' and bring yer new work tomorrow afternoon," Teddy called down the hall.

"Thanks."

Mrs. Tyler brought a paper bag each with four cookies inside. "Pick his work up tomorrow after school so we have the day to work on it," she said. "You can drop off his new assignments then as well. That way it's only one stop and we have a day to get each assignment done." She handed them their cookies as she spoke.

"Okay."

"Whenever you are totally well, you can come in. Michael will be so happy to have time with you. Thanks for doing this."

"You're welcome," Miles replied.

"Bye, Michael," the two waved.

"Bye. See ya tomorrow."

The boys left as Mrs. Tyler closed the door behind them. She picked up the schoolwork and took it to the kitchen. Looking around, she found a place on the side board near the flour cabinet and placed it there. "We're not doing schoolwork in the evening time." Turning from the books to face the boy, she continued. "Schoolwork is a daytime thing."

"Thanks, Ma. I'm so glad for that." He picked up a warm cookie and nibbled on it from the edges in.

\*    \*    \*

The new routine began. The boy continued to help his brother with chores. After Adam and his pa left for work each day, Michael and his mother worked on his school assignments. Each afternoon, Teddy and Miles picked up his finished work and left the new, and Mrs. Tyler gave each a bag of cookies. After they left, schoolwork was set aside until the following day. During some afternoons Michael read Mark Twain while his ma worked on his new buckskin coat. The two worked on preparing dinner. The boy ran to the cold cellar for whatever produce was needed or to the smokehouse for dinner's meat. Evenings were family time. Checker games were quite the challenge. The boys had become equally good and most games went to the wire. Many ended in a draw with no winner.

Jay stopped that first Friday afternoon and was very concerned when he learned the seriousness of Michael's illness. He was not aware of the danger that existed and offered that Michael could spend a day in Number twenty-one's cab with his crew when his schoolwork might permit. There was a break in schoolwork on Monday of the fourth week of January. Michael was able to spend the day with Jay and his crew, fully outfitted with the coveralls from his first day and his Christmas gifts – bandana, cap, and gloves. The day was spent delivering the freight cars from the previous day, making up the outgoing mixed freight, then double-heading with "Kidd" to run the freight, with passenger station stops, to Arlee and return with the new freight consist to Snow Shoe. For the most part, Michael served as apprentice fireman, working with and learning from Scott.

Teddy and Miles were able to visit early the last week of the month. Neither had any signs of illness and no one was sick in class. But by week's end, a case of measles was reported, though the sick child was kept home. Most of the older children had already had many of the childhood diseases, and while individual cases of chicken pox and others were reported, few others came down with the illnesses and those who did were kept home from school.

For much of the month, the weather continued to dominate life in the community. Finally, the heaviest winter weather began to abate during the fifth partial week of January with sunny days and temperatures in the forties. The snows began to melt as January slipped into February.

*   *   *

In the wee hours of the first Friday of the month, Michael awoke as usual, with Adam standing in the doorway with lamp in hand.

"That time already?" the boy rubbed the sleep from his eyes as he sat up to light the lamp on the side table.

"Yep. See ya downstairs." He turned to go, but stopped suddenly. "Listen."

Michael stopped to listen. "I don't hear anything."

"That's just it. It's silent downstairs. No noise from the kitchen. Somethin's wrong."

The boy dropped the johns he was about to pull on and dashed after his older brother in his nightshirt. Gaining the lower hallway, all was dark. The two rushed to their parents' bedroom. Both were still in bed, sound asleep.

"Ma?" Adam ventured. He approached the bed. Michael hung back in the doorway.

"Huh?" she responded drowsily.

"Are you okay?"

"Go away. Let me sleep."

"Pa?" He held the light to better see his parents' faces.

His pa stirred but made to effort to respond. Michael approached his side of the bed as Adam placed a hand on his mother's forehead.

"She's hot," he observed.

"So's Pa," Michael reported as he put his hand on his father's forehead. "What's a fever without a cough?"

"Let them sleep," the teen decided. "You get dressed then put on some tea and feed the stove. Get the kitchen real warm." He led the way to the door. "I'm goin' fer Doc Blevins."

Adam went to the kitchen to bundle up and left his lamp on the table. Michael used the glow from the lamp in his bedroom to find his way up to get dressed as his older brother left by the front door. The black of night just before the first hint of dawn, was lit by the quarter moon, hanging near the western horizon, as it cast its glow across the snow scape. Adam hurried out the lane toward the doctor's office and residence, across from the train station.

Michael dressed quickly, took up his lamp, and hurried down to the kitchen. The first order of business was to heat up the room. He opened the firebox on the large range and stirred up the hot coals before adding more firewood. Opening the damper on the stovepipe and on the cleanout door below the firebox, he created a draft and a quick fire. While the fire grew, he pumped water into the empty teapot and placed it over the hottest fire. Closing both dampers, he controlled the flame as it settled to a steady glow and radiated growing warmth into the room. He then reached down the tin of tea from the cupboard.

Soft footsteps entered the room. The boy turned from the stove.

"Ma? You need to be in bed?" He paused with tea in hand.

"I'll be okay. Let me help you with that." Dressed in her night gown and robe, she crossed the room to take the tea strainer from the drawer.

Michael opened the tin and she spooned the tea into the container. Kissing the boy on his forehead, she turned to the tea pot and hung the tea inside. The boy returned the tin to the cabinet. The woman pulled her robe closed and tied the cloth belt. They both walked to the table and sat down.

A blast of cold air rushed down the hall as Adam returned with the doctor.

"Should you be up, Ma?" he asked, reaching his coat and hat to their peg.

"I think I'm okay," she turned to her son and the doc. "I do feel really rotten." She smiled a half smile that seemed more like a grimace. "Yer Pa's not lookin' too good neither."

The teapot began to sing and Michael moved it off the high heat. Adam left for the bedroom to check on his pa.

The doctor touched his hand to her forehead. "You're hot with fever, but your other boy here had you beat with his the other week. No cough?"

"No. Pa neither."

"Seems like a cold without a cough, though I've not dealt with that one before." He hung his coat across the back of a chair.

"Let's see what tea and bed rest can do." He pulled out a chair and sat down.

"I'll put on some coffee," Adam volunteered.

"Sounds good. Is your pa awake?"

The older boy filled the coffee pot from the pump at the sink as he answered over his shoulder, "Not yet."

He put it on the cool side of the range while he filled the basket from the can of ground coffee. He dropped the spindle into the pot and moved it to the heat, then returned the coffee can to the cabinet. He turned to the doctor and repeated, "Not yet."

"I'll go check on him." The doctor left the room.

Michael brought a cup of tea and placed it in front of his mother. He then brought the sugar bowl and a pitcher of cream from the ice box. She added sugar and cream, stirred, then wrapped the cup in her hands momentarily before raising it to her lips to sip its warmth.

Doc Blevins returned from the bedroom with a very unsteady Bill Tyler.

"Pa!" Adam called. He rushed to his father's side.

His father raised a hand and shook his head. His son stopped. The doctor helped him to a chair and Michael set a cup of tea in front of him.

Doc sat down as Adam brought his coffee. Each of the boys took a cup of coffee and joined the adults at the table.

"You folks are somewhat of a mystery," the doctor began. "I'd feel sure you had colds it you were coughing. It seems you have the fever half of a cold. If you just feel miserable like a cold and not any worse, I suggest plenty of tea and bed rest. If you get worse, I'd suggest laudanum." He paused to drink his coffee. "Let the boys take care of you and just rest. Eat if you're hungry. Otherwise keep it light until you get your strength back." He finished his coffee then stood to put his coat on. "I'm heading back to the office. Leaving you boys in charge." Looking to the parents. "You two need to go back to bed."

"Okay," they chorused.

"You boys feed yerselves whatever ya find," their mother instructed. She finished her tea and stood, looking at her husband. "Finish yer tea, Bill. I'm goin back ta bed."

The woman started across the room toward the bedroom as her husband finished his tea and followed.

Doc Blevins started toward the hallway. "I think they'll be okay." He wrapped his scarf around his neck, placed his hat on his head, and pulled on his gloves. "Come for me if they get any worse."

"Bye, Doc," Michael called.

"Bye." He followed behind the Tylers and headed down the hall as they turned into their bedroom. A blast of cold air and he was gone.

The boys put the cups in the sink and sat down.

"Hungry," Adam asked.

"Hot oatmeal?"

"Sounds good."

"Ya wanna feed the animals while I cook?"

"Olay, Little Brother." He went to the door and bundled up. "I'll bring back some eggs if ya wanna cook them, too." He left and the storm door banged behind him.

*   *   *

Following breakfast, Adam left for *The Herald* by way of the Stewart Creek office, to alert Mr. Tompkins of his pa's illness. Michael cleaned up from breakfast and moved the pots of tea and coffee to the warming plates on the range. He then settled to the table with coffee cup at his side, to work on his school assignments. His parents slept. Fixing a light lunch of a sandwich and an apple, he brought paper and envelops from his bedroom and wrote letters for back home. Jay stopped late in the afternoon as he had been doing on Fridays.

"Coffee?" Michael offered as his friend settled at the kitchen table.

"Thanks. Sorry to hear about your folks." He sipped the hot liquid. "How are they doin'?"

The boy poured himself a cup. "They've slept most of the day. I've looked in on them and they seem to be all right."

"Before I forget, these letters came for you today." He reached in his pocket and passed three envelops to the boy.

Checking the postmarks, he chose the one with the RPO first to see what Scot had to say. The two sat in quiet as the boy read.

"Scot said he was glad to get my last letter and hope's I'm doin' okay. The railroad arrived at Livingston near the Yellowstone River in the southwestern part of Montana Territory, on January fifteenth. They expect to build a major shop and rail center there. His pa is working on makin' arrangements ta go to Savage fer Keith Summer's gatherin'. He thinks it's gonna be sometime near the end of March or beginning of April."

The man had finished much of his coffee during the boy's report on Scot's letter. Michael paused and brought a tin of cookies from the side counter.

"That's not a far way off," Jay observed. "It's already the first week of February. I'll have to follow up with Mr. Marlow when I run to Arlee next week." He took a cookie from the tin. "Who's next?"

The boy read a letter from Keith Summers while he drank his coffee and worked on a cookie.

"Keith said he hopes the snow's not causin' any trouble here. They've had some heavy storms which have closed off the town from the outside world for days at a time. Trader Mattson was delayed on his travels and just returned the day this letter was sent. The gatherin' is planned for the second week in April, after spring starts, when the weather is expected to begin to warm up. My family sent word with Mattson that they will be there. Keith says that Lawrence and his pa have seen buffalo grazing on his land about eight miles out from the fort. He hopes to invite Roaring Wing to summer on his lands where his people will be able to hunt buffalo again." He lay the paper on the table. "I hope they can and are able to come down in the spring." He smiled a dream of things he hoped might happen.

The last was a quick note from Trader Mattson to say his folks were fine and Prairie Flower was surprised and delighted to receive the deerskin. She planned to make something very special from it, but hadn't decided what.

The boy gathered his letters and set them on the counter to share with Adam when he got home.

There was movement in the bedroom.

"I'll be right back," Michael turned from the counter and headed for the bedroom.

The engineer walked to the stove and poured himself another cup of coffee. "Ma, ya sure ya wanna be up?" he heard from the bedroom.

The boy and his mother returned to the kitchen.

"Hi, Jay," she greeted in a hoarse voice. Michael walked her to the table and pulled the chair for her. She turned from leaning on the boy to resting her hands on the table.

The boy went to the large range and moved the pot of tea to the heat, opened the firebox door, and stirred up the hot coals into flames. He returned to the table.

"Janet," the man asked, "are you feelin' any better?"

"Yes, the extra sleep is working wonders." Michael touched the back of his hand to her cheek. "Any change?" she asked.

"Yer not as hot, but yer still warm," he responded.

The teapot began to steam and hint of a whistle. The boy picked it up, poured a cup for his mother, then set it on a warming plate.

"Here," he offered as he went for the sugar bowl and cream, and laid out a spoon from the drainer.

The clock in the parlor struck five o'clock.

"Time for me ta go," Jay stood and pulled on his coat. "Got a train ta take out." He turned toward the hall. "Thanks, Son," he nodded at the boy. "Janet, you take care and take care of that husband of yours." He pulled on his gloves. "Hope you're both better, soon."

"Bye, Jay."

"Bye, Michael. See ya'll next week."

The front door opened before he got to it.

"Hi, Jay."

"Hi, Adam."
They passed at the door as it shut behind them.

\*     \*     \*

"Good night, Little Brother," Adam greeted as he paused in the doorway on the way to his room. "Ma and Pa are in bed and the fires are banked for the night."

Michael set his lamp on the small desk by the window, then turned toward his brother. "I never saw my parents sick like our folks here." He sat down on the chair by the desk. "Eagle's Claw, our medicine man, always seemed to have things under control. I remember the day Grandfather was so sick and Eagle's Claw came and took care of him. We never worried that Grandfather wouldn't get better. I don't know why, but I was so worried when ma and pa weren't up this morning. I was afraid for them. I sure feel better that Doc Blevins was here and they seem to be getting better."

Adam stepped into the room and set his lamp on the chest by the door. "We've all been sick before. It's a regular part of winter. This is yer first winter here, so yer seein' it for the first time. I 'spect to be sick at some point before spring." He crossed the room and reached out to his brother. Placing his hands on Michael's shoulders, he guided him into a comforting embrace and held him close. "We're family, Little Brother. Together, we will get through this."

Michael reached around his brother's waist and held him close. "Thanks, Big Brother."

Adam let go and stepped back. "Sleep well. See you in the mornin'."

Michael stepped back as his brother turned to the door and reached down his lamp. "Good night."

"Good night." He was gone to his room.

Michael walked to his bed and changed into his nightshirt, turned down the covers, walked to the desk and blew out the lamp, then sat down at the desk. Gazing out at the moonlit snow scape, he reflected on the day just ended. He fingered the letters and thought of home and how much he missed everyone. And he thought back to his fears when his new parent's illness became the day's worry, and how close he felt to them, family. He was truly deeply connected to two families, his real family and his new family. He so loved them both. As deeply as he longed for home, he would long for his present home were he to leave, even to go back to his frontier home. He felt comfortable here. He had an older brother with whom he shared this life. He had Scot's friend who looked in on him on a regular basis and cared for him as a son. He felt safe. He was home.

# Winter's End

A steady snow fell in silence as the boys climbed the side porch steps on their return from the barn and morning chores. Stomping the snow from their boots, they set down the basket of eggs and bucket of milk to brush the snow off their clothes. Picking up the containers, they entered the warmth of the kitchen, kicked off their boots, and hung up their outer garments.

"Smells great, Ma," Michael complimented as he placed the eggs on the side counter then walked over to where she was flipping hotcakes on the range, and slipped an arm around her waste. "Sure is great to see you up again." He lay his head on her arm.

"Thanks, Son." She set the spatula aside and folded the boy into a warm embrace. "You want ta flip some?" She handed the spatula to the boy.

"Sure."

He watched as the batter on the griddle bubbled and burst and when it solidified, he flipped each pancake to finish cooking.

"Here's the milk, Ma." Adam informed as he set the pail in front of the ice box. "Is Pa up yet? Is he any better?" He reached the egg bowl from the ice box, emptied the basket into the bowl, then returned it to its cold storage.

"I'm okay, Son. Thanks." His father entered the room and sat down at the table. "I definitely feel much better. What's the weather like?" He accepted a cup of coffee from his wife.

The teen reached for a clean bottle from the counter top and skimmed off the cream, then took the cream pitcher from the ice box and set it on the counter to refill it. "It's not looking good." He filled the pitcher and placed it on the table. Facing his pa he continued, "I think we're gonna see another major storm."

Adam took the empty milk bottles from the side counter and proceeded to fill them as Michael and his mother took the food to the table. Placing the milk in the icebox, he then pumped water into the bucket and rinsed it out, then set it on the floor next to the door to the porch. All gathered and sat down at the table to breakfast of hot cakes, sausage, and biscuits.

The four ate in silence as they passed the platters of food around the table.

Mr. Tyler spoke up. "I think this is a good day to stay home and take it easy as much as we can." He paused to take some coffee. "Your mother and I need to regain our strength and will depend on you boys to get things done around here today."

Adam finished the food on his plate and carried it to the drainboard. "I'll go over to the company office to see what today's plans are and to let Mr. Tompkins know you're home improving, Pa," he offered. "Then I'll be back to help around here."

"Thanks, Son,"

The parlor clock struck the hour at seven as the older boy bundled up for his trip to the logging company. "I should be back within the hour."

He left the room toward the front door and was gone.

"I've got the dishes, Ma," Michael volunteered.

"Thanks, I'll take care of the leftovers, then we need to tend the stoves and enjoy their warmth."

"The least I can do is tend the stoves," Mr. Tyler acknowledged. He headed for the side door to bring in firewood from the porch.

\*     \*     \*

The storm continued through the noon hour, then began to ease off leaving accumulations of an additional five inches, more or less. Town life went on as usual with little more needed than some extra cleanup at each business and residence. School let out at its normal time and Michael's friends brought his classwork to the house.

Mrs. Tyler answered the door. "Hi, Boys."

"Hi, Mrs. Tyler," Miles greeted. "We have Michael's schoolwork."

Teddy added, "There's been no one sick in class in the past couple days and we've finished our colds. Do you think we can come in today?"

"Sure." She stood back and opened the door fully. "Michael's making hot chocolate and we've just finished a batch of sugar cookies. Go on in to the kitchen."

The boys walked past her to the kitchen and dropped their outer clothing on a chair by the side door.

"Hi, Guys," Michael greeted. "These are fresh from the oven."

He finished removing the cookies from the baking sheets onto a serving plate and took them to the table. His mother stirred the chocolate and poured it into a pitcher, then set the rest aside on a warming surface of the stove. Plates and cups were passed around and all settled to enjoy the snack.

Mr. Tyler entered from the living room. "Hi, Boys," he greeted. "Just finished tending the living room stove. Adam's outside cleaning off the path to the barn."

Adam entered from the porch. "I see the schoolwork has arrived." He paused to hang up his outer clothing, then took a seat at the table and helped himself to chocolate and cookies. "These are still warm and really soft," he complimented.

"I think they're best when they're fresh from the oven," Mr. Tyler added as he bit into his second cookie.

Teddy set a half eaten cookie aside as he reached into his school bag and took out a pile of papers. "Mrs. Miller checked yer figuring and only found a couple of mistakes. Adam can go over them with you tomorrow." He set the assignment aside. "Most of the rest of her corrections she made comments to explain and also pointed out items that were particularly good." He set the rest of the papers aside with the figuring, then looked toward Michael. "She said to tell you that you are doing really swell. She's really proud of how well you've done while not being able to be in class. She looks forward to warmer weather and your being back in school." The boy shifted his attention to the food.

"Thanks, Teddy," Mrs. Tyler said. "We sure appreciate all you two have done."

Mr. Tyler added, "Your friendship has meant a lot to the whole family. Little did I know when you asked to run yer trap line that you'd end up such a part of this family."

"Thank you, Sir," Miles added. "It sure has been great havin' Michael as a friend. It's made this year so much more fun."

"Pa," Adam acknowledged. "These two have had a lot to do with my little brother's gettin' to feelin' at home here in Snow Shoe. Do you agree, Little Brother?"

Michael had to swallow his cookie before answering. "They took me as a friend the first day I started school. And that made the whole first day special. You bet."

"So, Pa. What ya say they get to go with us ta visit Michael's home?" He took up his cup to savor the hot chocolate.

"What!?" Teddy and Miles exclaimed.

"That's a powerful question, Son," he choked on his food, coughing to regain his voice. "I'll have to think on it," he continued hoarsely.

"Can they?" Michael asked hopefully.

"Son," his mother added, "There's too much to consider to give an answer right now. We'll talk about it." She set her cup down. "Why don't you go get last week's school work so Teddy can put it in his school bag to take to Mrs. Miller tomorrow."

"Okay." He left the table to retrieve his assignments from the counter in the corner of the room near the flour cabinet.

* * *

Dinner was finished and darkness had settled outside. The family gathered in the living room as the boys tended the stove and their parents lit the lamps. The boys settled on the floor with their games, but didn't set them up sensing a serious conversation about to begin. They looked toward their father.

"Adam, I wish you hadn't brought up adding Michael's friends to the trip, in front of them, without saying something to me first."

"Sorry, Pa. The thought just came to me at the moment and I asked."

"Can't we try, Bill," his wife asked. "Those boys are such a major part of his life and I'm sure his parents and friends would love to meet them. It will help them to feel at ease, knowing their boy has a family and good friends." She looked toward Michael to check his reaction.

"Pa, I know Ma's right," the boy added. "Thunder Eagle and Prairie Flower have always honored my friends and thought very highly of them." Pleading eyes hoped for his father's permission.

"I agree with you both and with the idea of their going with us, but I'm not sure their parents will. We've never met. The boys' fathers work at the saw mill and we haven't spent time with them at church."

"Why don't we meet them next Sunday?" Mrs. Tyler suggested, realizing how important it was to her younger son.

"We can ask Teddy and Miles tomorrow when they bring my assignments," Michael offered.

"I think it would be great to have them along," Adam added. "We could ask them over for refreshments after church."

"They have brothers and sisters," his brother warned.

"The other kids can play in the snow," their mother said. "And we can do refreshments in the dining room."

"Agreed," their father conceded.

*     *     *

The following day, Michael wrote letters to his family and friends to share the idea and find out how they would feel about extra guests. That afternoon, he and his ma told Teddy and Miles they were considering their going on the journey and sent a note with each to invite their families over next Sunday after church. They could hardly contain their excitement.

Periods of snow continued throughout the week. Each storm left less than five inches and was easy to clean up, but each added to the general accumulation across the landscape. Continued freezing temperatures and overcast resulted in snow lingering on surfaces be it fences, rooftops, trees and shrubs, and more, leaving a winter wonderland of white as far as the eye could see.

Wednesday morning, Michael walked with his pa and his brother as they left for work, so he could stop at the mercantile and mail his letters. He decided to walk home by way of the school and see if Mrs. Miller might be in. It was far too early for any of the kids to arrive and maybe too early for the teachers as well. There was light in his classroom as well as one on the first floor, so he entered the building.

His teacher was at her desk.

"Mornin', Mrs. Miller," he greeted upon entering the room.

She looked up in surprise. "Why, Michael!" she greeted, "what a nice surprise." She put down the student work she was reading and turned her chair. "Pull up a chair and let me get a good look at you. It's been such a long time and it's so good to see you."

The boy found a side chair and pulled it to his teacher's desk.

"It's good to see you, too." He sat in front of the desk facing the woman. "I was at the mercantile to mail some letters and thought I'd walk home this way and see if you were in."

"I'm always in early to enjoy the quiet time and review some of yesterday's classwork." She rested her arms on her desk and leaned toward the boy. "How have you been doing? I know you're keeping up with your schoolwork and doing quite well."

"We've been busy at home keeping up with storm cleanup. Our folks were sick last week, but they're better now. Ma and me bake cookies every day." He opened his coat to let out the heat from his body and to cool off from the heat of the classroom.

"Did you get sick again when your folks did?"

"No. Doc said my sickness made me stronger against colds. He still worries about other sickness that I could die from and said he told you about that."

"He did. I can't wait for warmer weather and the day you can return to school. I know some of your classmates miss you. Jamison asks Teddy and Miles about you often."

"If no one is sick at the time, he's welcome to come with them some afternoon when they bring my schoolwork."

"I'll let him know." She sat back in her chair. "What's this I hear about you folks taking a journey late next month?"

The boy slipped off his coat, dropping it over the back of the chair. "Keith Summers, the owner of the freight company where I worked before coming here, is putting together a reunion with my family and friends. I hope Teddy and Miles can go with us. We leave the first week of April and plan to be gone about a month. I hope that won't be a problem with missing school."

"Why don't you boys keep journals during the journey as your school assignment. They should prove very interesting, and you can share them with the class when you return. For arithmetic you can keep an account of your expenses in the back of your journal. I'll give you some copy books to take with you today to use during your trip."

"Thanks."

Mrs. Miller left her desk to walk to a storage cabinet and take out a half dozen copy books and a box of pencils to go with them. Returning to her desk, she placed them on the desk in front of the boy. "If you feel like it, you can add some sketches of things you see and do."

"We'll do that. What a neat idea."

Children's voices were heard from the schoolyard below as the first arrivals brushed the snow from the swings and climbed on.

"I better go now." Michael stood and pulled his coat back on. "It was good to see you." He picked up the copy books and pencil box. "Thanks."

His teacher rose from her desk and extended her hand. "I'm so glad you stopped in." They clasped hands. "I'll give your message to Jamison and look forward to your return to school." She walked with him to the door. "Take care."

"Bye."

The woman stood at the door and watched her student down the stairs and out of the building, then returned to her desk.

*   *   *

Michael walked home by way of Jeffers to Cedar in order to enjoy the snow scape along the way. The streets were quiet. In a few short minutes they would come alive with children as they headed off for the new day at school. Before that happened, the boy reached the lane to the farm and home. He paused at the front of the lane to enjoy the peaceful scene of the farm, blanketed in snow and silence. The smoke rising from the chimneys brought a sense of warmth and the desire to hurry in and enjoy it. He hurried in the lane and up the porch steps to the kitchen door.

"Hi, Ma," he burst into the kitchen.

"Hi, Son. Cold?"

"Yea."

She poured a cup of hot chocolate and brought it to the table as the boy set the copy books and the pencil box on the table, hung up his coat and hat, and sat to the table. His mother sat across from him as he wrapped his cold hands around the cup to enjoy the warmth.

"I stopped at school on the way home. There was light from my classroom, so I thought I'd say 'hi' to Mrs. Miller." He put the cup to his lips, blew on the hot beverage and took a tentative sip.

His mother drank from her cup of coffee, already sitting on the table. "Was she glad to see you?"

"Oh yes. She gave me copy books and pencils so we can keep a journal as our school assignment. We visited some and she said that Jamison had asked about me. I told her that any day no one was sick in the class he could stop with Teddy and Miles." He drank from his cup.

The woman set her cup down. "I'm sure he will and look forward to meeting him."

Michael set his cup down and rose from the table. "I think I'll get started on my assignments." He walked to the far corner of the room where he kept his schoolwork, left the copy books and pencil box on the counter, and brought his schoolwork to the table. His mother went to the stove and added more wood to the firebox and adjusted the dampers to help it catch fire quickly and add more warmth to the room. She turned to leave the room.

"While you work on that, I'm goin' ta get your coat and work on that." She left the room.

*   *   *

There was a knock at the front door.

"I'll get it." Michael slid the hot cookies from the spatula onto the cooling towel, set the spatula down, and turned to the front hall. "Go on in to the kitchen," he instructed as his friends stomped the snow from their shoes on the front porch and entered down the hallway.

Three boys entered the kitchen as Teddy instructed, "Throw yer coat on the side chair, Jamison, and have a seat at the table."

The boys quickly peeled out of their warm clothing and found a seat at the table. Michael shoveled warm cookies onto a serving plate while his mother brought the hot chocolate to the table.

"I'll get an extra setting," she offered as she set the pitcher down.

"I'm guessing this is Jamison," she said as she placed the cup and plate in front of him.

He met her smile with one of his own. "Thank you, Ma'am."

"Help yerselves, Boys." She pulled up her own chair to the table.

The red head teen hesitated as he watched the others help themselves to cookies and pass and pour the pitcher of steaming chocolate.

"Go ahead, Jamison," Michael encouraged. "I'm glad you could come today."

"Thanks," Jamison reached for the pitcher. "I wanted to come as soon as Mrs. Miller gave me your message. But my mom doesn't know and I don't want to be too late. So I can't stay long."

"I understand," Mrs. Tyler comforted. "I'm so pleased to meet you. I've heard about you over the weeks and wondered when you might come. Thank you for helping Michael to learn how to play baseball. He's really enjoyed the game." She turned her attention to her snack.

"I was hoping you'd come," Michael greeted between mouthfuls. "I miss not being in class, and can't wait for warmer weather and spring and getting back to school." He drank from his cup. "Maybe I'll get better at the game once we start playing again."

The visit with the older boy lasted a short time more until he felt he had to go.

Standing from the table, Jamison excused himself. "I really do have to go now. Thanks, Mrs. Tyler. I'm glad I could come today, but really must go."

He bundled up against the cold and Michael walked to the door with him.

"Thanks for stopping."

"Thanks for the note." He started out the door. "See you in school one day." He waved and headed down the steps.

The boy closed the door and returned to the kitchen.

* * *

The week drifted on into Friday afternoon. The snow had stopped mid morning and the sun had slipped out as the clouds retreated eastward leaving a clear blue sky by early afternoon. Jay stopped for his weekly visit.

As the engineer enjoyed his cup of coffee he offered, "All rail traffic has been running normal this week, and in spite of the deep snow on the ground, the logging operations have gone fairly well. Just not as many train loads as it has taken longer to cut each." He paused to eat and drink.

The boy and his mother ate and listened as the man continued. "As a change of pace, do you think Michael can go on tonight's run to Arlee, stay the night, and return with me in the morning?"

The boy looked to his mother. "Can I, Ma!?" he asked excitedly.

"Won't that be inconvenient for the Johnstons?" she asked.

He finished the coffee and set his cup down. "Hank and Nancy have told me that Michael is welcome any time I can bring him. No advance notice is ever needed."

"Okay, I'll let Adam and yer pa know when they get home that they'll see you next some time tomorrow."

"Oh, thanks." He jumped up from his chair, gave her a quick hug, then dashed off to his room to pack.

"You spoil him, Jay."

"I know. I love him like a son and am glad I can do it." He smiled a contented smile and finished off his last cookie.

Mrs. Tyler poured another cup of coffee for each and they enjoyed them in quiet while they awaited the boy's return.

Shortly thereafter the boy bounced back into the room, dressed for work in the engine's cab with extra clothes packed in his carpet bag. The two bundled up for the weather and headed out the front door leaving the woman standing there and waving them on.

At the station, Michael stowed his bag in the baggage room on the combine and climbed into the cab for another trip's adventure. Jay let the boy run the train for the entire trip to the main line switch. There he took over and finished the trip into Arlee. Michael helped service Number twenty-one in the engine facility. The train was made up for the trip back the following day and parked on the siding at the station. Scott banked the fire for the night and joined the crew and the boy for a late dinner at the hotel.

Jason and his parents were delighted at the surprise visit. Following dinner, Scott returned to the train where he spent the night on a cot in the baggage room where he could check on the engine from time to time throughout the night. The rest of the crew retired to the bunk room above the station freight room. Jay and Michael retired to the hotel kitchen with Jason's family where they visited into the late evening and brought each other up to date over the past months' events over cups of coffee and hot chocolate. The boys went up to Jason's room while the adults banked the fires and retired to their own bedrooms.

Michael and Jason fell asleep mid sentence as they lay in Jason's bed and visited into the night. Michael woke to the distant whistle of the night express freight, crept stealthily out of bed, and sat at the window to watch it pass. Slipping back under the sheets, he quickly fell back to sleep. He was still sound asleep when Jason woke him the next morning. It was still dark outside as the two entered the kitchen and bundled up to do Jason's chores of bringing in firewood for the day and tending the stoves and the lamps in the dining room, and setting out table settings for the guests and breakfast. The front halls came alive with commotion as the guests came down for breakfast. The boys helped Mrs. Johnston put the food on the table, and all settled to eat and share conversation.

Following breakfast, Michael left with Jay to prepare the train for the trip back home. Just before departure time, Jason walked over to the station to watch preparations and to wave goodbye to his friend as the train departed with the passengers heading up the line. Once through the switch off the main line, the boy was again given charge of the engine and took the train to Day's End and back to Snow Shoe. He stayed with Jay as the train was spotted on its station track and the locomotive was turned on the wye track, taken to the yard, serviced, then bedded down in the engine house for the weekend.

The boy gathered his carpet bag from the baggage room as he and Jay walked back past the station then across Railroad Avenue and up Main Street toward Cedar Street and home.

*     *     *

On Sunday afternoon, following church, Teddy and Miles and their families walked home with Michael and his family. With all their brothers and sister, the boys' families totaled eleven. Adding the Tyler family of four, it was quite the crowd. Refreshments were served for the adults, in the dining room, and for the children, in the kitchen. Seven children packed around the kitchen table, but Adam and Michael stayed on their feet most of the time serving food for the others. The six adults were comfortable in the dining room. Mrs. Tyler having placed the food on the table upon arriving home, allowed for the parents to meet undisturbed and get to know each other. Meanwhile, the boys escorted all the children outside after they had eaten. They decided to break into teams by family and create snowmen, to compete for the most unusual. In the end, they were all so unique they declared it a tie. More than an hour passed before the children returned to the kitchen. Their parents were still in the dining room sharing a rather noisy conversation.

Adam and Michael heated up more hot chocolate and set out a plate of an assortment of cookies that Michael and his mother had baked up during the week. The young voices raised their own noisy conversation as they bragged about their snowmen and shared some of their own lives as the guests asked about life on the farm. Finally, the adults entered the kitchen to gather their children and get them bundled up for the return trip homeward.

"What did you decide?" Teddy asked as Michael and Miles listened for the answer.

Mr. Tyler spoke for all. "In short, the answer is yes. You will have to get the details from your parents when you get home."

The boys burst into smiles and hugged each other briefly as their siblings looked on inquisitively not knowing what this was all about.

"Let's go, Kids," Mr. Hart encouraged. "It's time we get home."

Mr. Latimer added, "We'll explain more after we all get home."

A short period of confusion followed while each child worked to sort out his own clothing and they all bundled up for the cold outside. Soon, the commotion moved down the hall to the front door where the two families left to walk together on their way home.

Quiet settled within the house as the front door was closed.

"We'll sit down after dinner to go over all we discussed," Mr. Tyler explained.

His wife added, "For now, we need to clean up these rooms and I need to start dinner."

All set about bringing dishes and leftovers in from the dining room and clearing the kitchen table to the counters and the sink.

*   *   *

Later that evening, the parents shared with their sons the nature of the conversation. Preparations were to include a meeting with their teacher to plan a course of study for the four weeks of school they would miss. Teddy and Miles would be expected to send a letter home at least twice each week for the first three weeks. Together, the four boys would plan what to pack and each would have a travel trunk to pack as they gathered what each would need for the journey.

February quietly slipped away. Toward the end of the month, the boys met with Mrs. Miller. She shared with Teddy and Miles what she had discussed with Michael and made sure each boy had the materials needed for their journals and budget record keeping.

Winter began to loosen its grip. By month's end snow depths had fallen to the point where Michael and Of-The-Wind could spend time together wandering in the meadow behind the barn. During the earlier weeks of the winter, the boy had spent time each day with her in her stall, sometimes brushing her while talking about anything that came to mind, sometimes sitting on her back and lying forward on her neck while he stroked her affectionately or just let his arms hang on either side, and sometimes sitting on her feed box watching her eat or stroking her neck as she stood before him and rested her head on his shoulder.

Routines continued with daily chores, school assignments, visits from Teddy and Miles, weekly visits from Jay, an occasional day in the cab of Number twenty-one, daily baking with his mother, occasional trips to the mercantile to pick up the mail, and some Fridays with Adam at *The Herald*. Mrs. Tyler continued to work on the boy's new coat for a time each morning with periodic fittings to be sure it would be plenty large enough for Michael to grow into for at least a year or more. By mid month the coat was assembled and it was time for the tedious detail work to finish off the edges of the coat and collar and to add pockets, buttons, and button holes. Finally, it was finished. He wore it to the barn that afternoon, to show it off to his pony. Adam saw it and admired it a little later when he arrived to do chores. Upon returning to the house following chores, he shared it with his father. He beamed with a sense of pride as he shared his new coat, a union of his mothers and his Sioux father who made it possible.

The last week of February ended with the first days of March. On Friday, Mr. Tyler came off the mountain on the midday train for a meeting at the bank to arrange for money to be available midmonth for the journey. Afterwards, he went home for a late lunch with his wife. Adam stopped in unexpectedly mid afternoon. He had dropped off the day's issue of *The Herald* at Jenkins' General Store and picked up the mail. There were letters for Michael which he brought to the house before continuing with his paper deliveries.

"Do you have time for a snack?" his mother asked.

"Yea." He sat down to the table with his pa and watched his brother study the letters, deciding which to open first. "Well?" he asked without even picking up his first cookie.

"I guess I'll check Mr. Summers' letter first." He tore the end off the envelop, withdrew the paper, and opened it to read first before sharing its contents.

The others waited in anticipation, ignoring the food.

He read the letter out loud. Mr. Summers expressed his concerns for the Tylers' illness and glad that they were getting better. Walt Mattson had taken the letter to Michael's parents on the delivery run to their people and reported that they were so happy that the boy's friends were coming and couldn't wait to meet them. Mr. Summers had invited the village to stay the summer on his land and to hunt the buffalo that had been seen toward the far end of the land along the river. They would all come down together when the family came for the reunion and set the village outside the fort as in earlier summers.

"Wow!" Adam exclaimed. "We'll get to meet your people!"

"This is stunning news!" Mr. Tyler added.

"So very special!" his wife noted.

"I can't believe this is happening!" Michael exclaimed. "I will really be going home!"

He paused, reflecting on what all he had just read as he consumed a cookie and some chocolate. Putting the cup down, he picked up Scot's letter. He, too, wrote of looking forward to meeting Teddy and Miles and the excitement he and his pa felt as they looked forward to gathering at the old fort. Trapper Murray's letter was brief, but he and Lawrence both looked forward to meeting Michael's friends and family and could hardly wait for all to be together again.

Each letter began the same way – 'Dear Prairie Cub.'

"I'm going home," the boy whispered. "I'm Prairie Cub and I'm going home."

The Tylers looked at each other with a serious expression of concern. Adam, too, looked upset. Michael was suddenly struck by their upset expressions and became deeply aware of the bond that all had come to share and a fear on the part of the family that it was about to fall apart.

"Ma, Pa, Big Brother?" he implored. "I feel torn up inside. I can't wait to go home. But I know, too, that I am home. I'm two people..." he started to cry. Tears came and he couldn't talk. He looked at his family with a look begging understanding.

His mother reached out and took his hand in hers. "I cannot begin to say 'I know how you feel.' We have always known that you are not just Michael, but that you will always be Prairie Cub as well. We know this is hard for you and will always be here for you in any way we can help." Her eyes watered and she wiped them with her sleeve.

"Son," his father spoke up hoarsely, "this will always be your home away from home, knowing full well that your real home is with your people, whether or not you are there."

Adam could only stare. He had no idea of what he could say that might help. He simply put a hand on Michael's shoulder and the boy turned to him and smiled. "Thank you." He could say no more.

After a moment of silence, the boy continued. "I know I am Michael and I live here. But when we go on this journey, I go as Prairie Cub, for that is who I am. And I will be Prairie Cub until it is time to come back. Then, I will be Michael.

"I want to see Of-The-Wind." He stood, put on his new coat, and left for the barn.

Adam got up from the table.

"Let him be," his father said. "He needs some time by himself."

"It's time I got back to work and finished delivering the paper." He put on his coat and hat and left down the hall and out the front door.

*   *   *

Early March brought warmer weather. After the crossover week with no new sickness, Doc Blevins gave the okay for Michael to return to school beginning the first full week of the month. Temperatures rose into the 50's and the snow began to melt. Rainy weather moved in and helped to wash away the heavy snow accumulations and turned the landscape into a mudscape and the roads to mud as well. Michael's classmates were glad for his return and whenever there was a break from class for recess or lunch, many gathered and asked what it was like being home all day. The sun made a comeback beginning the middle of that first week and by week's end, baseball returned to recess. Jamison picked up where he left off before the snows put an end to the game, and coached his young friend on how to hit the ball. The lessons paid off and Michael developed a working style for getting hits and getting on base.

Jay stopped for his regular visit Friday afternoon.

The man and the boy leaned on the gate to the meadow and watched the pony as she rolled in the grass not far from the gate.

"She looks like she's really enjoying herself," Jay observed.

"My pony is so happy to get out of the barn more and play in the meadow," Michael said as he watched the energy with which his pony rolled about on the ground. "I think she might get a green color about her if she keeps this up much longer."

Finally, Of-The-Wind got back on her feet and wandered to the gate for some attention. The boy obliged by running his fingers through her main and rubbing her muzzle. Then he reached in his pocket and gave her an apple he had brought from the cold cellar, among the last of the previous season. She stood there and crunched it, then turned to the water trough for a drink.

"It's getting close to the time when we must seriously plan to pack for the journey," Jay shared as he watched the pony. "Mr. Marlow stopped to see me while we were servicing the "King" this morning to say the Pullman Company is sending the two sleepers he ordered and that they will arrive this coming week." He turned to the boy. "Want to go with me next Friday when I stay over and see what they look like?"

"Sure do!"

"We'll work it out with yer folks tonight." He turned to the house. "What ya say we head up for yer ma's snack?"

Michael turned and started toward the house. "Good idea. Come on."

Upon returning to the kitchen, the two sat down for cookies and coffee and chocolate, and Jay talked to Mrs. Tyler about making plans for the following Friday. She would talk it over with Bill when he got home and Michael would join him at the station after school. He would have his travel bag and could take dinner with the engineer at the hotel before leaving for Arlee.

The week passed in tantalizing anticipation of Friday's trip.

*     *     *

The two skipped dinner before leaving. Jay explained they would eat when they arrived at Arlee.

Michael took the throttle for the routine run to Arlee. As they serviced the engine, Jay asked Scott to take her back to the train for the night and informed him that the boy and he had a dinner appointment in the yard. Michael looked at him wondering where they would eat in the engine yard.

"Just come with me," the man said as the two descended from the engine cab at the water tower.

Scott took the "King" down the track toward the station as the two stood there.

"Over here," Jay instructed as he led the boy to the track where he had previously seen the company president's car and the parlor car.

Michael stopped and starred at the presidential car. There were lights inside and Jay was leading him in that direction.

"What?" the boy exclaimed.

"We have a dinner invitation with Mr. Marlow."

"But we're filthy!"

"I had your bag sent over by one of the trainmen." They approached the front end platform steps. A stool had been placed at the bottom. "Come on. We can clean up inside."

A steward in a white coat with black pants met them on the platform and led them to the galley kitchen at the head end of the car. He wore a cap like Dan Seegers, but his gold plate had the word 'Steward.' Of average height, he was striking in his long face and the vague smell of cologne mixed with cigar smoke.

"It's not the ideal place to clean up," he stated, "but your bags are here and you can wash up at the sink and change."

The steward provided a paper sack for their work clothes and the two cleaned up for dinner.

"Leave your things in the back corner for after dinner."

He led them to the dining room where Mr. Marlow was waiting and the table had been set with white linens, silver flatware, and custom designed dinner ware complete with the V&T logo in the center of each plate.

"Thank you for joining me, Michael. Won't you be seated?" He pointed to the chairs at the table for Jay and the boy to be seated, then he took his chair across from them. "I wanted to work out this dinner for you with Jay so I can show you the new Pullman sleeper and talk about the plans for your train." He pulled his napkin from its ring and spread it across his lap.

Jay motioned for the boy to do the same and they both took out their napkins. They were a soft cotton fabric of generous size, complete with the company logo.

"Howard," Mr. Marlow called the steward. "You may begin."

The meal began with a tomato bisque soup with crackers. It continued with a strip steak, baked potato, string beans, coffee, and water. Dessert was cherry pie with a scoop of ice cream on top. When all had been cleared away, the president invited his guests into his office/sitting room in the back of the car. They walked the passageway past the sleeping compartment and into the open office area with sofa, upholstered chairs, roll-top desk, bookshelves, file cabinets, and a fire in the fireplace. Michael remembered the car from its previous visit to Snow Shoe back on New Year's Day. The steward brought cups and coffee and hot chocolate along with a plate of assorted pastries, which he placed on the desk behind Mr. Marlow.

"Make yourselves comfortable," he invited as he took a seat in his oak swivel arm chair. "I have worked out a travel schedule with the various railroads along the way of your journey and arranged for schedules and clearances along the way. It's all in this file case which I am giving to Jay for study and management." He handed the leather belted case to the engineer. "Your train will have four cars and Number twenty-one. You'll have a baggage car with stalls for two horses as I understand Michael has a pony and the Tyler boy has a saddle horse. The other end of the car will be packed with food and other supplies for the trip, including an extra ice box for refrigerated items." He paused to drink from his coffee. Jay and Michael ate of the pastries with their beverage as they listened to the president's explanation. "The parlor car will be next for daytime use with a kitchen for preparing meals. It has a sitting area in the front and a dining area in the middle. It will be followed by the Pullman. Finally, there will be a caboose for the train crew. I will send the train out with "Lauer" Number forty-three on Monday, March 26th. The "Lauer's" crew will be replacing the "King" beginning that week and while you are away. That way, you and your crew will have the rest of the week to prepare the special and take it for a practice run while Number forty-three's crew operates the branch line." He stood. "If there are no questions, I'll show you the sleeper. It's on this track behind the parlor car."

Mr. Marlow led the way to the Pullman car. Howard had gone ahead and lit the lamps within the car, that hung from the ceiling along the center aisle. Upon entering the car, there was a lavatory room beside the door. The car contained compartments down both sides of the aisle comprised of facing cushioned benches and an overhead berth. A board pulled out to cover the space between benches and make into a bed and the overhead folded down on guide rails at both ends to make a bunk bed over the first. Curtains at either end were drawn closed at night for privacy. The back end of the car also had a lavatory. Rosewood and mahogany woodwork adorned the interior throughout.

"Michael," he turned to the boy. "I really hope I have been able to provide for your journey. Your story is one of great challenge. I feel privileged that you are a part of our community and that I can contribute to this journey that lies ahead."

"Thank you, Sir." He offered his hand in appreciation. The two shook.

"It's late," the man observed. "I expect you two will want to pick up your things and head over to the hotel for the night."

"We greatly appreciate this, Mr. Marlow," Jay thanked. "This is a truly wonderful thing you are doing."

Mr. Marlow started to the end door toward his private car. "Look at it this way," he offered. "It will make for a great story which the papers will take up and give our little railroad some publicity. Who knows. We might become a tourist attraction, if only for one season." He chuckled to himself at the thought. "Your little train might have a brief moment of fame and people might travel here just to see it. But I won't hold my breath."

They arrived at Mr. Marlow's car and paused at the steps. "Jay," the man instructed, "we'll meet in my office on Monday to go over details of supply and personnel. I'll have your schedule altered to give you an extra two hours. You make arrangements for others to handle things at Snow Shoe." He started up the steps. "It was great to share this evening with you, Michael. Take care of yourself. I hope to see more of you in the future." He reached the top of the steps and departed into his car.

The two turned to the front of the car to retrieve their clothes from the kitchen.

"He sure is a nice man," Michael noted.

"There aren't many like him," Jay replied.

They collected their clothes from the kitchen, said good night to Howard, and headed through the yard to the hotel.

# Departure West

Upon returning home on Saturday, Michael shared the story of his trip with the family and they were deeply impressed with the effort Mr. Marlow put toward their forthcoming journey. That evening the boy wrote letters to his frontier friends, acknowledging that they would be the last before he would see them in the weeks ahead. He told of the events of recent weeks and of the train that would take him home along with the details of dinner with the president of the railroad company. As always, he signed them 'Prairie Cub.'

During the social hour following Sunday services, the Tylers sat with the Harts and the Latimers to share the events of Michael's Friday trip with Jay and dinner with Mr. Marlow, and to inform them of the scheduled arrival of the special train on Monday of the following week. It was time for them to begin getting their boys packed for the journey. Teddy and Miles stopped after school on Monday for snack and making plans. The boys' parents had ordered travel trunks from the mercantile. Ephram, from Wells Fargo, was to deliver them on Tuesday. They agreed that they wouldn't bother to reset the traps until after the journey. After eating, the boys wandered down to the barn to visit with Of-The-Wind and Cheyenne.

"Want to see what it's like to sit on my pony?" Michael offered.

"I don't know," Teddy hesitated. "I never rode a horse before."

"Me either," Miles added. "But I'll try it."

The three walked through the pony's stall as Michael led her out to the meadow. He took her to the fence.

"Easy, Girl." He held her by a handful of mane. "One of you climb up on the fence and sit on her back."

"You first."

"No, you first."

"Okay." Miles climbed the fence rail.

Cautiously he reached out for the pony's neck as he lifted his right leg across her back and sat down. The pony shivered at the extra weight of a rider unfamiliar, yet confident in her young master's presence at her head.

"I don't know about this," Miles quavered as he looked at the distance between him and the ground.

"Just hold her mane." The boy put his hand under her chin and guided her at a slow walk along the fence line and the back of the barn.

"This is pretty neat," Miles reported as he began to relax.

Teddy followed alongside as Michael took his pony along the far fence, then cut back across the meadow. Once back to their starting point, Miles used the fence to dismount.

"Me next?" Teddy volunteered.

"Okay, same as Miles. Use the fence."

Teddy climbed up and mounted the pony's back. Michael lead him on the same pathway as he had Miles. Once back, he thanked his pony, petting her neck and face and talking to her in the language they had shared all their lives. Once finished, Of-The-Wind walked away to the meadow and stopped to graze.

"You are so lucky," Teddy commented. "That was so incredible."

"Would you like to ride like that when we go to my home?" Michael asked.

"Could we?" Miles responded.

"My people have many ponies." They turned toward the house. "Any of the boys would gladly lend you one. But you would need to ride as you did today, without a saddle. We will only have Adam's saddle and he will want to use it with Cheyenne."

They walked toward the porch.

"If you want, come over each afternoon and you can practice riding without me leading Of-The-Wind. I will show you tomorrow."

They mounted the steps and entered the house. The screen door slammed shut behind them.

\*     \*     \*

The following day the trunks were delivered to the boys' homes. The three gathered at the farm and Michael showed his friends how to mount his pony from the ground. He held her head as each tried. After several failed tries, they used the fence to mount. Michael showed each how to hold his pony's mane and use their knees to guide her along with a sideways pull on the handful of mane. He walked alongside as each took a turn at trying to ride unassisted. It was awkward, but each managed the same trip as the day before. They tried again after school on Wednesday. First were several attempts to mount from the ground followed by the use of the fence, then an unassisted walk along the edge of the meadow. On Thursday, each managed to get a leg up, but needed a push from Michael to fully mount. Michael spoke quietly to his pony, then stepped back and let each ride on his own. Of-The-Wind was very patient and allowed each boy to guide her unaccompanied by her master. Friday was a repeat of Thursday, though the boys' mounting technique was almost successful. They agreed to an extra attempt on Saturday. The added day was the charm. Each was able to mount unassisted and to ride unaccompanied throughout the meadow. They celebrated their triumph with cookies and hot chocolate, then returned to the meadow with an audience to show off their new skills for Adam and his parents.

Returning to the kitchen, Mrs. Tyler gave each a sheet of paper and a pencil and they made their own lists of what to pack in their trunks. The task brought with it a sense of excited anticipation. The train was to arrive on Monday. Jay and his crew would begin the process of gathering the necessary supplies for the journey and packing the baggage car. The boys' trunks would be loaded next Saturday and final preparations made for a Monday morning departure following the return of the Monday run to Arlee. Arrangements were made for Brett Tompkins to tend to the farm while the Tyler family was away. The milk and eggs from each day would go to his family. They could sell any surplus to the mercantile or to friends. There was a sense of excitement at school as well. Michael's classmates would be able to walk with their teacher to the station on departure day for a special send off gathering. Michael had talked to Jay about letting his class visit the train for a tour of its cars on Wednesday after its arrival. Evan Clanton would be there as well so he could share a story of the upcoming event in the week's edition of *The Herald*.

\*　　\*　　\*

Monday the 26th dawned with a low-hanging mist across the countryside. Following chores, the Tyler family gathered for breakfast. A sense of anticipation hung on the air.

"I understand you boys have permission to arrive late to school today," Mr. Tyler announced. "And Adam and me don't have to report to the mountain until the midday train."

"I can't wait," Michael said, a sense of anticipated excitement in his voice.

There followed a moment of quiet as each consumed bacon and scramble eggs and washed it down with orange juice or coffee.

Mrs. Tyler set her fork down on her plate. "I feel your excitement." She looked at the boys. "I'm trembling some myself." She looked toward her husband. "I find it hard to believe this special train is arriving today, and in only a week, we will depart on the most fantastic journey imaginable." A broad smile lit her face.

"Will your friends meet us at the station this morning?" Adam asked. He picked up a piece of bacon and munched on it as he awaited an answer.

"They'll be there," Michael confirmed, reaching for his orange juice.

"Any idea what time?" his mother asked.

The boy finished off a piece of biscuit. "Jay said it should be a half hour behind him when he returns from Day's End."

Another period of quiet followed as the family continued to finish their breakfast. Empty dishes and utensils were gathered to the sink.

"What can we do to help, Ma?" Adam asked.

She pumped some cold water into the sink. "Son, you can bring some hot water from the range and your brother can tend the fires." She added soap powders to the water and began to wash and rinse the dishes then set them into the dish drainer to dry.

There was a knock at the front door.

"I'll get it." Mr. Tyler headed down the hall to open the door. "Hi, Boys. We didn't expect you here."

The two entered the hall, pushed the door closed behind them and followed the man to the kitchen.

"Our folks said we could come over here and go to the station with you when it was time." Teddy tossed his coat on the side chair by the door along with Miles'.

"I don't have any hot chocolate made," Mrs. Tyler turned from the sink as she dried her hands. "But the coffee's hot."

"That's okay," Miles replied as he took a seat at the table. "We've had it before."

Mr. Tyler set the coffee pot on its hotplate on the table while his wife brought the cups. Extra chairs were brought up from the side of the room and all gathered to await the time to head for the station.

Each enjoyed a cup of coffee in the silence of waiting. Mrs. Tyler added a tin with heavy donuts.

The hours slipped by amid quiet and excited conversation in anticipating of events to come. A whistle pierced the air as it quickly drifted past the station crossing at Main Street.

"That's Jay on the way to Day's End," Michael shared. "Can we head for the station now?"

"Let's go," his father replied.

All bundled up in coats and hats and headed down the hall to the front door. It was mid morning and the sun had burned off the early morning mists and shown warm in the east, well into its journey toward noon.

The excited group walked out the front lane, turned left onto Cedar, then took Main Street to the station. There they paced the platform as they waited for the train to return from Day's End. Jarrett and his father joined them from within the station building.

"Today's the big day," Jarrett volunteered as he approached Adam.

Adam stopped pacing. "Today's the beginning of the greatest adventure of our lives." His voice betrayed his high sense of excitement.

Several minutes had passed when the whistle of Number twenty-one announced its approach. Jarrett hurried off to throw the switch into the station. The train backed in from the main, wrapped in the screech of brakes, the rhythmic ringing of its bell, and a cloud of steam, and was spotted on the station track, centered on the platform in front of the building. A single short blast of the whistle announced it was stopped and the brakes were set. The few passengers stepped off the cars and proceeded to leave the station for their business of the day or await their luggage from the baggage car before moving on.

Jay climbed down from the engine. "We have to wait for the train to empty, then move the cars to the track behind the station," he announced. He approached the boys. "A really big day today?"

"Yea," they choroused.

"Can't wait ta see the train," Teddy stated. "You have already seen it."

"Not put together," Jay explained. "This will be a first for us as well."

"We're clear," Scott shouted from the cab.

"Coming." Jay turned back to the engine.

Once back in the cab, Dave Seegers shouted the all clear, the engineer responded with three short blasts on the whistle, the engine blew steam into the piston chambers and blasted the rods into motion as the engine drifted the train backwards to clear the switch to the back track. As the train cleared the switch, Jamie threw it. The train cleared it to the back side of the station and Jamie closed the switch and returned to the train. All watched as the train was backed past the building, uncoupled, and the engine taken to be turned on the wye, serviced, then returned to rest on the track behind the station. The crew left the train for the station building and coffee from the station office. They came through the building to the station platform and stood waiting with the rest of the crowd as they sipped slowly on their cups of coffee.

A sense of tense excitement permeated the air as all stood quietly awaiting the arrival of the special train. Fifteen minutes passed, then five more. A whistle sounded in the distance. All eyes were on the trees as they watched for the column of smoke to arrive, moving toward the station.

"There!" Miles pointed.

"It's comin'," Michael whispered in eager anticipation.

The whistle blew the crossing as the engine came into view flying the white flags of a special on either side of its headlamp. The cars followed in view, a consist unlike any other ever seen to arrive at Snow Shoe station, pulled caboose first with the cars in reverse order, already lined up to be in forward position when the train would leave on its journey westward. The train approached through preset switches, with bell ringing and brakes screeching as it slowed, wrapped in its blanket of steam, in its approach to the station. It slowed to a stop.

The engineer climbed down from the cab and approached Jay.

"Hi, Jay." He pulled off his glove and they exchanged handshakes. "Here's your train." There was a tinge of envy in his voice.

"Abner, welcome to my world." He turned to the gathered families. "Folks, this is Abner Matthewson with Number forty-three, the "Lauer." He and his crew will be taking the place of my crew while we are away. They start today and we are officially detached to take care of preparations and the journey ahead."

"Hello, Folks." He approached Michael. "And this is the boy who this is all about." He offered his hand. "I'm honored to meet you Michael." They shook hands. "I've read your story and am glad to help make your journey possible." He looked around at the gathered family and friends. "These must be your family who are going with you."

The boy smiled. "Yes, Sir. Thank you for helping to make this possible."

"You are most welcome." The engineer turned to the engineer. "Jay, can you help us get acquainted with your world and the rest of today's schedule. We also will need to know where we will be staying while we're here."

"Leave the train here. Jamie and I will take you to the yard and introduce you to those who will tell you your schedule."

At the mention of his name, Jamie joined Jay and the two headed toward the "Lauer" to climb aboard. But first, Jamie uncoupled the engine from the train, then rode the front pilot to be able to jump off and throw switches as needed. The engine let out two blasts of its whistle and set its bell to ringing as it began its noisy move toward the yard.

All approached the train and started to walk its length and examine the four cars. The Pullman car was next in front of the caboose, then the parlor car, and finally the baggage car. They all paused to admire the gold design work on the side of the cars. Fancy end scrolls matched the same as on the parlor car, the same as on the president's car. A fancy oval design on the side under the center windows had the name "Voyager" while the parlor car had the name "Walton," just like the president's car which had the name "Lage." They turned their attention at the sound of footsteps.

Dan approached the family group. They paused to hear what he had to say. "Jay's going to be busy the rest of the morning. Perhaps you could catch up with him this afternoon."

Mr. Tyler suggested, "Why don't you invite him to our house for lunch? Adam and I were supposed to take the midday train to South Camp. We might just have to skip today. We've already had substitutes assigned for our jobs 'til we return. Could you get word to Bob Leary to tell Teddy we're tied up?"

"That should work and I'll talk to Bob. I'm not sure what our schedule is going to be for now. I know there have been changes and Leary's crew will stick with the "Scott" and Matthewson's crew will handle all of the "King's" work."

"We'll head on home and wait for him." He turned to the family and friends. "Let's head home for now. We'll drop you three at school on the way. Whatever happens with Jay, we'll fill you in after school."

The six left the station and headed past the school toward home. The younger boys turned off into the schoolhouse as the remaining three continued on home to wait for Jay.

\*   \*   \*

By the time Jay arrived for lunch, he had already coupled the "King" to the special and moved the train to the main track at the edge of the station platform. There it would remain for the days of preparation while all through traffic used the pass track. The white 'special' flags had been transferred to the "King" as well. All of his crew would be with them for the journey along with Jamie. They were given the rest of the week off to have time with their families before their upcoming four-week absence. They would remain on call should Jay need them for any reason and return later in the week for the practice run of the special.

At lunch, Jay shared all this information with the Tylers and a concern about finding rooms for Number forty-three's crew. Mr. Tyler suggested he move into a spare room in their house so Clara Stauffer could add another bed to the room and rent his room out to Matthewson and one of his crewmen while he was away. If she has another room or two available, she could double them up as well. Jay accepted the idea and would see Clara after lunch and arrange for Ephram at Wells Fargo to move his things to the farm. He also learned that Mr. Marlow's steward, Howard Roth, would be arriving Friday morning to take charge of the kitchen in the parlor car and the care of facilities in the Pullman sleeper. He would also be bringing all refrigerated items for the iceboxes on the train as well as crates of fresh fruits and vegetables to be added to the stores in the baggage car. Jay would assign Jamie to work as Howard's assistant in any way needed. Dry goods and supplies had already been loaded onto the baggage car along with hay, and bags of feed for the horses and straw bedding in their box stalls. The front end of the baggage had been converted into a stable area and a ramp had been loaded into that area for loading and off-loading the horses. Provision had also been made for Adam to store Cheyenne's saddle and bridal as well as any added halters, tack, and blankets.

Jay left to meet with Clara and to arrange for Ephram to move his belongings to the farmhouse. He returned with Ephram and was at the house when the boys got home from school. All were invited to go with him to the station for a private tour of the train. A very silent "King" stood coupled to the front of the train. Michael wondered at its silence. He had rarely seen the engine so totally shut down. He climbed into the cab, looked in her fire box, and found it to be completely empty of any hot coals. It was lined with fresh cord wood and kindling scrap, ready to be ignited when the day arrived for its practice run. A newly filled can of coal oil stood on the cab floor beside the firebox door, ready to be added to the wood and kindling when it came time to start a new fire. The tender was stocked full of firewood, piled as high as possible without danger of falling over the side.

He climbed down to rejoin the family on tour. The parlor car had a kitchen and serving counter in the back and a section of four tables, two on a side, set for four persons each, in the middle. The seating area had the stove in the front corner, a cushioned side bench across from it, and an additional eight cushioned benches, four on a side. They walked through the side hall around the kitchen area through the door to the open platform. As they passed through the sleeper, it was seen that the upper berths had been made up with sheets and blankets and folded into the ceiling. Each was part of a compartment comprised of two facing cushioned benches with the overhead berth. Sheets and blankets were stored under the back end of the benches for the lower berths. Each cushioned bench had a drawer built in underneath the aisle end for the passengers' belongings. There was a lavatory room at each end of the car with wash basin and toilet. They passed through into the caboose. The front end had one set of bunk beds, a side bench across from them, a table with four chairs, a stove with wood box, and a small wardrobe closet. The cupola had a bed under each side with storage underneath each and ladders to the observation seats. The back room was a combination office and storage room with pegs along the sides for clothing items.

The party descended the steps from the back platform of the caboose. They headed back toward the farm. The four boys walked in front, thoroughly engrossed in conversation about the train. The group of adults followed, wrapped in their own conversation. As they walked up Main Street toward Cedar, Teddy and Miles turned off at Maple Street for home. Michael and Adam continued on by themselves.

*   *   *

On Tuesday, all went to work or school as usual. Wednesday morning was the class tour of the train. Teddy hosted the caboose, Michael the sleeper, Miles the parlor car, and Adam the baggage car. Jay and his crew took turns leading small groups of six students through the train, entering the front of the baggage car by way of the ramp and exiting the back of the caboose down the platform steps. Before the class began, Michael took Mrs. Miller on her own private tour of the train. Evan Clanton captured the whole event for the Friday edition of *The Herald*.

Thursday was the last day for school and work schedules. Howard Roth arrived on Friday's morning train and got right to work with Jamie's help and Jarrett and a baggage cart, transferring all he had brought to the special train. In addition to all that had been previously expected were two surprise gifts from Mr. Marlow – a blanket for each, horse and pony, with the railroad's logo in the corners on each side and their names on each side as well. They were hung on the front wall of their respective stalls with name showing.

During the afternoon, the travelers loaded their personal belongings on the train. A practice run was planned for Saturday morning to Kingston, then Day's End, and back. Jay wanted everyone to get a feel for the train before they left on Monday so any needed changes could be made during the afternoon. Howard said he would serve breakfast before they left so he could do a practice run of the kitchen.

Saturday dawned with a misty drizzle, damp and cold. In the early dawn light, the boys rode their horse and pony as their parents walked alongside – out the lane and down the streets to the station. As the train came into view, smoke rose from the engine's stack and those on the parlor car. The absence of the cloud of steam that normally wrapped the engine was a sign that the fire had been newly lit and it hadn't yet built up a head of steam.

Once on the station platform, the boys dismounted and led their steeds up the ramp and into the stable area. Cheyenne was unsaddled and turned in to her stall. Of-The-Wind was turned in to hers as well. The boys pulled the ramp in, closed the door, then went for breakfast. Their parents were already seated at a table with their breakfast.

Teddy and Miles arrived with their families. They had been invited along for the ride. Their parents took breakfast at one table, their siblings at another, and they with Adam and Michael. As the children finished breakfast, Michael and friends took the brothers and sister on a tour of the train. The train crew took their tables and enjoyed breakfast and conversation with the parents. Jay sat with the Tylers. The remaining four members of his crew sat at the table across the aisle.

Following breakfast, Jay and his crew left to prepare the train for the trip, the Tylers took the other boys' parents for a tour of the train, the children returned and found seats in the front of the car, and the adults returned to sit once more at the tables where Howard provided them with cups and coffee.

Michael and Adam excused themselves to ride the first leg of the trip with their horse and pony. They stepped out onto the front platform of the baggage car to listen to the "King" as it built up enough steam to operate. They heard the safety valve pop and the hiss of steam, and saw the steam cloud roll out and envelop the locomotive. They heard, too, Jay's voice as he informed the conductor that they were ready to go. Dave returned to the parlor car to call 'all aboard' and climbed inside to announce the train's departure. Two whistle blasts acknowledged the call, steam blasted through the cylinders, the drivers began to turn, and the train rattled into motion as the couplers pulled taught and the floorboards vibrated with the train's movement. A sense of excitement pervaded the car's occupants as the train eased into motion toward Kingston.

The boys reentered the stable area and stood near their respective stalls. Of-The-Wind was happy to have Michael at her stall and went to him for attention as soon as he reentered the car. She was calm and at ease having spent many days on a train less than eight months previously. Cheyenne, while glad for Adam's attention, was a bit skittish, having never before stood in a stall that was moving. By the time the train reached Kingston, both were at ease. The boys returned to the parlor car to ride with their friends. Meanwhile, the train waited on the pass track for the return train from Arlee to make its stop and proceed the Day's End and back to Snow Shoe.

At mid morning, the train returned to Snow Shoe. It pulled in on the main in front of the station, the coaches having been left on the station track just west of the platform and the "Lauer" having been serviced and put away in the engine house. The families detrained and left for home, the boys retrieving their horses from the baggage car. The engine crew took the "King" to the engine yard, serviced it, dumped the ash pan, and parked it in the engine house in front of the "Lauer" for the rest of the weekend. Howard and Jamie cleaned up the kitchen area and then the tables and seating area of the parlor car.

All had gone well. The train was ready for its journey to begin on Monday morning. Departure was scheduled for 10am, after the return of the morning passenger run to Arlee and before the daily freight run was scheduled to depart. It was to run as a special under its white flags, pass through Arlee, switch over to the southbound track, and continue to Truckee. There it was to lay over to await instructions and clearances to proceed westward on the Baltimore and Ohio Railroad with connections onward through multiple rail lines to the Northern Pacific Railroad and a terminus at Savage, Montana, the endpoint of its journey. Overnight layovers would be established in route according to the traffic movements on the various railroads along the way, and with the prearranged instructions in the package of materials Mr. Marlow had given Jay.

*   *   *

Later in the day, Brett Tompkins and his parents joined the Tyler family for lunch. After lunch, they toured the farm and went over the chores Brett would need to attend. Mr. Tyler offered that they could take the livestock to their place if it would be easier. The only needs that would remain were to keep the smokehouse fire burning so the meat wouldn't spoil and to keep the kitchen fire burning so the water pipes wouldn't freeze, should there be a temperature drop. In the end it was decided to leave the livestock in place since the fires needed tending anyway.

Following church and the social hour on Sunday, Teddy and Miles and their families stopped for light lunch and time for the kids to play hide-and-seek in the yard and the parents to visit in the house, so the boys' families could better know the family that would be caring for their sons in the month ahead.

Monday, the second day of April, dawned clear and cool with a thin band of yellow glowing in the eastern horizon, shedding dim light through Michael's window on the west side of the house and a dark moonless night sky.

"Hey, Little Brother." Adam stood in the doorway, a dark shadow without his lamp. "You ready for our last morning chores until month's end?"

"Huh?" the boy stirred.

"See ya down stairs." He was gone.

Michael stirred, sat up, and rubbed the sleep from his eyes.

He looked toward his trunk to reach for his clothes. But it wasn't there. Then he remembered, it was on the train. His clothes were on the chair. He dressed, made up his bed, then glanced about the room and on the desk to be sure he hadn't forgotten anything. The room was empty. All had been packed in his trunk. The boy left the room.

Entering the kitchen, he reached for his buckskin coat and hat. Adam was already dressed and headed out the door. Michael followed. The older boy had the milk pail and egg basket. They paused at the chicken coop to tend the smokehouse fire, feed the chickens, and gather the eggs. Moving to the barn, they left the egg basket outside the door and entered.

"Adam, I'll milk the cow while you take care of the feeding?" he offered.

"Okay."

Michael grabbed the stool on his way into the cow's stall. He had become very proficient at milking and was more than willing to make it his portion of the daily chores. Adam put the feed in the manger boxes along with the hay, and brought water in from the outside water trough to dump into each tin basin beside the grain box. Setting the milk pail and stool outside the stall, Michael climbed to the upper barn and threw down the day's hay.

"We'll be back, Girls." Michael announced as he picked up the milk pail and headed out the door.

Adam followed behind and picked up the egg basket as the two walked on to the house. In the kitchen, pail and basket were tended to as the boys hung up their outer garments and sat down at the table.

"Does everyone have everything needed for the journey?" Mr. Tyler asked as he reached for the platter of sausages. "Do a mental checklist. Look about the kitchen. Did you check your rooms one last time?"

"I can't think of anything," Adam responded. "Everything for Cheyenne is on the train. She has her halter and just needs to walk to the station with us." He forked two pancakes onto his plate and reached for the syrup.

Michael took sausages from the platter and passed it on. "Of-The-Wind just needs to walk to the train. I checked my bedroom this morning and couldn't see anything I forgot."

Mrs. Tyler set her cup down. "I've looked about the house and can't think of anything. I also did a mental checklist of what is already on the train. I think it's just my coat and hat. I also have several tins of cookies in a basket to take for Howard to put out for snacks. We should also take today's milk and eggs as well as that which is in the icebox from before." She began eating her pancake.

All ate in silence for the next several minutes.

Michael finished his breakfast and pushed his chair back. "Ma, I can't believe this day is really here! I'm goin home and feel so funny inside!"

"Me, too," Adam added. "I can't wait to meet yer people and see the world you come from." He wiped up the last of the syrup on his plate with a final forkful of pancake. "I can't feel about this the same as you, Little Brother. But I sure do feel a whole lot of excitement."

"We're all looking forward to this adventure," Mr. Tyler commented as he drained his coffee cup. "I know your friends are really excited, too. Their folks told us how they envy their boys going with us and look forward to their letters along the way."

The clock in the parlor struck the quarter hour past seven.

"Time to clean up from breakfast, bank the fire in the kitchen range, and close up the house. The fire in the living room stove is almost out and the dampers have been set." Mrs. Tyler rose from the table and started to clear it to the sink.

Each took his own dishes to the drain board and the boys returned to the table for the empty serving dishes. Their father took a towel and wiped the table down, then poured himself a last cup of coffee.

It was time.

The boys put on their coats and hats, hung scarves loosely around their necks to take should they be needed, and stuffed gloves in their pockets. They glanced around the room one last time to be sure they hadn't forgotten anything. The quivers of bow and arrows were already on the train along with Mr. Tyler's rifle.

"We'll get the horses and meet you in the lane," Adam said as he headed out the door, followed close behind by Michael.

"I'll carry the milk and eggs," the younger boy offered as he paused in the doorway. "Of-The-Wind does not need a halter. She will walk with me as she always does." He closed the door behind him.

As the boys returned from the barn, Michael picked up the bucket with the jars of milk and the basket of eggs, and all headed down the lane toward the center of town and the station.

\*　　\*　　\*

As the family approached the station, they saw the train sitting on the track beside the station platform. The "King" was in full steam, wrapped in the white vapor as it hissed from cylinders and fittings, accompanied by the rumblings in the belly of the boiler and the whoosh of white smoke from the locomotive's stack. The area was packed with townspeople who had read the article in Friday's Herald and had come to witness the departure and gaze upon this special train, the likes of which might never be seen again. The totally unexpected crowd and noise frightened the horses. Cheyenne was secured by her halter lead and Adam held her close to try and sooth her. Of-The-Wind pulled away and Michael had to hand the eggs to Adam in order to have a free hand to grab her mane. His touch calmed her enough to get past the crowd and onto the ramp. The air was thick with the noise of multiple conversations within the crowd. The ramp was out for the horses and the boys pushed their way in that direction. Michael spotted Howard standing at the steps beside the parlor car and forced his way to take the milk and eggs to him. Adam put an arm over the pony's neck to hold her long enough for his brother to pass his burden to Howard.

"I'll have to put these in the ice box in the baggage car," he shouted over the noise of the crowd. "The one in the kitchen is full."

He followed the boy back to the ramp and entered the car behind the horses. The boys put their horses in their stalls, pulled in the ramp, and slid the baggage door closed, latching it from the inside. They left the car by the front platform and joined their parents on the wooden platform.

Mrs. Tyler approached Howard as he descended from the back steps of the baggage car. She shouted to be heard over the constant drone of conversations within the crowd. "Here are several tins of cookies I baked this week for you to put out along the way for snacks and the like!"

"Thanks," he shouted back.

She walked with him to the parlor car then turned away to rejoin her husband.

Teddy and Miles were in the crowd with their families.

"Gotta go, Ma." "Bye, Pa." With kisses and hugs they slipped through the constant motion of the growing crowd to find their way to Michael and Adam.

"Janet, I had no idea it would be like this!" her husband shouted. "Maybe we should get on board where we won't be pushed and squeezed to death."

"Lead on, Bill. I sure do agree. We can say good-bye to the Harts and Latimers if we pass them on the way."

"I can see them and will try to push in their direction."

While the crowd had come to see the travelers off, no one seemed to pay attention to who they were. Some wished them well as they pushed through, but many saw them as in the way of their movement to see the train.

Jay and the train crew remained on the train where they could watch the gathering without being caught in the crunch. Jamie stood on the end platform of the parlor car and watched for the family and friends to make their ways to the steps and climb aboard.

Suddenly there was a new wave of movement surging along the back edge of the crowd. Mrs. Miller had arrived with her class. Her face said it all. She was shocked by the presence of so many people. What was worse, most of them had no interest in the departing travelers, they just gawked at the train and the rest of the crowd. It was nearly impossible for the children to see or say good-bye to their friends. Teddy and Miles had finally pushed their way to Michael and Adam, standing by the steps to the front of the parlor car.

"A group of kids just arrived with their teacher," Howard remarked.

"Where?" Michael asked.

"They're way back near the station building," the steward pointed.

"Let's go," Adam instructed. "No one's paying any attention to us. We can push our way around the edge of the crowd and you can see your friends."

The four worked their way along the edge of the crowd by way of Main Street and broke clear to walk to the station.

"I don't believe this mob!" Mrs. Miller exclaimed. "They don't even seem to be paying any attention to you boys, just standing around and talking amongst themselves and staring at the train."

"We came to see you off," one of the girls announced.

Another shared, "I sher am glad we were able to tour your train last week. This is just a mess."

Jamison pushed closer. "I hope you guys have a great journey. I understand you're each keeping a journal. I hope you'll read them to the class when you get back."

"Can we, Mrs. Miller?" Miles asked.

"I think that's a marvelous idea. Thank you, Jamison." Her smile showed her appreciation. "Now you boys better work your way back to the train and climb on board." She glanced down at her pendant watch pinned to her blouse. "It's just past 9:30 and I understand the train leaves at 10:00."

"Yes, Ma'am," Michael responded. "Thanks for coming and bringing the class. I hope to send at least one letter to the class. But I know I will be very busy. I'm going home to be with my people and to see my family and friends again." He suddenly felt a thickness in his throat and could say no more.

His teacher put a hand on his shoulder and said for him alone, "I think I understand. For this journey, you are Prairie Cub, and I wish you God speed. May the Great One watch over your journey and all who go with you. Your parents can be proud of you. They have raised you well." She squeezed gently, then stepped back.

The boy smiled a teary smile, then turned to work his way back to the train. The others followed.

"Good-bye." "Safe journey." "We'll miss you." "Take care." The classmates called as they waved their friends away.

A single sharp blast from the "King's" whistle cut through the morning air, piercing the noise of the crowd.

The boys got as far as the baggage car where they climbed the steps to the front platform to work their way through the train. They passed from car to car across the adjoining platforms as they entered the front of the parlor car. Howard had climbed on board and stood on the open platform as they crossed into the car. Their parents had worked their way to the back platform of the parlor car and stood there with Jamie. The boys passed through the car to join them, and stepped across to the platform of the Pullman for more room. From the vantage point of the platform they could look out and see Teddy and Miles' families and make out the faces of others from the church. They saw the boys' class with its teacher, far in the back near the station building. They waved and friends waved back. Standing across from their parents the boys, too, waved to family, friends, and classmates.

Dave Seegers came out on the platform with Howard.

"It's almost time to leave," he said. "This sure is a mess of people." He gazed out across the sea of faces. "Do they all know what's happening here?"

Howard ventured an opinion. "If you ask me, most have no idea what this is all about. They're just here because something different is happening and there's a strange train involved."

"I think you may have something there. It will be good to get away from all this noise and enjoy each other's company and the peace of the journey." He looked at his watch. "It's time." He stepped down to the station platform and waved toward the engine.

"All aboard," he called in a loud voice, then climbed back aboard.

Two loud blasts screamed from the engine's whistle as the bell began its rhythmic ringing. Family, friends, and train crew cleared the platforms with one last wave as they disappeared into the parlor car.

A loud chuff burst from the piston chambers on the locomotive followed momentarily by another as the drive rods slowly turned the large driver wheels. A loud clunking sound echoed from the train as the couplers pulled taught and the brake shoes clattered loose on the wheels. The chuffs came more quickly as the train began to move and to pick up speed. The wheels clattered across the rail joints.

In the crowd friends and classmates, family and teacher waved the travelers on their journey.

Some wept who knew how personal this journey was for one boy, torn between two worlds.

The train picked up speed and disappeared around a bend in the wooded landscape, its column of smoke following above the trees, until it, too, disappeared in the distance.

The crowd began to disperse.

Mrs. Miller took her students and started back toward the school.

# EPILOGUE – REUNION

# MICHAEL PC FREEMAN

SCOT ROBINSON

# LAWRENCE KAYMOND

# ADAM TYLER

## TEDDY LATIMER

# MILES HART

Prairie Cub was no longer that scared and grieving little boy, fresh off the frontier, who got off the train at Truckee some eight months ago. He had grown in stature. He had grown in confidence. He had a new sense of security and belonging as he sat by the window of the speeding train car and gazed out at the predawn blackness of night. He smiled at his reflection in the glass, dressed in his buckskins, lost in dreams of anticipation.

The boy was alone in the car. He had risen early to walk to the baggage car, dress in his native clothes, and spend time with his pony. Michael was packed away in his trunk and would stay there until the day they departed for the return trip to Snow Shoe. The others on the train were still asleep in the Pullman car. Only the train crew was awake – Jay and Scott in the engine cab and the rest in the caboose with their morning coffee.

Prairie Cub was going home, home to a world he could only visit, journeying from a new world he had come to love and feel safe and at home in. He had come to terms that he truly was two people, living in two very different worlds with two very different families, each of whom he loved dearly. Each of whom loved him dearly in return.

Suddenly, an engine wrapped in its blanket of steam, with lighted cab, flashed by outside the window, followed by the dark silhouettes of freight cars and the flash of light from its caboose. After a night's layover, the special had left Bismarck, North Dakota Territory, an hour back, with clearance through to Savage, Montana Territory. Eastbound traffic was to hold on its respective pass track as the westbound special passed by. All had been prearranged by the president of the Virginia and Truckee through the president of each other railroad along the way. Arrival was expected by late afternoon.

The door at the back of the car opened letting in the noise of the moving train and a whiff of cigar smoke. It closed. Howard Roth headed to the kitchen to prepare breakfast. As was his custom throughout the journey, he enjoyed his cigar while he lit an overhead lamp and gathered materials together for preparing the meal. He then put it out in the water from the sink and set it aside for his midmorning break, and cracked open a window to let the smell out and the noise of the running train in. Daytime smoke breaks were taken on the open platform so as not to offend any aboard the train.

Waiting for the cigar smell to clear the air and the window to close, the boy rose from his seat and walked back to the kitchen.

Howard looked up in surprise from the mixing bowl of pancake batter. "I didn't know anyone else was up yet," he turned to the boy. "Are these your native clothes?" He set his measuring cup down to give the boy his full attention.

"Yes, Sir."

"I assume from your story that today you are Prairie Cub."

"Today I will be home with my family."

"I understand. That is this journey's destination. Can I get you anything?"

"Coffee when it's ready. Can I help with anything?"

"Would you like to light the lamps and set up the tables?"

"Okay."

The steward put on a pot of coffee, then returned to his breakfast preparations while the boy lit the overhead lamps throughout the car, then took the utensil trays from the counter and began to set the tables, a job he had done previously throughout the journey.

The two worked quietly at their respective jobs.

Again the open door and the clattering of the train rattling along the tracks announced the arrival of another. Adam entered the car, yawning at the effort to wake up. He closed the door and cut off the noise then looked at his brother, no longer wearing his brother's clothes.

"I guess you're not my brother just now." He approached the table area.

The boy paused in his work. "I am Prairie Cub until we start back for home. And I am still your brother, wherever we are." He smiled as he continued to lay out the place settings.

"Mornin', Mr. Roth," Adam greeted, turning to the kitchen. "I smell coffee."

"Mornin', Adam," the man replied as he vigorously stirred the pancake batter. "Coffee has to perk yet, then you can put out a cup for each of you."

"Thanks, I'll help my brother here." He entered the kitchen and gathered the stack of plates to set out on the tables.

All worked in rhythm with the rocking of the train and the vibrations of its movement through the floorboards. They had become accustomed to the motion over the previous days of travel, even anticipating the occasional sudden shift when the train hit a section of rough track. The sizzle of sausages added a new aroma to the air as the coffee rattled to a perk and the table setting was finished. Adam poured two cups of coffee and passed them to his brother, then reached the cream from the ice box and settled at the table with Prairie Cub. They enjoyed their coffee in silence while they watched Howard at work, juggling the various preparations of the breakfast meal.

The outside noise of the moving train once more exploded through the open door as Jamie, Teddy, Miles, and the Tylers entered the car. The door closed and the noise was cut off.

"Hi," the boys greeted.

"I smell coffee," Mr. Tyler announced.

"And the aroma sausage," his wife added.

"Breakfast will be ready shortly," the steward announced.

"What can I do?" Jamie asked.

"You can start the pancakes on the grill."

The young assistant entered the kitchen and went to work on the grill.

Outside the windows the moving landscape began to brighten with the predawn light of a rising sun in the eastern sky behind the moving train. Within minutes, the sun peeked over the horizon, its light flowing through the windows to cast the shadows of the car's occupants. Outside, a vacant land of rolling hills and plains with scattered clusters of trees and low vegetation and little evidence of civilization, flowed past the windows. Nearly a hundred miles of wilderness lay between Bismark and Dickenson, the next town along the railroad.

"Breakfast is ready," Howard announced as he and Jamie brought the food to the tables.

All helped themselves and began to eat as they gazed upon the wilderness outside the windows.

"Look!" Miles pointed to a distant spot on the land. "There's a huge cloud of dust and it seems to be coming this way!"

All looked to the unknown spectacle.

"Buffalo!" Prairie Club exclaimed. "Hundreds of them. And they're coming this way."

Howard and Jamie rushed over from the kitchen as family and friends moved to the chairs closest to the windows where Miles had seen the animals. The train began to slow. Teddy looked toward the front of the train as a water tower came into view in the far distance. It approached rapidly as the train slowed and the brakes began to screech. The train slowed to a crawl as the engine approached the tower and the engineer lined the tender up with the water spout. It stopped and a sharp whistle chirped. A large pile of firewood lay beside the water tower.

Scott climbed up onto the tender to open the hatch, pull down the water spout, and fill the tank. Jay climbed down from the cab to pass firewood to his fireman. The rest of the train crew walked up from the caboose to help with the task. The herd of buffalo came closer and the shaggy beasts could be seen within the dust cloud.

Once the engine had been serviced, the train crew walked to the front of the parlor car and came aboard. As they opened the door, the tremendous thundering of the approaching buffalo herd rolled into the car with them.

"We're not going anywhere until they pass," Jay announced. "So we might as well join you for breakfast."

The boys and their parents moved away from the two empty tables as the men pulled out their kerchiefs, wiped their hands, and took their seats at the tables. Jamie and Mr. Roth brought platters of food to the remaining tables along with the coffee pot and cream to be passed around, then joined the Tylers at their table. As the diners watched, thousands of buffalo passed across the tracks about a quarter mile in front of the train. The herd seemed to stretch for more than a mile. Nearly an hour passed before the last of the herd crossed over and disappeared to the south.

"We can get underway now," Jay announced as he stood from the table. "Howard, can you send a pot of coffee up before we start?"

"There's one brewing now," the steward replied. "It'll be along shortly."

"We're goin' up to feed the horses," Adam informed.

The four boys followed the engine crew out the door to cross over to the baggage car to tend to Of-The-Wind and Cheyenne.

"Dan," Mr. Tyler spoke up, "You and your crew might as well settle here with us. Once the boys get back it will be time for them to update their journals."

The Tylers and the train crew moved to the lounge area in the front of the car. Charles, the brakeman, tended the stove, keeping the fire low. Dan brought the coffee pot from the table and set it on the stove top. Howard and Jamie cleared the breakfast dishes and set out the journal books from their place on the far corner of the kitchen side counter. Jamie took the pot of coffee to the engine where he would ride the next part of the journey.

The whistle sounded and the train began to move. The floorboards vibrated with the clatter of releasing brakes, couplers pulling tight, and the rumble of steel on steel as the wheels turned and the train picked up speed. The next scheduled stop was Dickenson.

*     *     *

The sun still hung high in the late afternoon western sky as the train began to pass through the farming country outside of Savage, Montana Territory. The engine whistled the first grade crossing in nearly a hundred miles. Prairie Cub stared in disbelief at a countryside that had been empty when he had left at the end of the past summer, but was now dotted with cultivated fields.

"Boys," Mrs. Tyler interrupted, "it's time to gather your things from the Pullman and your journals, writing materials, and games, and pack your trunks. We'll be leaving the train shortly and putting it to rest for the next two weeks." She stood from her bench in the seating area and moved to a table to briefly watch the approach into Savage, before joining her husband.

Mr. Roth gathered the rest of the boys' materials from their place in the kitchen and moved them to a table. Prairie Cub remained in his seat while his brother and friends left for the sleeper to gather clothing and anything else from their sleeping compartments. He had removed all his things when he went to the baggage car before sunup to change into his clothes. Mr. and Mrs. Tyler went with the boys to gather their belongings to take to their trunk in the baggage car. Shortly thereafter, all passed through the car to the baggage car to pack their trunks, then returned to watch out the windows as the train entered the town and approached the station. A few local folks paused to stare at the train as it screeched to a halt and sounded a single sharp blast from its whistle, but moved on when no one appeared on the car platforms to step down from the train. Jay sent Jamie back from the engine cab with instructions for everyone to wait aboard the train for further instructions.

"We're to wait here until Mr. Summers meets with Jay at the engine," Jamie informed. "When we stopped at Dickenson, Jay wired ahead where we were and about what time he expected we would arrive. Mr. Summers replied that he would meet us here and see that the train was moved to his company spur inside the company yard, then come aboard and meet with us."

"I'll set out coffee and the last of Mrs. Tyler's cookies if anyone wants," Mr. Roth announced.

Jamie went to the kitchen to help put out cups and plates as the family and friends took seats at the tables where they could watch out the windows at peoples' reactions to the arrival of the special train. Dan and the rest of his crew joined them to enjoy the refreshments and observe activity outside the windows as well. Moments later, Jay entered through the door to the front platform, followed by a large built man in glasses.

"Mr. Summers!" The boy rushed out of his chair toward the man who waited with open arms.

"Prairie Cub!" he called in return.

The man folded the boy in an emotional embrace, grateful to be together once more.

Jamie brought a freshly poured cup of coffee for each of the two as Howard moved an empty chair to the boys' table.

The boy pulled the proprietor to the empty chair while Jay took a seat with the Tylers.

Keith Summers explained, "I didn't want any ruckus here in town. Everyone's at the fort. Stay on the train until Jay pulls it onto the company track inside the yard and we close the gates. Walt's there with two wagons, ready to go. Unload everything into the wagons, including all remaining supplies." He paused to drink some coffee. "The Robinsons and the Kaymonds have thoroughly cleaned up the barracks so you can move in as soon as you arrive. Howard has full use of the kitchen where all supplies will go. Walt will work with him to restock whatever he needs. Prairie Cub, Roaring Wing has set the village right in front of the fort with Thunder Eagle's lodge closest to the gate." Again, a coffee break. "The stables are ready for Of-The-Wind and Cheyenne. Take all the stores and tack from the baggage car. Fresh will be supplied for the return trip. Tomorrow, my staff will do a thorough cleaning of the train under supervision by Howard and Jay. Walt will stay at my house in the fort to be with you while you are here. He is very fond of you folks and doesn't want to miss a moment of your stay. Any questions before we move the train?"

"Keith," Jay asked. "I don't suppose you have an ash pit around here. Is there any way we can empty the "King's" fire box?"

"If you can keep here under steam while we move everything to the wagons, I think we can uncouple the train and I can ride with you to the water tower. Fill your tender with water and wood. Then we can dump the hot coals under the water spout, back away, water the coals, then return to the yard."

"That'll work."

Several minutes passed as the engine crew returned to the locomotive, moved the train from the station to the spur inside the freight company's yard, then returned to the parlor car.

"Let's put all personal gear in the front wagon and supplies in the other." Summers emptied his cup and stood from the table. "We'll leave for the fort as soon as all is done here." He started toward the door. "Jay, let's you an me take care of your engine."

The train crew followed to help service the engine.

The boys and the family followed out the front door to empty the baggage car while Howard and Jamie started to clean up the tables and the kitchen.

*   *   *

The freight wagons advanced up the hill on the wilderness road out of Savage. By the sun, it was nearing five o'clock in the evening. The lead wagon, driven by Walt Mattson carried the engineer and his crew. Mattson wore the coonskin hat he had made from the skin bought from Teddy. The boy noticed it the moment the families started to load the wagons and told the man how great it looked.

The second, driven by Keith Summers carried the Tylers, the boys, and the steward and his assistant. Prairie Cub and his brother rode along either side of the wagons. The boy wore his new buckskin jacket so his friend Walt could see it. Walt had admired it as they loaded the wagons in preparation for the trip to the fort.

A lone rider approached from the front. Prairie Cub broke from the wagons and rushed ahead.

"Prairie Cub!" the teen shouted as he drew near.

"Hi Scot!" the boy returned as he raced to greet his friend. "I'm home," he cried.

"I know. I couldn't wait!"

The two drew alongside each other, their faces glowing in the pure joy of reunion. They reached out and locked forearms in greeting.

"I like your new coat," Scot observed.

"Thanks," the boy grinned. "My ma made it from skins Prairie Flower had tanned."

Scot urged his horse to the first wagon to ride beside at matched speed. "Hi, Jay. Hi, Guys," he greeted.

"It's so good to see you, Scot," the engineer replied as he reached out to the offered hand. "Boy, have you grown these many years."

"I've missed you all," the teen shared. "Are you teaching this boy, here, how to run the "King"?"

"He sure is," the fireman cut in. "And this boy has gotten really good at it, too."

Dan added, "Now when we run the branch, Prairie Cub runs the whole trip all the way to the switch to the main line."

"You know, the "King's" here?" Jay asked.

"Heard tell it got ya here, but it don't make sense."

Matt explained, "Prairie Cub's story made it to Mr. Marlow, the president of the railroad and he took a personal interest in it. He provided a whole special train for us to make this trip."

"I can't wait to see it," Scot responded. "I'll see you all later. I have to get back and report to Pa that you're here. He's working on supper and needs ta know about when ta have it done." He turned his horse. "Gotta meet the family first."

The teen rode to the second wagon and turned his horse to ride alongside.

"Hi, Scot," Mrs. Tyler greeted.

"Hi, Mrs. Tyler. I met you folks in the newspaper article Trader Mattson brought back. You're his ma and pa back in Snow Shoe."

"And you're his railroad friend who once stayed in Snow Shoe," Mr. Tyler greeted. "We are so glad to meet you." He offered his hand and the youth reached out for it. "This is our other son, Adam," he pointed to the teen on the horse.

"Hi, Scot," Adam waved from the far side of the wagon.

"Hi," Scot waved. "I haf ta go now," the teen continued as he turned his horse and headed back toward the fort.

"I'll go with you," Prairie Cub shouted.

"Pa said as you should stay with your family and make sure no one gets lost." He put his horse into a run and hurried on up the road to quickly disappear over the horizon into his trail dust.

*　　*　　*

The wagons' occupants and their outriders gazed ahead at an approaching scene absolutely amazing in its scope. Exiting the bluffs of the Yellowstone's river valley, the land was open with a few rolling hills, as far as the eye could see into the higher foothills of the mountains beyond. In front stood the old wooden trading fort with a village of dozens of tepees with lodge pole crowns, spread out in front of its gate. As the party drew near, they could detect people, hundreds of them, all standing in a large mass, watching the wagons come in.

"Oh my God!" the Tylers exclaimed. "They're all waiting for us!"

"You have a very special son," Walt explained. Without pausing his wagon or turning to face the family he went on. "It was his arrow that killed the officer who led the attack on their village. He wears the coup feathers in his headband that were awarded by their chief, Roaring Wing. As his family, you, too, are held in high honor by his people. As his friends, Teddy, Miles, and all his friends, here, are honored as well. This homecoming is a much anticipated and longed for event. Nothing else could have brought these people together. And for this gathering, we are all indebted to Keith."

"I have to go!" Prairie Cub cried.

"I know," his mother acknowledged. "Go."

The boy leaned forward on his pony's neck and she broke into a wild, joyous run as she charged toward a familiar tepee just outside the front of the fort. All from the wagons watched as the two slid to a halt in front of those standing there and he slipped to the ground and stood momentarily. Thunder Eagle, Prairie Flower and Granny Woman lost all composure as they reached out and wrapped their son and grandson in an emotional embrace for which they had longed ever since he had left the village on that last visit near the end of the past summer.

The wagons arrived at the gathering. Janet Tyler looked down on the four, still locked in their emotional embrace. She could not contain her tears or think of anything to say. Trying very hard to maintain some semblance of composure, Thunder Eagle looked up to the woman.

"We'll keep our son with us for now." He could say no more.

The woman smiled and nodded her head. No words were needed.

Trapper Murray stepped forward from the families near the gateway. "Walt," the bearded Frenchman began, "Supper is ready in the barracks. Unload the wagons and have the folks wait inside. Take the wagons to the stables and Scot and my son will help put the horses up and back the wagons into the sheds. Roaring Wing's people will have their own celebration tonight and will meet with you tomorrow. We will get to know each other at supper."

The wagons moved on into the fort where they drew up in front of the barracks building and their occupants began to unload. The family and the boys felt a sudden loss at the unexpected separation from the younger son.

\*     \*     \*

Thunder Eagle and his family sat to dinner in front of their lodge as members of the tribe stopped to welcome their son home and pay their respects. Roaring Wing and his squaw were the first to visit. No one else arrived out of respect, until the chief had left. Little Bear and his family were the next to stop. Others followed throughout the evening. The boy was lost in the ecstasy of the moment. He was home.

\*     \*     \*

Within the barracks, Keith Summers took charge and briefly organized the chaos of arrival. The personal trunks and possessions had been unloaded along the front wall. Within the great room, many of the individual tables had been lined up to form one grand long table.

"Everyone find a seat while we make some quick introductions and supper is brought to the tables." The proprietor moved to a chair near the end of the table.

The gathering tended to settle in by family groups with the train crew sitting in their own group. Mattson sat with the Tyler group. Howard sat with Jamie and the train crew. All took a chair.

"Most of us have heard of each other," Keith began. "I'd like to take this moment to introduce folks." He started along the table. "Here, we have Prairie Cub's family from the East: Bill and Janet Tyler and their son, Adam, with Prairie Cub's friends, Teddy Latimer and Miles Hart, and you all know my Business Manager, Walt Mattson." He paused as each stood in turn and nodded to the gathering. "On this side are Northern Pacific Railroad surveyor Clint Robinson and his son Scot." Another brief pause. "On the other side, Murray and Marian Kaymond and their son Lawrence." He concluded by asking Jay to introduce the railroad personnel.

The meal was served by the Kaymond family as they moved the serving dishes to the table to be passed around family style.

*    *    *

In the hours that followed, Mr. Summers showed the new arrivals to the accommodations he had created in the upstairs rooms. Back at the end of summer, after Prairie Cub had gone east and the fort had become a ghost town of sorts, he had continued to make changes to convert the barracks into a hotel for Easterners who might come west as tourists. Many had been grouped together to create suites with a common room and two or more bedrooms. In most cases, walls had been removed and bedrooms were doubled in size. The Tylers moved into a two-bedroom suite with generous room sizes wherein the three boys had a comfortable room with two bunk beds and plenty of space for four wardrobes. two desks, and open wall space for the four travel trunks. Jay and his crew had rooms set up for two and a three-room suite for Howard and Jamie with a room each and a work area where they could work to coordinate the business of operating the kitchen and the barracks as a hotel complex. Janet and Marian offered to take charge of the kitchen and were given that responsibility for the duration of their stay. Jamie was to be their assistant. The entire complex had been previously cleaned by the Kaymond family with help from the Robinsons, as they prepared for the visitors from the east. All trapping paraphernalia had been removed to storage in the trading post storeroom. The great room had seating areas scattered about and the long table down its center at the kitchen end of the room. Larger seating areas were established at the opposite ends in front of the large stone fireplace that centered on each end wall. As the warmth of spring set in, the fires were allowed to die out.

Once moved in, Adam asked his pa if they could take Prairie Cub's bundles and weapons to his lodge in the village outside the fort. He approved and the boys left.

The three boys approached the family, gathered at their fire in front of their tepee.

"Okay if we bring these for Prairie Cub?" Adam asked.

"Yes, of course," Thunder Eagle replied as he stood to greet the boys. "Won't you join us?" he invited. "This is our son's mother, Prairie Flower," he introduced, "And this is Granny Woman." He indicated a small wiry woman with wrinkled skin and a warm glow from sparkling brown eyes.

The two looked up to the boys and smiled.

Prairie Cub stood up. "This is my big brother, Adam," he introduced as he accepted his possessions and set them near the tepee door, "and my closest friends, Teddy and Miles."

"Welcome," Thunder Eagle greeted. "Have a seat by our fire."

All sat down, the three boys awkward and unsure of their welcome.

Prairie Flower attempted to put them at ease. "We are so grateful that you were able to come on this journey." She looked to each in turn. "Our son has written so much about you and the joy that Teddy and Mile's parents would allow them to come. We have looked forward to meeting you and hope you will enjoy your time here."

Thunder Eagle added, "We have only arrived a few days ago ourselves. Trapper Murray and his son took a small party from the village to scout the far reaches of Keith's lands to search for the buffalo. They have come and are grazing several miles to the west of here."

"We will have a hunt!" Prairie Cub added excitedly.

"And this time you will be part of it," the aged voice crackled.

His father continued. "The council met and the buffalo dance is planned for two suns from this day. You are all invited to witness this. Our son tells me Adam has his own horse and Of-The-Wind has allowed Teddy and Miles to learn to ride. I will find you ponies so you can ride with the women and children to watch the hunt and help with the harvest. Prairie Cub tells us you two have been running a trap line, so you can help his mother with the skinning and gathering. This will be the first hunt that he will be with the hunters"

"Wow!" the three exclaimed as they looked at each other then at their friend and his family. "Wait 'til I tell Pa!" Adam added.

"Lawrence and his father were here for the buffalo hunt last spring, but left following the ceremony," Thunder Eagle informed. "This year, they might join the hunt, too."

"Would you three like to stay the night with us?" Prairie Flower invited. "We can crowd you into our home for the night or the four of you can sleep out here by the fire."

"Inside," her son chose. "They can know what our home is like."

"Are you sure?" Adam questioned. "This is Prairie Cub's home-coming and we don't want to interfere."

"Our son has let us know that he has two families," the warrior answered. "This journey will allow both families to get to know each other and become one."

Adam confirmed, "We'll go back and tell my folks and get our blankets."

The three stood.

"Thanks," Prairie Cub stood. "I'll bring some more firewood and see you when you get back."

The three boys left on the run to share their invitation with Adam's parents and return with their blankets.

*　　*　　*

The first full day of the adventure dawned with a bright red sun peeking over the horizon in the east and a chilly coolness in the air within the tepee. As the boys rose, dressed, and rolled their blankets, Teddy asked Thunder Eagle if the family would join them for breakfast in the barracks. He looked to his wife to confirm his approval and it was agreed. The boys picked up their blanket rolls and the six of them headed for the gateway into the fort and the barracks building within.

Upon entering the barracks, the boys found Howard and Jamie setting the tables for breakfast.

"Do you have room for three more?" Adam asked the surprised pair.

"Of course," Howard replied. "Jamie, help me add another table to this end of the tables."

The two quickly moved another table and its chairs from the side of the room along with complete place settings. Hearing the conversation from the kitchen, the women entered the dining area to greet the family. They introduce themselves to Prairie Cub's family and asked his mother if she would like to help them in the kitchen. Thunder Eagle remained with the boys and menfolk and watched as they completed their work.

Janet and Marian had several cast iron frying pans filled with sizzling sausages and chopped potatoes with onion. A large bowl of scrambled eggs was waiting on the counter to be cooked fresh after the rest of the gathering arrived for breakfast. Trays of biscuits had been placed in the oven to bake and stay warm. Prairie Flower accepted a spatula and took over the constant stirring of the potatoes.

In the dining room, the noise of the arriving menfolk filled the room as all began to gather for breakfast. The families and the train crew came down from their rooms and introduced themselves to Thunder Eagle and shifted their seating to accommodate Prairie Cub's family. Mr. Summers and Mr. Mattson arrived from the proprietor's house, where they would stay for the first few days, and took their places at the table. As food preparations finished and the meal was gathered into serving dishes, Howard, Jamie, and the women brought it to the table and all seated themselves to enjoy the meal and each other's company.

"Mr. Tyler," Thunder Eagle began. "My son would like to take his brother and his friends for a ride into the hills and show them some of this country." The warrior glanced with fatherly pride at his son. "I understand that he and his pony have begun to teach them how to ride and that Adam has his horse here as well."

Bill Tyler glanced at his wife. "How safe is this wilderness?" he asked. "I know it's Prairie Cub's home and he knows it well. But we are responsible for Teddy and Miles' well being entrusted to us by their families. Will they be safe?"

"They will be in no more danger than any of our boys ever are." He looked toward Scot then Lawrence. "They will be with friends who know this country well. I expect Scot and Lawrence will go with their horses as well and we have well trained ponies the boys may ride."

"Can Little Bear and White Hare go, too?" Prairie Cub asked.

"I think they will all make a fine scouting party and can tell us what they see in their travels," his father observed.

Following breakfast, the three boys saddled their horses while the fourth led his pony and the remaining two walked with the others, and all six walked back to the village with the warrior. Prairie Flower remained to help the women in the kitchen and get to know them better. Thunder Eagle led the boys to the pony lines where he selected two ponies for Teddy and Miles. On the way, Prairie Cub told his two friends what they were planning and invited them to go along. Several minutes later the unusual party of eight boys rode out from the village toward the hill country west of the fort.

The boys were eager to get to know each other as East met West and all shared their lives and curious queries with one-an-other as they rode out from the village. Little Bear and White Hare were the same age as Prairie Cub. In stature they were slightly shorter and of stouter build, thicker through the chest and legs. Little Bear was the taller of the two. Brown hair was loose and straight. Brown eyes sparkled with curiosity and the joy of adventure. Neither boy spoke English, so their part of the conversation was translated by Prairie Cub, as was that of the other boys.

Little Bear asked, "Prairie Cub, are these friends of yours strong enough for this ride? I know Lawrence and Scot have skills."

Prairie Cub translated and let Teddy make the reply. "Little Bear, while we come from Prairie Cub's other life, we share an interest in trapping, and with his help, are learning to ride. We will never be as good as you because we don't get the chance back home."

Miles added, "Our worlds are very different. Prairie Cub has invited us to share this journey and learn what your world is like. And I am so glad he did and so glad to meet you and all his friends our here."

Again, the boy translated and Little Bear was satisfied. "I like your friends and the feel of their respect. With them, we are equal."

White Hare joined in. "Little Bear speaks for both of us. I want to get to know all who have come with you. Your people show respect that so many others from your other world don't have."

"Thanks, White Hare," Teddy acknowledged. "I think that's why we enjoy such a close friendship with Prairie Cub."

After a mile of travel with the village and fort lost from view, the boys began to see a growing presence of wild life. Rabbits and other small game scampered through the grasslands. In the distance, an elk herd grazed as it slowly crossed the land. A large bird floated on the airwaves and Scot called the younger boys' attention to it.

Pointing skyward he announced, "Look there, it's an eagle. He's probably hunting for food for his young'uns. Watch and see."

The boys halted their ponies and watched the eagle's moves. Suddenly it dropped from the sky at surprising speed, opening its wings at the last moment as it extended its talons and snatched a small rabbit from the grass before flapping its wings and rising once again, high into the air. The eagle banked to the side and disappeared toward the distant hills.

"Wow!" Miles exclaimed. "That was awesome!"

They moved on. From the south, a loud honking racket approached. The boys looked up to witness a constantly shifting flying wedge of geese in their migration flight northward.

"That's the sign that it's time for the buffalo migration and the annual hunt," Lawrence offered. "My pa and I were witness to last year's buffalo ceremony before the village left for the hunt and we left for the rendezvous." The fourteen-year-old French teen looked toward the Indian boys. "We've already seen the buffalo this year. They're several miles further west from here, grazing along the Yellowstone."

White Hare invited, "The ceremony is only one more sun from now. You can all attend."

Prairie Cub translated and added, "With your trapping and skinning skills, Teddy, Miles, and Lawrence can probably help with the hunt as well."

"All right!" the three responded.

The party had arrived at the hill country.

"You call these hills?" Teddy smiled. "They're higher than Fisher Mountain is back home!"

Prairie Cub looked to his native friends, "You can't imagine how small the land is where we've come from. I really miss this open space back there."

As the boys climbed above the open grassland, they entered stands of pine trees. They came into a clearing where they stopped to look out across the land below.

Scot reflected, "This is so different from when I stayed back east in Snow Shoe. You can't see open land like this. Everything is so cramped."

"Yea," Miles whispered, awestruck. "I've never seen anything like this!"

"Little Brother," Adam added. "I'm beginning to truly understand you. It has to be really hard to leave this all and live in my world. I can see, now, why you hurt so much."

"Do you miss us?" Little Bear asked.

"Always."

"And that is so true," Adam confirmed. "And now I'll know his pain."

"Yea," Teddy whispered.

Miles could only nod his head in agreement.

Lawrence added a personal note. "In all our years of trapping, Ma always stayed home and took care of our home place while Pa and I lived in the mountains. She always said she understood. But she was hesitant about taking the train from St. Louis to join us here when Keith Summers asked if she would come. Now that she is here, she has said how she always thought that she understood our need for this country, but that really wasn't true. After she had been here a week, she told Pa and me that she finally truly did understand. If we agreed, she would close up the house in St. Louis and come with us in the future."

Prairie Cub translated. No one spoke for several minutes as the enormity of what Lawrence shared sunk in.

"Is it time to start back?" Scot asked.

"It's time," Prairie Cub agreed.

*   *   *

While the boys rode the countryside, the families and the train crew gradually became acquainted with each other. The three women quickly bonded as they worked together in the kitchen. Keith Summers had explained that it was policy that each person took his dishes to the kitchen and the kitchen help took care of things from there. Once finished breakfast, the dishes were cleared to the kitchen and Summers invited everyone to gather in the sitting area at the end of the room by the large stone fireplace. The boys had quickly cleared their places and waited for Thunder Eagle. Thunder Eagle paused as the others cleared their places, thinking for a moment that Prairie Flower would take his dishes. When she didn't return from the kitchen, he followed the example of the others. His squaw asked to stay and help the other women and he agreed, then left with the boys. The women sent Howard and Jamie to join with the rest of the men.

"This is becoming a truly eye-opening experience," Marian commented in her pronounced French accent. She was the shortest of the three by a couple inches, fragile in appearance, but surprisingly strong in the way she flung the cast iron cookware about. "I thought I understood Murray and our son's fascination with the wilderness as they left each season for his cabin in the mountains and his trap lines for beaver." She paused in drying the dish in her hand. "It was a man's world and I stayed behind to care for our home while they were gone. And I missed them so much. When I received Mr. Summer's letter asking me to come here, I wasn't sure about coming. It seemed it, too, was a man's thing. When I realized it was a family reunion of some sort, I wanted to be here, too." She finished the dish, set it aside, and picked up another.

Janet picked up a handful of flatware, dipped it in the rinse water, placed it in the drainer, then paused with her hands in the dishwater. "When Walt Mattson visited us during the Christmas season, there were many emotional moments as Prairie Cub constantly hurt in his longing for home. All that got us through the pain of his leaving to return here was the knowledge of the planning for this reunion and that we would see him again and our boy was going to be able to go home again." She paused to wipe away a tear and to regain her voice, cut off by emotion.

Prairie Flower moved a stack of clean dishes to the side counter, then turned and leaned against the counter top. "Thunder Eagle and me have known the pain of separation these past months and worried greatly if we had done the right thing in sending our son back into the world of his birth. We have felt his pain as well in his letters, yet he believes we did right. Now that we can be with his eastern family and our son's new friends, we know it was right, but it will always hurt. I hope this reunion will be able to happen each year." She picked up a handful of flatware and started to sort it into its storage tray.

"Prairie Flower," Mrs. Tyler asked. "Do you think that you and Thunder Eagle would ever be able to visit us. We would be grateful, too, if our boy's friends from here could come as well. And that includes the Robinsons and the Kaymonds."

"That would be a really big challenge," Mrs. Kaymond offered. "There's no way we could have our own train to make the trip."

"And I don't think people would accept any of us traveling in our native clothes without making trouble," Prairie Flower added.

"I understand," Mrs. Tyler responded. "We have been very fortunate to have the friends back home who have accepted Prairie Cub's background. And at our end, it's a very different situation in that he lives as Michael in Michael's world. Our son is two different boys from two different worlds and has said as much. When we left home, he said he comes here as Prairie Cub and will be Prairie Cub until we return home. Then he will be Michael again." She dumped the dirty dishwater, then continued. "We have a truly remarkable boy, you and me. I hope through this visit we will truly become one family and our son will be able to live in less pain."

The two women stood looking at each other, unsure of their feelings and how each felt about the other.

"If it's okay with you two, you can hug each other," Marian suggested.

Janet opened her arms and Prairie Flower accepted the invitation. The two approached each other and embraced. After a moment, they reached out to Marian as well. It was a precious moment of union and the three women became fast friends in that moment.

\*    \*    \*

Thunder Eagle returned to the barracks and joined the men by the fireplace. He was familiar with those from the frontier, but not yet comfortable around Bill Tyler and the railroad folks. Mr. Summers had just finished sharing the background story of the fort and its future plans when the warrior returned and found a chair to the side of the group.

"Folks," Jay began. "I sure do feel that we are outsiders in this visit, yet I know we are connected by two boys here. I am thrilled that we are able to bring Prairie Cub home and to once again visit with Scot and to meet his family. I know this is not in the plans, but if there is an opportunity, we would like to take you folks on an overnight trip on the train. We don't have to go any place in particular, just go out where there's a siding we can park on for the night, and return the next day."

Mr. Summers responded, "I think it would be a great idea and I'll see what I can do to make it happen." He looked toward the warrior. "I think Thunder Eagle has some plans for later this week."

Thunder Eagle stood. "Trapper Murray took a scouting party out a few days ago and found the buffalo grazing to the west of here. It is the season for the buffalo hunt and preparations begin with tomorrow's ceremony. You are all invited to join us at sunrise for a day of preparation for the hunt on the following day. Trapper Murray has been to our celebration before, so any who come, come with him and he will be your guide. As soon as the women have finished, I will take Prairie Flower and we will go to prepare for tomorrow."

The women entered from the kitchen to join their men, and the warrior and his woman bade all farewell and left to return to their home.

\*    \*    \*

Trapper Murray and his family led the large party of visitors from the fort. The Robinsons followed close behind with the seven railroad men close behind him with Jay at Scot's side. The Tylers brought up the rear with their three boys in tow and Walt Mattson at their side.

"Jay, you have looked very uncomfortable since you arrived here," Scot observed.

"It's just that everyone else is so connected and we have nothing to do with these people and this place." He watched the scene ahead as he spoke with the boy.

"But you and your crew are connected. To me and to Prairie Cub. We wouldn't be here if it weren't for your part in caring for us." He looked up to the drawn face in its discomfort at feeling out of place, then he slipped his arm around the man's waist. "You are a very dear part of our lives. You cared for us when we so badly needed someone to care. And you still do, and we care for you."

"Thanks, Scot. I guess you're right. But I still feel so out of place as do my people."

Clint cut in. "Jay," he looked toward the man. "I and Prairie Cub's family may not know you from the past, but we know you through our sons. We may be too involved to say so just now, but be assured we know so. You all stick with us and it will get better."

"Thanks."

As the party approached Prairie Cub's family's tepee, Mr. Kaymond gave instructions. He stopped and turned to his group. "Today, we are outside observers." All stopped to listen. "Yes, we have been invited to be here, but we must realize, this is a sacred event to these people and their full attention is on each person's place in it. Stand here and wait for the boy's family to finish preparations. When they leave for the ceremonial grounds, I will take you there and show you where to sit. My son and I were here last year and it is truly a wondrous event few get to see."

He turned his attention to the tepee and waited.

Thunder Eagle and his family emerged in full ceremonial regalia, in their finest buckskin clothing with beaded decorations, quillwork, feathers, and anklets with jingling bells. Prairie Flower glanced toward Scot and saw he wore the necklace she had given him and smiled. Then she noticed her son's knife worn by Trader Mattson. Surprise quickly turned to understanding as her eyes caught the man's and she nodded with a hint of a smile, her approval. The trader nodded back his thanks. The family left to follow others to the ceremonial dance ground. Mr. Robinson led his party along the outside of the village to the edge of the ceremonial grounds then showed all where to sit. Shortly thereafter, the rest of the village gathered and the drums began.

Granny Woman approached the visitors.

"I'm too old to do a whole lot. I do want to, but my body doesn't," the voice crackled. "If you don't mind, I'll sit with you and watch."

"Sit here," Mrs. Tyler offered.

The people stood in a circle surrounding the dance ground, keeping the area open where the guests sat so they could see. The buffalo dance began with dancers wearing buffalo headdresses entering the area and dancing as though they were grazing on the grasses. A short time later, the hunters entered waving their lances and dancing around the buffalo. They pantomimed the attack as they struck out with their lances and the buffalo fell. The hunters moved on. The women arrived in their dance and pantomimed the skinning of the dead animals and the butchering of the naked bodies. The visitors watched in fascinated awe as Prairie Cub and his father danced their part as buffalo and hunter, and Prairie Flower danced the harvesting of the dead animals. All stopped momentarily as others took on the headdresses and a new cast of characters repeated the dance story. The constant change of cast and story repetition continued throughout the morning. After the sun passed its zenith at high noon, the focus of the dancing changed to personal dances telling individual stories by various members of the tribe. Each dancer yielded the ground to others in turn throughout the afternoon. As the sun dipped toward the western horizon late in the day, families drifted back toward their lodges to prepare the first meal of the day and to start to settle in for the night. Murray Kaymond signaled when it was time to leave.

He led his visitors back to Thunder Eagle's tepee where Granny Woman joined Prairie Flower to help prepare the meal, and Mr. Kaymond thanked the warrior for the honor of witnessing the ceremony and made arrangements to meet the following day for their assignments for the hunt.

Tomorrow would begin during the last darkness before sunrise.

\* \* \*

All arrived in the last darkness in the broken light of the setting moon. Walt Mattson drove a freight wagon with those who were on foot. Lawrence and Scot and their fathers were on horseback along with Adam. Thunder Eagle and Prairie Cub were mounted on their ponies and had ponies for Teddy and Miles. Prairie Flower was mounted on a pony with a travois dragging behind. She had skinning knives for Teddy, Miles, and Adam, and led a second pony with its travois. This was the first hunt for Prairie Cub and his friends and they rode ahead with Thunder Eagle and the hunting party to begin the hunt. As the hunters departed, the women and children followed behind to their appointed place to follow the hunt and harvest the fallen buffalo. Prairie Flower took charge of Mattson and his outriders, and led the party to their place on the distant prairie where they would witness the hunt and the harvest.

Hours passed as they travelled the miles to the western prairie to await the hunt. After their arrival, Scot and his pa stayed with the wagon and its passengers. Lawrence and his pa joined with the three boys and waited with Prairie Flower for the hunt to pass and the harvesting to begin. They had declined an invitation to join the hunt, explaining it was not their place to be there. All waited in quiet anticipation.

The first sign of the hunt was a trembling in the ground and a distant sound of thunder. Then the sharp cries of the hunters became audible as the thundering crescendoed and broke over the distant rolling landscape as the stampeding buffalo charged into view, running wild with the warrior hunters riding within their numbers firing their arrows into the sides of the animals. Bleeding buffalo ran until their life blood gave out and they dropped in mid motion and those behind broke around them. They passed from right to left in front of the waiting women as the living thundered on and the hunt gradually passed from view. Prairie Cub and his friends passed with the herd, each firing his arrows into the closest animal. Thunder Eagle passed close behind.

Suddenly, Little Bear broke from the chase and rode hard toward the waiting women, followed close behind by a charging wounded buffalo. They were just about to crash through the horrified watchers when the wounded beast brought down the boy and his pony. Bill Tyler, jumped from the wagon, stripped off his coat, and charged to distract the animal as it turned to gorge the pony and its rider. The man shouted and waved his coat and the bleeding buffalo turned in confusion to face him. It stood there momentarily focused on the man, then dropped dead in its tracks. In the meantime, the pony got back on its feet, bleeding from a tear in its neck, and wandered to check on the boy.

As soon as he could break away, Thunder Eagle rushed to the boy's side. Mr. Tyler had dropped his coat and knelt by the fallen boy. The pony wandered aside to graze.

"Don't move," the man instructed as he placed his hand on the boy's chest to keep him on the ground.

It was obvious from its strange position that his leg was broken. Mr. Robinson quickly joined Bill Tyler as Thunder Eagle slid from his pony. Adam approached.

"Is Eagle's Claw with you?" the teen asked.

"You know of him?" a surprised warrior inquired.

"My little brother has told me of his medicine. He has great respect for how he healed his grandfather and now Little Bear needs him."

Prairie Cub and White Hare had left the hunt to see if they could help their friend.

"He is in the village," Thunder Eagle informed.

"The boy really shouldn't be moved," Mr. Robinson advised. "But I have done some medical work with the railroad on occasion and would be glad to see if he could be made safe to put in the wagon and taken to the medicine man's lodge."

"See if that can be done," the warrior requested. "If not, I will send my son and his friend to bring him back." He turned to Mr. Tyler. "That was a brave thing you did. I did not think a white man from the east could be so brave or care enough."

"I'm sorry you would think that, but I can understand why." He stood aside to let Mr. Robinson check out the boy's injuries. "I love my son dearly and through him, his people, too. I am truly blessed to have this chance to be here and to come to know who he really is."

Little Bear cried in pain as Mr. Robinson examined his condition. "I think we can stabilize the boy and take him back in the wagon. There are two bones in the lower leg. It appears that the thinner one is broken and the stronger one is okay. We can leave the others here to help Prairie Flower harvest this beast, take the boy to Eagle's Claw, then return for the rest of the party."

"What do you need?" Thunder Eagle asked.

"I can use four arrows and some strips of fabric to stabilized the leg. I wish we had some blankets, but as many coats as possible might cushion the ride and we have to keep him warm so he doesn't go into shock and get worse."

Prairie Cub reached four arrows from his quiver and passed them to the man. "These are very strong. My father made them."

The warrior smiled in acknowledgment of his son's praise.

Marian climbed down from the wagon. "Rip what you need from my petticoat," she offered. She lifted the hem of her dress and started to tear strips of fabric from her petticoat.

"There's more where that came from under my dress if you need," Mrs. Tyler offered as she reached under her dress and tore off a strip.

Mr. Robinson accepted the strips of fabric as he spoke to the boy. "Little Bear, this is going to hurt somethin' fierce when I set the broken bone in your leg and wrap it tight so it won't move on us." He looked to Scot. "Son, can you hold him under his arms to give him support while we do this?"

The teen dismounted to do as his pa asked. Prairie Cub slipped from his pony to kneel by his friend's side with words of encouragement. In their common language, he told how Mr. Robinson had taken care of him when he was hurt and that he would take good care of Little Bear, too.

Little Bear screamed in pain as the leg was pulled straight to set the bone and wrap it tightly with the arrows to keep it in place. Jay and his crew vacated the wagon and any who had coats removed them to make a bed for the boy's journey back to the village. Carefully supporting the leg, the two men and their sons lifted Little Bear into the wagon bed.

Adam had an idea. He unsaddled Cheyenne and used her saddle blanket to cover the boy. The saddle was left on the ground and the boy tied his horse's reins to the saddle horn.

"Mr. Mattson, please bring the blanket when you come back."

"I certainly will, Adam."

"I'm going with them," Prairie Cub announced.

"Me, too," White Hare added in his language.

The wagon left with its two outriders.

Thunder Eagle dismounted. His pony turned aside and began to graze. He stepped aside as Prairie Flower and her large party of helpers began the task of skinning the buffalo that lay by their side, and lining the travois to carry the meat. The railroad crew stood by to pass the butchered pieces to the two mothers who carefully loaded the travois to pack as much as possible on the hide. Once loaded, Prairie Flower showed the two how to use the rawhide ties that hung from the travois to tie the hide across the pieces of meat and hold the load secure. What wouldn't fit was tied to the second travois. As they focused on their work, they became aware of other family groups that had gone to identify their warrior's kill and begin their harvesting as well. As all in the large gathering worked to prepare the harvested beast for travel to the village, Thunder Eagle took Mr. Tyler aside.

For a moment the two observed the work.

Then the warrior spoke. "Come with me, Bill Tyler. Let's walk." He led the man aside, out of earshot of the working party.

"I know now that our son is truly fortunate. He is in a good place with you and your family." The two fathers wandered off a short distance more then stopped again to observe their women working together for the family's welfare.

"I am deeply honored by your trust," Mr. Tyler stated.

"I know now that he really does have two fathers and two mothers. Now we can send him home with you and know that his new parents will honor his heritage. We can trust that he will be okay knowing that he loves you and is safe with you."

"Thunder Eagle, you must know that though he loves us dearly as we love him, and he and his big brother are as close as any brothers can be, in his heart, you are his true parents and we are only temporary. We know that. He knows that and has said as much."

"He seems so happy here. What will happen when you leave?"

"Prairie Cub has told us that he is two people. He is Prairie Cub and he is Michael. As we prepared to leave on this journey, he told us that he is Prairie Cub from the time we left home, and when we start on our journey back, he will be Michael. He has come home to his true home. But he has also left home behind and will return home when this journey ends."

"Then somehow, we must help our son to know he is one person and should not feel divided, that we are one family. We just happen to have two different heritages based on the lives we live. Our son truly is *our* son."

They turned their attention once more to the women at work, harvesting the dead beast.

"Our women work together as a family," the warrior observed. "They seem so happy together."

"They are happy," Mr. Tyler agreed. "I watch this group of families and friends and feel the bonds of friendship and of family are tighter than I ever realized."

The two men started back to join the rest of the party and prepare for the trip back to the village.

*     *     *

By late afternoon, all hunting parties and families had returned to the village. One of the families stopped at Thunder Eagle's tepee to return the arrows from the buffalo he and the boys had killed, but forgotten during the crisis with Little Bear. They shared that they had harvested the buffalo and would gladly bring the meat. But the warrior thanked them for the returned arrows and for taking care of their kills. They should keep the meat and share it with others who might be in need.

The large party with Thunder Eagle's family gathered in front of his tepee.

"Will you all wait here and help the women divide and prepare the meat. I wish to take Scot and Adam and their fathers and my son to Eagle's Claw and learn of Little Bear's healing." The warrior left with his party as the rest took instructions from Prairie Flower and began to set up racks and fires to cook and smoke the meat.

*     *     *

Eagle's Claw welcomed Thunder Eagle's party into his tepee where Little Bear lay on a buffalo skin bed, covered with a bear skin blanket.

"How is the boy?" the warrior asked as he knelt beside the patient.

Eagle's Claw knelt beside him. "Your Mr. Robinson did a great thing in caring for the leg. I have prayed over him with the Great Spirit and put a poultice on his other wound. The leg is good and should not be changed. It will take a long time to heal. He should stay down for many suns and then only walk with a stick for support."

The fathers and sons watched and listened as Prairie Cub quietly translated the words spoken. They saw for the first time where the medicine man had lowered the torn legging above the splinted leg to reveal a deep gash in the boy's thigh, and had wrapped it with a piece of buckskin to hold a poultice in place. Little Bear asked his friend to thank the men for saving his life and fixing his leg. They replied in turn that they were glad he is alive and that he will heal from his injuries.

"Thunder Eagle," Mr. Tyler asked, "if you want, we can carry Little Bear to his tepee so his mother can care for him."

Eagle's Claw agreed. Mr. Robinson removed the bear skin and handed it to the warrior. The four took positions on the four corners of the buffalo skin and lifted the boy on his bedding, then followed Prairie Cub and his father through the village to the wounded boy's home. All along the way people stopped to watch them pass in reverent quiet. There, Little Bear's father held open the door covering while his mother led the group in and showed them where to place her son. Once on the ground, Thunder Eagle covered him once more with the bear skin. He was quickly surrounded by his younger brother and sister and a shower of questions.

Little Bear's parents expressed their grateful thanks to the men for saving their son's life and helping to take care of his injuries. Thunder Eagle translated, then led the group back to his lodge.

The railroad men were deeply involved with the tasks needed to prepare the fires, smoking racks, and meat for the slow process of curing. Lawrence and his pa actively shared their expertise in a process they had done many times over the years. Marian and Janet added their talents too.

"Prairie Flower and Granny Woman have given us part of the meat as well," Howard announced as he stood to meet the party's return with Thunder Eagle. "It's wrapped in a piece of buckskin in the wagon."

Jay stood from a fire he was tending. He stepped toward the arriving boys. "We have learned new skills, today. Definitely nothing to help run a train, but still a lot of fun in its own way."

Prairie Cub smiled. "Welcome to my world."

Mr. Roth lay the strips of meat he had just prepared, across the cooking rack and stood. "I think it's time to get this gift of meat to the kitchen and into the ice box." He handed the butchering knife back to Granny Woman. "If anyone's hungry, we can start dinner while the rest get cleaned up."

Mr. Tyler turned to Prairie Cub's family. "I know you have a lot of work to do here. But if you're able to take a break, you're welcome to join us for dinner. As a matter of fact, we'd be honored if your family would take as many meals as possible with us while we're here."

Thunder Eagle responded, "We cannot stop until all the meat has been prepared, or it will spoil and be wasted. This day is always planned with the moon's passing in mind. We will have light and work into the night. We will join you in the morning."

Mr. Mattson spoke up. "Thunder Eagle, after I get these folks to the barracks and the meat unloaded, the boys and I will load the wagon with firewood from Mr. Summer's pile of the remains of the south wall. We'll dump it here, near your tepee, and any who need can take from the pile."

"That would be a great help," the warrior replied.

The gathering of families and friends bade farewell and walked with horses and wagon back toward the fort.

*   *   *

The next two days were spent tending to the fires and the buffalo harvest. Buffalo hides had to be cleaned and salted down in preparation for a meeting with Keith Summers at month's end for their sale at the trading post. The meat had to be cured for storage for future use. The boys spent the mornings together riding the land and exploring distant hills. They rode to the valley where the buffalo had grazed on the first day and reported back that the herd had moved on. In the afternoon, they visited Little Bear and spent time in games with the other boys of the village. They gathered at the edge of the village to run races and contests of skill such as the moving hoop throw.

Prairie Cub and White Hare demonstrated. White Hare rode his pony with his lance and threw it through a hoop, with web lacing that Prairie Cub rolled across the ground in front of him. The two took turns. Prairie Cub was very out of practice and missed most attempts. White Hare was very good.

Seeing the two play the game, other boys came from the village and joined in.

Teddy and Miles tried a race to see if they had enough balance to stay on their ponies. They found they weren't ready yet and decided to watch the other boys instead. Prairie Cub showed his two friends how to roll the hoop so they could be part of the games.

The boys had so many new experiences to write about in their journals. Each evening, before the families gathered near the fireplace at the end of the room, the boys wrote in their journals. Since his family joined them for dinner, Prairie Cub was there, too. Howard appointed himself 'keeper of the journals' and saw to their bringing out while dinner was cleaned up, and their storage in the kitchen afterward.

Thunder Eagle made it a point for the family to join the families and friends at mealtime in the morning and in the evening. Prairie Flower helped in the kitchen with the other women. On the second evening, the family stayed for the gathering at the fireplace. The evenings evolved as a time to share stories as Murray shared stories of the trapping season and the rendezvous, Clint shared stories of the railroad construction, Jay and his folks shared stories of the Virginia & Truckee as well as personal stories of life in general, and Bill shared stories from the mountain. Thunder Eagle offered a story.

He settled in his chair, comfortable with the others in the gathering and secure in their interest in what he might offer. He began, "Many summers ago, nine counting back from the summer to come, Prairie Flower and I journeyed to a trading fort in the foothills of the Wind River Mountains. They were said to have very fine porcupine quills and she hoped to get enough to do quillwork on a knife sheath for my father. We were able to trade a tanned deer skin for a large bundle and started back to the village. Crossing the western edges of the prairie, we saw a settler wagon and its campfire, just barely whisping smoke, and headed over to visit. But no one was there. On closer look, we found a man and a woman inside the wagon. They had both been dead for at least two days. There was no sign of why or how they had died. The woman was lying in a bed on the floor and the man was sitting beside her, both in the stiffness of death. We heard a movement under the wagon and saw a blanket roll to the side and a small boy roll out. He was a half starved little yellow hair, very steady on his feet as he stood up to come and greet us. He pointed to himself and said 'Michael' then to us and asked 'you?'"

Prairie Cub interrupted. "That's my story?" he asked.

"Yes, Son. It is your story," his father responded.

"You never told it before."

"There was never a need to."

"And now?"

"These families and friends who are such a part of our lives, need to know." Thunder Eagle paused and looked toward the Tylers. He continued. "We looked to see if there was anything we should take for the boy and decided there wasn't. Not knowing if his parents had died from some sort of disease, we decided to rekindle the fire and burn the wagon. We took the two horses and the boy and continued home. He didn't cry. He didn't seem to understand what had happened. Once home, we gave the horses to Roaring Wing and asked if we could adopt the boy. The council gave permission and we named him Prairie Cub because of how we found him. I knew then that I had to learn his language and see to it he would always know his language as well as ours. It has helped, too, because I am able to translate for my people. We all can. At the same time, my parents learned the language of the English as well."

There was a loud silence in the room.

"Thanks, Thunder Eagle," Mrs. Tyler barely whispered.

"We are so grateful to learn more of our son's heritage," Mr. Tyler added.

Keith Summers announced. "I have to returned to the company tomorrow. Walt will be staying in my house as long as we are all here and will see to any needs that arise and work with Howard to coordinate supplies for the hotel needs." He stood. "I'll head to bed now and see you all at breakfast."

"Before you go," Thunder Eagle spoke. "Tomorrow is to be a day of celebration for these families and friends. Chief Roaring Wing and the council have asked me if you would join us at the ceremonial grounds when the sun is at its highest."

"I will stay an extra day," Summers announced.

"Please tell Roaring Wing that we will all be there," Mr. Mattson acknowledged.

"Thank you." Thunder Eagle stood and looked to his family. The three gathered and left for the night.

There were 'good nights' around as the gathering broke up and the families headed upstairs to their rooms.

\*   \*   \*

The warm April morning advanced to its noon hour as the gathering of nineteen walked toward the ceremonial grounds in the center of the village. A tarp canopy stood on one side with buffalo skin blankets covering the ground. Prairie Cub's family stood there and indicated the arriving families and friends were to join them there, too. Roaring Wing and his chiefs sat together along one side. All were dressed in their finest clothing. Little Bear had been carried to a place near where Prairie Cub's family sat. White Hare was there, too. The hundreds who comprised the tribal families were gathered around the edge of the large ground with a scattering of deer skins spread about the area on which various dance regalia lay waiting.

Roar Wing stood to face the gathering and Thunder Eagle rose to translate.

"Our chiefs have asked that we celebrate in dance and song, and with food, this great family of our son, Prairie Cub. We are grateful to this boy because he ended the cruelty of the officer who brought death to our people. Now, this season, his father gave life as he saved Little Bear from a wounded buffalo that was about to take his life. This day we celebrate life." The aged warrior returned to his seat and the drums began.

Dancers from many families took to the open ground and began a variety of individual dances, many accompanied by personal songs. Over the course of the next three hours, individual and group dances, songs and choruses, and story dances brought life and animation to the ceremonial gathering. Among the stories was the eagle dance, involving over a dozen dancers, each telling the story at his own pace. Prairie Cub shared in this dance. His mother helped him into the eagle costume with headdress and eagle wings. The dance began in a crouched position telling of the birth of the eagle as the boy stood and stretched his arms to the full extent of his wingspan. He danced in a step-hop fashion, flying and soaring in the joy of life. Then he slowed and stooped, then lay out on the ground in death. After a brief pause, he fluttered a wingtip and gradually returned to life as he rose once more to fly again in triumphant after-life. The dance was repeated several times by several different dancers.

The afternoon drew to a close. Roaring Wing rose to address the gathering in closing.

"After the fight when Prairie Cub was sent to the world of his birth, the council awarded him coup, for it was his arrow than ended the life of the cruel captain. He wears his coup in his headband today. Three days ago at the buffalo hunt, when a wounded beast brought down Little Bear and his pony, it was this boy's father who stood before the beast with nothing more than his coat, and drew him away from the boy. Because of this bravery, the boy and his pony both live. Because he is Prairie Cub's father, he understands what the council has done as it met this morning before this celebration. For our people, the council has awarded him coup and I give him this eagle feather as its sign."

There was a gasp of astonishment from the assembled guests as the significance of what had just happened sank in. The chief stood before a shocked man as his family pushed him to stand and both his sons helped pull him to his feet. The chief presented a large grandly decorated eagle wing feather of curved beauty with bright red wrappings containing beautiful soft breast feathers. He could say nothing, nodded his gratitude, then returned to his seat. A joyous chant arose from the people.

The chief announced that a feast was to be served and any who wished could stay. A number of squaws brought a multitude of dishes to place before the guests and bowls from which to eat.

*   *   *

Thunder Eagle asked Mr. Tyler to bring his family to their fire later in the evening.

The sun hung low on the western horizon as the Tylers and the three boys approached the warrior's tepee. The three-generation family was gathered around their low fire in front.

"I wasn't thinking about Prairie Cub's friends when I asked you to come. But I think it is good that they are here." He turned to his son. "Would you ask if White Hare can join us. I wish Little Bear could come, too."

The boy left.

"Would his father let me carry him here and back?" Mr. Tyler asked.

"We'll go together and ask," the warrior replied.

The two left to see if the boy could come.

"Prairie Flower," Mrs. Tyler asked. "This sounds so serious. What is happening?"

"I do not know," the mother answered. "He has seemed so serious these days since the hunt."

"I hope everything's okay," Adam offered.

Several minutes passed. The boy returned with his friend.

"What's happening?" Miles asked.

"I don't know," Prairie Cub replied. He shared the question with White Hare.

The fathers returned carrying Little Bear. Mr. Tyler carefully set him down near his son. The men settled on the ground.

"We need to solve a problem," Thunder Eagle began. "Prairie Cub."

"What?"

"Michael."

"What!? You have never called me by that name."

"It is your name?"

"Yes."

"You have two names."

"Yes."

"But it's still just you, Son"

"What do you mean?"

"We are here, sitting together at out fire. There are four of your friends and seven of your family."

Prairie Flower quietly moved to the other side of Granny Woman to sit with White Hare and Little Bear to translate the conversation in soft whispering.

"I know," the boy agreed.

"We are one family, Bill and Janet and Adam Tyler, Prairie Flower, Thunder Eagle, and Granny Woman, and Michael Prairie Cub Freeman."

"How did you know?"

"Your mothers talk to each other. Your fathers do, too. And you know that name is all one person."

"But I am not one person. Here, I am Prairie Cub. In Snow Shoe, I am Michael."

"Son, you are one very special person who happens to have two very different heritages. I told your story last night to help you know who you are and to let your friends know that, too. Come, sit here." The boy moved to sit beside his father. "Adam, please sit here beside your brother." The older boy moved as asked. "Bill, would you sit next, then Janet." The two moved as asked.

Thunder Eagle continued. "On this side you have your Sioux heritage. On your other side you have your white heritage. But you, like your name, are one person. We are one family. With your two heritages you have two sets of parents. You have two sets of friends. Look around you." The boy glanced at the people around him. "We sit here as one family with one set of friends." He paused for everyone to think about what he had said.

"Your father tells me that you came here as Prairie Cub and you will return home as Michael. But you are both and have come and will go home as both. We call you by different names because we know you by different names. But you are still the same boy. We know that you hurt terribly at being separated from our part of the family. We wish we could take away your pain. We know we can't. Yet we do know and are very grateful, that you have come to love your new world as well and feel safe with your white family as well. We, your parents, have come to know each other as one family, too. But we don't want you to feel torn between two people, because you aren't. You are one son with two fathers and two mothers and a terrific older brother."

"I never thought of it that way. Ma? Pa? my father is right?"

"Yes, son. Your father is right," his parents confirmed.

# ABOUT THE AUTHOR
# J. ARTHUR MOORE

J. Arthur Moore is an educator with 42 years experience in public, private, and independent settings. He is also an amateur photographer and has illustrated his works with his own photographs. In addition to *Twelfth Winter* Mr. Moore has written *Journey into Darkness,* a story in four parts, *Blake's Story,* Revenge and Forgiveness, two Civil War historic fictions, and *Summer of Two Worlds,* a Native American historic fiction set in Montana Territory in the summer of 1882. *Twelfth Winter* is the sequel to *Summer of Two Worlds* and tells the story of Prairie Cub after he is forced to return to the world of his white heritage, the world of his former name, Michael. It is the emotional journey that followed.

He recently published a third Civil War era historic fiction, *West to Freedom.* His previously last work, *Summer at Stewart Creek,* is pure fiction, set in the fictitious territory of his Virginia and Truckee Railroad of West Virginia, which he has recreated in miniature and used to illustrate this story. It is the same world in which Michael finds himself.

Moore's next project is another work started forty years ago during the same time that *Summer of Two Worlds* was written and *Twelfth Winter* was started. It is the prequel to *Summer of Two Worlds*, titled *Stranded in Snow Shoe*. This book is the story of Prairie Cub's friend, Scot Robinson, whose experience led to the story of *Twelfth Winter*.

A graduate of Jenkintown High School, just outside of Philadelphia, Pennsylvania, Moore attended West Chester State College, currently West Chester University. Upon graduation, he joined the Navy and was stationed in Norfolk, Virginia, where he met his wife to be, a widow with four children. Once discharged from the service, he moved to Coatesville, Pennsylvania, began his teaching career, married and brought his new family to live in a 300-year-old farm house in which the children grew up and married, went their own ways, raised their families to become grandparents themselves.

Retiring after a 42-year career, Mr. Moore has moved to the farming country in Lancaster County, Pennsylvania, where he plans to enjoy the generations of family, time with his model railroad, and time to guide his writings into a new life through publication. It also allows for the opportunity to participate in a local model railroad club as well as time for traveling to Civil War events, and presenting at various organizations and events about the boys who were part of that war. He also shares the process of writing, and readings from his work, and does book signings at a variety of locations.

Mr. Moore can be reached through the contact page of the website for his books at **www.jarthurmoore.com** with links to his Facebook and Twitter pages; and a blog page focusing on the stories of the boys who served in the Civil War.

CPSIA information can be obtained
at www.ICGtesting.com
Printed in the USA
BVHW042322090521
606879BV00001B/2

9 781952 874505